The Starter House

SONJA CONDIT

CORVUS

First published in the United States in 2014 by William Morrow, an imprint of HarperCollins Publishers

Published in trade paperback in Great Britain in 2014 by Corvus, an imprint of Atlantic Books Ltd.

Book design by Diahann Sturge

10 9 8 7 6 5 4 3 2 1

A CIP catalogue record for this book is available from the British Library.

Trade paperback ISBN: 978 1 78239 212 5
E-book ISBN: 978 1 78239 213 2

Printed in Italy by Grafica Veneta

Corvus
An imprint of Atlantic Books Ltd
Ormond House
26–27 Boswell Street
London
WC1N 3JZ

www.corvus-books.co.uk

For Brent, Ethan, and Rebecca

Acknowledgments

THANK YOU, FIRST OF ALL, to the wonderful faculty at Converse College's MFA program: my mentors, Leslie Pietrzyk, R. T. Smith, Marlin Barton, and Robert Olmstead; and to Rick Mulkey, Susan Tekulve, and Melody Boland, who kept the whole thing going. Thank you to Jenny Bent and Carrie Feron, for dragging me through the process, and to Nicole Fischer, for answering all of my questions so patiently. Most of all, I would like to thank my husband, Brent, for believing in me even when I doubted myself.

Chapter One

IT WAS ALREADY JUNE, and the Miszlaks still hadn't found a house. Eric wanted guarantees: no lead, asbestos, mold, termites, crime, or trouble. Lacey wanted triangles.

"Triangles," Eric said, as if he'd never heard of such a thing. They shared the backseat of the Realtor's Tahoe, he with his binder of fact sheets organized by street name, she with her sketchbook, outside of their one hundred and eighth house. Lacey wanted to like it. She wished she could say, *This is the one, I love it,* for Eric's sake, because he was getting anxious as their list of houses dwindled from the twenties to the teens, but she just couldn't. This house with its square utilitarian front, so naked and so poor—if Eric settled for it, he'd be miserable by Christmas. They'd had enough of square houses, bland rooms no better than the motels she'd grown up in and the apartments they'd lived in together, houses without memory. They couldn't live that way anymore, with the baby coming.

"Triangles," she said, shaping one in the air with her hands. "Gables. Dormer windows. Look at that thing; a person could die of actual boredom. What about the one with the bay window?"

Eric flicked through his binder. "Bad neighborhood. Two title loan stores and a used car lot right around the corner."

The Realtor turned in the front seat. She was on the phone with her office, trying to find another house in the neighborhoods acceptable to the Miszlaks. Although three thousand homes were for sale in Greeneburg County (many of them in the city of Greeneburg itself) this first week of June, the Miszlaks' requirements limited them to Forrester Hills, on the northeast side of town. Lacey, three months pregnant and planning her baby's perfect childhood, had mapped the attendance zones of the good schools. Eric drew a circle around his uncle's law office, so he would have no more than a twenty-minute commute. The circles crossed only here.

CarolAnna Grey, the Realtor, had become steadily less blond over three weekends of driving the Miszlaks from house to house. Lacey felt sorry for her; she kept taking them to houses that failed one or more of their criteria, usually Eric's. He had grown up in Glenaughtry, Greeneburg's finest golf neighborhood. He had standards.

"This is my neighborhood," CarolAnna said. "I've lived here all my life."

"I'm not buying anything that's walking distance from Austell Road," Eric said.

"You're going to have to open up your search."

"No," they said together, and Eric turned pages in his binder and said, "What about the blue house around the corner, Lacey? It had those windows you like."

Lacey fanned her sketchbook and found her impression of the house: a toadstool with fumes rising from its gills. "Smelled of mold." It smelled like a basement apartment with carpeting so dirty it sticks to your feet. She'd spent too much of her life in rooms like that already.

"Why don't you just look at this house?" CarolAnna Grey said.

Eric and Lacey got out of the Tahoe. "We could look," Eric said.

Lacey looked. It was a square, no question. She dug in her purse for the bag of pistachios. In the last three months, besieged by morning sickness, she had gained ten pounds, though the baby itself was smaller than her thumb; she had to eat all the time, dry salty food, to keep the nausea under control. She wandered to the corner, seeking shade.

The neighborhood was exactly right. She loved the way the streets curved. She loved the cul-de-sacs and the big trees, the gardens all flashed with pink and white as the last dogwood flowers withered in June's green heat. She loved the big lawns prettified with gazebos, fountains, swings, wishing wells. A flock of little boys on skateboards flurried through the next intersection. Their voices hung in the air behind them like a flight of bells. She could live here forever, in the right house.

Forrester Lane curved counterclockwise, an arc of lawns and trees. She poured the pistachio shells back into the bag and walked along the sidewalk. It was broken in places, shattered from below by the heaving roots of oaks and maples. She liked that. It showed that the people who lived here valued trees more than concrete. Here was shade, under the biggest maple she had ever seen, effortlessly shielding two houses at once.

She looked up suddenly, her eye drawn to some motion not quite seen, and there was the house. She looked at it and her heart turned, like a key in a lock. Her house: a Cape Cod, dusty rose, its face naked and bruised. The shutters were piled on the porch, a sheet of plywood sealed the upper-right dormer window, tire tracks rutted the lawn, and a blue Dumpster stood crooked on the grass, filled with rolls of brown carpet and green foam-pad. A rust-stained claw-foot bathtub lay upside down on the porch.

Eric came up behind her and touched her arm to pull her away. "Look," she said. It spoke to her. Its brokenness and emptiness called her, and the discarded carpet was a mark of hope. This house had been someone's home; it had suffered and been damaged, and it was ready to be a home again. "Look, this is our house," Lacey said.

"It's a mess."

"You're not looking." She pointed to the house on the left. Also a Cape Cod, it gleamed immaculate in the shadow of the big maple. Its siding was a yellowed cream, the shade of egg custard, and the shutters were golden caramel. Three white rockers sat at friendly angles on the porch, under hanging ferns. Someone had mowed the lawn in perfect herringbones. "They're just the same. It could look like that, if we took care of it." She couldn't turn her back on this house; there was something in its expression, the angle of the dormers, so quizzical and innocent and appealing. It *needed* her. "It's just so cute."

"Cute? Be serious. The down payment, it's all the money we have."

The porch steps were broken. Lacey got her left knee onto the porch and hauled herself up, ignoring Eric's protests. The front door, scraped of its paint, swung open to her hand, and she walked in.

The entrance was surprisingly wide. To the left, an open arch led to the formal living room: two big windows and a gray marble fireplace. The floor was bare wood, with a sander standing in the middle. Lacey was glad the carpets were gone; they must have been horrible. To the right, another open arch, and a smaller room, with the same big windows. A roll of carpet stood in one corner, its underside stained in broad circles of brown and black. Straight ahead was the bright heart of the house, a stair-case beautiful even under its mud-colored Berber. A porthole window, a quartered circle, shed yellow western light down into Lacey's eyes. The last six steps broadened and curved out and back, with the lowest step describing a complete circle around the banister post.

Lacey could see her someday children there. They would sit on that round step in the sunshine. She saw a boy folding paper airplanes, which he meant to throw from a bedroom window. She saw a girl leaning against the post with her head bent over a book. The girl tucked a lock of hair behind her ear. She read as Eric did, biting her upper lip, her eyebrows tucked into a frown. The light hid their faces from her, but she already knew them. Someday, here. They had chosen their home in this house.

Eric took Lacey's elbow and pulled her out of the house. "You can't just walk into someone's house," he said. "You don't even know if it's for sale."

Lacey let Eric help her off the porch, where CarolAnna Grey caught up with them. "This is the house I want."

"You don't want this house," CarolAnna said. She looked as if she could say more, but Lacey didn't want to hear it. After one hundred and eight shoeboxes, she knew a real house when she saw it.

"We don't want a fixer-upper," Eric said. "I won't have time to work on it, and you can't, not by yourself."

"Someone's fixing it up already. Fixing it to sell."

"You can't know that," Eric said, but Lacey knew it by the

house's emptiness. Her someday children would never have appeared in another family's home. A family would have moved their furniture from room to room, not taken it all away. This house was getting ready for a new life.

The maple cast a green darkness over the lawn, a whisper of busy hands, and CarolAnna shuddered and moved away from it. "There's a real cute condo in a new development west of the mall," she said. "With a swimming pool."

Eric walked backward across the lawn, squinting upward. "Roof looks good."

"They're getting ready to paint," Lacey said. "If we make an offer fast, we can choose the colors. Inside and out."

If the shutters were green, dark mossy green . . . She wanted a green door, like the door of Grandpa Merritt's house, which had closed behind her forever when she was six, her last real home. They'd paint the baby's room sky blue and stencil stars and butterflies on the ceiling. They could do whatever they liked and not have to ask a landlord's permission or worry about the damage deposit. They would have a dog. She added a golden Labrador to her vision of the someday children on the staircase; then she pulled out her sketchbook and roughed in a drawing of the house's face and the maple.

The house looked happy in her picture. This was why she preferred to take sketches of the houses, rather than photographs. Snapping a picture was quick and easy, but the drawing told the truth, like the difference between e-mail and real conversation, websites and books.

"You could rent an apartment and wait a couple months," CarolAnna said. "Come July, there'll be thirty more in your area."

"Is there something wrong with this house?" Eric said.

Next door, in the twin Cape Cod, the front door opened and a tall white-headed man came out onto his porch with a watering can. He looked over and said in gentle surprise, "Well, it's you, CarolAnna Grey. This isn't Tuesday."

"It's Sunday."

"And how's little Madison; is she practicing?"

"Not so you'd notice."

The tall man courteously left a space in the air for CarolAnna to introduce Eric and Lacey. She set her mouth and said nothing. Lacey stepped into the painful silence, folding her sketchbook open on the picture of the house, and said, "I'm Lacey Miszlak and this is Eric. What do you know about the house next door?"

"Harry Rakoczy." He smiled at CarolAnna. "I've known this one since she was tiny, and now her little girl's taking lessons with me. Violin. You're interested in the house? I'm getting ready to sell."

Lacey said, "Yes," but Eric said, "Maybe. What's the history?"

"Harry, they don't want it." CarolAnna touched his arm. He looked at her hand until she let go. "It's not right," she said.

Harry ignored CarolAnna and smiled at Lacey. "It's been a rental for years. Roof's two years old, heat pump's practically new, and I'm renovating." He waved his watering can at the old bathtub. "Get that thing out of there. It's time."

"Harry," CarolAnna said. She glanced at the upstairs window of the empty house and moved away, as if someone might see her. "Harry, no. She's pregnant."

He set down the watering can and smiled at Lacey. "Looks good on you."

"The second trimester begins today," Lacey said. "And my due date's Christmas." She told everybody she met, now the first trimester was over and it was safe; she wanted the world to know.

"What are you asking?" Eric said. He was never lost, not in a confusing map or a meandering conversation. Eric always knew where he was going.

"A hundred ten."

Lacey was surprised. The other houses in Forrester Hills ranged from a hundred fifty to over two hundred.

"Harry," CarolAnna said anxiously.

"Is there something wrong with the house?" Eric asked again. Lacey wished he wouldn't. The house was obviously perfect. They could deal with anything—termites, mold, radon—but they could never make an ugly house their true home.

"Yes," Harry said to CarolAnna, "is there?"

CarolAnna licked her lips, then wiped her mouth with the back of her hand. She looked at the bathtub on the porch and said to it, "People died here."

"People die everywhere," Lacey said, though the words gave her a shiver. Poor house, no wonder it was lonely. "When did it happen?"

"A long time ago," Harry said. "It was very sad."

"If it doesn't bother you," Eric murmured, and Lacey shook her head—she didn't care at all. These houses were thirty, forty years old. People must have died, had babies, gotten engaged, married, divorced, hurt each other in a thousand ways, reconciled and forgiven, passionately hated and desperately loved; if you abandoned a house whenever something significant happened, people would live in tents. This house had known life.

"Ninety-five," Eric said to Harry. "Pending the inspection."

"Ninety-five," Harry said thoughtfully, as if he might actually consider the offer—it had to be worth a hundred seventy at least. Lacey felt she should tell him so. Just then a green Hyundai pulled into his driveway. "Here's Lex and the baby, I've got to go. CarolAnna, send me the offer and we'll talk. And you tell your

Madison, ten minutes of bow exercises every day, and I'll know if she hasn't done it."

A tall man got out of the Hyundai and unbuckled a baby from the back. He stooped under her weight, and she seized two fistfuls of his colorless hair and pulled his face up. The baby's voice pealed in a high wordless cry of greeting, bright as a bird.

Harry shook Eric's hand again and hurried back to his own front door before Lacey had a chance to ask about the bathtub. She loved old-fashioned furniture, and the claw-foot tub was beautiful. She wanted to know if it was rusted out, or if it might be refinished and reinstalled. While Eric and CarolAnna returned to the Tahoe, Lacey picked a few flakes of white enamel off the tub and rubbed the rusty iron beneath. The tall man stared at her from Harry Rakoczy's front porch, the baby squalling impatiently, until Harry urged him inside.

The Tahoe honked. "Come on," Eric said. "She says there's a new subdivision zoned for Burgoyne Elementary."

Lacey patted the bathtub. She already knew everything that mattered about the new subdivision: small lots, no trees, the houses all alike. "You stay right here," she said to her house. "Wait for me." They'd have to be quick; if Harry meant to accept Eric's offer—ninety-five thousand, practically giving it away—they'd have to grab the chance. There was no time to waste on condos and subdivisions.

Chapter Two

SEVEN WEEKS LATER, on the first Tuesday in August, the Miszlaks moved into 571 Forrester Lane. CarolAnna Grey got over her inexplicable reluctance to sell the house when Harry Rakoczy added an extra percentage to her commission. He told the Miszlaks he needed to sell because he had retired from the orchestra and would soon be moving to Australia to be with his son's family. Lacey was disappointed. She'd been looking forward to taking her baby next door for violin lessons with the old man in five years.

Though Eric called it their starter house, Lacey planned to live in it for ten years and maybe forever. She wanted her someday children to attend the same school from kindergarten through fifth grade, to have teachers who'd seen them grow and friends whose toddler birthday parties they'd attended. Her own childhood had been furnished with cardboard boxes and duffel bags, always moving, always ready to move. Lacey had attended eight different schools, and she couldn't count the moves or even define them. There were times they'd slept in the car. Was it *moving* if they parked in a different spot? Did a shift to another room in the same shabby motel count as a move?

She knew what she wanted for her baby. She wanted the home that had been hers when she was six, when she and her mother had lived with Grandpa Merritt in the white house with the green door and the big magnolia tree. Grandpa Merritt's house, like 571 Forrester Lane, had a smiling face, a sense of welcome. She wanted to be able to walk in the dark and recognize the sound and texture of every room.

Everything would be different when they were settled in the house. She hated moving, but if she had to do it, it might as well be in August, her New Year. For Lacey, a teacher, January was the trough of the year, when the children faced her across a barricade of desks, both sides exhausted beyond compromise. Now in August, the crayons were fresh in their boxes, bright as the children themselves. Every year, she bought new sketchbooks, leaving the last pages blank in the old ones. As soon as they moved in, she'd go from room to room, sketching doors and corners, making it her own.

They'd driven the route a dozen times in June and July, viewing the house, meeting with the Realtor, the bank, the lawyers, Harry Rakoczy, and the painters. They'd both driven it yesterday, coming up in two cars to leave Eric's Mitsubishi in the Greeneburg U-Haul parking lot. It had always been an easy drive; they'd never seen traffic like this.

Highway construction delayed their arrival until seven thirty. Eric had planned for noon. Being late put him in a terrible mood, and if they didn't deliver the empty U-Haul by nine, they'd be charged an extra day. "Let's get started," Eric said. "We can pile everything on the lawn for now. Just get the van empty."

"Can't we pay the fifty bucks and do it in the morning?"

"I'm not paying just so we can park overnight. Come on. I'll get the books and furniture, you get the light stuff. Forty minutes and we're done."

"Can we give it a rest, this once?"

No, they could not. He was right and she knew it; she wished he wouldn't be so completely right, all the time. He backed the van into 571's driveway. The west was fat with gold, and most of the houses on the street already had a few lit windows. Harry Rakoczy's house was dark and his car was gone. Lacey had hoped Harry could talk some sense into Eric, but they were on their own.

"I'd rather unload the futon and finish in the morning," she said.

"We can do this." Eric yanked at the van's back door. It accordioned up into its slot and stuck halfway. He started pulling out boxes and laying them on the lawn. "Get the light stuff," he said.

Lacey leaned into the van, breathing the smell of their lives, the years of their young-married student poverty: clothes washed with never quite enough cheap detergent, the orange Formica dinette, the futon Lacey bought for fifty dollars from an old roommate. The smell of garage sales and thrift shops, old textbooks, off-brand coffee, slightly irregular sheets worn thready at the hems.

She grabbed the nearest box, which gave a glassy jingle. She balanced it on her belly bump long enough to get her right hand under it, turned toward the house, and tripped over the curb. As she stepped high to get over it she could not see, a bell rang. Surprise made her stumble, and she caught her balance, the box chiming in her arms; she hoped nothing had broken. A child rode a bicycle along the sidewalk. She hadn't heard him coming until he rang his bell, though the ticking of the wheels was loud enough. He had sprung out of the grass in the tree's shadow. Her heart closed and opened. She took a breath and talked sense to herself: *Just a kid on the street, settle down.*

Her teacher's eye said *Nine, but small for his age:* a boy with fair, wavy hair and a gray T-shirt stained with long rusty streaks. Trouble at home. Something about the way he stared straight ahead, something about the grip of his small fingers on the handlebars. She hoped he didn't live too close. He rode his bike along the sidewalk to the edge of Eric and Lacey's new property, still marked with a row of orange survey flags—he rang the bike's round bell once, *ting,* and then turned and rode to the row of flags on the other border. He braked by jamming his heels into the sidewalk and rang the bell again. *Ting.*

Lacey started across the sidewalk and there he was again, suddenly, pedaling in front of her. His shoulder brushed the box, and she dropped it. Salad plates and dinner plates, bowls and coffee mugs, hit one another in one great shout of destruction. "Do you have to do that?" Lacey cried. "Right here? Do you have to?"

The boy stared at her, a look of challenge, like a dog too long chained: *Come closer and see if I bite.* "Who asked you to come here talking to me?" he said. The strange ferocity of his response made her step back and raise her hands.

Eric ran to the box. "I said leave it alone!" He opened the box to a mass of splinters and shards, with one intact dinner plate on top from the stoneware set they had bought at the Dollar King last June, on sale for nine dollars (marked down from fifteen). "These were good plates. They could have lasted us for years. Look at this, all this waste." He laid the pieces out to match the bigger parts together and see if some of them could be saved. White ceramic dust drifted in the bottom of the box.

Lacey could hardly believe how a single impact destroyed the dishes so completely. "We can get another set," she offered. "They were cheap."

"Nothing's cheap when you're living on borrowed money. You don't know," Eric said. So angry, like it was her fault, the traffic eating up the day—like she'd dropped the plates on purpose. "You don't know what it's like," he said. "Just this. Just everything. But if it's what you want, fine, we'll do what you want, like we always do. Buy new plates. Buy new silverware while you're at it. New tablecloths, why not. Spend a hundred dollars. Five hundred. Whatever, what difference does it make, I don't care." He pulled the accordion door down in its slot so hard it bounced, and he had to catch it and force it down again.

"Wait," Lacey said. The day had been just as hard on him as on her—harder, because he'd been driving. "We can finish. We're almost done."

He got into the driver's seat, and the slamming door was his only answer. At the corner, he stopped and signaled before turning left. His carefulness so exasperated Lacey that she had to chew on her knuckles to keep from shouting after him.

She sat on the grass, holding her knees and rocking, with a dozen fragmented conversations rattling in her mind. *You should have known—you think you know so much—I could have told you—why don't you ever listen to me?* Another stupid argument, their fourth this week. He said she spent too much, they had no money, why couldn't she understand—which was good, coming from a guy who'd grown up with all the money in the world, a two-million-dollar trust fund and a vacation home on the Isle of Palms, until it all disappeared. And he was telling her what poverty was like, as if he knew. This wasn't poverty; this was just a temporary low point between her job ending and his beginning. They were building up some debt, but it would all be gone in two months, except the student loans. If they couldn't handle the stress of moving, what kind of parents were they going to be?

She breathed quietly and listened to the maple. Eric always left when they fought. When he came back, he would be all love and sweetness, and neither of them would mention this fight again.

She lay back. After a while, she began to hear the sounds of the grass. When the wind brushed her face, the blades rubbed against each other, sharing friendly news. Bees worked the blossoms of the tall purple clover and the short white clover, the small sweet buttercups. A wood dove called, "*You-u. You-u.*" Children's voices rang, far off. The ticking of wheels gathered in the rustling stillness. And the little boy rode his bicycle up and down the sidewalk, turning at the property line.

The whirring wheels seemed loud but distant, like a recording played back at too high a volume, and each time the rhythm of his stop and turn was identical, his heels bouncing and then scraping on the sidewalk, the wheels slowing, his quiet grunt as he picked up the bicycle and turned it, and then the bell at last: *ting*. How did he do it exactly the same every time? More and more, Lacey felt she was listening to a recording, and not a real event. If she opened her eyes—which she would not do, nothing could make her look—she would see the sidewalk empty except for a boom box playing a CD on infinite repeat: *Ting. Ting.*

Chapter Three

THE HOUSE WAITED, its windows golden in the evening light. Lacey yearned to be inside, to open the windows and let the fresh air carry away the smell of new paint, to decide where to put the futon—opposite the window, or diagonally in a corner? She'd have to wait for Eric to come back with the keys. She lay on the grass with her hands lightly woven over the belly bump, sensing the odd fishlike twitches, the clear sense of something in her that was not herself, a stranger in the dark red heart of her life. Her favorite pregnancy website, YourBabyNow.net, said that at eighteen weeks she wouldn't feel the baby, but she'd felt it from the first day. For two months they tried, and halfway through March she woke up one morning with a blunt, foreign feeling in her cervix. Something new, hello, little stranger. She waited two weeks for the test, but she knew, and she felt it now, though the website said the baby was no bigger than a large olive. She breathed quietly, and the child knocked and twisted, and finally lay still. Even in its stillness she felt it, the hard wall of her womb under a half-inch shield of fat.

Someone alive, someone new. On the day she took the test—the first day of her first missed period—she had parent-teacher meetings, three hours of parents, variously nervous, belligerent, businesslike, guilty, proud. She discussed handwriting and spelling, recommended math-game websites. The only meeting she remembered was the last, a young mother who sat in Lacey's classroom with her three-month-old daughter on her lap. The baby was bald except for a tuft of transparent hair. She wriggled and murmured, and her round eyes never left her mother's face. Ten minutes into the meeting, the baby began to fuss. The mother, never missing a word, lifted the baby up to her face, and the baby lunged forward, then latched on and suckled on the mother's chin. Lacey had never seen a gesture so intimate. She forgot what she was saying about the woman's older child and simply blurted to this stranger, "I'm pregnant."

The young mother shifted the baby to her shoulder and rubbed the back of the round fuzzy head. "Your first, right?" she said. "It's worth it in the end."

The life inside Lacey was a mystery, not a communion. In its first weeks, this child, a creature smaller than a fruit fly, took her body by storm, three months of nausea. The baby filled her ankles with water, unstrung her knees, and tormented her with a starving hunger worse than she had felt on even the strictest diet.

The world was full of other people's babies, so beautiful, with their big round eyes; they looked at her with a deep gaze, knowing something she had long forgotten. Even if she'd known it would be this hard, she would have welcomed it, the someday baby coming closer every day. But the struggle was hers alone. Not even Eric could understand.

Cloud shadows shuttered across her eyelids, cool, warm, cool again, and a small wind walked around her, plucking at her hair with teasing fingers. A darker, nearer shadow fell over her. She became aware of presence, the sound of breath, a weight in the air. How vulnerable she had made herself, lying on her back, half asleep, in a place where she knew nobody. She opened her eyes.

Harry Rakoczy from next door, whom she had last seen in Eric's uncle's office during the closing, loomed over her like a mild-mannered predatory bird, dangerous only to the fish in his shadow. Most people loomed over Lacey, but Harry was at least a foot taller than she, though he couldn't weigh a pound more—probably five pounds less.

She felt she was seeing him for the first time. Before this, she'd looked at him through the house, her desire for the house; he was the owner, the opponent, the obstacle, her ally when Eric got cold feet; his was the signature that made the house hers. Now she looked at him as if she meant to draw him. He had the habitual stoop of the unusually tall. The length of his strong narrow hands and the height of his thin face rising to the black widow's peak of hair made him seem even taller. She gathered herself out of the grass, brushing the dry bits of thatch off her clothes, hating to be caught like this, sweaty and scruffy, waiting for Eric to come home.

"Are you okay out here?" Harry said.

"Eric took the van and he forgot to leave the key." She was appalled to feel herself on the verge of weeping. "And I left my phone in the van, so I can't call him. It's just the whole day, I don't know. Moving. And then we got stuck in traffic forever."

"Moving is hard," Harry said. "Come inside and have some tea."

In five minutes, Lacey was in Harry's kitchen with a glass of sweet tea. His house was everything she hoped hers might some-day be. The maple floors shone, and every piece of furniture had its own light, from the red sun shining off the polished tabletop to the rainbows flaring from the beveled edges in the china cabinet's doors.

He seemed restless in the beautiful room, putting down his glass and picking it up again, fidgeting with a dishcloth. "Come to the front room and see where I teach," he said. She thought he'd been about to say something else and had changed his mind at the last moment.

In the front room, she found the same glossy oak floors, two wooden music stands, a framed five-by-six-foot charcoal drawing of a young woman playing the violin in a whirl of long hair, and a collection of amethyst carnival glass on the mantel. Harry raised his glass of tea to the drawing. "My sister, Dora. When she was very young."

"It's beautiful. Who drew it?"

Harry's face smoothed to a deliberate flatness, a public face, neutral as the image on a coin. "Her husband. They lived next door, in your house."

Lacey nodded, abashed, unable to fathom what she had done wrong. She bounced on her toes and wished she could find a way to leave without seeming rude. She followed Harry to the kitchen and accepted more tea. "Did the painters do a good job?" he said.

"I can't get in." Eric could at least have left the key. She forced her mind away from the house, still withholding itself from her after all those weeks, the forms they'd signed, the down payment, and she couldn't even get inside. A thought came to her. "The little boy on the bike. Who's he?"

She didn't like the way he'd turned at the property line and kept himself so exactly in front of her house, as if he had a right to be there. It made her uneasy. Harry looked like the neighbor who knew everyone's business, the plant waterer for friends on vacation, the third name on everyone's emergency contact list. Lacey's mother depended on people like this to hold her mail when she was vagrant. Lacey hoped the boy was someone's grandson visiting, or the child of renters who were leaving in a month. Someone she wouldn't have to worry about.

Harry set his glass down hard in surprise, and tea spilled onto the bright tabletop. "You've seen him?" he said.

"You know the one I mean?" Lacey was disappointed; if Harry knew the child so well, he must live nearby and be a problem in the neighborhood.

"Children on bicycles, they come, they go. . . ." He busied himself with a napkin and wouldn't meet her eyes.

She leaned forward across the table. "Does he live on the street?"

Long after the table was dry, Harry kept rubbing the napkin in circles, staring at his hands. At last, he looked across the table, but his eyes were fixed on Lacey's glass, not her face. "No. He's never shown himself to me."

Lacey had seen this kind of evasion when she asked other teachers about certain children. If the child's first-grade teacher said, *I didn't know him well* or *he's probably changed since then,* she knew she had trouble. Refusal to answer was the answer. "Thanks for the tea," she said. She'd watch for this neighbor boy and get to know him; trouble was her specialty. "I'd better get back. Eric will be home soon." Maybe—she hoped.

"I'm thinking, CarolAnna changed the locks, but did she get the back door?" He opened a drawer next to his sink. "Key, key. Let's see if this works."

She followed him out the back door, looking over her shoulder for one last glimpse of his sister, Dora, with her violin in the front room, her predecessor in the house. They walked between the two Cape Cods, underneath the maple where no grass grew. New mulch left a sulfured scent in the evening air. The back lawn was mowed in diagonals down to the row of cypresses, and around the brick patio the sentry boxwoods stood neat and tight. Lacey knew that Harry had been maintaining the Miszlaks' yard along with his own. She hoped she and Eric would be able to keep it this nice.

Harry offered her the brass key. "Give it a try."

Lacey wriggled the key into the lock. She pressed it hard, and something pushed back. Her hand jerked with a reflexive shock, as if she'd touched a centipede. She hated the touch of many-legged things, so wrong, unnatural. The key dropped to the doorstep. When she picked it up, it was warm in her hand, and it wouldn't enter the lock at all.

"No," she said, suddenly furious. The whole bitter, frustrating day came down to this: the door, the key, the lock. She wasn't about to let Eric find her waiting to be let in, like some stray. She had found this house and chosen it—it was *hers*. She forced the key. The lock yielded slightly, then seized and would not let the key release or turn.

"Wait," Harry said. "I'll go get the WD-40."

It was too much. Her house had shut her out—*her* house, the house she had loved when it was broken and dirty—now clean and beautiful, it shut her out? No. She found a chunk of gray stone under the boxwoods and hammered the window, ignoring Harry's protest. Her anger felt entirely reasonable to her; one way or another, she was going in. The glass clung to the frame for three seconds before releasing to shatter on the kitchen floor. She put her hand through to reach the inner lock, and something *bit* her—no, it was broken glass in the window frame. Blood ran down her palm from a diagonal gash, shockingly cold, as if she'd reached into a freezer and grabbed the coils. She gripped her wrist and looked at Harry, so disoriented by her own behavior that she could not imagine what to do next. And the angry thought, rooted in her mind as deeply as the baby in her body, pulsed relentlessly, *My house, mine, mine.*

"Wait," he said. "Don't go in." He hurried across the grass to his own back door.

She saw a roll of paper towels on the kitchen counter, so she reached through the broken window and unlocked the door. Fat handfuls of blood spread on the newly grouted floor. They had chosen light blue tile for the floor and gray granite for the countertops. She hoped her blood wouldn't turn the blue grout black. She squeezed her hand around a clump of paper towels. Numb cold rayed through her wrist.

Inside, the dining room and hallway were unexpectedly dim with a darkness gathering like water in a cup, and pressing into Lacey's eyes and filling her throat. Her teacher voice, the careful adult Lacey, warned her to stop, go out and wait for Harry, but she ignored it because the house was *hers.* Nothing could keep her out. She clenched her injured hand between her breasts and reached out with the other hand to feel her way.

She could not understand this darkness, here where the lowest step turned in a full circle and she had seen her someday children and their maybe dog in the bright afternoon. Evening light came in through the two windows in the living room and reflected off the newly polished and sealed floors, a sheet of brilliant amber. In the kitchen, red sunlight glittered in the granite's mica flecks. Yet no light reached here, where the stairs began, though it should have poured in a shower of gold down the porthole window. She looked up to see what was wrong—had the painters blocked the window with cardboard and forgotten to remove it? Was the glass broken and boarded up?—and she saw nothing, not even darkness. A mist pressed against her eyes, and her mouth tasted of cold gray water, the taste of fear.

There was a step on the front porch, too light for Harry, and a hand tapped the door. Lacey held her breath and pressed her hand over her breastbone to muffle her rushing heart. She felt like a child put to bed in a strange room, knowing silence was safety, head under the blankets no matter how hot, suffocating on terror and her own used breath. But the teacher voice said, *It's time to act like a grown-up,* and the hand tapped again. *Nothing to be afraid of,* it said, *just a neighbor at the door.*

"Coming," Lacey called. Something caught her ankle. Something that gripped and squeezed. Her feet flew out behind her and she tumbled forward, twisting as she fell.

She landed hard on her right side and curled around the belly bump. "No," she said. "No, no." This could not happen. She held her breath, keeping the child in through will alone; she clenched her fists, regardless of the pain in the slashed palm.

The back door opened, and with Harry's entrance, light flowed into the hall, rising from the polished floor. The porthole window burned. "Lacey? Where are you?"

"I fell." The middle of her body tightened, relaxed, and tightened again around a feeling too dense and slow to call pain.

"Are you hurt?"

Something touched her thigh. "I'm bleeding."

He took her right hand and pulled her fingers away from the red clot of paper. "You'll need stitches."

"No. I'm *bleeding.*" Lacey reached under the pink dress to touch the thing on her thigh, soft and insinuating, a wet feather, a tickling tongue, the faintest sticky stroke of warmth sliding on her skin. "Ambulance," she said, her voice perfectly steady. Her heart hummed in her ears, and she kept her face stony. If she let go, let her mouth shake even once, she would fall apart and the baby would die. She tightened her thighs to hold everything in, blood and baby and all. She would not allow this to happen.

"This is too soon," Harry said. He reached down to take her elbows, as if to pull her to her feet. She shook her head. His hands jumped away from her.

"Ambulance," she said again. She showed him her left hand, the blood on her fingertips. "Please."

Chapter Four

AFTER TEN MINUTES in the emergency room, Lacey was wheeled into a semiprivate room in Labor and Delivery. Pink and blue balloons floated above the doorknobs in the hall, each announcing someone else's baby. She waited for a long time and no one came to tell her if her baby was alive or dead. If only she had her phone so she could call Eric—even if she had the phone, the battery was probably drained; she was forever forgetting to plug it in. It made Eric so impatient with her; he was always waiting for her to call, or trying to call her. Where was he? She closed her eyes and whispered to the baby, "Hold on, hold on," and still the blood trickled, sticky and slow.

The door opened. "The cut's closed up on its own," Lacey said without opening her eyes. "There's no point stitching it now." They'd brought her into this room and left her here, surrounded by other people's happy balloons, and didn't care enough to come in with so much as a stethoscope, let alone an ultrasound. It was so unfair, and she was all alone; she needed help and no one cared. Not even Harry had come with her, and where was Eric? Her underwear was soaked through, and every time she touched it, the blood was still warm and fresh.

"Lacey, what did you do to yourself?" Eric, at last. "All you had to do was sit there in the shade. I wasn't gone for fifteen minutes, and I come back and there's the window broken, blood all over the floor, anything could have happened, I had no idea."

"You shouldn't have left me."

"I was only gone a minute. Just to get my temper under control. My parents used to fight about money. They went on for hours, shouting, breaking things. I don't want to be them."

"Then you can't leave. You have to stay and talk to me."

He sat on the bed and lowered his face to hers, kissed her forehead, her eyelids, and her mouth. His face was wet. He was crying, right out in the open, defenseless. "Lacey, can you ever forgive me? I am so sorry."

It terrified her, the way Eric could turn like this. He dropped everything all at once, all his competence, his confidence, everything that made him right, and gave her his naked heart, a thing she was afraid to see, let alone touch. No one else had ever seen him like this—and now, when she didn't know if the baby was dead or alive, now *she* had to comfort *him*. She knew he needed more, but she couldn't make herself speak.

His face sank into her neck and he lifted her shoulders into a dense, trembling embrace. "I was so scared," he whispered into her skin. "I thought you were dead, I thought the baby was dead."

And he assumed the baby was fine, that she'd taken care of everything while he was out soothing his own hurt feelings. "Nobody's looked at the baby yet," she said. "Nobody's told me anything."

He pushed himself off the bed. "They haven't looked? Are you still bleeding?"

"I can't tell." Her voice cracked, and she closed her mouth hard. As the blood dried, her skin tightened and itched. She didn't want to touch whatever was happening under the sheet, fearing to find something more than blood—a tiny curled body, already cooling in the mess. No; her fingers imagined it, but she shut her mind. She wanted a doctor. Someone who would tell her quickly, as quickly as the pregnancy test: *yes* or *no*.

"I'll be right back," Eric said.

He returned in four minutes with ultrasound machine and doctor in tow, a dry small woman with pearl earrings and the cleanest hands Lacey had ever seen, fingernails like bleached shells, palms pure white. "Let's look at you, Mrs. Miszlak," she said. The gel was cold, and the doctor slid the wand over Lacey's belly and said brightly, "There's the heartbeat."

"Are you sure?" Lacey couldn't let go of the fear so easily. The doctor touched a panel on the machine, and the heartbeat sounded through the speakers, a quick watery *hush-hush, hush-hush*. Lacey cried without noise, weak in relief, pressing the backs of her hands against her cheekbones.

Eric sank into a chair. "Thank God."

"You want to know what you're having?" They nodded. She slid the ultrasound wand over Lacey. "Definitely a boy." It looked like a star map to Lacey, a sweep of cloudy constellations, gray in a black sky. "There's his profile. Look at that pretty face. Now, about this bleeding."

The ultrasound machine printed out a picture, and Lacey saw the child in the gray stars, the large curve of his head, hands under chin, thin legs drawn up and crossed. There he was, a real person, already alive. It was good to think *he* instead of *it*. She was bleeding, the doctor told her, because the placenta had partly torn away from the wall of her womb. There was no surgery and no medication, no help but rest, and no promise that rest would help. If the placenta tore away—*unzipped,* the doctor said, if it unzipped itself from the wall—the baby would die. If it scarred, the baby would survive. She spoke as calmly as if she were reading a recipe. "We want to keep you overnight for observation," she said.

Lacey wished the doctor would leave the machine hooked up to her so she could listen to it all night. *Hush-hush, hush-hush.* Even more, she wished the doctor would stay and interpret the pictures and sounds. *Still alive,* the doctor would say every hour, on the hour. *It's a boy, and he's still alive.* "Will he be okay?" Lacey asked, and the teacher voice admonished her, *Don't ask if you don't want to know.*

"Most likely," the doctor said. "You relax." She left, taking the ultrasound machine with her. Lacey put the picture on the bedside table. Every few seconds, she touched it, imagining the baby's heart, *hush-hush.*

Eric slumped in the chair with his hands over his eyes. After a while, he said slowly, with a weight in his voice, "I have to get down to the office."

"The office?" Resentment flowed up Lacey's left arm into her heart. "You're not staying?"

"I've got to. Uncle Floyd's given me a dozen divorces, and I've got to get up to speed." He stroked her belly and then bent down to kiss her. She let him do it, holding her lips stiff under his mouth. Then she was sorry, and it was too late, he was gone, because his work was important.

Eric's work was always more important than hers; when they were dating, he would cancel on her without a second thought if he had a big test or paper due, and she never did. Even when she was working to put him through school, his work was a career and hers was a job. The first thing he said when Uncle Floyd offered him the position was *now you can stay home till the baby starts school,* as if that had been their plan all along. She thought not, and she'd let him know in good time.

Eventually, the nurses fed her a flat gray piece of turkey, or possibly a boiled sponge, along with a dinner roll, boiled carrots, boiled spinach, and a boiled potato, with cherry Jell-O. She drowsed, propped up in the bed with her hands folded over the belly bump, feeling her son spinning and dancing inside her. "We'll go home tomorrow, baby," she said. "We'll get moved in; I just have to unpack a few boxes."

The door opened. If it was another nurse with another needle, Lacey would beat her off with the dinner tray. But it was the bicycle boy from Forrester Lane, little mister trouble-at-home. "I could help," he said. "Maybe I could."

Grayness whirled over her, the same strange gray panic that had closed her sight on the stairs; she disappeared into it. This child should not be here. It was wrong. She searched for the call button, but it had slipped away and its cord was caught in the machinery of the bed.

"Why are you here?" she said. She found the cord and pulled it sideways. It gave an inch and then stopped.

"My mom came here."

"Your mom had a baby?" Though Greeneburg was a small city, it surprised her to land in the hospital at the same time as some near neighbor. She yanked the cord, and the call button jumped into her hand. Its solidity in her palm gave her strength. Why was she so flustered by this ordinary child? Stupid hormones. "Why aren't you with her?"

"I can't find her."

The child looked terrible, dirty around the hairline and neck, clean-faced as if he had been washed carelessly and against his will. He sniffled and smeared the back of his hand against his nose. "Have you been lost for long?" she asked him.

"Ages. They left me and they took the baby and I can't find them."

"I'll call the nurse."

"They're no good. Nobody listens to me."

"I'm listening. What's wrong?"

His body swayed, as if he meant to run over to the bed and cast himself upon her. He held himself tense by the door, twisting his dirty hands. "It's the baby," he said. "She cries, and Mom's real tired all the time, and I only wanted to help."

Parents never knew how sweet their children were. At conferences, when Lacey said something good about a child, especially a boy, the parents often responded with *Are you sure that's my kid?* right in front of the child. So this little guy wanted to help, and his parents wouldn't let him. Probably they were afraid he'd drop the baby.

"Let me buzz the nurse; all you have to do is tell them your name and they'll take you straight to your mom's room," she said.

"No, they won't. They never will."

Lacey's eyes flooded for his sake. It was partly the hormones that made her weepy, partly this one dirty, hopeful, affectionate child, this one loving and wounded heart, the emblem of so many. She pressed the call button, but when she said, "They're coming," the child was gone.

"What do you need here, Mom?" the nurse asked.

"There was a little boy. He couldn't find his mother."

"I'll find him."

Lacey waited for her to come back and tell her the child had been found. She never did. The hospital hummed and whispered, and every time Lacey fell asleep, a door banged, or someone's footsteps ran fast and hard outside her room. She counted boxes, everything that needed to be unpacked, all that work she had to do tomorrow, the empty house waiting to be filled. She drifted off and spent the night working in her dreams, unloading box after box after box of things she didn't even know she owned, opening door after door in a house that had no end.

Chapter Five

THE NEXT AFTERNOON, when Eric brought her home in the Mitsubishi, she discovered he had done more than turn in the U-Haul and pick up the car. He opened the front door and Lacey stepped into a room she didn't recognize. He laughed at her surprise. "The magic of same-day delivery," he said. "You like it?"

When they were dating and he'd had money, Eric had been the master of romantic surprises. He took her on the most astonishing extravagant dates: a balloon ride, a cabin in the Smokies, a cruise to Alaska. Even when the money went away, he'd live on peanut butter sandwiches for two weeks to save his lunch budget for a special meal. And now he'd furnished the house. He'd bought real furniture: sofa, loveseat, and chair in dark red leather—end tables and a coffee table, dark walnut—and the most perfect lamps, ornate brass columns with gold linen shades and tassels. Everything had ball-and-claw feet. Her whole life, she had longed for furniture with ball-and-claw feet, furniture that announced itself: *I am here, and here I stay.*

"If you don't like it, we've got three days to exchange it," Eric said.

"It's perfect. Oh, bookshelves! Real wood, no more plastic.

I feel like such a grown-up." The bookcase was bolted into the wall, baby-safe already, and Eric had left the bottom three shelves empty, perfect for the baby's books and toys.

"There's no art. You can put up some of your things. I always liked that big coffee cup."

Lacey looked at the blank wall between the two big windows, and her mind flashed to the same wall in Harry Rakoczy's house next door: his sister, Dora, charcoal under glass, her face tilted against the violin, her long wild hair.

She loved the furniture, but what had Eric done? He'd been counting pennies ever since her last day of school; he'd lost his temper over fifty dollars to keep the moving van overnight, twenty dollars to replace the dishes, and now this? "Are you sure?" she said.

She wanted the furniture. It was everything she wanted: a houseful of things that couldn't be packed up and moved overnight, a home with weight, an anchor for her life. This was the home she'd drawn in her school notebooks, all those nomadic years with her mother. These beautiful rooms. Eric knew what she wanted; but she knew what he needed. She tried again, knowing she had to voice her doubt as a true question; she had to give him the chance to change his mind.

"Are you sure we can afford this?" she said. "If it's too much, we could wait."

"There's no interest for six months. Don't you like it?"

He sounded disappointed, and of course she liked it—he always knew what she liked. It would have been fun, though, to have chosen the furniture herself, to have hunted through the store with Eric. An ungrateful thought, and she pushed it away: in the end she would have picked precisely this. "I love it," she said. The bookcases stood on either side of the fireplace, and there were all the books and CDs, along with his grandmother's Ukrainian Easter eggs in Waterford crystal eggcups. All that work. She knew, without asking, that he had unpacked every box except those marked *Lacey Classroom,* flattened the boxes, and tied them in a stack in the garage. And the *Classroom* boxes were up in the attic, and when she opened them a year from now, maybe two, they would smell of crayons and the future. "And you unpacked all this," she said, sighing. "I worried about it all night."

"Come see the bedroom."

Lacey grabbed Eric's hand, ignoring the pain that shot across her palm. "How did you do this? All in one night?"

"You don't get through law school by sleeping. Come and see."

Eager to see and approve the bedroom, she pulled him to the foot of the stairs. They were finished with the same deep-amber oak flooring as the rest of the downstairs, with a runner of red carpet coming down, held in place by brass rods on each step. That was so typical of Eric, the exact detail, his concern that she might slip on the glassy wood. In the kitchen, she knew, he had already replaced the broken window.

She sensed something—not a sound, but an approach—and she looked up the stairs. Something dark rushed down, something too dense and hectic to see. Blackness seized her by the knees. It hit her all at once, driving into her breastbone. She coughed and pulled for air, and her lungs resisted, unwilling to open again. To breathe felt like an effort against life, as if she had to open her mouth underwater.

"Lacey," Eric said urgently. "What's wrong?"

Something in the house. Something pushing back against the furniture—the thing that had tried to keep her out, sealing itself against the key, slashing her with the broken window. When she was eight, her mother had had the chance to house-sit for a friend of a friend who was traveling to Tanzania: six months in a big house, free rent and utilities, and even some extra pay for taking care of the dogs. Her mother had walked into the house and out again. *This house doesn't want me,* she'd said, and so she and Lacey spent the winter moving from one motel to another. Lacey thought she felt it now, some resentful force pushing down the stairs, pushing her out.

Unacceptable. Not *this* house. This house had loved her from the moment they met, the house stripped of shutters and carpet, Lacey with her hand full of pistachio shells on the sunny street. This dizziness was nothing, loss of blood, maybe. She shook her head. "Some kind of weird vertigo. I'm fine."

"You looked like you might pass out." Eric glanced up the stairs, then took her elbow and steered her into the kitchen. "I bet you're hungry."

Lacey seized on this explanation. "If you saw what they fed me . . . I'm starved."

She was disappointed to see their old dinette in the kitchen. "We're eating in here for now," Eric said. "We can't do the dining room till we've paid off the rest. Baby's room first. We'll do that when you feel better."

"Maybe in a month." Yesterday the doctor had told her the baby would be viable in six weeks. *Just barely viable, and you have to keep him in the oven as long as you can. Take care of yourself. Don't lift anything over ten pounds.* Just six weeks to go. She wouldn't buy a crib until then: it would be tempting fate.

They sat at the Formica dinette, and it was just like back in Columbia, when Eric was in law school and Lacey taught fourth grade, the two of them in their nest, so cozy and sweet. Eric frowned at the chipped orange table and said, "Butcher block.

After the dining room." He slid two slices of pizza onto a paper plate.

She loved it when he made pizza. He made the dough from scratch, and somehow, in the midst of buying the furniture and unpacking all their things, he'd found time to pick up her favorite ingredients. The anchovies and the meaty little black kalamata olives, the artichoke hearts cured in olive oil. She craved such salty, intense flavors since getting pregnant. He'd left one-third of the pizza plain cheese for himself.

"So I called your mother," he said.

Lacey put the second slice back down onto her plate. "What for?"

"The doctor says you're on bed rest. Your mother's coming to help us out."

"No." Lacey wasn't hungry anymore. The anchovies, so delicious a moment ago, turned her stomach. "She makes me crazy."

How could she make him understand? She knew how to be Eric Miszlak's wife, hardworking and sensible and supportive, a girl who kept her head in a crisis; she knew how to be Ella Dane Kendall's daughter, quiet and sensitive, gifted with spiritual talents not yet developed. She could not possibly be both at once. And what if Lacey's mother came in and felt that force pushing down the stairs, something in the house denying her right to be there? Furniture wouldn't anchor Ella Dane Kendall to any house; she would insist they leave, which Lacey would never do. Ella Dane wouldn't believe what it meant to Lacey, to have a real home at last.

It was already too late to explain her mother to Eric, years too late. Lacey had told him stories of her unsettled childhood as adventures, comedies, when they were dating. She hadn't wanted to be *that* girl, the one who was needy and damaged, the work in progress, the fixer-upper, and so she laughed and made faces and shaped the stories with her hands. *Did I ever tell you about the time . . . ?* she would say. The time Ella Dane's then boyfriend poured bleach on all their clothes; the time Ella Dane smuggled a litter of puppies into a motel; the time they had spent three weeks one July sleeping in the car outside a fancy hotel in Myrtle Beach, sneaking in to the breakfast buffet and the swimming pool. It was too late to tell the stories again as the humiliating horrors they had truly been—to Eric, who had fallen over himself laughing at the idea of a fancy hotel in Myrtle Beach. She hadn't even known that was funny.

"You don't know how crazy she makes me," Lacey said.

"She means well."

"She'll do some kind of moon ritual and burn weird candles." She would pray for the baby, in her way; Lacey couldn't stand the idea. She didn't want Ella Dane having any opinions about this pregnancy, advising Lacey what to eat and what to avoid. If Lacey had been thinking clearly, those first few weeks of her pregnancy, she wouldn't have told Ella Dane about it at all—not until the baby was born. After the mess she'd made of Lacey's childhood, she had no right. "You'll hate it," Lacey said.

"You can't stay here alone all day in bed. What if you need something?"

"I could call you."

"I'll be working. You can't always get me." He turned his back on her to wash his hands at the sink. "Finish your pizza," he said. "You've got to eat. For the baby."

Lacey's stomach twisted again. She couldn't tell: Was it hunger, nausea, rage? They all felt the same. Eric was right. The baby needed food. She waited until he left the room before she took another bite.

Chapter Six

TWO WEEKS LATER, on the first day of school, Lacey woke at eight, breathless, with her conscience biting her heart. Having been student and then teacher since the age of five, she could not shake the feeling that she was urgently wanted somewhere else.

By eight thirty she was at the kitchen table, her laptop open and a cup of decaf cooling beside her. She was supposed to be choosing an obstetrician. It had taken her half an hour to find her way into the provider list for Eric's new insurance; everybody else had grown up with computers and cell phones since elementary school, but Lacey had been lucky to have a working calculator, and she still wasn't entirely comfortable on the Internet. Now she was passed from one your-call-is-important-to-us hold to another, from receptionist to nurse, each handing her along as soon as she said *placental abruption*. Every nurse told her the doctor's schedule was full. She jumped to YourBabyNow.net to see what her baby was doing at eighteen weeks. She loved this website, her online home.

He was growing a layer of fur called lanugo all over his body. He was the size of a lime. Lacey cupped her hand. The entire hairy child could fit into her palm, and she wouldn't even stretch her fingers. And in a month, he'd be big enough to survive on his own—just barely, and two months would be better, or three—she could hardly bear to imagine it, after all that bleeding. Better, safer, to think of other things.

Her mother came up behind her and started rubbing her shoulders. Lacey sighed and let the roots of her neck relax under Ella Dane Kendall's strong hands. "I can't find a doctor," she said. Last week, Eric had taken an afternoon off work to drive her to her old OB in Columbia, but that wasn't a long-term plan. In all Greeneburg, there had to be one doctor who would take her.

"You should look for a doula and not a Western death doctor."

"Insurance only covers the Western death doctors. And they don't want me because, you know, I might die."

"I know what you need." Ella Dane stopped rubbing Lacey's shoulders and busied herself at the stove, making some kind of tea.

"No herbs," Lacey said. When she went to college, her mother's life became an unending self-improvement project: cruelty-free cosmetics, organic clothing, veganism, bearded spiritual men. Ella Dane meant well, but what kind of life was it, when the woman's only long-term relationship was with the world's nastiest dog? She came to their aid without complaint, keeping their house clean—well, cleanish—even though she refused to use the vacuum cleaner (it scrambled the feng shui, she said). Lacey tried to be grateful, without much success. *She means well, means well, means well* was Lacey's mantra; Ella Dane threw out all the cleaners and used vinegar for most purposes, oil with a few drops of essential sage for the furniture, and now the living room smelled like an Italian salad. And Bibbits the vegan poodle, whom Lacey remembered as a frisky thing with a habit of nipping, had taken to vomiting in corners and coughing for hours, rolling his bloodshot eyes in the most pitiable way. Lacey wasn't the only one who needed a Western death doctor, but Ella Dane had shaken off her suggestion of a vet. Her dog didn't need chemicals. But she meant well. And she had sensed no angry, unwelcoming presence in the house. *A happy house,* she'd said. *You did well.*

Then what was that darkness, the thing that had fallen down the stairs? Nothing at all. Low blood sugar. Vertigo.

"I'm going to lie down for a while," Lacey said to Ella Dane. She'd find a doctor later.

She paused at the foot of the stairs. Something had moved in the living room. She closed her eyes against the gray wash of panic and forced herself to look straight into the room. Her mother, who had refused to spend a winter in a comfortable house because it felt unfriendly, had entered 571 Forrester with a smile two weeks ago, telling Lacey she had never felt a home so glad to be lived in. There was nothing wrong. There could be nothing wrong.

The thing in the chair was Bibbits, turning and clawing the red leather seat, nesting in the shredded remnants of a green and gold brocade cushion. Relief made Lacey furious. "Down!" she shouted. "Off! *Bad* dog." A thing her mother had forbidden her ever to say, because all dogs were naturally good. The fringe of the cushion hung from either side of Bibbits's mouth in an extravagant green mustache. "*Bad,*" she said, and swept him off the chair with her hand.

He landed hard, with a yelp of more surprise than pain, and instead of bouncing to his feet, he jerked backward as if something had struck him and shrieked aloud.

"Bibbits?" Ella Dane rushed into the room with her hands full of letters and catalogs and scooped him up. "What's wrong, baby love?"

In Ella Dane's arms, Bibbits bared his teeth at Lacey. His body twitched, and he stretched his lips and began to cough, dry and deep. Ella Dane pulled a brown glass vial from her pocket and squirted a dropperful of something into Bibbits's mouth. His cough eased, though he still panted.

"He fell," Lacey said. She couldn't admit having hit him. She hadn't hurt him; something else had made him shriek. The red leather was clawed and the cushion ruined beyond repair. "Keep him off the furniture, please," she said, hoping she sounded patient and reasonable, and not like a whining child. She picked up the mail and went upstairs.

Lacey had been thirteen when Ella Dane picked Bibbits up from the side of the road. His vet bills used up Lacey's birthday present, all the money Grandpa Merritt sent—it was one of those times when Ella Dane was in grudging contact with her father, though she wouldn't let Lacey talk with him—and for years Ella Dane maintained the fiction that Bibbits was Lacey's dog. How many friends' houses, garage apartments, basements, and motel rooms had the Kendalls been evicted from, because of Bibbits. . . . That dog had made her life miserable.

Ella Dane loved him. Lacey went upstairs, carefully, two feet on each step, gripping the banister hard. Downstairs, Bibbits began to cough again.

Chapter Seven

ERIC SAT AT HIS DESK looking at his lunch. It was the most depressing sandwich he had ever seen. Nobody else at Moranis Miszlak brought their lunch to work, but whenever he went to a restaurant, the money he'd spent over the last month sprang up and seized his throat. They had good reasons for every cent, and yet the more reasons he thought of, the weaker they seemed. He felt like the criminal defendant who wouldn't stop explaining why he walked into the drugstore with a gun. Because his girlfriend's ex was threatening him. He forgot it was in his pocket. He was going to the pawnshop to sell it and only stopped for a Coke. It wasn't even his gun, he'd never seen it before.

So Eric bought furniture because it was on sale, and they needed all those things anyway, and a pregnant woman on bed rest couldn't sleep on a futon, and it was all delivered for one fee, and, and, and.

Because. Because Lacey looked so small in the hospital bed. Because of the long, long ten seconds before the doctor found the baby's heartbeat. Seven thousand dollars on the Discover Card. Because he walked into the house and it was empty except for the bloody footprints, and one small handprint, still sticky, on the lowest step.

He bought the furniture so the house would never be so empty again.

Seven thousand dollars, and then the hospital bill. Eric's uncle created this job for him when the firm could have gone another year without hiring. Uncle Floyd and many of his clients had lost money when Eric's parents' investment firm, Foothills Financial, went bankrupt, so Eric's salary was maybe half what it should be, and Floyd expected Eric to be grateful.

Lunch at the desk. It was nice of Lacey's mother to make his lunch. He wished she wouldn't. She was a gluten-free vegan, and what looked like cheese in his sandwich was actually some kind of pressed fermented soy by-product, and the bread was made of turnips and rice. Lacey had warned him Ella Dane would light candles and sing strange chants, but it wasn't that bad, apart from the food. And that rotten little dog.

Voices washed through the front office as the personnel of Moranis Miszlak returned. They brought a wonderful smell, becoming even more wonderful as it approached his office. Uncle Floyd opened the door. The old man was fabulous in his pink three-piece seersucker suit, green bow tie, and white shoes. He shoved Eric's untouched files to the side of the desk and set down a white Styrofoam box. "Brought you Abernathy's orange bourbon ribs. Baked potato. *And*"—he indicated the slice of orange, twisted and stuck into the ribs with a toothpick—"salad."

"Thanks, Uncle Floyd."

"Heard from your parents lately?"

"No." After the Foothills pyramid collapsed, Eric's mother had gone to Indiana to stay with her sister, and his father was still in jail. Eric wondered if Floyd had given him the job to find out if there was money hidden somewhere. If only. "Mom wrote once, but not Dad. I guess he's ashamed."

"He should be." Floyd reached across Eric's desk to finger the files. "Loaded you up with judies, huh?" Those were the clients who picked Moranis Miszlak because they saw the ads on afternoon television, airing during Judge Judy: cheap cases, hardly worth the cost of his time. People suing each other over undocumented loans, minor car accidents, and of course the low-income divorces. These cases belonged in small claims court, except for the clients' inflated value of their own pain and suffering. The divorces were people who had seen trouble coming and married it anyway. "Poor people need lawyers too," Floyd said. "You'll get better cases soon."

Eric straightened the picture of Lacey in its clear plastic frame. She stood beside the bumper cars at Myrtle Beach, with a snowcone in her hand, her hair blowing across her face in wavy strands of brown and gold. When Foothills went down, two weeks after Lacey and Eric got engaged, she kissed him and comforted him and promised to get him through law school. And she did it. Now she lay in bed with her feet elevated, wearing an adult diaper to catch the trickling blood.

"I've got enough to keep me busy," Eric said.

Floyd took the picture from his hands. "It ain't good enough to be busy. You got to be smart." He laid the picture on the desk, facedown, and took the orange slice off Eric's ribs and ate it, peel and all. "You know why they call this a doggy bag?"

Eric nodded. This sounded like the beginning of an Uncle Floyd life-skills seminar, and the quickest way through it was to nod and smile.

"Because you are that little girl's bitch is why," Floyd said. "Women all over God's earth have babies and they don't whine and carry on."

Eric couldn't let this pass unchallenged. "She put me through law school."

"Good for her. Now she's putting you through hell."

Eric pushed his keyboard away and tore a rib off the rack. It was still hot. These weren't leftovers. Floyd must have ordered for him just before leaving the restaurant. He was such a terrible old man, and then he had moments of disarming generosity.

"You got to be ready," Floyd said. "You were smart about the house, not spending much; she'll get half, but in a few years you'll hardly notice."

"She's my wife. I love her."

"There's never another wife like the first. My Marian, I still dream of her. Doc gives me Xanax for it. That girl of yours, her mother's some kind of witch."

Eric and Lacey had a courtroom wedding; Floyd Miszlak and Ella Dane Kendall, their witnesses, had made a bad impression on each other. Ella Dane interrupted the ceremony to invoke the four elements and the four directions to bless the young couple, bringing them fertility, abundance, harmony, and joy. Floyd followed her incantation by declaring it the deepest pile of crap he'd ever stepped into, including the summer he'd worked cleaning the elephant habitat in the Greeneburg Zoo when he was sixteen. "It prepared me for the law," he concluded, "but it didn't prepare me for this." He never missed a chance to remind Eric that all women turned into their mothers.

"Thanks for the ribs," Eric said.

"Best barbecue in town. I'll swear it on my deathbed." Floyd left the room.

Eric wiped his hands. On the surface, Floyd was all chicken-fried grammar and happy fat charm, like a rustic chair with bark on the wood, but under that were layers of cunning; the man could write a contract that would make Satan weep. But he was wrong about Lacey.

When Eric told her there was no money, that his parents had drained his trust fund to string their clients along, she took off her engagement ring, a one-carat marquis barricaded by ramparts of smaller diamonds, three carats total. She put it in his hand.

"You don't want to get married?" he said. It had been his first thought when he heard the news on morning television. *Upstate investment firm closes its doors.* He turned toward the television, toaster waffle steaming in his fingers, to see the Foothills storefront with its doors chained, and a crowd of clients—people whose accounts he'd handled during his internship last summer, when everything was fine—milling in the parking lot, funneling their hands and peering in the windows as if they might see boxes of money on the desks. *Lacey's gone,* he thought. The ring flashed in his hand.

"Do you still want to?" she said. "Things won't be like we thought."

He nodded but could not speak.

"So return this ring. Get me a little topaz, and use the money for tuition."

He put the ring on her hand, sold the BMW his parents had bought for his sixteenth birthday, and applied for student loans. While applying, he learned his parents had stolen his identity to open several lines of credit, so Lacey took out extra loans to cover his tuition. She finished her degree in three years and started teaching fourth grade, also after-school tutoring and summer school. A dozen divorces a month passed over Floyd Miszlak's desk, but he didn't know everything. He saw only the failures. Nobody came to the lawyer on their twentieth anniversary to file a legal declaration that they were happy and faithful.

Eric picked up the phone to call Sammie Vandermeijn, Moranis Miszlak's office manager. "I need you to order flowers for my wife," he said.

"What do you think this is, 1963?" she demanded.

"What?" Eric said, completely thrown.

"I don't work for you. I don't order flowers, and you can make your own damn coffee. You got something for me to do, it better be a billable hour with a client's name on it. Your wife doesn't want flowers."

"I want to do something nice for her. She's having a hard time."

"She asked for it, marrying a Miszlak." His door opened, and Sammie entered, phone in hand. She leaned against the door frame, her gray skirt pulled tight across her hips. He didn't take it personally. Sammie flirted by instinct. Everybody knew she was sleeping with Floyd. "You know what's nice?" she said. "Sapphires."

"What about food?"

"Miszlak. The little birds in the trees have a name for you. Cheap, cheap, cheap."

She swayed out of the doorway, and he watched her walk down the hall. He could watch Sammie enter and leave rooms all day long. Sapphires: that showed how shallow she was. The way to Lacey's heart was through onion rings.

Chapter Eight

ELLA DANE HAD BEEN E-MAILING her clients. She had taken to the Internet with astonishing ease and had become an online pet psychic. Mostly she tried to persuade people their dogs wanted to be vegan. She told them dogs felt compassion for all living things and truly preferred hydrolyzed soy protein to beef, and in return, the owners deposited twenty dollars a month into her PayPal account. Surprisingly, she had over fifty clients. Lacey couldn't understand it.

Somehow, Ella Dane had supported herself and Lacey ever since the day they left Grandpa Merritt's house forever, a day just as hot and sticky as this, though it had been September. Lacey was six, a first grader, when her teacher held her back at the end of school to say, "You're not riding the bus today, your mom's picking you up."

Ella Dane arrived at school not in Grandpa Merritt's extended-cab Ford pickup but in a blue car Lacey didn't recognize, a sickly hatchback lunging against its wheels. She had to get in the driver's door and slide over Ella Dane, because the passenger door was punched in, and it was terribly hot. "Can't you turn the air on?" she said.

"There's no air." Ella Dane lowered her window. The passenger's side had no window, only a sheet of thick plastic duct-taped to the crumpled frame.

The hatchback was full of black garbage bags. One of them was open, and Timmy the bear peered out of it. Lacey grabbed him and said, "Why's my stuff in garbage bags?"

"I packed our things, we're leaving."

That was all Ella Dane would say, then or later. That morning, Lacey had kissed Grandpa Merritt good-bye and gotten onto the school bus with her Barbie backpack and sparkly sneakers. That night, she and her mother slept in the car on a strange street. A week later, they moved into a motel in a new town halfway to the coast, and Lacey found a palmetto bug in her book bag. It ran across her hand. Each individual thorned foot clutched her at a particular point. She couldn't get the feeling off her skin.

Grandpa Merritt had lived in an old neighborhood in Columbia. The magnolia was twice as tall as the house, and in September when the furry cones fell, little Lacey picked out the ruby-red seeds. Grandpa Merritt suspended a hula hoop from the ceiling and hung gauze curtains from it, so she could have a princess bed. After that day, she never saw that house or that room again. By the time she was old enough to visit Grandpa Merritt on her own, he had suffered three strokes and was trapped in the nursing home bed. He clutched her with his dry claw and mouthed words she couldn't understand. The hair on his arms was a wiry white fleece. Long ago, he used to swing her up over his head and catch her, swing her and catch her again.

They'd lived with him for a year. One year of coming home to the same house every day, one year of having a real house, her own home, and then back on the road with Ella Dane, always on the way to somewhere else, just as it had been for the first five years of Lacey's life, since before she could remember.

"Because we can't," Ella Dane said, whenever Lacey wanted to go home, when things were worse than usual and they were sleeping in the car again. "Because I had to," she said, when Lacey wanted to know why, why, why had they left Grandpa Merritt. "Because I had no choice."

After his stroke, Grandpa Merritt lay on his kitchen floor for two days, the telephone out of reach on the wall. If the Kendalls had been there, he might not have been reduced to the wet-mouthed stammering thing strapped in the nursing home bed. There had to be a reason.

"That's done," Ella Dane said. "Now I've got to write the blog." She blogged about the challenges of raising a vegan dog. She'd taken Bibbits off his vet-prescribed medication and was treating his heart condition with a tincture of *Taraxacum,* which when Lacey Googled it turned out to be dandelion. Hundreds of people read what Ella Dane wrote and took her advice for their own dogs. Astonishing.

Eric passed through the kitchen, on his way to somewhere else. "I'm going back to the office," he said. "A client's coming to give a deposition."

"At night?" Lacey asked.

"I'll call if I'm going to be later than eleven."

For a moment she had felt the old connection with him, the sympathy that had been the root of their love. Now he was gone again, living a real life in the real world while all she had to do was keep the baby alive inside her, a thing even a sheep could do. Lacey tried to be understanding. Eric's life was so much harder than he'd thought it would be. He was supposed to be writing contracts in Foothills Financial, making a six-figure income on four days a week, not putting in twelve-hour days in the back room of Moranis Miszlak. And she couldn't even look at Ella Dane without seeing Grandpa Merritt's green door in the shadow of the magnolia. She hauled herself out of the kitchen to relax on the living room sofa with the latest issue of *Early Learning,* to read about literacy readiness for at-risk kindergartners.

Dizziness walked through her. She closed her eyes and leaned back into the new-leather smell of her sofa. She breathed deeply, four, five, six times, and the doorbell rang on a single note, like a clock chiming the half hour. She waited for the second, falling tone. It didn't come. She folded her magazine open on the kindergarten article and dragged herself into the hallway.

She didn't want to answer the door. That black vertigo was gathering on the stairs, the terrifying sense of something spinning inward, closing in, pulling her down. She reached out to the banister as if she were groping in the dark, as if she could pull herself up the stairs. From nowhere, something tumbled toward her, a plunging boneless thing, falling without will and without resistance, all blood and hair. Lacey grabbed the banister with both hands. The thing fell into her, fell through her, leaving her hollow and cold.

She wanted to scream and run, cover her face and sob like a child; she bit her lip and stared right into it, the whirling vertigo. Whatever it was, it was *wrong.* Standing just here, she had seen her someday children and their maybe dog on the stairs, that first day. That was the truth, not this. There was nothing to see. Ella Dane would have sensed it and warned her.

She lifted her face. Light filled the porthole window and overflowed in the stairwell like water in a clean glass. Her beautiful house. Her family's life would be beautiful here. It wasn't yet, but it would be. The vertigo drained down her throat, leaving her head clear but her stomach full and sour.

The bell rang again and she opened the door. The evening light slanted on the porch. She blinked into the glare, blazing red with the blood in her own eyelids, and she swayed for a moment. The house at her back supported her, and she rubbed her eyes clear. "What do you want?"

It was little mister trouble-at-home. He smiled and said in one quick rush, "Hello-my-name-is-Drew-I'm-selling-popcorn-for-my-school-how-many-boxes-would-you-like-please-and-thank-you-ma'am-you-can-write-a-check."

What kind of predatory PTA fund-raisers did they have in Greeneburg, sending the kids out to start their sales on the first day of school? "No," Lacey said.

He clutched a clipboard in one hand and a plastic bowl of popcorn in the other. "Don't you want a sample? Just one piece." He shook the bowl. The unpopped kernels rattled, and Lacey choked on the hot chemical smell of artificial butter.

"No," she said with her hand on the inner knob, ready to swing the door shut.

"There's low fat," he offered.

"I don't eat low fat."

"Yes, ma'am, I can see that. If you wanted to, you could."

"I'm pregnant. I'm supposed to look like this."

Drew's blond eyebrows jumped, a surprisingly adult expression. "Yes, ma'am, if you say so. There's also extra butter. It's only fifteen dollars a box."

Bad trouble, said her teacher's eye. *Shut the door, shut it quick.* But what kind of teacher was she, what kind of human being, to feel revulsion rather than pity? There was something wrong with him, and it wasn't his fault. It never was. She was shocked by his condition: the flush on his fair face, the light hair sweat-browned along the hairline, his sunburned ears, and the white dead scale on his lips. "Sweetie—Drew, how long have you been out here in this heat?"

"Since school was out, six hours, ma'am. If I sell ten more boxes, I get a pocketknife with three blades and a screwdriver," he said.

A warning sounded deep in her. Since when did a PTA fundraiser offer a knife as a selling prize? "How about you come inside and cool off?" She would persuade him to give her his number and call his parents to take him home. And she could get a look at these parents. "I've got orange juice," she said.

She stepped back to let him in. The whole house quivered like water just below the boil, and Lacey's heart stuttered into the rhythm of the baby's heart, three times as fast as her own. Blood whistled in her ears. She pressed her right hand against her throat, and the boy caught her left hand and said, "Are you okay?"

In the kitchen, Bibbits barked once, and Lacey clutched Drew's hand. "I have to sit down," she said. Threads of black whirled in her vision. She'd never fainted, but she'd felt like this after she and Eric double-dog-dared each other to ride the Bungee Slingshot at Myrtle Beach; when she landed, the earth felt rubbery and unreliable, and this was worse. Drew pushed her down, and she sat on the second step of the stairway, her left side and shoulder pressed against the banister post.

"Can I come back another time?" Drew said.

"Yes, yes," she said, panting, "later." She closed her eyes and pressed her head against the post, breathing slowly to steady her heart and make the world stop spinning.

Bibbits's claws rattled on the hallway floor, loud enough to make Lacey wince. Her mother was there, a hand on Lacey's shoulder and an urgent voice, "Do you need an ambulance, baby?"

Cautiously, she opened her eyes. The house had stopped shivering; the sense of near-to-the-boil anticipation was gone. Through the open door, the sounds of distant traffic pulsed smoothly, calm waves washing on sand, and her home was all peace and brightness, just as she meant it to be.

"I got dizzy for a second," Lacey said.

"Stay right there," Ella Dane said briskly. "I'll bring a hot honey and lemon. I got these for you." She draped a strand of rough red gems over Lacey's head. Garnet, to strengthen the blood.

Low blood sugar. Hormones. Perfectly normal. Lacey relaxed against the banister post and watched as the front door gradually pulled itself closed, hesitated, than latched with a solid click. Bibbits licked her hand. Was this going to happen every time a sound surprised her—doorbell, footstep, sudden voice? She'd spent too much time online, reading about everything that could go wrong with the pregnancy. The Internet was full of terrible pictures, warnings of disaster, horror behind every click of the mouse. She had to limit herself to YourBabyNow, and not go browsing in the Google wilderness, crowded with new fears. Blood pressure too high or too low, preeclampsia, diabetes, blood clots. This body was not her own, it had become a house of death.

Chapter Nine

LEX HALL NEEDED A LAWYER. In the telephone book, there were ten pages of lawyers. Some of them listed only their names, and he didn't trust them because they didn't say what kind of lawyers they were; he remembered there were different lawyers for different kinds of trouble. Some of them had a whole page in the book, with pictures of themselves smiling, and he didn't trust them either, because why were they so happy? The law was a terrible thing. So he called his uncle Harry, and the old man said, "I sold the house to a lawyer. Call him."

The woman who answered the phone had a friendly voice. Lex came into the lawyer's office holding the big manila envelope across his chest. It had arrived yesterday, Monday, delivered by hand at MacArthur's, when he was in the back sorting avocados. The soft avocados went into the "Buy Me Today" bin at half price. A man in a blue windbreaker came into the back, carrying a clipboard. "Andrew Lexington Hall?" he said and handed him the envelope and was gone before Lex knew what had happened.

The thing was only four pages long. It took a long time to read. Lex could read as well as anybody. He had his GED. He didn't have any trouble reading, but his mind slid away from the words. He worried about the avocados.

Petitioner. Respondent. Dissolution of marriage. He thought someone must be suing him and Jeanne, because her name was all over it. On his lunch break, he called the old man and read it to him, even though the break room was full of cashiers, listening to him and giggling behind their hands.

"It means divorce," the old man said.

"Then why is Jeanne's name here?" He still couldn't understand. And so many of the avocados were already soft. The delivery truck must have parked in the sun. These things weren't supposed to happen.

"Jeanne's divorcing you," the old man said. "You need a lawyer."

No lawyer had ever helped Lex, no matter who paid them, the old man or the state or whoever. They knew one another, lawyers. They went out together and drank in the same bars. He wasn't stupid; he knew. "Jeanne's got a lawyer," he said. He'd found the name on the last page. Cambrick MacAvoy. One lawyer was okay. You only got into real trouble when there were two lawyers.

"That's Jeanne's lawyer," the old man said. "You need your own."

So here was Lex in the front office of Moranis Miszlak, an expensive room that smelled of perfumed men and dry-cleaned cotton and fancy magazines. At the back of the room, at a big curved desk, sat a golden-skinned black woman with soft straight hair, and she looked at the manila envelope all greasy from his clutching hands, and she judged him. People always did. They looked at him and they knew. Even if they didn't know what they knew, they smelled it on him.

The shiny girl looked away from the envelope, like she was sorry for him. She pressed a button on her desk phone and said, "Eric, your four o'clock's here," and then she went back to her computer. Not once had she raised her hazel eyes to look at Lex. People didn't, especially women.

"My wife's divorcing me," he told her. Petition for dissolution of marriage. Petition meant asking. Just because you asked for something didn't mean you'd get it. "It's not right," he said to the shiny girl.

Now she looked at him. Her eyebrows were as black and clean as if they'd been drawn with a Sharpie. "Mr. Miszlak will take care of you," she said.

The Miszlak lawyer was shorter than Lex expected, and younger, too young to have his name on the front door of the big office. It was thirty years since Lex had much to do with lawyers, but he remembered if your name was on the door, you were the big dog. This was not the big dog. He was short, with reddish-brown hair and a tight mouth. Lex followed him down a white hallway with glass doors.

The young lawyer's office was around two corners and past a water fountain. It was a little room with no windows and a torn-up vinyl floor. "Your name's on the door," Lex said, to get that clear in his mind. Names were hard. "Miszlak, that's you."

"I'm Eric Miszlak. Floyd Miszlak's my uncle. Technically it's his name on the door, not mine."

"And you're my lawyer."

"If you retain me, yes."

"Really my lawyer. Not the court's lawyer. Mine." Lex knew about the court's lawyers. They promised to do all they could, to help if he told them everything, but they never did. He knew not to talk to any lawyer but his own.

"Absolutely," the young lawyer said.

They weren't allowed to lie. Lex pulled the old man's check from his windbreaker. "Mr. Rakoczy's paying your retainer?" the young lawyer asked. He sounded surprised. Lex didn't know why. Everybody knew the old man.

"Can you help me?"

"What do you want, Mr. Hall?"

"Can I stop her?" The lawyer was shaking his head. Lex tried to make his question clear. "Can she divorce me? She's my wife."

"It's the law, Mr. Hall. She can divorce you whenever she wants. All I can do is represent you and make sure the settlement's fair. I need information. Any kids?"

"Theo. She'll be a year old in October. Can she do that? Jeanne? Can she just take her and leave?"

"Where did she go?"

"She went to her mom's house and she won't let me see Theo. Can she do that?"

"No. You have parental rights. We'll get a temporary order. The court will appoint someone to represent your daughter. They're called the guardian ad litem and they'll get in touch with you." The lawyer pulled a pad of yellow paper onto the desk and started making notes. "So she left you in the marital home. Do you own or rent?"

Lex didn't care about the house. He'd bought it with the money the old man gave him for the other house. Jeanne could have the house, but she couldn't have Theo. The lawyer had to understand. "I want my baby," he said.

"The court usually leaves a baby with the primary caregiver. Is that you?"

"Are you the court's lawyer or my lawyer?"

"Yours, your lawyer. I can't help you by making false promises. We can go for joint custody. That's the best you'll get. Sole custody, not a chance, unless there's abuse and you can prove it. That gets very ugly, very fast. I'm not going to waste your money and your time fighting for something you'll never get."

Lex reached into the greasy envelope for the pictures he'd brought. There was Jeanne, with her gold-blond curls and her bright pink face that spread out onto her shoulders. Her cheeks were wider than her forehead, her neck wider than her cheeks, her chin a pink bump in the broad meat of her throat.

"She's a lot younger than you," the lawyer said.

"She's twenty. She was always big." Lex knew he wasn't being clear. "I bring fruit and vegetables. She takes my money that I bring home and she eats cheeseburgers for breakfast, and she feeds my baby." He brought out the second picture: Theo with her fluff of dandelion-seed hair, her laughing face. She wore a white lace dress. Her arms bulged out of the short sleeves, and her cheeks were round pads of fat.

"Your wife's unfit because she feeds the baby too much?"

"I need to take care of her." That was as clear as he could be. It had to be enough.

The lawyer laid the pictures on his printer. "I'll scan these into your file. We'll depose the pediatrician. You need evidence. That means you need to be able to prove—"

"I know what evidence is."

The lawyer gave him the pictures. "Mr. Hall, I'll be honest with you. It's a long shot. You're calling it child abuse, the way your wife's feeding Theo?"

Lex nodded hard. The lawyer was young, but he was quick. Child abuse.

"You'd have a better case if you'd filed on her."

"I was going to." And it was true, though he hadn't known it until he heard himself saying it. "I told her, you keep feeding my baby cupcakes and corn dogs, I'll take her and leave you. I told her, you can't do that to my baby."

"You said you didn't want her to divorce you."

"What I meant was, I wanted to go first and take Theo, because it's not right. Jeanne was quicker than me is all." It should have been true; it was as good as true.

The lawyer typed as Lex spoke. "Good. You get me Theo's medical records, and I'll get your custody hearing on the calendar."

Lex stood up. "You're a good lawyer," he said. "You like avocados?"

"What I'd like is evidence good enough to make a family court judge take a ten-month-old baby away from her mother. If every chubby kid got taken into protective custody, we'd have to build a ranch the size of Texas to keep them in."

"I can take more pictures. Better pictures."

"Do that. I'll get started on custody and visitation."

The lawyer walked around the desk to shake Lex's hand. People didn't get close to Lex. Men, when they shook his hand, kept their arms straight to hold him off. Women crossed their arms when he came too close, and they never shook his hand at all. This was the first time a man who had a desk had walked around instead of reaching across. Lex let the hand drop—he was never sure how to stop shaking hands; was he supposed to pull away or let go or squeeze harder? There was a way to do it and he never found out how—and he backed out of the room.

Chapter Ten

ERIC WAS RIGHT, as he so often was. It made Lacey tired. One of these days he'd be wrong about something, and his head would explode. She laughed at the childish thought, though she was ashamed of it. He was the living twin of her teacher voice, an essential part of herself. He'd suggested she call the OB who'd seen her at the hospital, because sooner or later she'd end up in the hospital anyway. Dr. Vlk, it turned out, had a private practice, and her nurse found room in the schedule for Lacey on Monday, August 22.

The baby was twenty-two weeks old. Dr. Vlk, dressed not in scrubs but a gray skirt-suit and pearls, turned the ultrasound machine so Lacey could see him. He grabbed his umbilical cord and pulled on it.

"Can't you make him stop?" Lacey said.

"The placenta's stabilized. See the white band? That's scar tissue. It looks good."

Lacey wanted to ask *will he live?* but she didn't trust her voice—this good news brought her closer to tears than all the weeks of fear and doubt. He was the size of a Cornish game hen. Half his body was head. He turned his face, and Lacey saw his profile, his beautiful little nose, his short upper lip. Dr. Vlk took the picture and said, "We're getting a good heartbeat and lots of kicking. You can start exercising a little, short walks, but still no heavy lifting."

Lacey felt safe in Dr. Vlk's hands. *Will he live?* A good heartbeat and lots of kicking: she'd take that. She even tried a little joke. "Dr. Vlk," she said, "wouldn't you like to buy a vowel?"

Dr. Vlk was not a woman for jokes, not with those pearls. She had the look of the veteran teacher who'd mentored Lacey through her first semester of practice teaching, a natural mind reader, terrifying but comforting too. Dr. Vlk looked into Lacey and through her, as Mrs. Ravenel used to look at students. "Tell me what's wrong."

"If the baby's fine, I'm fine."

"We don't have time for me to be your psychiatrist."

Some bedside manner. "What happens if I start bleeding again?" Lacey asked.

Dr. Vlk's eyes were a silvery blue, almost as light as her hair. This was a woman who could not lie. "He's about viable," she said. "The longer he cooks, the better he's done. The outcome's not what you'd want till you're past thirty weeks. Thirty-five is better. Tell me what's wrong."

Lacey swung her feet off the examination table. "We're fine," she said. As a teacher, she'd known when students were in trouble, often before the students knew it themselves. More than once, she'd kept a child in before recess to ask what was wrong and received a wide-eyed *Nothing* in return, only to find the child in tears a week later: parents divorcing, big brother on drugs, Grandma terminally ill. If Lacey, with only three years in the classroom, could see this much, how much more could Dr. Vlk see, having given good news and bad for thirty years or more.

"You're not fine. How does Dad feel about the baby?"

Lacey wanted to say Eric was thrilled, they were both so happy, and her own voice surprised her: "Scared. He's got this new job, and we moved. It's hard."

Dr. Vlk handed her a box of tissues and said, "Have you talked with him?"

"Oh! Talked with him! I'd have to make an appointment. He's working twelve hours a day, and I'm going to whine about some weird feeling? There are noises."

"It's an older house?"

"My grandpa had an old house. You could hear things, voices in the walls; it's only noise, I know that." Her mother had always said there were ghosts in Grandpa Merritt's house, but not to be afraid of them, because they were peaceful spirits, interested only in each other, a family from long ago. "But there's this feeling on the stairs. What's wrong with me?"

What a relief to ask the question, to admit something might be wrong—a thing she could never say to her husband or mother. To Lacey's surprise, Dr. Vlk took her seriously. "Pregnancy makes your body wise," Dr. Vlk said. "Morning sickness keeps you from eating dangerous food. Fear keeps you from doing dangerous things. Fear is your friend. Trust yourself. Can you live downstairs?"

The idea was so startling, Lacey had to take a moment before she answered. "You mean, don't go upstairs in the daytime at all?"

"Sleep downstairs, too. Your weight has changed, your ligaments are loose, you're scared because you could fall. Pretend you live in a one-story house."

"It's that simple?"

"Most things are. Try it. Any bleeding, call me. If it's more than a drop or two, call 911. Make an appointment on the way out. Two weeks."

Lacey went home dazzled by the revolutionary simplicity of Dr. Vlk's idea. She was afraid that Eric, who came home exhausted every day, might resent the work and trouble of moving her downstairs. But his reaction was like hers: Was it this easy, solve her problems by keeping her off the stairs? Perfect. He came home early and spent the afternoon organizing Lacey in the dining room. He ordered a twin mattress and a simple metal frame, paying extra for immediate delivery. They still had some old sheets from Lacey's dorm days.

A twin bed. She wanted to ask why he didn't order a double, or even a queen, so they could still sleep together, but since the thought had so clearly not entered his mind, she couldn't quite find the words. She curled in the red armchair, watching him trot up and down the stairs, organizing her new life while her mother brought her a mug of jasmine tea and a plate of gingersnaps; jasmine for serenity, ginger for nausea. It was as if they were breaking up, as if he were moving her out of more than the bedroom. Out of his home, out of his heart. How careful he was to make sure she had everything she needed! He folded her maternity clothes into a couple of the big plastic tubs they'd used for moving; he brought all her things to the downstairs bathroom. He went upstairs again for her sketchbooks and magazines.

Lacey left her tea and gingersnaps on the side table. She stood at the bottom of the stairs and lifted her face, surprised by a rush of sadness. This was a good day: the placenta healed, the baby strong, a doctor who listened. One of the best days of her life. "You should be sitting down," Eric said, edging around her with his arms full of sketchbooks, boxes of pencils and pastels balanced on top. She hoped he didn't drop them. Those colored pencils were so brittle, the leads shattered if they were ever dropped.

"You should be resting." He set his pile on the lowest step and took her back to the red chair.

"What if I'm lonely downstairs?" she said.

"I'll check on you." He touched the mug. "Your tea's gone cold; you want me to nuke it?"

"What if I can't sleep alone?"

"Lacey, be reasonable. That room's not big enough for a big bed. And this mattress and the frame—this can be the baby's bed when he's bigger. It's only for a little while. I'll keep my cell phone on at night and you can call me if you need me."

"The tea's fine," she said. Call him at night on the cell phone. Maybe she could send him an e-mail. Train Bibbits to carry messages. Eric was still standing there, as if waiting for permission to complete this separation. "Everything's fine," she said. He rubbed her shoulder, then carried her books and art supplies into the dining room.

A wonderful day, she told herself, a perfect day, but she was losing half her house. It hurt unexpectedly; it hurt like a death. Her first real home. Good-bye to the master bedroom, good-bye to the shiny new bathroom, see you in four months, good-bye. Like a child again, she was camping out in a temporary bed. She told herself it was just a makeshift arrangement, but that was what it had always been. *Just for a little while,* Ella Dane said, and now Lacey could not convince herself she would ever sleep in her own bedroom again. Everything she had wanted and worked for, gone. She wiped the tears from her face and tried to smile.

The doorbell rang. "That's the bed," Eric said. He directed the men to set it up in the empty room, their formal dining room someday, and by the time they were done, it was past nine. Lacey was as tired as if she'd hauled the furniture around the house herself. Ella Dane made a pizza-shaped article consisting largely of potatoes and seaweed. Lacey, not wanting to eat, sat on her new bed and looked at her white walls.

Eric knocked and entered on the echo of his knock, laughing as he pulled the door shut behind him. "Happy housewarming," he said as he handed her a greasy paper bag.

"That's not a cheeseburger? And onion rings?" She hadn't even heard him leave the house. "I love you," she said. He was so sweet; she didn't tell him so often enough.

He kissed her just above the right eyebrow. "I've got to get some work done."

"Can't you stay?" she said, disappointed.

"I'm in court all morning, got to get these motions written up. You want to go shopping this weekend, look at baby furniture?"

No. Lacey's instant revulsion surprised her. Absolutely *no,* no crib, no car seat, no highchair, no. She felt as if he'd asked her to hold a tarantula. "It's too soon," she said. *What if the baby dies.* She wouldn't say it; she shouldn't have to. He should know. "What if it doesn't work out," she said. "Then we'd have all the things and not use them. No."

He sat beside her on the bed and pulled her into a one-armed hug, pulled her head down onto his shoulder and stroked her hair. "It would be the worst thing ever. But we'd keep the things. We'd still use them sometime."

"No," Lacey said, implacable. To buy the furniture before the baby was safe was asking for trouble. To use for a later, living child the things that were bought for the dead—no. Ella Dane would understand this fateful feeling; not Eric.

Eric breathed hard for a moment, and she felt him control his temper: everything he wanted to say to her, things he said when they disagreed, that she was irrational and difficult, her mother's daughter—his thoughts pressed in on her, but she did not yield. She couldn't have baby furniture until she was sure she'd have a baby. "Okay," he said finally. "If that's what you want." He hugged her again and pushed her away. "Got to get my work done. Good night."

Lacey sat on the bed eating onion rings and reasoning with herself. It was all right if Eric didn't understand. Later, when the baby came, he'd know she was right. He was angry, but he'd get over it. And he had brought her onion rings. She liked to nibble a hole in the crust, suck the onion out, and then eat the crust like a crunchy onion-flavored cookie. Delicious.

A voice snorted under the door, "Huh. Huh. Huh." Hard claws tapped back and forth, and the snuffling voice traveled from one side of the door to the other. "Huh."

Poor little Bibbits. Under all his fluffy apricot poodlosity, he was a sweet dog. Lacey pulled off the cheeseburger's lower patty. She opened the door, and Bibbits stood on his rear legs and danced in a circle for her. She dropped the patty in front of him.

He sniffed it, licked it, nudged it with his paw. Then he looked up and barked. "Seriously?" she said. She tore the patty into four pieces and fed them to him. When he was finished, he trotted back into the kitchen and knocked his bowl of rice upside down.

Lacey brushed her teeth, took off the garnet strand, and went to bed, though it wasn't yet ten. She let the garnet strand fall into the clay bowl beside her bed, along with all the other gemstone strands and amulets Ella Dane had given her over the last few weeks. Rose quartz for her uterus, amethyst for serenity, citrine for cleansing, moonstone for new life. Ella Dane was concerned for Lacey, but she had not sensed anything wrong with the house itself. The baby rolled inside her. What a busy boy he was, playing peekaboo in the dark.

She fell asleep with the child dancing under her hand, and she woke gradually to a pain above her heart. Too many onion rings. She needed milk. The room was dark. She had a confused sense that it was later than it seemed, that midnight was long gone and yet morning had come no closer. The night had taken a turn into a different kind of time, bubbling out of itself into a circle of nameless hours between three and four.

She needed milk. She pressed her hand against the mattress to lever herself upright, and her palms sank into a swampy warmth. She pressed deeper into the mattress. The slow liquid rose over her fingers, over the tops of her hands.

Blood. So much blood, too much. While she was sleeping, the thing she most feared had happened, and it was already too late. Where was Dr. Vlk's firm voice now? The window was a gray square in the wall, white with moonlit clouds casting no light into the room. She threw the upper sheet aside, and the bed was a black pool, a deeper black around her hips. She felt the warmth on her left thigh, the dark stain from her waist to her knee. Where the child had danced, stillness. She stood up, expecting pain, feeling only the old pain over her heart, the wetness cooling on her legs and hands. Eight steps to the light switch. Every step was a prayer. Please God no. Let it not be true. No no no.

She touched the light switch, and the bed was blazing white. The lower sheet was translucent, water soaked. Warm water, with drifts of bubble-bath foam, planes of rainbow where the bubbles met in flat walls, a continental mass of bubbles mounding where she had slept. In the middle lay a green-and-blue plastic tugboat.

Impossible, intolerable. She could not believe in the tugboat. She had never owned it, never had it in a classroom, never seen it in her life. It lay in the bubbles and the wet bed, so real and so specific, so exactly that particular tugboat, a real thing.

She had to wake up now. She felt herself standing by the light switch with her hand on the wall. She also felt herself lying in the bed, on her left with her knee drawn up, breathing hard, trying to move a hand, to make a sound. Between the real self and the dream self, only the pain over her heart was the same. She breathed harder but could not engage her voice. She brought her whole mind into her left hand lying softly next to her breast. If she could tighten the fingers, if she could move at all. . . .

The baby kicked. Lacey opened her eyes. She was in her clean dry bed, no blood, no water, no tugboat. The window was lighter than in her dreams, gray clouds scrawled over a deep purple sky, and she could see everything. Even so, she turned on the light and searched for the tugboat. She couldn't find it in the bed, under the bed, or in her boxes of clothes. There had never been a tugboat. She needed milk.

There was a pale light in the kitchen, where the refrigerator stood open. Everybody was asleep, and Drew was there, pushing plates of leftovers along the shelves. Trouble-at-home was in her house now, hungry at midnight, and she accepted him without surprise or protest, only a dark recognition: she'd known he was coming. Midnight, though. She had to find his parents.

He stood in the refrigerator light in his blue striped pajamas, looking from one shelf to another. "What's that thing?" he said.

The teacher voice said, *Tell me your phone number,* and Lacey was surprised to hear herself answer his question: "Some kind of pizza. You want milk?"

"Is there Coke?"

"You're lucky there's milk." She took the milk from the refrigerator and closed the door. In the suddenly darker kitchen, the milk jug sent an alarm of cold through her hand. She put the jug on the counter and looked at Drew. Like the tugboat, he was real and not real. "Why are you here?" she said. These words took strength; she had to lift them past a dense weight in her mouth. She pushed her voice out and said, "Go home."

His eyes glimmered, catching a light from outside. "I live here."

"It's my house."

"It was my house first."

Child's logic, unassailable. Two children scuffling over a classroom toy. *I had it first.* "It's not your house anymore," she said. There was always one question to ask a lost child. "Where's your mother?"

"Can't I stay? You can be my mother."

"No. That can never happen. Go away."

"I'll be good this time, I promise, please."

Lacey felt herself weaken. This was her failing as a teacher, and when she went back to the classroom, she would have to harden her heart. She let children turn in their homework late. She accepted their excuses, not because they were believable, but because of the urgent young voices, the supplication so utterly sincere. She couldn't say no. Teachers learned to deny even the pleading of angels; Lacey didn't know how.

"If you're good," she said, hating her own weakness, unable to refuse.

He rushed toward her with a sweep like the wind. She closed her eyes and stepped back, covering her belly with both arms. "Don't touch me. No, no." She took another step backward into vertigo, and she stopped moving and sank down. She found herself sitting on her bed, in the dark, her head awash in dreams and echoes of dreams.

None of it had happened. Panic burned in her throat, just the same. She took her pulse and it was one hundred fifty. She'd read an article on YourBabyNow.net about dreams. It was all completely normal. Real. Not real. She listened to the quiet creaking of the walls. There was no blood, no water, no tugboat, no abandoned child. Only the crazy pregnancy dreams, one after the other. They never happened, they meant nothing at all.

She folded her pillow and clutched it under her head. The milk. She saw the milk in her mind, she knew where it was: sitting on the counter where she had left it, the white plastic jug sweating big beads of condensation. By morning, the surface would be dry and the milk sour. Eric would be irritated and Ella Dane would lecture her about waste.

She wasn't getting up again, to risk walking into another dream. She might be dreaming even now. Better to lie here quietly. In the kitchen, all by itself, the refrigerator door swung shut, and the quality of light coming in under Lacey's door changed from blue to dull orange.

Chapter Eleven

ERIC HATED TO ADMIT IT. and he'd never say it to Lacey who loved the house so much and had been determined to buy before the baby was born, but the Realtor had been right. They should have rented for a year or two. Yes, it was a bargain, ninety-five thousand for a house that would be worth twice as much in five years, but he couldn't afford problems at home; he had to focus. There was the stickiness of the air at the threshold, the house's resistance every time he entered, the sense of a complete life, compact, hidden, self-sufficient, going on without him.

Lacey needed the house. All pregnant women nested, and it had hit Lacey hard. And he was the same—he'd bought the furniture, he'd summoned Ella Dane Kendall to live with them. They'd rushed into everything together, on the run from the families that had failed them, wanting the marriage, the house, the baby all at once. They should have waited.

Too late; they were committed now, and they'd have to see it through. Even though he had no money, less than no money, he went out to eat with his uncle and colleagues. He needed better cases, and so he had to stay in communication with the firm, not lurk in his office like a guilty secret shut away in the dark. It was better than going home, where every day he felt less necessary and less welcome—Ella Dane made little shrines on plates, here a lavender candle on a layer of rock salt, there an amethyst crystal in a dirty old bird's nest, and she was furious if he moved them. And now that Lacey was sleeping downstairs, her memory dwindled from the bedroom along with the light rose-citrus scent of the sachet in her lingerie drawer. It was no longer *their room,* it was any room; he slid his shirt hangers into her side of the closet, put his razor by one of the double sinks and his toothbrush by the other, and it was as if she'd never lived there. Her room downstairs was a different world, smelling of dog and Ella Dane's spices. Some days, Lacey didn't even brush her hair. Who was this woman?

Uncle Floyd had a standing reservation for Abernathy's large corner booth. For the third evening in a row, Eric joined the rest of Moranis Miszlak for beer and wings. "Good work today," Uncle Floyd said. "It helps when the judge is a moron."

"Can't count on that," Eric said. He'd argued in family court on behalf of a client who had discovered his six-year-old wasn't really his; surprisingly, the judge rescinded the child support order until the ex-wife located the child's biological father.

Floyd mused on Eric's victory. "You'll lose on the next hearing. You get a judge with an IQ higher than room temperature, which is at least half of them, and he'll slap your guy with child support. Back child support. With interest."

Eric had already warned his client. "Maybe the biological father will pay."

"Maybe pigs will fly out my ass. How many clients you got?"

"Hundreds," Eric said glumly. "They're all judies. It gets me down."

"They're the peanut butter in your sandwich, boy."

Eric's mind slid to his new client, Lex Hall, whose bill was being paid by Harry Rakoczy. He'd depose the pediatrician. Maybe he could get together with the wife's lawyer. "What do you know about some guy called Cambrick MacAvoy?" he asked.

The lawyers and paralegals laughed, and Sammie the receptionist's Bambi eyes got even bigger and darker. "Here's a joke," someone said from across the table. "How many lawyers does it take to screw in a lightbulb? Depends on how many Cambrick MacAvoy can drag in there."

"Who is he?"

"She," four voices said from various points across the table.

"Ex-wife," Floyd said. "Mine. You're up against her?"

Eric was surprised. His family hadn't been close with Floyd, seeing him only at Thanksgiving. When Foothills Financial collapsed and Eric's father went to prison, it was Lacey who called Uncle Floyd and asked him to hire Eric. Eric didn't remember the name Cambrick. Could he have missed an entire marriage and divorce in his uncle's life? It was too bad. He should have sent a card. Maybe two. "It's a divorce. A judy."

"Not with Cambrick on the other side. Trust me, that woman will hang your kidneys on her Christmas tree. Don't tell me there's custody."

"There's custody. I was hoping to work something out."

"Could be, could be," Floyd allowed. "If you give her your kidneys right off the bat, she might could let you keep half a lung and a pound of liver."

The food arrived. Floyd had ordered a variety of wings with

names ranging from Sweet Caroline to Inferno. "I'm serious," Eric said, as the lawyers passed the plates. "I need to talk with her."

Floyd raised his voice and yelled across the bar, "Cambrick MacAvoy!"

Eric dropped the wing on his plate and hastily wiped his hands. "She's *here*?"

"You've got a little something," Sammie murmured, leaning across the table to dab at the corner of his mouth with her napkin. Sometime in the last few minutes, her blouse had mysteriously slipped lower on her breasts.

"Thanks, I'm good," Eric said. He reached for his beer. If she kept lunging at him, he'd have to spill it on her. An image of Sammie with her pink blouse soaked in beer crossed his mind, and he quickly amended the thought: he'd have to spill it on himself.

Floyd chimed his beer glass with his knife. "Cam-*brick*!"

A tall white-haired woman in a blue dress slid over to the table. "I see you've gained weight," she said to Floyd.

"Looks like you overdid the Botox, darling."

"That's my natural expression when I see you. Rigid horror."

"You go to court in that rag?"

"Only if I'm meeting the judge in chambers afterward." Her white hair was wound into a Sunday-grandma pouf of a chignon, and the blue dress showed a body that made Sammie look like a middle schooler playing dress-up. Her gaze wandered around the table. This might be the perfect moment to spill beer on himself. Then she said, "I'm looking for some larval Miszlak thing."

"That would be me." He looked directly into her face, ignoring all distractions; and then he recognized her. "Aunty Marian?"

"He remembers. Do you know, once I divorced your uncle, I

never heard from any one of you Miszlaks again? It was like I fell off the earth."

"I was only eight." He stood up to kiss her cheek, as he had been trained since infancy—*kiss your aunty, kiss your grandma*—though she felt not at all like the usual sort of aunt. Something dreadful had happened to her. "You're looking great."

"I dropped three hundred pounds of ugly fat; that'll do wonders for a person. You're representing some nut, I hear."

"Lex Hall, Aunty Marian."

"I'm not your aunty anymore, and I'm not Marian either," she said. "It's Cambrick, as in, what the hell just hit me upside the head, some kind of brick? Lexington Hall! He's got dirt in his past, and his dirt will bury him. Remember."

"Yes, ma'am." That childhood training again. "I surely will remember."

She tousled his hair as if he were eight years old and she the aunt who showed up once a year with a can of cranberry jelly. "You want to discuss Jeanne Hall's spousal maintenance and child support, call me. You make an offer, make it worth my time." She handed him a business card with a dogwood embossed in gold.

"Yes, ma'am," Eric said stupidly. She rippled away.

Floyd gave him another beer. "Boy, you done good."

Eric wiped his burning face. "I done what, I mean, I did?"

"Never seen her off her game like that; the Botox must have worked its way in through her skull. Numbs the cerebral cortex something fierce, they tell me. She gave you something, and you gave her nothing."

"What did she give me?"

"Your guy's got a past," Floyd said. "Don't ask him, he'll

never tell you. They never do. Pure as woolly baa-lambs, every one. Use an intern. Sammie, get on it."

Sammie looked around the table and shook her head. Her gold hoop earrings swung against her cheeks, and all the lights in the room flashed along the flying curves. "I'll do it myself," she said. "I wouldn't trust these clowns to track a car title."

"Thanks," Eric said.

"Don't thank me. It's a billable hour. Now go home to your wife."

Chapter Twelve

ON FRIDAY AFTERNOON, just after six, Lacey gave up waiting for Eric. She'd slept downstairs since Sunday, and every evening this week, Eric had gone out with his uncle and the rest of Moranis Miszlak, drinking beer and eating the kind of food she hadn't seen in weeks. Wings, nachos, chili cheese fries.

She hadn't been out with friends since spring, when she and Eric started spending their evenings online and weekends in Greeneburg looking for a house. She used to go out with her college friends and a group of young teachers. House and baby had sucked her in, and she hadn't called her friends, or answered their e-mails, or even checked Facebook. Lacey's life had kaleidoscoped inward, the same images mirrored and mirrored again. Husband, house, baby. House, baby, husband. Baby, husband, house. Phyllis, her best friend and roommate all through college, must have tried to get in touch with her on Facebook. There must be a thousand messages. The thought exhausted her. She'd get around to it.

She and her friends used to go dancing, ending the night at a dive in Five Points for chili cheese fries at three in the morning. She was that girl, four months ago.

Chili cheese fries. Hunger leaped on her with no warning, filled her like helium, making her head float. She had to sit down for a minute. Low blood pressure, Dr. Vlk said—another good reason for staying off the stairs and not driving, not that she could drive anyway; she and Eric had sold her car when they moved, because they wouldn't need two cars until after the baby came. Worst decision she'd ever made, letting Eric sell her car. Because it meant this: now, when she would sell her soul for chili cheese fries, the car in the driveway belonged to a vegan.

Restaurants delivered. She could have all the chili cheese fries she wanted. She could even have steak. A deep-fried onion blossom, the whole onion cut open and fanned out and battered and fried, with ranch dressing for dip. She used to share an onion blossom with four friends. Now she was hungry enough to eat one by herself. She got up from the bed and headed for the kitchen to look up restaurants in the Yellow Pages.

The doorbell rang. Lacey closed the phone book and listened. Her skin tightened, and she held the phone book over her belly like a shield—if it was Drew again, mister trouble-at-home—why wouldn't Ella Dane answer the door? The bell rang a second time.

"It's your house," Ella Dane called. "Answer the door. Bibbits, come to Mama."

Lacey walked toward the front door, Bibbits bouncing around her feet. Whatever Ella Dane had been giving him from the brown glass vial, it seemed to be working; he hadn't coughed for days. "Why won't you go to your mama, anyway?" Lacey asked him, and he licked her ankles with his slimy pink tongue, telling her as clearly as a dog could that as long as she kept giving him meat, his mama was on her own. She glanced up the stairs as she passed them, and there was Drew, standing at the top, with one hand on the banister.

When he came with popcorn, he'd asked her if he could come back and she had said *Yes, later.* Now here he was, inside the house. Without warning, she was back in the world of the dream, accepting Drew's presence, his right to be present, though some far part of her mind wanted to shout *go away, get out.*

"Don't answer that door," he said, with a childish ferocity that triggered her teacher's instinct to take him to a quiet place and ask what was wrong. The doorbell rang again. "Don't talk to her."

Who? Her thoughts scattered. There was something important, something she had to tell or ask him, but some mute heavy thing sat on her tongue and resisted her. She pushed through it. "Where is your mother?" she said, but that wasn't what she needed to know. She opened the door and saw CarolAnna Grey and a little girl with a clipboard.

"Hey, Lacey," CarolAnna said. "It's nice to see you. This is Madison." She pushed the child forward. Lacey glanced back up the stairs. Drew was gone.

"You want to buy something for my school?" Madison thrust a dog-eared catalog at Lacey: Academy Notions, a collection of Christmas gift wrap, scented candles, and outrageously expensive chocolate. The PTA at her old school used the same firm. Waxy chocolate, magnolia-scented candles, flimsy gift wrap and plastic Christmas banners: dollar-store goods at boutique prices, and the PTA got 5 percent of the profits.

At least this child would leave, not hang around the house, appearing in nightmares and sliding around corners. "Sure," Lacey said, taking the catalog. Madison showed no enthusiasm at this possible sale, but CarolAnna took a step forward, holding out a pen. "Do they still have the candied pecans?" Lacey asked.

"I dunno."

"Madison! Page seven," CarolAnna hissed.

Madison rolled her eyes. "What she said."

CarolAnna handed Lacey the pen and the order form, and Lacey said, "My checkbook's inside. Come in and cool off for a minute."

CarolAnna hesitated, glancing along the empty street as if someone might be waiting for her. "Thanks," she said just before the silence became awkward. "I'd like to see what you've done with the place."

Lacey was as delighted as if a carload of her old friends had come up from Columbia. Maybe CarolAnna would stay a while. Sit on the back porch, drink iced tea, try Ella Dane's black bean paste fudge. "I'm so glad you came," Lacey said.

Madison jumped backward down the porch steps. "I'm not going in there. It's the murder house." Her voice hung and echoed off the porthole window.

"Murder house?" Lacey said blankly. *You know this already,* the teacher voice admonished her.

"I told you when you were looking at it," CarolAnna said quickly, as if responding to an accusation. "There were deaths."

"Not murder." Lacey kept her voice steady. She was surprised— she *wanted* to be surprised—but the shock felt more like recognition. The murder house, of course; what other house could it conceivably be? CarolAnna's well-trained face was blandly open, making the moment ordinary; it was nothing, happened every day, just two adults chatting about the strange ideas of children. "Murder." Lacey pushed the word at CarolAnna. She hadn't spoken it in July, so she'd have to hear it now. "Murder. I'd have remembered that."

She wrote her address on the order form. She thought she was moving slowly, performing large simple gestures for an audience far away, but the handwriting was a panicky sputtering scrawl, not her own teacherly script.

"Nobody's ever seen it and lived," Madison said pertly. "The thing in the house. It eats babies. There's never been a baby in this house."

On cue, the baby kicked. "There's one now," Lacey said. What would Eric say to this? She needed his voice. He would laugh. He would give no more credence to a child's superstition than to a squirrel hissing in a tree.

"You wait," Madison said.

"*Maddie,* stop. There's nothing at all wrong with this house," CarolAnna said.

"The kids at school told me about it," Madison said. "Everyone knows."

Lacey had to stay calm to get the rest of the story. "It's perfectly normal. Kids always tell stories. Where I taught, the fourth-grade girls wouldn't sit at this one table in the cafeteria. It had the poison touch, that's what they said. So what about this house, Madison?" She wrote out the check: fifteen dollars for three ounces of candied pecans. Ridiculous.

"The kids told me when I started taking violin with Mr. Harry. They told me, Don't go next door or the thing will get you, the thing in the murder house. Because of all the people that died here."

CarolAnna, flushed under her makeup, was already reaching for the check. Lacey had only a few seconds to get more information from Madison, and she needed to know everything—was there danger, was the baby in danger? "How many people?" she said.

"All of them!" Madison flew down the steps and along the sidewalk, stopping only when she was past Harry's house.

"I'm really sorry," CarolAnna said, with irritation. She was apologizing for Madison's rudeness, not for the house and its secrets. "It's just rumors. You got a good deal on this house. You should be happy here."

CarolAnna followed her daughter down the street, and the front door ripped itself from Lacey's hand and slammed. Drew stood there, red-faced and shaking. "Don't listen to people!" he said. "Don't let them in. I told you not to!"

"I want to know what it means," she said.

"I don't have to tell you anything."

Lacey leaned against the door and locked her hands on the doorknob behind her. "Where do you live?" she said.

"Here. It's my house."

The doorknob pressed into Lacey's back. That was hard and solid, a real thing. She pressed against it to the point of pain. This was happening, not a dream; Drew was the unseen thing in the murder house—she didn't have the luxury of disbelief, not if the baby was in danger. "How long have you lived here?"

"Since forever. I never left." His breath hitched (his *breath,* she noticed, what breath?), and he snorted and wiped his nose with the back of his hand. It was too real. *Ghost,* she thought, but she could not believe it. Her mind flurried with images of last fall's PTA fund-raiser, Spookapalooza; she had supervised the haunted bouncy house, and the little spooks lined up with their faces painted, zombie, vampire, witch, just as physically present as Drew was now. He was barefoot, and his left big toenail was bruised black. How could that not be real? He snorted and wiped again, and she couldn't resist; she let go of the doorknob and opened her arms to him, as she would to any unhappy child.

He burrowed in her arms, and his hair smelled of salt and dirt.

This had to be real, this living child, this warmth, the softness of his T-shirt, his shoes squeaking on the floor. "You can cry if you need to," she said. "It's okay."

"I'm not crying." Drew let go of her, pushed her away, and ran for the back door. He was gone, and the door neither opened nor closed; Ella Dane, with her laptop on the kitchen table, didn't raise her head as he passed. Ella Dane, who claimed to be a psychic. Crystals and candles, and communion with the spirits of strangers' dogs. Drew's feet pounded behind her chair—he ran so close behind her, she could have touched him as he passed—and she sensed nothing. Her blindness to Drew shook Lacey more than Madison's story or CarolAnna's obvious discomfort.

Maybe the hormones of pregnancy had opened some long-locked door in Lacey's brain, and Drew was not a ghost, but madness; she was haunting herself. It was just as likely—more likely. Lacey's knees gave way, and she sat down and leaned against the door. Her life was filled by a child she did not know; was Drew her someday baby, the imaginary become real? But the other children told Madison Grey a scary story when she started violin lessons. If the house had a dark history, the children would remember.

The fourth-grade girls shunned the table with the poison touch. Not all the fourth-grade girls, just a particular group, too old for their years, with double-pierced ears and ironed hair. They were obnoxious, all rolling eyes and jutting hips and supercilious, impatient groans. They were hysterical, superstitious, irrational. But they weren't wrong. At that table, a kindergartner had almost died of a peanut allergy three months earlier. The fourth graders and the kindergartners never crossed paths, yet the girls knew. *Don't sit there, it's got the poison touch.*

Who would know about her house? She couldn't ask Carol-Anna Grey, who had already concealed so much and would be on guard against further questioning. Ella Dane was obviously no help. *It eats babies,* Madison said. Lacey had to know before the baby came.

Chapter Thirteen

ALL LACEY'S LIFE, she had watched her mother know the un-knowable: she'd kept Lacey home from school the day of a tor-nado, she could always find a lost thing by standing still and repeating its name. *Social studies book, social studies book—you were studying in bed and it's fallen between the mattress and the headboard.* Coincidence, Eric called it, when Ella Dane greeted him by name on the telephone without benefit of caller ID. Lacey always car-ried an umbrella if Ella Dane suggested it, no matter how bright the day seemed. So if the house was dangerous, how could Ella Dane not know?

Lacey went into the kitchen and said, "Mom, did you feel something come through here just now?"

Ella Dane had closed her computer and was stirring a pan of refried beans on the stove. "We're having burritos," she said. "Grab some plates, would you?"

Lacey opened the cabinet and pulled out a couple of plates. "Did you?"

Ella Dane moved the pan off the heat. "There was a draft on my neck."

Lacey took a breath and held it. Ella Dane used to read tarot for her friends, and then stopped, five years ago, because (she said) she was getting too good at it and did not want to open herself to demonic influences. Her last boyfriend, Jack McMure, specialized in spiritual cleansing, coming into homes that had suffered violent crimes or unhappy deaths and chanting until the spirits left. If anyone would believe her, Ella Dane would, but Ella Dane had lived in the house for a month and sensed nothing. And if she *did* believe, she'd call Jack in, and Lacey would have to explain it to Eric.

"Are you feeling something in the house?" Ella Dane said. "Bibbits has been nervous. He's an old soul, you know. Very sensitive."

"There's a little boy; he keeps coming in," Lacey said, and something crashed upstairs: broken glass, and then something heavy, tumbling and shattering as it fell.

"Bibbits!" Ella Dane cried, and the dog barked once and then retreated to the safety of a cage of chair legs. He was shivering, with his black lips pulled off his teeth in a soundless snarl, and the stub of his tail tucked low. His panting accelerated and deepened into a cough.

The house rang with cracks and claps, and a long rending splinter, some thick piece of wood, twisted until its fibers ripped, and the air conditioner surged on again, flooding chill air from every vent. Ella Dane rushed for the stairs, with Lacey following more slowly. Footsteps crossed the upstairs hall, which was visibly empty, with a fat serpent of dust drifting and the afternoon light striking slant columns through it. The footsteps hurried through the dust, and not one mote turned in their wake. The bathroom door slammed open and rebounded from the wall.

"Who's there?" Ella Dane said in a soothing voice. "We won't hurt you."

Her courage took Lacey's breath away. This invisible thing shook the house from door to roof, and Ella Dane promised not to hurt it? Lacey wished she herself could be so bold.

All the upstairs doors stood open, except Ella Dane's. The dust rotated through the sun-slant, and behind the white door Ella Dane's room exploded. Lacey shrieked and covered her face, while Ella Dane hugged her. The noise went on and on, a pounding fury, footsteps racing around the room, splintering wood, flying objects crashing into walls; such a sound should have been the harmony to a scream of rage, yet they heard no voice. It ended at last, and Lacey saw she had squeezed her mother's hands white.

"Who's there?" Ella Dane said again, massaging her knuckles. She opened the bedroom door.

The window was broken and its frame hung in long deadly shards from the wall. The room was shattered, destroyed, the furniture broken to bits. Ella Dane's clothes and books were shredded. Pieces of the dresser and the bed jutted from the drywall. Parts of the ceiling were shattered; Lacey saw the beams, and shreds of pink insulation bulging down from the attic. It looked like the kind of damage left by a tornado, dresser drawers freakishly impaling the wall, a paperback book driven into the ceiling.

Lacey pressed her hands over her mouth. She couldn't think about Drew, angry for a reason she couldn't guess and dangerous in his anger, or about Ella Dane who owned so little, that little now ruined—she could only think of Eric. He couldn't see this, his mind didn't work this way, he couldn't stand it. She thought of the way he'd been ready to give up their engagement, their life together, everything, just because it turned out his parents were crooks. His mind didn't change easily. That was her job, to find out the new life and lead him into it. This, though, was a life he would not live. She started gathering shreds of purple batik cotton, the remains of Ella Dane's favorite skirt. "We have to clean it up right now," she said. "Help me."

There was no glass on the floor under the empty window. The window had been broken from inside. Ella Dane took the purple cotton scraps from Lacey's hands. "What's in your house?" she asked. "Is this a poltergeist? How long has this been happening?"

"How come you don't know?"

"You said there was a little boy. A spirit?"

"I don't know."

"A ghost? He talks to you, you see him? And he's hidden from me—that's not just an imprint, that's intelligent. Maybe even demonic." Ella Dane seemed to take to this idea with a gleeful excitement. "Has it touched you?"

"No." Lacey set aside the conversation with Drew, her dream, every eerie sensation she'd had. The murder house. She wouldn't tell Ella Dane; she rejected it completely. This was a thing she would not allow. And she had touched Drew; she had hugged him—he was real. "He lives in the neighborhood." He was trouble; he knew 571 Forrester's reputation, just as Madison Grey did, and he'd tried to make her believe he was the thing in the house, but she would not believe it, would not, would not.

"No child could do this," Ella Dane said, waving at the ruin of her room.

"You have to keep the doors locked. He's been coming in."

"All right, Miss Clever, if a little boy did this, if a *child* broke my bed and smashed the ceiling, where is he? We came up the stairs. There's no other way out."

"The window. He must have climbed down the tree." Tree climbing: an old-fashioned skill. A tree-climbing boy was now as rare as a candy-making mother. The branches closest to the window were thinner than Lacey's wrist.

Ella Dane shook her head. "You've got big problems here, Lacey. You've got to take it seriously."

Lacey picked up a handful of shredded rags, something that used to be one of Ella Dane's long cotton dresses. "Go get some garbage bags," she said. "We can get most of this picked up before Eric comes home."

"The window," Ella Dane said. "The ceiling."

"I'll ask Harry; he's got to know a handyman. I don't want Eric to worry about this."

"*I'm* worrying," Ella Dane grumbled, but she caught Lacey's urgency and ran downstairs for the box of garbage bags.

Chapter Fourteen

THE YOUNG LAWYER needed evidence. Lex well knew what evidence was. It was what they showed in court, to tell the things you did and make a story of it. The lawyers told the story to each other until the thing that really happened disappeared. When you tried to remember, only the story was left, until in the end you told the story yourself, the same story everybody else was telling. Evidence, they called it.

If he wanted to save Theo, he had to tell his own story. Nobody else was going to do it. The lawyer? Five hundred bucks wouldn't pay the lawyer to find out the truth. Lawyers on TV did that, not real lawyers. Lex bought a camera for seventy bucks and spent another twenty for the memory card. He took pictures of cars in the drugstore parking lot, figuring out how to zoom and take video. By then it was dark.

The streets around Autumn Breeze Apartments, where Jeanne had taken Theo to stay with her mother, Big Jeanne, were busy as always. People drove through the complex's parking lots at all hours, with their car stereos so loud the Dumpsters in the back lot shivered like big metal drums. The complex had twenty buildings, twelve units per building, three stories each with one apartment in each quarter.

He liked the design. It made sense, like a stack of oranges. He didn't like the yellow lights, too few and too far apart. He didn't like the skateboarding kids who zoomed out from the darkness between the buildings. They didn't care what kind of place they lived in or what it would do to them. The place was loud and senseless; everybody shouted, and laughter sounded like screams. The only good thing about it was the azalea bushes around the back walls of the buildings, so he could get right up to Jeanne's windows and nobody could see him.

It was after nine at night, and Theo wasn't in bed. He'd been raising her right, training her to sleep and wake and eat on a schedule, the way he lived his own life, the way the old man taught him: now you do your homework, now you practice the violin. Here it was 9:15 and Theo was strapped in her car seat on the kitchen table, alone, red-faced, shiny around the nose and chin. She'd been crying. Lex took out the memory card and put it back in again twice, to be sure. He zoomed on the window.

Theo started crying again. Lex had a perfect view, and he couldn't hear a thing. It was like watching a life-sized TV screen with the sound muted.

Jeanne came in with a bucket of chicken, a thigh piece in her left hand. She tore off a chunk of the skin and waved the thigh piece toward the next room, talking with her mouth full.

Seeing her mother, Theo waved her arms and legs. Lex knew from the look on her face that she wanted a clean diaper. Theo hated to be dirty. Jeanne gave the baby a chicken leg. Theo threw the chicken leg on the table. Jeanne gave it back to her. Theo threw it again. Jeanne put it in the baby's left hand, wrapped the fingers around it, and forced the chicken leg toward the baby's mouth. Theo turned her head away. The car seat held her in place, and with the chicken in her mouth she had to eat it or suffocate.

Lex threw the camera through the window. It was all he had. He realized, as it left his hand, that it was a bad idea; he needed the camera. Too late. The window shattered, and the noises of the apartment started, as if he'd turned the mute button off. For a moment, he couldn't quite believe what he'd done. Because he couldn't have thrown the camera through the window. It was the kind of thing crazy people did.

Theo threw the chicken leg, and it fell in the broken glass. Jeanne shouted, "Call the cops, Mom! He's busted out the window!"

Evidence. The memory card was evidence, even if the camera was broken. He had to get it back. He took off his windbreaker, wrapped it around his left arm, and broke the rest of the window glass. "Get out, get away from me, get away," Jeanne panted. She couldn't shout for long. She couldn't do anything for long, the way the fat squeezed around her heart, and this was what she wanted for Theo.

He wanted to tell her. "You'll die," he said. "What you're doing. You'll die."

Jeanne crushed her small white hands together over her sick heart. She had such pretty hands, the prettiest part of her. "He says he'll kill me," she said.

"I called them," Jeanne's mother said from the living room. She didn't come into the kitchen. She hardly ever got out of the recliner because her knees hurt. "The cops are coming, Lex!" she shouted. "They gone shoot you in the head."

He didn't believe her. The phone was on a sideboard across the room from the recliner. Big Jeanne wouldn't be out of the chair yet.

He hadn't meant to threaten her. It was so hard. His thoughts were real, and the words never came right. Jeanne's pretty hands. There was a pleat where the fat folded over her wrists, and then the fine small hands, like they were sewn on. The rest of Jeanne could be like that, fine and pretty and perfect. "You're sick," he said.

"*You're* the one who's sick, taking pictures through my window!"

"I love you," he said. That could never be the wrong thing to say.

"That's some sick crazy love," Jeanne said. "I was fourteen when we met."

Lex unbuckled Theo from the car seat. "She needs a clean diaper."

"I'm her mama and I'm the one who says what she needs. You put her down."

The camera was next to Jeanne's right foot. Another second and she'd see it and stomp on it, and where would his evidence be then? "I need to take care of you," he said.

"Mama! Call the cops. He's threatening me."

"I need you to listen to me. I need to take care of you. You're sick."

"Mama!"

A metallic groan and a thump came from the other room: big Jeanne lowering the footrest of the recliner. Lex had no time, and he had to get the camera. "Here," he said, pushing Theo into Jeanne's arms. Theo laughed and grabbed her mother's cheeks. Lex lunged for the camera. The view screen was broken off, but the memory card looked okay. "I want to take care of you," he said. He took out his wallet and gave Jeanne a twenty-dollar bill.

She laughed angrily. "Twenty bucks, and what about the window?"

"I'll send you a check tomorrow." The old man would have to pay for it. Lex couldn't afford it, that big window, three or four hundred bucks. And it must have been cracked already, otherwise there was no way the camera could have broken it. He wasn't going to argue with Jeanne, though. "Don't call the cops."

"I got my finger on the nine," Big Jeanne said from the other room.

Jeanne looked at the camera and the window. Too late, Lex remembered she was clever; people forgot that about her. Her eyes looked dull and small, but her mind belonged to the pretty hands, so clever and so quick. "I can take pictures, too," she said. "My lawyer knows your lawyer. She says she can eat him for lunch. I'll get a restraining order. I'll have you arrested. Get out of my house."

"I only want to help you."

"I've had enough of your help." She held the baby out to him. The thick little legs, thicker than zucchinis, kicked in the air, and the baby fussed, protesting against the lack of support. "Say good-bye," Jeanne said. "In five years, she won't know your name."

Lex left through the window. He grabbed the frame as he jumped from the room, and the broken glass cut his hand. He bled all the way back to his car. When he took the memory card out of the camera, it was still whole. He had his evidence.

Chapter Fifteen

ELLA DANE CLEANED THE ROOM while Lacey went outside to pick up the glass. Lacey kept looking over her shoulder, sensing Drew's proximity. She never saw him, and the house had a dull, sulky feel that made her lower the thermostat, though it wasn't exactly heat. The air pressed in through her pores and left a sour taste in her mouth.

Eric rolled his eyes at Lacey's story about how the wind had thrown a branch through Ella Dane's window, but he was glad to let Lacey take care of the repairs, and Harry Rakoczy's handyman was quick about the window, though he kept promising to come back to finish the ceiling and then canceling at the last minute. Had something in the house disturbed him? More likely it was Lacey's own fault, for paying him in full for the entire job instead of withholding half until the ceiling was done.

All through Labor Day weekend, Ella Dane filled the house with lavender candles and spent ten minutes in every room each day, meditating and singing lullabies. She phoned her friend Jack and told him her experiences. A chill in the kitchen, another in the hallway. Lacey didn't think the candles and lullabies would help, yet there was no sign of Drew, so maybe there was something to it after all. She felt uneasily that Drew was only waiting, biding his time; lullabies would not sing him away.

Whatever their effect on Drew, the lullabies got rid of Eric very effectively. He spent the whole weekend holed up in his office, and he didn't ask why Ella Dane had switched from "Om Mani Padme Hum" to "Hush Little Baby," which was just as well. Lacey had no intention of telling him.

Lacey felt less married every day. The last time she'd felt truly in harmony with Eric was—when? Coming home from the hospital, when she saw the furniture—could she truly be that shallow? Now she was just a chore on his list: water the grass, answer e-mail, check on Lacey. Solitude gave her time to think, but the time did her no good; her thoughts chased each other in an endless circle. Was Drew a trespasser—was he a ghost, so tangible, so real? Should she ask for Ella Dane's help or should she deal with Drew (whatever he was) on her own? Should she tell Eric, and if she did, then *what* should she tell him? The only way Eric would believe in Drew's existence would be if they met face-to-face, and maybe not even then. Lacey imagined herself saying to Eric, "This house is haunted"—no, there was no possible way that conversation could end well.

She had to take care of Drew herself. To hand that responsibility to Ella Dane would be to abdicate control of the house. Whatever he was, she could handle him—civilize the trespasser, tame the ghost. Real or not, he was a noisy boy, and she a teacher who kept a lively room. By her third year, her principal knew her strengths and gave her the loudest of the loud, the unmedicated ADHDs, the brilliant and bored, the illiterate and belligerent, the squirmy worms. Usually those boys were separated, spread out two or three per room. This last year, Lacey'd had ten of them. They all ended reading at or above grade level, not one of them suspended or expelled. If she could handle that crowd, she could take care of Drew.

On the Tuesday after Labor Day, she went shopping for school supplies as if buying for a classroom: crayons, construction paper, copy paper, safety scissors—the talismans of her competence. Though she waited for Drew all day Wednesday, and Thursday morning, the house was quiet. Nothing fell but sunlight from the porthole window. On Thursday afternoon, she came home from her appointment with Dr. Vlk full of good news with no one to tell.

The baby weighed slightly more than a pound, by Dr. Vlk's estimate, perfect for his age, and he could hear. Lacey laid her hand over the bump, and when Dr. Vlk clapped, the baby twitched. She didn't want to disturb Eric at work, and Ella Dane had picked up a part-time job in the gift shop of a holistic spa. But she had to tell *someone*.

She paid off the taxi and stood in her driveway as it left. She really needed a car of her own. Dr. Vlk said she could drive again, and she was officially off the semi-bed-rest limitations, except she still should stay away from the stairs.

She'd been putting this off day by day, waiting for the perfect time to ask Harry Rakoczy about Drew. But there would never be a perfect time to say *Did you sell me a haunted house?,* and he had already deflected her earlier questions about Drew; she had no rubric and no plan for the conversation. What did he know about her house, and why hadn't he warned her?

Music rang from Harry's house, as always. He came to the door with a remote in his hand, and when he saw her, he clicked a button and the music stopped. "Lacey Miszlak!" he said. "What a pleasant surprise. I have a student soon, and I made coffee. It's one of *those* students. About as musical as a constipated frog, poor kid. Come on in."

"No coffee for me, thanks. Baby no like." She patted the bump.

"Orange juice? And how is baby?"

"Twenty-four weeks and he's perfect; he's growing. Dr. Vlk did ultrasounds; look at him! Isn't he beautiful?" She showed him the grainy blur, arcs of black and white crossing through the image. "Look. There's his face. Look at his tiny nose, it's so cute. Those are his knees. He's got toenails. Imagine, real live toenails."

Harry took the pictures. "Is he sucking his thumb?"

"Adorable, right?"

Harry led Lacey to the kitchen and poured her a glass of juice. She tried not to make faces at the smell of his coffee, because she wanted more than a few oohs and aahs over her baby. She'd hoped the words would come, but she couldn't bring herself to say, *I think my house is haunted and I want you to tell me what you know.* That was crazy talk.

"How are you liking the house?" Harry asked.

There'd never be a better opening. "Have people ever said anything about it? Anything weird?" Not even Ella Dane went so far as to say the house was haunted, even after what Drew did to her room. *Troubled* was what Ella Dane said. *Psychically active. In need of intervention.*

"Are you hearing noises?" Harry's face was smooth, and his dark eyes met Lacey's with warmth and concern. But he was a performer; he'd spent half his life onstage and the other half teaching, which was another kind of stage, individual and intimate. Harry leaned forward across the table and lowered his hands over hers. Lacey had used that exact soothing touch on children who were frantic over some disagreement with a friend. Distress flashed across his face, wrinkling the skin above his eyes, leaving his mouth unmoved. Whatever he said next would be a comforting lie.

"There were squirrels in the attic three years ago," he said. "Maybe they've gotten in again."

On the day they found the house, CarolAnna had tried to warn them. *People died here,* she'd said, and Harry had smoothed the words away: *A long time ago.* True, and also a lie. She pulled her hands out of his and said, "There's something in the house."

"I tested for mold," Harry said. "The termite contract never lapsed." He looked so honest and innocent, such a sweet old man. But he kept talking, as liars always did. "The radon test came up negative."

"Something's not right. Didn't anybody see something?"

He was shaking his head. The teacher voice worked on some adults, but not this one. Something moved deep under the skin of his face—a flick of the lower eyelids, a downward pull on the corners of his mouth—then he caught himself and pulled the mouth up into a smile, even forced a laugh. "What could there be to see?" he said.

Lacey couldn't stand it another second, sitting at his table, drinking his tea. She pushed her chair back and took her glass to the sink. "Is there something wrong?" he said behind her, and if she hadn't seen that false face a moment ago, she would have found his tone of warm solicitude entirely convincing. She filled the glass with cold water and drank it quickly.

There were framed pictures on the kitchen windowsill, pictures filling every foot of wall space, more pictures on top of the refrigerator. He must spend hours dusting. She found herself staring at half a face, a frame hidden behind another frame. Carefully, she put the glass in the sink. Glass chimed against steel, loud in the breathless room.

"Who is this?" she asked.

It was a small boy in a tuxedo. Behind him, a black piano mirrored stage lights and swallowed the child's black suit, leaving only his face and hands. His left hand clutched the side of the keyboard, and his blond hair fell across his forehead.

Harry reached for the picture, and Lacey held it in both hands, turning it in the sunlight. "This is my son, Ted," he said. "When he was little."

"He's in Australia, right?"

"Yes, he's a baritone, sings at Sydney most of the time, a bit of Rossini all over the world, you want the barber of Seville, Ted Rakoczy's your man."

He was babbling. Trying to talk his way over something. Too much explanation; truth did not need this much defense. This child was almost Drew, except the hair was darker, the eyebrows brown instead of blond. "Did you ever have any other kids?" Lacey asked, looking at the little boy's sweet smile.

Harry moved faster than she expected, twitching the frame from her hand and putting the picture back in its place. "Why do you ask?"

It was Lacey's turn to babble. "We can't decide if we should try for another baby right away, or wait a few years. Some people say you should have them quick, and other people say you should space them out, what do you think?"

"I think nobody can tell you what to do," Harry said firmly, "but I'm not the one to ask. We only had Ted."

She kept up the chatter of siblings and family spacing as she let Harry lead her from the house. So that was his son the opera singer. Not Drew, and not a brother if Harry was telling the truth about Ted being an only child, but a close relative. Harry knew Drew, no matter how he went on about termites and radon, but he'd never admit it. She'd have to find some other source.

Chapter Sixteen

"HAPPY THURSDAY," SAMMIE SAID, coming into Eric's office with the Hall file.

"What's so happy?" Eric looked up from his computer. He had just finished transferring money from savings to checking to cover Lacey's check to the handyman who had fixed Ella Dane's window—whatever Ella Dane had been doing in there, moon dances or some kind of hyperactive yoga, there was no way a branch had caused that damage. It was easier to pay than to argue. He'd have to close the savings account; this transfer had put the balance below the minimum, and the bank would charge ten dollars a month to keep it open.

And this was his life now. He couldn't even keep three hundred dollars in a savings account.

Sammie laughed. "After this, the rest of the week's wall-to-wall judies. You need to get this guy in on Monday or Tuesday. Thursday's too late."

Eric shrugged her suggestion away and snapped his fingers for the file.

She shook it at him. "You don't get like that," she said. "Snapping your fingers at me. I don't *think* so. You listen. These nut clients, you don't want to deal with them on a Thursday or Friday."

"Why not?"

"You give them bad news early in the week. They go back to work. By the weekend, they're mad at somebody else. You've got to take him seriously. Always take the nuts seriously, 'specially the ones who know where you live."

"Lex Hall doesn't know where I live."

Sammie dropped the file on his desk. "You wish. Happy Thursday."

The top page was Sammie's précis of her investigation into Lexington Hall. His legal record: twice, he'd reported neighbors to DHHS, and both cases were dismissed. Both families sued, and one lost the case because Lex had recorded the noises. The second family settled for three thousand dollars. The child was hospitalized with a fractured shoulder four months later and was removed from the parents' custody.

Then there was one case of simple assault. Could this be the dirt that Cambrick MacAvoy mentioned? Again, children were involved. Last year, Lex Hall, recently promoted to produce manager at MacArthur's, had seen a woman send her children through the store to shoplift. Three children, the oldest only eight, loaded up on meat and over-the-counter pharmaceuticals. He tackled the woman in the parking lot. Lex and the mother were arrested. When the dust cleared, the prosecutor dropped the charges against Lex; the children were taken into the system.

So: righteous indignation in defense of the young. Not exactly a deal breaker in family court. What had Sammie meant, Lex Hall knew where he lived? He riffled Sammie's printouts and photocopies—if all this represented billable hours, she must have blown through Lex's retainer and then some—and he had only five minutes before the man arrived.

Sammie's note:

Records of Lexington Hall begin at age 20. No information prior to 1983. No birth certificate, no educational records, no military record. First legal appearance of LH: sold 571 Forrester Lane to Harry Rakoczy in 1983.

Eric felt as if he'd walked around a corner and met himself coming the other way. The Miszlaks' house, Harry Rakoczy's house, Lex Hall's house . . . What did it mean?

Sammie buzzed him. "Mr. Hall is here," she said in her receptionist voice.

"Thanks, Sammie. Listen, about that property, what about its title history?"

"Yes, sir," she said. "I'll look into that. Mr. Hall's coming right in."

He opened the door for Lex, who entered with a blue nylon shopping bag from MacArthur's, and the scent of pineapple. He thumped the bag onto Eric's desk. "Could you move that to the floor, please, Mr. Hall?" Eric said mildly.

Lex set it on the floor, then reached in and pulled out a pineapple, the largest Eric had ever seen, and put it on the desk. "This is a big pineapple," Lex announced.

"It truly is, Mr. Hall."

"I brought it for a present." Most of its scales were golden, some streaked with orange, and juice glistened in its seams and creases. "It's ripe. Most people buy the pineapple green and eat it green."

"Mr. Hall, we need to go over some things. There's a temporary custody and visitation order."

"When do I get my baby?"

Eric hated this part. "There were problems. The test you took, the MMPI—the personality test—it came back unresponsive."

"Did I fail?"

"It means you were nervous on the day you took the test, and they couldn't get a clear reading on you." He couldn't get a clear reading on Lex, even face-to-face. The man was opaque. The flesh around his eyes never moved, and his mouth twitched as if he were talking to himself, practicing what to say. He was forty-eight, supposedly. If he claimed seventy, nobody would blink. "It means you'll have to take it again. You just relax and answer the questions truthfully."

"I didn't understand the questions. It's forever the same test. They used to make me take it all the time when I was in that place. I never understood the questions. When do I get my baby?"

When I was in that place: Eric wrote these words on his notepad to ask Sammie about later. What place, why, and for how long? Theo's guardian ad litem had interviewed Lex at home and had reported the home was clean, child-proofed and well maintained, but recommended supervised visitation because Lex was hinky. *Hinky*. What did that mean in a court of law? The judge rightly disregarded it. "The temporary order is joint custody. The baby stays with Jeanne during the week, and you get her on the weekends."

"I've got evidence now. I've got pictures. She's giving my baby a piece of chicken. Force feeding. Look."

Eric laid the pictures on his printer to scan them. "We're deposing the pediatrician next week," he said. "I'm not sure if pictures of Jeanne feeding Theo are going to help."

"Force feeding."

"Do these pictures show force?" Eric didn't give him time to answer; this was not an argument. "Mr. Hall, I met your wife's lawyer, and she told me there's dirt in your past. I can handle it if I can get out in front of it. What I can't handle is a surprise. If she shows up with something I'm not ready for, you're done. Have you ever been arrested?"

This was Lex's test, and he passed it. He looked down, looked away, stroked the pineapple, and then told Eric, in short spitting sentences, everything Sammie had laid out for him. The child abuse reports, the lawsuits, the assault arrest, everything.

"Is there anything else?" Eric asked.

"I brought you a pineapple." Lex held out his hand to Eric. "Smell my fingers."

"No thanks, I'm good."

"When you touch fruit, you should smell of fruit. Then you know it's ripe." He reached into the blue nylon bag at his feet and pulled out a big heavy knife, as big as a chef's knife but heavier, the blade corroded black but the edge silver with use and sharpening. Eric pushed back from the desk. Where was the panic button? Did he even have a panic button? He'd taken a seminar in risk management in law school and now he couldn't remember anything except *make sure you have a panic button.*

Lex raised the machete over the desk, and the ceiling fan interrupted the light and sent it running along the edge like a string of boxcars. Eric couldn't stop looking at it. His hands touched and discarded potential weapons on his desk—pencil cup, iPad—and settled on his laptop. He raised it like a shield. Someone said strongly and calmly, "Put that down, Lex," and it was his own voice.

"I want my baby," Lex said. He brought the knife down on the pineapple and skinned off half its peel in one stroke. Four more strokes, and juice trickled from the naked pineapple, oozing into Eric's files and documents.

Eric set the laptop on the chair behind him and snatched his iPad out of the spreading pool. "Mr. Hall, please." The chain of broken light along the machete's edge sparked in his dizzy eyes, quick as his own pulse. Now the danger was past, fear crashed over him, and he tightened his hold on the iPad so Lex wouldn't see his hands shaking.

"My baby needs fruit." Lex cleaved the pineapple in two. Then he wedged the knife into the woody core and flicked it out, one half and then the other. "Jeanne won't feed her right. You have to tell them. Whose lawyer are you? Mine or theirs?"

"Yours," Eric said. He buzzed Sammie, to stop her if she was on her way in to see what he needed. He might need help; he certainly didn't need to see Sammie getting her throat cut in his office. "Okay out there?" he said.

"Enjoying your Thursday?" she asked cheerily before she hung up.

Lex's knife whirled over the desk, dismembering the pineapple in tidy slices. "This is a good pineapple," he said. He put the knife in his bag and left the room.

Eric moved the laptop to a dry corner of the desk. He sank backward into his chair, blinking the panic haze out of his eyes. As soon as the door shut, he buzzed Sammie again and said, "Does Lex Hall owe us money?"

"I need to go over his account."

"Don't. Just let him out. Lock the door behind him."

Eric heard doors opening and closing, and Sammie's professional voice: "Have a nice afternoon, sir." Then she was back, asking urgently, "Do you need the cops? What's going on in there?"

Eric looked at the pictures: the car seat, the woman forcing the baby's hand closed around the chicken leg. What must it be like to be Lex Hall, frustrated, indignant, boiling over with desperate love, lacking even the most basic vocabulary to explain himself? The pineapple wasn't a threat. It was a moral argument.

"Sure," he said, "everything's fine."

The pineapple was beautiful, translucent gold rayed with deeper gold veins, and it tasted sweeter than canned fruit, rich and fresh, without the gummy aftertaste of syrup. As a moral argument, it was pretty damn convincing. But it wouldn't go over well in court.

Chapter Seventeen

A WEEK AFTER Lacey questioned Harry Rakoczy, while she was still wondering how to find someone else to ask besides the obvious (Drew himself), Ella Dane came home with a sort-of-not-really-a-futon, a sofa-sized thing similar to a dog bed, stuffed with buckwheat.

Lacey nudged the sack with her foot. "We'll never eat this much buckwheat."

"It's a bed. My friend Jack McMure says buckwheat is a natural psychic buffer."

Ella Dane didn't want to sleep upstairs after what Drew had done to her room. She'd been camping out on the living room sofa, and now she dragged the buckwheat sack into the other front room, the future formal parlor. The next morning she claimed she had never slept better in her life, there was nothing for the spine like sleeping on buckwheat, and the grain gave off a life energy so beneficial to the lungs, "much better than your metal coils," she said, "and the cover's a mixture of bamboo and hemp." Lacey noticed Bibbits gnawing a corner of it and wondered how long it would take him to open it.

Lacey went online and searched for haunted houses in Greeneburg. She found dozens of websites for Halloween attractions, and surprisingly few reports of real hauntings, most of them not in the city of Greeneburg but in mountain palaces in the north of the county, summer homes of wealthy nineteenth-century families, all of them a hundred years old at least and most of them well into their second lives as bed-and-breakfast inns. Romantic haunted weekends abounded. Ladies in white could be seen in rose gardens, Confederate soldiers walked on porches, and phantom carriages raced down old roads, bearing doomed lovers to tragedy. The Confederate Museum in downtown Greeneburg was so thronged with haunted relics that no dog would enter the building, and a blind tourist from Pennsylvania had filed suit against it. There was a photograph of glowing orbs outside the old county courthouse; it reminded her of Ella Dane's ideas about ghosts. She found no information about 571 Forrester, and she preferred not to discuss her search with Ella Dane.

Though Lacey slept alone, Drew never came. Eric visited her room every evening, but he was far away even when present, doing something important in his mind, drafting documents and planning depositions. Dutifully he asked her about her day. Her day was fine. She was reading a book about Piaget. She had walked around the block. "Great," he said heartily and left her to sleep alone.

She saw less of him now than when they were first dating. She'd fallen in love with his car, to begin with, the powder-blue BMW Z4, a noticeable car on campus; she'd wanted to be seen in that car to make another guy jealous. Her friends, especially her roommate, Phyllis, warned her the driver of a car like that couldn't help but be a spoiled rotten kid and a jerk. She wondered if Eric's friends advised him he could never be sure if a

girl wanted him or his car. He'd been shy of her and so respect-
ful she wasn't sure why he'd asked her out at all. When the time
came for him to make the move, he didn't, for weeks. Finally,
one evening in his apartment, she took off her clothes and asked
him what he planned to do about it. He said, "I wasn't sure you
wanted to." She laughed, but it worried her; the next morning he
said he loved her, so that was all right.

Was he doing that again? Waiting for her to make the move, to
be certain she wouldn't reject him? She was off bed rest and Dr.
Vlk assured her that sex was safe, but Lacey thought it wasn't—
not with Drew in the house. It might upset him, and after what
he'd done to Ella Dane's room, that was not a risk she was willing to take.

When Eric's family money disappeared, he sold the car so she
could keep her ring. He said it was because the ring would keep
its value but the car would only depreciate. He'd done that for
her, and so she had to deal with Drew for him, and for that, obviously, she'd have to make Drew show himself. Now or never, she
decided.

"Drew," she called when Eric and Ella Dane were both at
work, "come here, I want to talk to you."

Then she listened to herself. *Come here, I want to talk to you.* No
noisy boy would obey a summons like that. When she wanted
her noisy boys' attention, she turned her back on them and got
involved in something they couldn't see. Chase them and they
run. Lead them and they follow.

She pulled a tube of sugar-cookie dough out of the refrigerator. Ella Dane said a person might as well eat marshmallows—
the worst thing she could think of—but it was Eric's weakness.
The only thing he loved better than a cookie fresh from the oven

was a chunk of raw dough hacked off the tube. He ate it in the middle of the night, went through three tubes a week, and probably thought she didn't notice.

She sliced the cookies onto a tray and slid them into the oven. It was going to work. She felt it already, a sense of gathering in, of presence, the feeling her senses had interpreted as darkness when she first entered the house. It wasn't darkness, though she couldn't see through it. It was more like pressure, breathlessness, as if the air had curdled into some denser substance. Like souring milk, or scabbing blood. Drew was watching.

Her body reacted with fear. The muscles of her belly pulled tight, and her womb hardened—breathlessness, pressure, and the baby shoved a knee into her ribs. A contraction, not a real one: they were called Braxton Hicks contractions, Dr. Vlk said at her last appointment, and they were for practice. Not to panic, it wasn't really labor. Lacey asked how she would know when real labor started, and Dr. Vlk laughed out loud.

Lacey practiced breathing. This was what she wanted: Drew to appear, so she could question him. She spread her school supplies over the kitchen table. The beautiful white paper, the colored construction paper, the crayons and markers and scissors and glue, the green binder. Lacey felt another pain under her heart, and this was no contraction. She wished she could be in the classroom right now, any classroom. Even if only as a substitute or an aide, she should be with real children, not Drew.

She took the latest ultrasound out from under the strawberry magnet on the refrigerator and laid the picture on the table. Crescent streaks of lighter and darker gray marred the black-and-white image. She chose a piece of light green construction paper and a gray crayon. When she had a good outline of the baby's profile, she reached for the blue, and then the oven timer went off.

The cookies were gold coins with bronze edges. She stirred cinnamon and sugar and sprinkled the mixture over the hot cookies, then spatulaed two of them onto a plate. When she turned, Drew was there. How real he seemed, down to the sunlight glistening white on the few individual hairs that haloed his blond mop, and the shadows of his eyelashes on his cheeks. He hunched over a sheet of paper, drawing fast and hard, the way little boys drew, concerned not so much with accuracy as with getting the idea down on paper while it was whole in their minds.

"Hey," she said lightly, while her heartbeat whirred in her ears. "Want a cookie?"

Could he eat? He'd been hungry the night she'd met him in the kitchen, but maybe it was a dream. "Sure," he said. He took the black crayon and drew hard, using the flat end. That was never good. She put the plate of cookies next to him.

His left hand crawled over to the cookies. He grabbed one and munched it, and the sticky crumbs fell on his picture. The black crayon whirled over them, pressing cinnamon and hot grease into the paper.

He ate the cookie. The cookie disappeared. Where could it be going?

"Milk?" Lacey suggested, and she interpreted his grunt as a yes. He drank the milk, and it beaded on the transparent down of his upper lip. "Can I see?" she asked.

He shoved the picture toward her. A thick black whirling of lines, disturbingly similar to her ultrasound, and behind the whirl, a stick figure family. Father, mother, three boys.

"That's your family? I'm drawing my baby," she said. She let the blue crayon float over the gray lines she had already drawn. She drew in rapid, nervy jabs, spidery lines, light shapes thickening as she became sure. She shaded the baby's arm and sketched a suggestion of umbilical coils, fleshy and serpentine.

"I didn't draw the baby yet," Drew said. He scrawled a stylized cradle with a big head and a stick-figure body, and a ram's-horn curve on the side of the baby's head. This was his symbol for female hair, because he'd drawn the same sign on his mother. "She was noisy," he said. "She cried all the time." He wrote WAH in huge letters over the baby's head, pressing with the flat end of the crayon to lay the wax down in thick flakes.

"All babies cry."

"All the time." Drew used the red crayon to change the flat mouths of his family to bloody downturned frowns.

"Some babies cry more than others," Lacey observed. She couldn't tell much about her baby's face in the ultrasound, so she drew a slight lift in his mouth, not quite a smile but a disposition to smile. Then she used the white crayon to touch up the highlights in the image. The illusion of three dimensions appeared under her hand. Drew left his own picture, having whirled a scarlet cyclone over his family, and stood next to her.

He was so real. She felt heat from his body, or maybe it was cold, or an electric charge—some palpable change in the quality in the air around him. He leaned against her left arm. She felt the cotton of his T-shirt against her skin, the yielding of his muscle, the solid bone beneath, the sturdy, resilient texture of boy. She cherished these moments with her noisy boys, when they dropped their shielding energy and let her touch the sweet child within. Soon he would hold her hand. Even as she thought it, she felt his fingers crawl into her palm. He had the prickly, grimy feel of a child who played hard and had no time for soap, with an overlay of warm sugar.

"I like your picture," he said. "How do you make it look round?"

"Here, get a new piece of paper, and let's start with a circle."

She taught him to use the lighter and darker colors over the construction paper's middle shade to turn the circle into a ball, and to draw the lines and angles of cubes and pyramids. Was he doing something like this in her mind, creating an illusion of surface, reality, wholeness? She pushed the thought away: to deal with him, she had to accept him as real. "Now you decide where the light's coming from," she said, "and let it be the bright side of your pyramid. Where do you think the shadows will go? Light moves in a straight line," she reminded him, just before he put the shadow in front of the lighted face, and he moved the brown crayon. "What's your baby sister's name?" she asked.

"Dor.othy."

"That sounds good together, Drew and Dorothy. Do your brothers' names begin with D? David and Donald?"

"No."

"Dexter and Dennis? Daryl and Dwayne? Help me out, kiddo. On Dasher, on Dancer, on Donner and Blitzen?" This would have drawn a smile, however grudging and shy, from even the noisiest boy. From Drew, nothing. "Doc and Dopey? Dimplecheeks and Droopydrawers? I'm running out of options here."

"James. Matthew." Drew pushed his pyramid drawing away. "I want to draw some more circles. Can I have the green paper?"

Drew, Dorothy, James, Matthew. If he'd give her the family name, she could search for them online. "Here you go. Have you always lived here?"

Drew gave a sullen don't-ask-me hunch and scrawled a lopsided oval on his green paper. "I messed up," he said. "I want another piece. I want to draw a green ball."

"That was the last green. You want orange?"

"Green." He looked at her drawing of the baby, which she was now touching with specks of purple to bring out contrasting lines in the eyelids and the curled hands. "I can draw on the back."

"This one's mine. See how the baby's head looks round? It's just the same as the ball. When you can shade all the shapes, you can draw pretty much anything."

"I want green!"

He snatched at the paper. She was ready for him and whisked it out of reach. "You can have it if you tell me something," she said. "The name of somebody who lived here before me."

"That lady. The one with the kid, they came here selling stuff. The one that goes next door for violin lessons. She lived here once."

"CarolAnna? Is that who you mean? *CarolAnna* lived here?" And she'd never said anything, not when showing the house, not when Madison told her story. What was she hiding, what did she know?

"We used to play tag. She said I was her best friend. Then she went away, they always go away, nobody ever stays. Give me the paper."

Lacey gave him the picture of her baby. He turned it over, drew another rough oval, and said, "I messed up again!" He tore the paper in half and crumpled the pieces. "I hate this dumb stuff!" he yelled, and he was gone.

Lacey gathered the pieces of the torn picture and all Drew's sketches and threw them away, except the picture of his family, which she slid into the green binder. She chose light blue paper and the gray crayon and started drawing the baby again.

She put the picture in Eric's laptop case. Later, when he found it, he thanked her and promised to put it in a frame in his office. Then she was embarrassed because that was a thing a little kid would do. *Look at this picture I drew for you.* He was gone all day, twelve, thirteen, fifteen hours, coming home only to sleep. Nobody should have to work this hard. It wasn't like he was appealing death sentences on the eve of executions. She didn't put him through law school so she could be married to an empty bed. She had to talk to him.

First, Drew. CarolAnna Grey had lived in the house, CarolAnna who had told them they shouldn't buy it, CarolAnna who didn't know what stories the children told. Once upon a time, Drew was her best friend in the world. Lacey found Grey and Associates in the phone book and decided she'd rather have this conversation in person, and without warning. Madison Grey took violin lessons from Harry Rakoczy, so Lacey went for a walk when he was pruning dead branches off his dogwoods and chatted with him about students. She'd tutored privately, last year, and she always had to have her apartment clean and her materials ready. How many students did Harry have? Was it hard to keep track? Madison Grey's lesson, she found out, was at four on Thursday afternoons.

On Thursday at 3:58, she ran out the front door, gasped, and stepped back in. After three weeks of dry air, with everybody's lawn turning blond except Harry's, all September's hoarded rain was coming down at once. The Greys' car swam along Forrester Lane, waves washing back along the gutter from the wheels. Lacey grabbed Eric's umbrella and hurried down the street as the Greys pulled into Harry's driveway. "Let me take you to the door," she said.

"No way am I getting under an umbrella that comes from the murder house," Madison returned sharply. She jumped from the car and ran up to Harry's door, shielding her head with the violin case.

"Want to come in?" Lacey asked. She held the umbrella over CarolAnna's door.

"Thanks," CarolAnna said. "I've been meaning to ask you something."

"Yes, me too." Water filled Lacey's sneakers and ran down her shoulders as she held the umbrella over CarolAnna, and the ten seconds from the car to the door soaked her to the skin. When she got inside, her wet clothes turned cold and stuck to her. She shook her head, feeling the wet hair flapping against her ears, and laughed. "There's sweet tea. Or I can make coffee."

"Tea's fine, thanks." CarolAnna sat down, put her elbows on the table, and shoved all her fingers into her hair, in the eternal gesture of the overworked mother. It took Lacey right back to the classroom, parent-teacher meetings with women who'd already put in a nine-hour day and had to get home to clean the house and make dinner.

Lacey wanted to tell CarolAnna not to worry, Madison was a good girl with the potential for high achievement, she simply had to apply herself, because that was true of them all. Nine-year-olds: their parents never appreciated them until it was too late. The only parents who knew how great their fourth grader was were those who had teenagers. She handed CarolAnna the glass of tea and said, "You wanted to ask me something?"

"Halloween. Will you decorate?"

"Not this year. No ladders for me, and Eric's too busy."

"It can get intense, so just leave your lights off. The Wilsons three doors down from you do a huge display, so there'll be traffic. Last year they had holographic flying witches. And if you think it's bad at Halloween, just wait till Christmas!"

They laughed, and Lacey said, "Have you lived in the neighborhood long?"

"We live a few blocks away, on Hills Place. It's a nice neigh-borhood. Very active. I didn't see you at the Labor Day picnic."

Lacey rubbed her belly. "I didn't feel up to it. Too hot." She took a deep breath, wondering how to get the conversation around to the house. Then Drew was there, sitting opposite CarolAnna. Lacey's body clenched and the hair on her arms stood up—the chair hadn't moved from its place, it was impossible for anyone to have taken the seat without moving the chair, yet there he was. She was living in her mother's world, where spiritual influ-ences permeated every daily act. Light the right candle, change your life . . . She became aware that some minutes had passed in silence, herself staring blankly at Drew's chair, and CarolAnna waiting for her to come out of her daze. She shook her head and laughed. "Sorry," she said, "just faded out for a second."

Drew put his elbows on the table, propped his chain in his hands, and grinned at her, eager to help, which surprised her after his furious reaction to Madison. According to Piaget, nine-year-olds were in the phase of *concrete operations*: Drew could reason abstractly and anticipate consequences. He could use deductive reasoning. She didn't feel that she was using any reasoning at all, just flailing around by instinct.

"Ask her if she remembers me," he said.

"Do you remember him?" Lacey said obediently.

"I should go wait in the car. Madison'll worry if she doesn't see me."

"Do you remember him? Drew?"

CarolAnna shook her head. "I don't know anyone named Drew." She kept on shaking her head, as if she'd forgotten how to stop. "I don't remember."

"Ask her," Drew said. He leaned across the table, until his face was only inches from CarolAnna's. How could she not sense him, his voice vibrating the air? "Ask her if she remembers what she saw underwater."

"What did you see underwater?" Lacey said.

"Nothing."

"And you left me!" Drew shouted at CarolAnna. CarolAnna mimicked Drew's previous posture, resting her chin on her hands. If she was mirroring him, wasn't she somehow aware of him? Lacey's head whirled. Drew was so close, CarolAnna must have felt his breath on her eyes. She never blinked. "You went away," he said. "You left me all alone and now you can't even see me!" He was gone, leaving a hum of anger that made Lacey breathless but didn't appear to touch CarolAnna at all.

"Why did your family leave?" Lacey asked. Her breath was short, and she was panting like Bibbits on the verge of a coughing fit, yet CarolAnna seemed to sense nothing unusual.

"My dad got a job in Atlanta. My mom had bad dreams."

"What else do you remember?"

"Nothing. We lived here the spring of 1991. The people who came after us, I remember their name because it was so unusual. Warm and fuzzy. I named a hamster after them. Honeywick. The hamster was orange with white paws. I'd better go."

Lacey walked CarolAnna to the door. CarolAnna dithered, waiting for a pause in the rain. "Maybe you shouldn't stay," she blurted. "Not with the baby coming. Maybe it's not a good house for a baby. You can't blame me, I tried to tell you." And she was gone before Lacey had time to answer.

Chapter Eighteen

SOMETIMES, INSTEAD OF GOING FOR LUNCH with the rest of the office, Eric stayed at his desk to browse baby-related websites. Lacey spent hours on YourBabyNow.net; she was always calling him into her room to share some new and interesting fetal fact. The baby's retinas were fully formed. He could recognize individual voices. But when Eric wanted to put together a list of names, she shook her head.

He'd been dreading the day when Lacey would announce they needed to buy the baby furniture they couldn't afford. The day never came, and now it was her silence he dreaded. She hadn't bought so much as a single baby blanket. Why wasn't she getting ready? Eric, sisterless, had an impression, distilled from movies and sitcoms, of the rituals of pregnancy. A baby shower. He asked why she didn't have one. "You can't give a shower for yourself," she said. "I don't know anyone in Greeneburg."

So he called a couple of her old friends, fellow students and teacher colleagues from Columbia, to let them know that Lacey was taking her pregnancy hard and felt lonely. He had disliked those women when he was dating Lacey, knowing she discussed him with them—what did she say? Did they advise her to hold on to him, or did they shake their heads and tell her she'd be better off alone? And even after they were married, she took it for granted that she'd go out with her friends without him, just the same as before. When they first moved to Greeneburg, he'd been happy to see those connections fade. The Lacey who came home from a night out with her friends was hard and loud with the smell of beer in her hair, not a girl he would ever have dated—not *his* Lacey. Now he found those friends on her phone and asked for their help.

A few days later, her old roommate, Phyllis, called to tell him that Lacey had vetoed the idea of a shower and wouldn't even let any of her friends come visit. "She's feeling superstitious," Phyllis said. "Don't push it. Let her do what she has to do." Eric noted on his calendar in November: *Invite Phyllis for Christmas party.* Lacey needed her friends; he didn't have to like them, but he had to welcome them for her sake. She wouldn't be drinking with them, anyway.

Alone, he wandered the infinite shopping aisles of Amazon and found everything babies needed. He marveled at the five-thousand-dollar strollers and fell in love with a tiny little newborn-sized tuxedo onesie with a red bow tie. That was his first purchase, and he was hooked. He bought clothes, diapers, chewable books, and tiny little socks. He bought crib bedding and stuffed animals, Eric Carle prints, and a mobile of Dr. Seuss characters. He bought a diaper presterilizer and a bassinet but decided to hold off on the crib until Lacey felt better; the baby would use the bassinet for the first three months.

He didn't buy a breast pump because looking at the pictures made him feel funny, and the YouTube video of a woman hooked up to a double electric pump was something he wouldn't forget in a hurry. He didn't buy bottles because they attached to various other pieces of equipment. They weren't just bottles, they were feeding systems. He eavesdropped on Internet chats among young mothers about the relative merits of Medela and Avent and decided this was one decision he would leave entirely up to Lacey.

He joined a chat on circumcision and found himself arguing, lawyerlike, for both sides. On a chat about postpartum depression, he asked diffidently if there was such a thing as prepartum depression, to which all participants unanimously responded *yes* and encouraged him to talk with his wife's OB. Dr. Vlk alarmed him, in much the same way as the breast pumps, but he called her to say he thought Lacey might be depressed.

"Lacey is doing very well," Dr. Vlk said. "You should come to the next appointment. You need to sign up for a birth class."

He was startled to realize their due date was that close. Lacey shut down the idea of classes. "Not yet," she said. "Not till he's bigger." Phyllis was right, then—Lacey wouldn't prepare till she was sure there would be a live baby. He complained on the postpartum depression chat that he felt he was going through pregnancy alone, and the women flamed him so badly for his insensitivity he didn't dare go back.

He had his purchases delivered to Moranis Miszlak so they wouldn't upset Lacey. On the Friday after the big rainstorm, with summer's heat finally broken, Sammie hauled a box in from reception. "More of your loot," she said. "What's this?"

"Got to be the bassinet."

"How come it's coming here and not to your house?"

He explained Lacey's odd behavior. Sammie laughed. "My grandma wouldn't let anybody buy anything for my sister," she said. "It's an old-country thing. They think they're going to jinx the baby. You better quit buying, she'll want to do it herself."

"We need the car seat."

"You've got three days after the baby's born to get the car seat. Listen, your four thirty canceled and I rescheduled your five for Monday. Go home. Try not to buy any diapers on the way."

Released early, feeling ridiculously free, Eric drove home in daylight for the first time in weeks. He had a boxful of files in the backseat, twenty hours of work for the weekend, but it was only 4:45 and he was home. He sat in the car to admire the house. Lacey had been right about the green door. It welcomed him. Voices came from the backyard, so he walked around the side of the house to see what was going on.

Lacey, looking like a peach in a pale orange dress, was running water into a big plastic tub, while Bibbits chewed the hose and Harry Rakoczy hung around his own back porch, spreading mulch and watching. "Come on, you stinker," Lacey said. She grabbed the dog and pushed him into the tub, holding him down with one hand while she squirted shampoo on his head.

Ella Dane came out of the house on the wings of her own raised voice. "What are you doing to my dog?"

"He's filthy. Look at this, his fur's all matted. Come and hold him while I scrub."

They hadn't seen Eric yet, and he hung back, unwilling to get involved with soap and water and matted dog filth in a suit that had to be dry-cleaned. Whatever was going on between Lacey and Ella Dane, he wanted no part of it.

"You haven't been taking care of him," Lacey said. This sharp tone surprised him; she'd never spoken to him in that voice.

"Oh, and you know so much about taking care of things. Who's been washing your dishes and vacuuming your floors and doing your laundry?"

"I was on bed rest. It's not like I asked you to come here." Bibbits's claws slipped on the plastic as he tried to climb out of the tub. Lacey pushed him down and squirted more shampoo over him. She dropped the shampoo bottle and held the dog in the water, working her fingers into the matted fur, scrubbing with both hands.

Lacey must be feeling better. Recovering from sickness always made her angry, and she worked her temper off by cleaning something. He'd learned to stay out of the house on the fifth day after she came down with a cold, so she could have the place to herself, although her furious bleaching usually ruined something, leaving rusty spots on her good black pants, or yellow stains on white Formica. It wasn't too late to drive back to the office—the women hadn't seen him yet.

"Let go of my dog!" Ella Dane said. "What's that stuff you're putting on him?"

"Shampoo." Lacey scrubbed the dog into a ball of foam. Bibbits paddled frantically in water three inches too deep for him, and Lacey's hand plunged through the foam and forced him underwater. "You've heard of it. It gets hair clean. Also dog fur. Have you smelled this dog lately? My bed reeks like a kennel."

The dog's legs were slowing down. Eric didn't want to get into the middle of this—it was worse than the breast pumps—but he couldn't stand there and let the animal drown. Harry laid down his rake. "Ladies," he called as he walked across the lawn. Lacey turned to look at him, and her hand relaxed on the dog's back. Bibbits surged out of the tub, and half the water sloshed out as he broke for freedom.

"Catch him!" Lacey and Ella Dane shouted. Ella Dane ran after the dog, and Lacey sank down where she stood, one hand pressed against the base of her throat. Eric stepped in front of Bibbits, who swerved to the right, directly into Harry's arms.

Harry picked up the still-running hose, held the dog flat in the grass, and worked the water into the fur until there were no more bubbles. Ella Dane picked up the shampoo bottle and read the ingredients out loud in tones of horror. "Sodium laureth sulfate," she said. "Salvia extract. So they dipped a sage leaf in it, big deal." She went inside.

Eric helped Lacey up. "Are you okay?" he asked. "Do you need the doctor?"

"No, I was dizzy, there was this feeling. Something came over me."

"You were rough on the dog." Such violence—this was a side of Lacey he'd never seen, and he couldn't help imagining her, a year from now, alone with a baby who needed a bath, angry and impatient as she was with Bibbits. She wouldn't. She would never lose her temper with a child, never. Of all the things Lacey would never do—but he kept seeing her hand, holding the animal underwater. "It looked like you almost drowned him," he said. He'd been several yards away; he couldn't be sure what he'd seen. But some of the things those women said on the Internet . . .

Lacey shrugged herself out of his arms. "Oh, come on. You think I'm going to take the dog outside and drown him right there in front of Harry and Ella Dane, really, you think that? How crazy do you think I am?"

"Of course not," Eric said, but he added something new to his ever-evolving mental shopping list of things he needed to buy for the baby. One of those plastic bath seats, with a seat belt, the tub formed to support the baby upright. He'd spent half an hour yesterday watching online clips of babies being washed in a variety of tubs and seats and even, one of them, in the kitchen sink, which didn't look safe at all. A plastic bath seat, for safety.

How crazy did he think she was? Not crazy at all, but maybe

Ella Dane could stay on for the first couple of months. Several women on the depression chat wrote about how close they'd come to killing their babies, one way or another. Shaking, dropping, and drowning. Mostly drowning. *It seemed so easy,* one of them had written, *it seemed like a thing I had to do,* and dozens had agreed.

Chapter Nineteen

OVER THE NEXT WEEK, Ella Dane was sweet and careful with Lacey. She drove her to all the used-car lots that Harry Rakoczy recommended, and when they found a three-year-old Camry, silver, with only forty thousand miles, Ella Dane bundled Lacey back into her car and drove her away, telling the salesman, "We might come back later."

They came back with Harry. Ella Dane insisted, and she was right. Harry made thoughtful sounds at the engine and doubtful sounds at the brakes, and the car cost three thousand dollars less than Eric had budgeted.

Something had changed between them, on the day Lacey gave Bibbits a bath. Between all of them. Bibbits took to licking her hand, or standing in front of her and wagging so hard his claws rattled on the floor. Gratitude or submission? Either way, it creeped her out, and something was wrong with Eric too. He watched her with a caution she knew well. This was how he evaluated any not-quite-adequate machine—would the car's transmission last till September? How soon before the air conditioner needed servicing?—but why was he looking at *her* that way? It was only a little water, nobody got hurt. And

Ella Dane stopped singing lullabies for Drew, stopped bringing home crystals and sprinkling rock salt in the fireplace. Instead, she began to talk about moving out. She wouldn't move far, and she'd come back for a few days when the baby was born, but it was time to get her own place. She paused as if waiting for Lacey to protest *Please stay, I can't manage without you,* but Lacey said, "That sounds great," although she'd miss Bibbits. The little dog had grown on her.

The weather changed. The sky was bright and open, and the rain came decorously twice a week. Lawns thickened, drooping shrubs revived, and a gilt edge began to show along the outlines of the maples and Bradford pears. Lacey took Dr. Vlk's advice and began to walk around the neighborhood. In the shining health of these autumn days, with the windows open and every room freshened, even with Drew her constant companion, she found it hard to imagine anything unwholesome in her house. Lately Drew was so sweet, he was good company and she liked him; it took some effort for her to remember his anger and the damage he had done to Ella Dane's room.

But CarolAnna said it wasn't a good house for babies. It popped into her mind at odd moments, spoiling her pleasure and making her feel nervous and guilty. She should do something about it—but what? Day after day, she delayed.

The days were so clean, and her skin craved the fresh air. On warm afternoons she put on a bikini and sat on the deck to sun her belly. Did the light come through the tight dome of her flesh, brightening her baby's dark world into red, like a flashlight shining through a hand? She thought it must; she felt him turn and stretch. One afternoon, when the wind was just a little too cold for sunbathing, she took paper and crayons out to the deck and taught Drew how to make leaf rubbings. It was one of his friendly days. He pressed the crayon too hard and laid the wax down thick and flaky.

"Lightly," she said. "Let go." She stripped the paper off the gold crayon. "Here."

He looked up, smiling. Her eyes prickled at his sweetness, as bright as the tall October sky. Stupid hormones. Only a sentimental idiot would feel like crying because a little boy had a beautiful smile. They all did, all the noisy boys, they all had that bright, soft, vulnerable smile; she had never seen it on a grown man. Something happened to them. Lacey's private classroom goal, one she never wrote down or told anyone, was not to be the thing that happened. She sent her boys into fifth grade smiling the same undamaged smile.

Lightly he rubbed the gold crayon, picking up the veins and edges. "You carry on," she told him. "I have to make a couple phone calls."

Not a good house for babies. Time was running out and she had to know the truth. She remembered the name CarolAnna gave her and found three Honeywicks in the phone book. The first was an insurance agency. The woman who answered the phone said, "There hasn't been a Honeywick here for years. Would you like Mr. Carruthers?"

"No thanks." If CarolAnna had been nine, that had to be twenty years ago at least. The Honeywicks might have moved to Oregon, Nevada, anywhere. For a moment, she lost hope. But even if her Honeywicks were gone, some of the others knew where. It wasn't like calling people named Jones and asking for their cousin Emily.

The second Honeywick number was answered by a teenager who seemed not at all able to understand what Lacey wanted. "How long ago?" she asked.

"Twenty years," Lacey said.

"Twenty, are you kidding me, *years,* and you're calling on the *phone*? Why don't you Google them? Or haven't you heard of Facebook?"

"I don't know their first name. I don't want all the Honey-wicks on earth," she replied, and the teenager snorted and hung up on her.

The third one was an old man who, again, had trouble under-standing what Lacey wanted. "Twenty years ago," she said for the third time.

"And what was the address?" he asked.

"571 Forrester Lane."

"And where did they move to?"

"Sir," Lacey said with desperate politeness, "I don't know. But I need to ask them a question. If you could just give me their first name," because, now she thought about it, the teenager's sugges-tion was not bad. And even if she had to search through all the Honeywicks on earth, how many could there really be?

"That's the bad house, isn't it, honey?" the old man said.

"Oh, yes, please," Lacey said. "Can you tell me their name?"

The old man put the phone down and wandered away. She heard household noises: water, a toilet flushing, more water, doors opening and closing, a burst of thin laughter from a TV or radio.

She could hang up. She didn't have to know these things. Drew was the same as any other boy, and as for the smashed room—everyone had a bad day, once in a while. Was she going to hold it against him forever, one little tantrum? It wasn't so bad, she could live with it. She squeezed the phone and wouldn't let herself put it down.

"Sir?" she said. "Hello? Are you still there?"

Slow footsteps neared the telephone. "Greeley," he said.

"That's in Colorado?"

"That's my niece. Greeley Honeywick. She's in Utah. The number is, here it is, I have to unfold the paper, the number is seven. Four. One. Four. Two." He stopped.

Lacey waited. "Are there more numbers?" she asked finally.

"No."

"Her name's Greeley Honeywick, and she lives in Utah?"

The old man didn't answer. He had wandered away from the telephone again. For five minutes, Lacey listened to the vague puttering of his day, and eventually she hung up; there didn't seem to be anything else to do.

"Greeley Honeywick," she said out loud and turned to find Drew, paper in hand.

"No," he said. "You can't talk to her."

"Let me see your leaf. Look how all the veins came up when you did it lightly."

"I don't want people talking about me. They keep doing it. Talking and talking."

"Drew," Lacey said in her patience-and-understanding voice, "sweetie, I understand that you're angry and upset. Can you tell me why?"

"No!" he shrieked and suddenly he flew at her, into her and through her, breaking against her body in a cold wave. The sense of the real child vanished, and he was a disembodied power, all will and fury. For a moment, the cold crawled over her like a tide of ants. Another moment, and all the ants bit and burrowed inward. Lacey sank into a kitchen chair. She tugged her blouse away from her body, expecting to see blood spurting from every pore: nothing. Was it all illusion, seeing, hearing, touching him?

The cookies disappeared when he ate them. His pictures were

real. These things happened, and this, the cold wave, *this* was the illusion. It had to be; anything else was insupportable. As Lacey sat at her kitchen table, she felt something else that was surely real. The vise of a Braxton Hicks contraction closed over her belly, and then kept tightening. She felt the feather tickle, the tongue of blood on her thighs.

No, no. Not after all this time, she couldn't lose him now, it wasn't *fair*.

Twenty-nine weeks. Third trimester, her baby would live, he would be born alive. She'd looked just this morning and the website said the chances of survival were 84 percent, a high C-plus, almost a B. She grabbed her car keys. No time for an ambulance. Her mind flicked into crisis control, no panic, no fear, time for that later, now she had to act. If the placenta unzipped, he wouldn't die right away. She had a little time. Dr. Vlk's office was ten minutes closer than the hospital, so she went there, stopping at red lights, signaling for turns. Careful, careful.

The problem was what to do when she got there. Lacey sat in the car in the parking lot of Women's Medical Services, Dr. Vlk's office. She couldn't get out of the car; standing was too dangerous. She pressed her thighs together, feeling the blood bubbles bursting as steadily as air reaching the surface in a large aquarium. One by one they grew, forced their way out of her body, and opened slickly against her skin. She couldn't move, but she couldn't stay in the car. "Help me," she whimpered, and answered herself with the teacher voice, "Stop whining and *think*."

She dug in her purse for her cell phone. She saw it in her mind, brilliantly lit as a stained-glass window in June: her phone, plugged into its charger, on the kitchen counter where she always left it. It drove Eric crazy. *Why don't you carry your cell phone,* he always said. *What do you have it for, decoration?* Help was as close as Dr. Vlk's receptionist. She dumped her purse on the passenger seat, and there it was. The battery was low, but not fully depleted. And Dr. Vlk's number was in her queue of recent calls. "Thank you, thank you," she said to the phone. She called and found herself in a maze of voice-mail options. Future appointments, prescriptions, "and if this is an emergency," the recorded voice concluded, "please hang up and dial 911."

What was the point of having a cell phone if no one would answer? She could call 911, they'd send an ambulance. No time. And not safe. 911 meant the hospital, and Drew could find her in the hospital. She'd seen him there.

Ella Dane—no, it would take her forty minutes to get here. Eric was in court. Dr. Vlk's windows were twenty feet away, and nobody would even pick up the phone. Lacey banged the steering wheel, and the horn beeped softly. This was no good, this stupid horn with its stupid little ladylike tootle. She needed some real noise. She leaned onto it with both elbows and pressed her upper body against the wheel. The horn sang out, and the blood bubbled faster. Nobody came. Were they going to let her sit out here and die—why wasn't anyone listening? She leaned into the horn again.

Dr. Vlk's office doors opened, and a nurse in Strawberry Shortcake scrubs ran out. Lacey lowered her window and waved. "Here!" she shouted.

The baby moved. Lacey laid her head on the steering wheel and held her breath to hold the life inside her. He moved again, pushing under her ribs. "Hold on," she told him. "Don't worry, you're okay, hold on."

The nurse dashed inside and came out moments later with

a colleague in Hello Kitty scrubs, pushing a wheelchair. Straw-berry Shortcake took Lacey's information while Hello Kitty low-ered the wheelchair's right armrest; they slid her into the chair and rolled her through the lobby straight into the exam room. "You really should have called an ambulance," Hello Kitty scolded, while Strawberry Shortcake helped her onto the exami-nation table, shoved the thermometer in her mouth, and strapped the blood-pressure cuff on her left arm.

"I don't have a fever," Lacey mumbled around the thermom-eter. "I'm bleeding, can you look?"

"Dr. Vlk will be right with you."

"It's an emergency, I need help *now*," and Dr. Vlk entered the room, pushing the ultrasound machine herself.

"I'd rather have my ladies go to the hospital in emergencies," Dr. Vlk said, cool and superior, as if she were ordering fruit salad instead of fries. Before the ultrasound machine even stopped roll-ing, she pulled the stool up beside the exam table and drew a pair of latex gloves from the box on the counter. "Now let's see what's going on here. Nina, get the feet."

Strawberry Shortcake slipped Lacey's feet out of her shoes, pulled her underwear off, and tucked her heels into the stirrups. "There's some light spotting," she announced.

Light spotting, they called it. Another bubble opened. "I'm bleeding," Lacey said. "It's twenty-nine weeks, is he okay?" She hadn't felt him move since that moment in the car. If the answer was *no, he's already gone,* she needed to know immediately, before she suffocated on the hope writhing in her throat. Light spot-ting, that sounded not too bad; it sounded survivable. "Can you tell me?"

"This will be cold," Dr. Vlk said as she squirted gel onto

Lacey's belly. She slid the ultrasound wand over Lacey's tight, slippery skin. She was quiet for a long time, and one of the nurses slid a pad under Lacey's backside. Another bubble burst. It was death, certainly death.

"There's the heartbeat," Dr. Vlk said at last, and Lacey broke into tears; the nurse was ready with tissues. Dr. Vlk turned the monitor so Lacey could see the gray swirling image. "There's a bit more placental abruption just at the top edge."

"It could unzip," Lacey said. She blew her nose and tried to control her hiccuping breath. Unzip, such an ugly word.

"We'll keep an eye on it. Nina, hand me the speculum."

Lacey braced herself, and Dr. Vlk told her to *just relax, now,* which was easy for her to say, as the cold metal slid into Lacey and opened inside her. She stopped her breath as if by doing so she could pretend that this most intimate door forced wide in her body had nothing to do with her.

"Good," Dr. Vlk said. She withdrew the metal tool and dropped it into a plastic bin marked *biohazard*. "There's no dilation, no effacement." Stripping off the latex gloves, she dropped them in a different biohazard bin. Gently, she squeezed Lacey's left arm. "It looks worse than it is. You're closed up tight, so all you need to do is rest and keep your feet up."

"The baby's not coming today?"

"He shouldn't. We need to get you home. Can we call your husband?"

"He's in court. You can try his office."

"I want to have another look, as long as the machine's here." Dr. Vlk put on a new pair of latex gloves and squeezed more gel on Lacey. She slid the ultrasound wand to the left. "Hey, little guy. Such a monkey. How did you get that bruise?"

"What bruise?"

Dr. Vlk touched a spot on Lacey's left side, below her rib cage. "There."

"That hurts! What is it?"

"Did someone hit you?"

"No. I must have bumped myself." Lacey tried to think of something that would hit her body at that height and leave a round bruise. "Maybe a doorknob."

"And you turned around and hit it on the other side?" Dr. Vlk asked, touching Lacey on the same spot on her right side. Lacey gasped. "Who touches you?"

"Nobody." Drew had touched her, Drew had rushed toward her with his arms open, and his hands would have touched her just where she was hurt.

Dr. Vlk was as smooth and elegant as ever, and her voice was calmly light as she said, "You don't have to go home. There are safe places for you and your baby. The hospital, to begin with."

"Can you call Moranis Miszlak and ask them to get Eric out of court?"

"You have choices."

Better to go home and face Drew there than to wait in the hospital, surrounded by strangers who couldn't see and wouldn't believe. Better to be home, where she had her things, crayons and paper to distract him, cookies, games, all the tools and tricks to keep him friendly and engaged. She couldn't go to the hospital to lie in the white bed in the empty room waiting for him to say, *I came here to find you.*

There was no way to explain any of this to Dr. Vlk. No way to explain it to Eric. She hadn't discussed it with Ella Dane recently—she'd let Ella Dane develop the idea that Drew had been soothed away. The silence between herself and her mother was uncomfortable, oppressive, but so was the communication; at least it was a change. She was all alone with Drew, and she had to do all she could to keep him happy, because if he got angry, he might kill her, or the baby, or both. He'd be sorry afterward, but he was only nine, just beginning to predict consequences, still impulsive and reactive. If she stayed away too long, what might he do, angry and alone? If he went on the rampage, and Eric arrived— She saw the shattered bed in Ella Dane's room, the book driven into the wall. She couldn't let Eric walk into that.

"I'd rather go home," she said. "Could you call my husband, please?"

Chapter Twenty

LEX HELD ON TO HIS PICTURES, waiting for his lawyer to call him back. After a week, he started calling Moranis Miszlak, but the shiny girl at the desk never put him through. "He's with a client," she said. An hour later, he was in court, then with another client, then taking a deposition.

"There's nothing new," the shiny girl told him in her bright, bored voice. "He'll let you know when the custody hearing is scheduled."

He kept calling, hour after hour—he wasn't sure she understood the danger Theo was in, drowning in cheeseburgers and white bread and fries—and by Wednesday afternoon, she stopped taking his calls. On Thursday afternoon, Lex printed out his shots of Jeanne shoving the chicken into Theo, copied the video to a CD, and drove down to County Place. If the lawyer wouldn't help him, he'd help himself.

He parked in the Heart Healthy Visitors section, as far from the front door as he could get. The buildings were gray and low and square, with big concrete triangles jutting out like broken bones sticking out of gray flesh.

Nothing good ever happened here. All the courts were here: the family court, where Jeanne would try to take Theo away from him forever. Criminal court, civil court. The county jail was here, in a back building hidden from the street, looking just like the big court building only with no broken-bone triangles and no windows. Juvenile detention was here, sharing a wall with the county jail, but with a different entrance. It used to have a playground, where the larger boys had put the smaller boys on the swings and tried to push them all the way over the top. Later, the playground disappeared, replaced by a community garden where all the vegetables died and only wild garlic grew. Probate court was here, where the judge gave him his parents' house. . . .

Nothing good. Nothing good ever happened here.

All the hallways looked the same. They were gray, like the outside walls, and colored stripes on the floor crossed each other, turning in different directions at each intersection. They meant something but he didn't know what, and all the doors were the same gray steel, and every third door had a red Exit sign, but none of them led outside. A person could get lost in here forever.

Long ago, once upon a time, his mother told him if he was lost, look for police. They were everywhere, cops or security guards at every intersection, and sitting on chairs next to the elevators. The courtrooms and the important offices were underground, two or three levels down. Some of the hallways underground, Lex remembered, connected the courtroom elevators to the jail elevators. What if he got into the wrong elevator and accidentally wandered into the jail? Was that a crime? Would they arrest him again?

He walked past three security guards, quickly, with his eyes on the colored stripes on the floor, hoping he looked like he knew where he was going. Like he was supposed to be there. Then he found himself at another set of three elevators, or maybe the same ones. The security guard sat with his knees splayed wide and his pants wrinkled. All the colored stripes headed into the elevators. Lex held back.

The middle elevator opened and a new security guard came out, a young woman with black hair in big waves around her face and a coffee cup in her hand. Lex smiled at her. He liked her. She looked like the Mexican women who came into MacArthur's. He always asked if he could help them, and he led them to the jicamas and the chili peppers. For them, he had persuaded the management to order sugarcane and mangoes and all the beautiful tropical fruits. She said, "Sir, are you lost?"

"I need help," Lex said. His voice was too loud. "I need the police."

"Do you want to report a crime?" she asked.

"Yes!" She was so kind and so beautiful. Tears ran down the inside of his nose, and he wiped his sleeve across his face. "A crime. I need to report a crime."

She handed the coffee to the fat guard. "Here, Jim, I'll be right back. This way, sir." She led Lex along the purple line through several identical gray turns and into a glass-brick lobby he hadn't seen before. He liked her young, strong walk, not panting and pigeon-toed like poor Jeanne. She took him past the lobby and into a maze of desks and cubicles, big messy offices with their doors flung open, telephones and shouts. It was worse than Moranis Miszlak. He wished he hadn't come.

"Here," she said, and sat him down at one of the desks in the middle of the room, opposite another messy cop, maybe the same one from the elevator, come here by a faster and more secret way. They looked just alike. "Officer Bennet will help you," she said firmly, and took herself away.

He held out his disk, and the messy cop didn't take it. People didn't like to take things from Lex's hands. He had learned not to touch the produce when the customers could see him. "It's a crime," Lex explained. "I had a camera."

The messy cop took the disk and slid it into the drive on his laptop. After he watched the scene, he looked at Lex, his face turning red. "You wasting my time?"

"She's poisoning my baby. It's a crime."

The messy cop sucked his big, pink lips and pressed a button on the phone. "Code L over here," he said, "family court type," and a few minutes later a woman appeared, not the kind Lex liked to look at but one of the other kinds, a short solid woman with stiff gray hair standing up in triangles just like the County Place building.

"Is there a problem, sir?" she said to Lex. She had a friendly voice.

"My wife is poisoning my baby. I took pictures." He gave her the pictures. She stood behind the cop and watched the video on his computer.

"Has your wife left you, by any chance?" the gray woman asked.

Lex nodded.

"And there's a custody hearing coming up, correct me if I'm wrong."

He nodded again.

"You have a lawyer? What's your lawyer's name?"

"Miszlak."

The cop pressed another button on his desk phone and said to someone, "Miszlak still down there? I got a Code L, one of his." Then he turned back to Lex. "Your lawyer's coming," he said.

But it was some other lawyer, an old man in a pink checkered suit with a yellow bow tie. "That's not my lawyer," Lex said. "Mine is a young one."

"You're one of Eric's clients?" the new lawyer asked.

The cop and the gray woman explained. The new lawyer gathered the pictures and the disk, took Lex's elbow, and led him out through the glass lobby. "You can't come to the cops with this," he said. "You let Eric take care of you. He knows what he's doing."

"My wife's lawyer says I'm crazy."

"Who's your wife's lawyer?"

"MacAvoy."

They had reached the front entrance of County Place. The new lawyer pushed Lex toward the big smoked-glass doors. "Oh, you're *that* one. Are you crazy?"

"I just want to take care of my baby girl."

"Eric never told you to come here with pictures. You've brought the cops into a custody case. You bring a gun to a knife fight, you better know how to use it, or you'll get yourself shot. You want your kid in foster care? Let Eric do his job."

"What's Code L?"

"That's L for loony."

Lex turned back. He could find his way along the purple line. "They can't call me that. There's nothing wrong with me."

The new lawyer grabbed his arm and towed him outside. "They call you whatever they want, and you say, *Yes, sir, may I have another?* Got that? Come here again before your court date, and you'll be finding yourself a new law firm."

"Yes, sir," Lex mumbled, and he began the long walk back to his Heart Healthy parking spot. Halfway along the first aisle of cars, he stopped and looked back. The new lawyer was standing by the glass doors, watching him walk away.

Chapter Twenty-one

ERIC WAS GLAD to have been called out of court. The case was the judiest of judies: a young man who had bought his ex-girlfriend a car and was suing her because she wouldn't pay the insurance. He was as passionate about it, as desperate and sincere, as Lex Hall about his baby, or any of the almost exes about their children, dogs, and houses.

The judge wanted to know why the young man didn't cancel the insurance and let the girlfriend fend for herself. Eric wanted to know that, too. This case, like so many others, should have been heard in small claims, but the young man was suing for the car as well as for the insurance, even though Eric had explained for twenty minutes (half a billable hour) that his having bought the car on the girlfriend's birthday and having the dealer put a big red ribbon on it made it incontrovertibly a gift.

"It's not right," the young man said. "She owes me. It's not right."

"For future reference," Floyd murmured as he stepped next to Eric to make his apologies to the judge and take over the case, "the customer ain't always right. You should never have let this goober near a court."

"Couldn't stop him," Eric said. "What's wrong?"

Floyd raised his voice. "Family emergency, Your Honor. Your wife's at Women's Health," he said to Eric, more softly, but loudly enough that everyone in court heard, while believing they were not meant to hear. Eric marveled at Floyd's instincts, using this trick on such a worthless case. "Trouble with the baby. Better get there fast."

Eric drove with his mind full of blood, unable to clear away the hateful, pragmatic questions his legal mind laid out as for a deposition: Would Lacey want to touch it, hold it, and say good-bye? He knew she would, and she'd want him to do it, too. Could he hold in his arms this not-quite-a-person who had never lived? Would he remember it forever, would it pollute his feelings for the living child who might be born someday? Would they have a funeral? Was there some law about disposal of medical waste, and would a funeral home be legally permitted to take a stillborn fetus? They hadn't chosen a name. They'd need a good name but not too good, not a name they would regret having wasted.

Dr. Vlk met him when he arrived, and the baby was fine, and Lacey was fine. All his questions disappeared, leaving a residue of shame. Before letting him see Lacey, the doctor questioned him stringently about Lacey's daily activities. "She bruises easily," Eric said. "Half the time she doesn't know what she did." He kept his tone concerned, eager to help, distracted: "You're sure the baby's okay?" he asked again. As if he didn't know what this was about. Lacey had a suspicious bruise, and the doctor wanted to know why. "I blame myself," he said, with sincerity worthy of Uncle Floyd. "I should be home more, taking care of her."

That did it, finally. The doctor led him down the hall to Lacey's exam room. Lacey was asleep. Seeing her in this medical light, pale and shadowless, Eric was struck by how terrible she looked. She was so small, and the huge round belly bulged like a parasite that had almost drained its host, a grossly overgrown caterpillar on a flower stem. The skin around her eyes was stained purple and black, and her mouth fell in as she slept. No wonder Dr. Vlk thought he'd been beating her. If a client came to Eric looking like that, he'd file a restraining order and drop her off at the women's shelter himself.

What could he do, what more could he do? He'd bought her the house, the car, the furniture; he'd called her mother here to take care of her; and he had to work to earn money for all that. He'd bought the bassinet and the newborn clothes, dozens of things they'd need for the baby, without troubling her about any of it. He planned to change diapers, get up in the middle of the night, hold her hand during delivery, all those good-father things his mother always complained his own father never did. Right now, there was nothing he could do. He couldn't take one moment of her pregnancy for her.

"Hey," he said, taking her right hand.

She blinked, turned her head toward him, and smiled. The smile hurt him, false and difficult, an ill-fitting shoe squeezed back onto yesterday's blisters. She shouldn't have to smile like that. Without his noticing, something had gone badly wrong between them, and no matter what he did, he couldn't reach her. "Bad day," he said.

"Not so bad as it might have been. We're still pregnant, anyway."

"So I've been thinking," which wasn't true, because the idea came to him only as he spoke, "I should get a house-cleaning service. Ella Dane shouldn't have to clean our house." Especially since she was so bad at it. "And if Dr. Vlk says bed rest, then you're going to bed. I'll cut down on my hours and ask Uncle Floyd if I can work at home more. You don't have to be alone."

She rolled her face away on the pillow. "I'm not alone. Never."

He waited for her to say more, but she drifted off to sleep again, unself-conscious as a little girl. He kissed her, and then touched her belly, feeling the baby rush up against his hand and slide away. Amazing. And still alive. Now, how was he going to get Lacey home, with two cars, not letting her drive?

He'd have to call Ella Dane. That would leave him with three cars and two drivers. If he drove Lacey home in his car, and met Ella Dane at home, and drove Ella Dane back here in his car, then she could drive Lacey's car home. . . . Planning and calculating, he walked from the room, his cell phone in his hand, and tripped over a little boy in the doorway. "Sorry, kid," he said, "you looking for someone?"

"I followed her back here," the boy said. A nice-looking child with thick blond hair and a late-summer tan, not yet faded in mid-October, a boy who'd spent the last seven months outside, climbing trees and playing baseball every minute he wasn't in school. Wholesome. Eric thought of the tiny being curled inside Lacey. He might be blond like her; he might have a strong body and an open face like this boy. "I can't find her," the boy said.

"Your mom's here somewhere? You're not supposed to be wandering around." What if he opened a door and found her with her feet up on one of those medieval-torture tables? That was no way for a boy to see his mother. "She won't leave without you."

He seemed unsure, but he allowed Eric to lead him back through the white hallways to the waiting room, where he slumped in one of the cushioned chairs and hid himself behind a ragged copy of *Highlights for Children*. Eric stepped outside to call Ella Dane, and when he came back in, the little boy was gone.

Chapter Twenty-two

LACEY LET ERIC help her up the porch steps. After all her fears, the house was as radiantly peaceful as October sun could make it. Eric brought the leather sofa cushions from the living room and set them at the head of Lacey's bed. She hadn't had so much attention from him in weeks. "Good?" he said.

She wriggled her shoulders against the cushions. "Perfect."

They looked around her room. Someday the china cabinet would stand here, where the head of her bed now touched the wall. They'd have an oval table in the middle of the room, mahogany with ball-and-claw feet. She'd take down the miniblinds and put curtains across the bank of three windows that looked out on the backyard, brocade and tassels and a layer of lace, a rich and elegant room. Now, her sheets smelled like an old motel, like dirty feet and sour nighttime breath. And Bibbits.

"Can you open a window?" she said.

He was so sweet, but already he was looking past her. He checked his watch; he was thinking about the courtroom she'd called him out of and all the work he still had to do. He put up a good show, she had to give him that. He opened the window, made sure she had a glass of water, and told her to stay in bed unless she needed to go to the bathroom, not to get up for anything. He brought her drawing supplies, her laptop, and the television from the living room. He went out to buy liver and bacon and even cooked it, although she knew the smell of liver made him gag. The smell would be his excuse to leave her alone; he would take his laptop upstairs.

The front door slammed in a meaningful way as Ella Dane left the house to avoid the smell of meat. Sulking. What was it now, apart from the liver? Maybe she was upset because Lacey had called for Eric's help and not hers.

"Your mom's got a bee up her butt," Drew said. Suddenly he was at the foot of her bed, as if he'd always been there, sitting with his knees drawn up to his chin. His light hair flopped over his eyebrows, and she couldn't see his eyes. He had mosquito bites on his ankles, some of them freshly raised welts, others scratched, scabbed, scratched again. He stuck his left pinky in his ear and rooted for wax, and Lacey marveled again at his persuasive reality. When he moved, the mattress shifted under her.

"Language," she said.

"I'm just saying."

"She's going out because she doesn't like liver."

Drew pulled his knees in closer and dropped his face, so all she could see of him was the crown of his head, the flat wavy locks of hair springing like separate leaves from the uneven part, the whorl at the back. He muttered something into his legs.

"Didn't hear you," Lacey said.

"I *said*." He burrowed his face into his knees and shouted through his own body. "I said I was sorry, okay? I only wanted to make you listen."

"You could have hurt me. You could have hurt the baby." Outrage and terror sank into the sand of her mind. So exhausting.

She'd had this conversation before. Children in classrooms had knocked over desks; they had thrown book bags, pencils, and binders at her; they'd hooked their feet around her ankles trying to trip her; twice, she'd been bitten bloody. Teaching was a perilous art. She coaxed, comforted, and challenged her difficult boys. *Use your words,* she said, and then she taught them better words. She'd never given up on a child, however troubled and strange.

"I said, I know! You have to be careful of babies. I know."

"Okay. Thank you." As in a classroom after talking down a tantrum-prone boy, Lacey sat quietly next to Drew and felt peace rising within him. She could do this, keep him calm, keep her baby safe. The heavy scent of liver cooked in bacon grease came under the door, and she swallowed again and again. She was hungry enough to eat the liver half raw, as long as there was a lot of it. But Eric, ever conscientious, would cook it gray, safe and sanitary.

Her door bumped open, and Bibbits trotted in, his nails tapping as he crossed the room. He stood up on his back feet so that he could see up to the bed, and when he looked at Drew, he whimpered and fell back to the floor.

Bibbits could see him, though not all the time. Ella Dane never had, nor CarolAnna at the kitchen table. Ella Dane was sensitive—she *should* have known there was something in the house. As a child, CarolAnna had actually seen Drew. Drew was in control of their awareness, he must be. Drew smiled at Bibbits, and the dog whined in the back of his throat. Eric called from the kitchen, "Almost done!" and Lacey patted the blanket next to her. Bibbits barked once at Drew, then jumped into the bed next to Lacey's shoulder.

"So," Lacey said. "Think you can tell me what upset you?" There was always a reason for the tantrum, and children liked to be taken seriously.

"You know." Drew plucked at the blanket. He raised his chin up to his knees and peered at her under the fall of hair. "I don't want you to talk to her."

"Who?"

"That lady. The one whose name you found out."

Greeley Honeywick. "Why?"

"She'll tell you bad things."

"Are there bad things?"

"She'll tell you I hurt her."

"Did you hurt her?"

"She was mean to me."

"What did she do that was mean?"

Bibbits barked, one shrill word. Lacey glanced up at the doorway, and there was Eric, with a tray in his hands. Liver with bacon, hash browns, and a big glass of orange juice. "I heard you talking," he said.

The weight still pressed at the foot of the bed, but Drew was gone. The weight gradually lifted, leaving her left foot numb. She could still smell his salty hair, the smell of a child who had spent a long day playing in the sun.

"Who were you talking to?" Eric asked.

And she couldn't say, *Smell that, it smells like a little boy,* because he didn't know children the way she did, and anyway the room smelled of liver now, also of poodle. Bibbits barked again and pulled at the blanket with his front feet. "Just the dog," she said.

"I don't think so." Eric waited as Lacey pulled herself up against the cushions. He set the tray on her lap and sat next to her, holding Bibbits firmly in spite of the little dog's growls. "Who got hurt? Who was mean? What's going on, Lacey?"

Lacey took a bite of liver, for time, and handed a piece to Bibbits, for peace. She took a mouthful of hash browns. Eric had cooked them in the bacon grease and they were wonderful. "There's something in the house," she said, "and I know you won't believe me." She should stop talking; the teacher voice warned her, *Stop before you say another word,* but it was too late. She had to tell him; she couldn't do this on her own, and nobody who made such perfect hash browns could be unsympathetic. "There's something in the house, and it's dangerous."

"Something?" Eric said.

"Somebody." She still couldn't say *ghost*. The weight on the bed, the part in his hair. He was too real. "A person. He's angry about something." A thought came to her. "Angry, or maybe sad." She gave a little bounce, and Bibbits took advantage of the motion to lunge for her plate and snatch a piece of bacon. Lacey grabbed the plate, and the liver slid off; she caught it with her right hand, and Eric pulled away from her with a sound of disgust. "Sad," she said, brandishing the liver at him, "that's what he is. Being sad makes him angry."

"So this person, what kind of person is he, and where did he go?"

He wanted to make her say it, but she wouldn't. Let him ask Ella Dane. "A sad person," she said. "I don't want to talk about it." She closed her face, a trick she had learned from Eric; nobody could slam shut the way he could. He couldn't make her say, *This house is haunted,* because then she'd be as crazy as her mother, and that was a thing no one could ever say about her. She bit the last piece of liver in two, ate half herself, and held the other half over the side of the bed. Bibbits licked it from her hand.

"Okay." Eric stood up and took the plate. "You don't have to tell me. I'm going upstairs to get caught up on my work." He left, just as she had predicted.

She sighed and rolled over. Bibbits fell asleep next to her. She jiggled her feet, rolled over again, and blew puffs of air on Bib-bits's closed eyes. He wrinkled his little nose with each puff, but didn't wake up. She was so bored. She wished she could get up and walk around the room, run screaming from the house, drive to a mall, anything. But the baby needed her to stay still and behave. Rock the cradle gently, rock him only with her breath. He turned, and she watched the bulge slide under her skin. What was that—his knee, his whole body? What was going on in there, double Dutch with the umbilical cord?

Her thoughts clattered, what-if chasing maybe-then. If she left the house, where would she go? Her beautiful house with the beautiful furniture Eric had chosen just for her, their first real home; it wasn't like filling up a couple of old backpacks with clothes and putting the boyfriend-of-the-month's stereo in a box and walking out toward the next place, the way Ella Dane had done so often, dragging Lacey along. To stand up, walk away, leave—to abandon her own real adult life, like a refugee—she couldn't.

And even if she left, Drew might follow, as he had followed her to the hospital. No point running, unless she knew she was running to a safe place. *Not a good house for babies:* How bad was it? She had to stop these racing thoughts. She had to rest. She had to give the placenta a chance to heal, to save the baby. She hitched herself up to a sitting position, dragged her laptop from the nightstand, and logged on.

First, she visited her favorite maternity-clothing website and ordered a new dress, dark brown cotton printed with purple flow-ers, all pintucks and lace, the skirt opening out in long elegant gores. She also bought a pair of amethyst earrings, because they matched. Then she remembered she was stuck here in bed, so Eric would see the mail before she did. He would open the Visa statement, and he would want to know what she needed a new dress for when they hadn't paid for the furniture yet. So she canceled the order. She'd order them again when she could get out of bed. Now that was motivation.

The room felt empty. "Drew?" she asked. Nothing, so it was safe to search.

Greeley Honeywick wasn't anywhere near Utah, as her ancient uncle had said. She lived in Vancouver, Washington, where she was a high school gym teacher and triathlete. She smiled out of the computer screen, her auburn hair in shining waves in publicity shots, ponytailed and severe at finish lines. She was a double amputee, having lost her left leg below the knee and her right foot at the ankle in a domestic accident.

A domestic accident. Lacey checked the time. Nine P.M., so it was only six in Washington. Greeley Honeywick was on Facebook, with a pair of six-year-old twins, as smiling and auburn haired as herself, with the confident, well-brushed look of children born to middle-aged parents, and a tall husband who stood behind her in the pictures and looked away to the left or down at one of the twins, never at Greeley herself. *Trouble at home,* the teacher's eye said, looking at the children's smiles, so wide and bright. Domestic accident. Greeley Honeywick had taught at Burgoyne Elementary in Greeneburg eighteen years ago.

That was the school Drew must have attended. Greeley couldn't have taught him, though; CarolAnna had known Drew before Greeley lived in the house. Lacey raised her hands from the keyboard and let her senses spread through the room, feeling for Drew's weight. Nothing—she was still safe. Maybe he didn't understand computers.

She found a phone number in the Vancouver, Washington, telephone book, attached to Honeywick Auto Repair. Lacey called, and within minutes she was talking with the tall husband. Lacey told him she had been a student of Ms. Honeywick's at Burgoyne Elementary. "In second grade," she burbled, "and I loved her so much, she was my favorite teacher! And now I'm a gym teacher myself, and I just wanted to get in touch with Ms. Honeywick and tell her how much she meant to me. She changed my life. She really, really did."

"Let me give you her number," the tall husband said, and Lacey noted: not *our number.* "I'm sure she'll be happy to hear from you."

Lacey called the number, and a small girl, one of the auburn-haired twins, answered the telephone. "Can I talk to your mom?" Lacey asked.

"I don't know," the little girl said slyly, *"can* you?" She giggled.

"Aren't you the cutest thing, you. *May* I speak to your mother?"

The little girl handed the phone over, and Greeley Honeywick said, "Who's this?" She had a PTA-mom voice, no time for non-sense. This was a woman who held a full-time job, kept her house perfect, was active in her children's school, and ran triathlons, all with no feet.

Lacey heard all that in those three words, so she said briskly, "Ms. Honeywick, I'm calling from Greeneburg, South Carolina, and we're doing a piece in the newspaper on alums and teachers from Burgoyne Elementary. Your name came up."

"How?"

"Somebody remembered, and I Googled you. Honeywicks aren't exactly a dime a dozen. Do you have a minute?"

Greeley launched into a well-practiced lecture on the impor-tance of physical fitness for young people, and an upcoming fund-raising triathlon for the Special Olympics. It was like listen-ing to Ella Dane explain how to sprout wheat. All that sincerity and well-meaningness. Please, no more. Drew could appear any second; there was no time for this. "And I understand you lost both feet?" Lacey interrupted.

"Yes. A domestic accident."

"Did it happen while you were teaching here at Burgoyne?"

"It happened at home. Domestic, that's what it means."

That vertigo, the terror on the stairs. Lacey held her breath for a moment, for courage, and said, "Did you fall down the stairs?"

"You're not from any paper. Who are you?"

"Did you live at 571 Forrester Lane?" Lacey asked.

Silence, so long that Lacey began to wonder if she'd been cut off, and then Greeley said, "Do *you*?"

"There's this thing on the stairs, something falling."

"It's not me. I mean, I fell down the stairs, but the thing was there when I moved in. It kind of came over me one time; it overtook me and I fell. I never told anyone what happened. The thing on the stairs. Nobody would believe me."

It was true. It was all true. After everything she'd felt and seen in the house, Lacey was still amazed. Ella Dane believed it, but Ella Dane believed anything. This sane stranger, her faith mattered. Maybe she felt the same about Lacey, maybe she had held her secret for eighteen years, waiting for this call.

"I believe you," Lacey said. "Was it a little boy?"

"My legs were broken, and then I got this infection in the hospital and lost my feet. And I was pregnant when I fell. Three months. What's it to you?"

That child should be seventeen. There was no teenager next to the auburn-haired twins in any of the pictures. Also, Greeley had sidestepped the question of Drew. "I'm pregnant," Lacey said. "Twenty-nine weeks."

"How've you kept it so long?" This question took Lacey's

breath away. Greeley went on, "I did some research on the house after we moved. There hasn't been a live baby born in that house since 1972. He doesn't like babies."

Madison Grey had known the truth: *It eats babies,* she'd said. That meant Drew, when he was angry. Lacey saw Ella Dane's room smashed. That could be her baby's room, six months from now. Stuffed animals shredded, cardboard books exploded in confetti, slats of the crib driven like spears into the walls. The corner of a blue blanket showing under the overturned body of the crib—blue satin turning red. And silence. Lacey's eyes burned. She swallowed and swallowed but could not speak.

Drew killed children. If Lacey doubted it, she could go upstairs (when it was safe, whenever that might be) and look at the ceiling of Ella Dane's room, the demolished plaster, the beams, the drooping swaths of pink fiberglass. The handyman still hadn't come to fix it; there was all the evidence a person could want.

"I have to go," Greeley said. "You'd better get out now, that's all I can say to you; get out now and hope it's not too late. He was in the hospital, and he touched my feet. . . . I felt them die. I felt the baby dying inside me. Don't you remember Beth Craddock? Get out." She hung up the phone.

Lacey laid her own phone on the nightstand and lay back against the cushions. Dying inside. She realized she'd felt no motion from the baby for an hour or two. With both hands, she bounced her belly, waited for some answering motion, shook it again. *Wake up, be alive.* Strong as an eel, the baby pushed against her hands and slid away.

Her ears rang and she counted her breaths, two counts in, five counts out, her lungs on fire. She wiped her eyes with the backs of her hands and pressed her face into her fists. Her first impulse was to put her shoes on, grab her cell phone, run from the house, and call a taxi. But she was on bed rest. She couldn't afford to panic and run; she had to rest and let the placenta heal. And Drew was a good boy most of the time. She'd have to keep him in a good temper, that was all. Until she had somewhere safe to go.

Weight shifted at the side of the bed, and there was Drew, appearing in answer to her thought. He rubbed Bibbits's ears. "You shouldn't have done that," he said mildly.

Lacey wanted to say something friendly and companionable. Greeley Honeywick's last words echoed: *Remember Beth Craddock. Get out.* "Who's Beth Craddock?" she blurted.

"Leave me alone, leave me alone! Why won't you leave me alone?"

And he was gone. For the first time, she was looking directly at him when he disappeared, and there was nothing. No change, no fading, no intermediate state. Just Drew and then no Drew, there and gone, vanished more utterly than lightning. He left nothing, not even a sense of warmth where he had been sitting.

"I'm not the only one who's seen him," Lacey said to Bibbits.

CarolAnna Grey, Greeley Honeywick, someone called Beth Craddock. And how many others, how many women and children and babies, how many families, over how many years?

Chapter Twenty-three

ON SATURDAY AFTERNOON, the second Saturday in October, Jeanne came to Lex's house to leave Theo for the weekend. The old man had given him five hundred dollars to pay for her window. When he handed it over, she said, "Don't think this makes any difference. My lawyer says she can make you pay her fees."

Lex lifted Theo out of her car seat. She must have gained another pound in the last week. "Da!" she shrieked, and smeared a fistful of melted candy corn along his cheek when she lunged in for a hug. "Da!" she said again, more urgently, and he knew she meant *down* and not *Daddy,* so he took her inside and set her down on the floor.

Theo sat in the living room, a pink heap of flesh and polyester, and she would be just like Jeanne and Big Jeanne and all those poor sad women who walked past the produce department like it wasn't even there, filling their shopping carts with ham and potato chips and wondering why their ankles hurt.

When Jeanne took her away, Theo was crawling and beginning to pull herself up by grabbing on to chairs. She'd been almost ready to walk, a month ago. Lex was forever having to run after her, she scooted around so quickly. Now she sat where he had put her. After a while, she rolled over onto her back and grabbed her feet. He knelt beside her and pulled her up to sit. "You want to stand up?" he said. "Stand up for Dadda?"

He held her hands and tugged her, but she didn't push up at all. She just sat like a half-melted marshmallow. He pulled her hands. "Stand up!"

She opened her mouth square, just the way Jeanne did, and shrieked. He dropped her hands and ran to the kitchen. While she cried, he stood behind the door with his hands over his ears, because he couldn't stand it; he couldn't listen to that noise. After a while, she stopped, and he wondered if she might be hungry.

Jeanne had given him a grocery bag, and Lex laid the things out on the kitchen table. Three cans of Vienna sausages. Three cans of peaches in syrup. A package of Hydrox cookies. White bread. He threw it all away and put a yam in the microwave.

A voice at his feet said, "Bub, bub, bub?" Theo had crawled all the way here.

"Good girl," he said. She made a wet, demanding noise. "Soon," he said, "not yet." The last two years, he'd made Jeanne wait for her food. She could eat as much as she wanted, he couldn't stop her, but he piled her plate with vegetables. Even when she was pregnant, she lost a little weight. She'd gained it back by now.

Theo didn't like the yam. He mashed it and added a little formula. She squeezed her red lips tightly together and flung her head from side to side. Gobs of yam flew everywhere. He got some into her mouth, and she poked it out with her tongue. She squared her mouth and screamed. He shoveled in a spoonful of yam, and it came out, an orange spray. Finally, she grabbed the bowl and dumped it over her own head. Mashed yam ran down her neck, and she screamed at him with her mother's own voice.

"Yummy," Lex said desperately. Why was she crying? A month ago, mashed yam was her favorite food.

She pounded her yammy fists on the tray. Her pink dress was orange, her white hair was orange, and she was so loud. The neighbors might call the cops. He would call the cops if he heard a noise like this. "Okay, okay," he said. He dug a can of Vienna sausage out of the garbage, opened it, and dumped it on a plate.

Theo hummed. She poked a Vienna sausage into her mouth, keeping her hand pressed against her lips. She ate the whole can in two minutes and shrieked again. Lex gave her two Hydrox cookies and a sippy cup of formula, slightly diluted. She made a suspicious face but was too tired to fight. He couldn't put her to bed like this, covered with yam. He carried her into the bathroom.

Lex had done everything for Theo since she was born. He had changed diapers, dressed her, fed her, played with her, and talked to her. Everything but the bath. That was one thing Jeanne always did. He couldn't do it; many times he'd put Theo to bed grimy or sticky rather than wash her, but this was too much. Trying to remember how it was done, he ran the water, half an inch at the deep end, barely covering the tub at the shallow end. Was it too hot? It felt like room temperature. Maybe it was too cold.

His mother used to test the water with her elbow. Lex lowered his elbow into the tub, and the bottom was higher than he expected. He whacked his funny bone on the bottom of the tub, the strength went out of his arm, and he collapsed against the tub, the tub's hard wall catching him under his armpit.

Theo screamed. She'd used the toilet seat to pull herself up, and then her fat little feet slid out, and she hit her chin on the toilet. Lex's right arm was useless, throbbing and tingling with funny-bone pain. He gathered her in with his left arm—he was wearing his last clean white shirt, and now he was covered with yam, but that didn't matter. "Baby, baby, baby," he sang to her.

Bit by bit, his right hand came to life, and he undressed Theo and lifted her into the bath. Instantly, she screamed and beat the water with both hands. "No!" she yelled. "No, no!"

The water was too hot. Or too cold. Lex retreated to the bathroom door. He wanted to go back to the kitchen and stay there for a while, but he couldn't leave Theo in the bath. *Never, never,* he said to himself.

Theo's screams crumbled into sobs. He'd never heard her sound so unhappy. The water must be too cold, because if it was too hot, she'd be crying in pain. Lex knelt beside the tub and turned the water on again, tilting the knob slightly toward warm.

Theo fell backward. Her head hit the back of the tub, and the shrieks began again. That big square mouth, just like Jeanne's. Lex pulled the towel off the rack, grabbed Theo, and ran from the house with her in his arms. He couldn't do this on his own. He needed help. He had to get to the old man right away.

Chapter Twenty-four

SATURDAY WAS BRILLIANT AND CLEAR, a perfect day, and Lacey was stuck in bed. Yesterday, Dr. Vlk had given her permission to get up for a couple of hours and maybe walk around the backyard. "Nothing strenuous," Dr. Vlk said. "Avoid stress," which made Lacey laugh. Whenever she tried to sleep, she heard Greeley Honeywick: *There hasn't been a live baby born in that house since 1972.* And *remember Beth Craddock,* whoever that was.

Google would tell her, in seconds. She'd rather talk to a real person, so she would know she wasn't imagining the whole thing, so she could ask questions, find out what Google couldn't know. What did it mean, and what could she do? There was no app for that. And every time she logged on, Drew was there, watching where she went.

Eric had grown up here in Greeneburg; he might know the name. Where was he on this gorgeous Saturday, when she had the doctor's permission to go outside? Was he enjoying the day with her, mowing the lawn while she sat on the Adirondack lounge and pointed out the spots he missed? No, he was at the office, meeting some rich old people about writing their will, showing them how to leave all their money directly to their grandchildren, bypassing their wastrel children. She missed him and resented his freedom to go where he liked and work as hard as he needed, while she was trapped by her leaky, defective, inadequate womb.

Harry Rakoczy was mowing the Miszlaks' yard. Lacey leaned against the cushions. Her bed stank like a swamp. She suspected that Bibbits had wet it. Even if he hadn't soiled her bed on purpose, he was old and getting weaker. She'd seen him at his business. He dribbled down his leg sometimes, and other times his aim was off and he peed on his chest, and that oily brown smell had grown on him again.

"I want cookies," Drew said. He was standing at the door, as if he had just entered the room, though the door hadn't opened. "You haven't made cookies for ages."

Not again. Not now. Lacey shut her eyes and thought, *Go away, don't be here.* Without opening her eyes, she said, "The doctor told me to stay in bed."

"You got out of bed yesterday," Drew said.

"That was to go see the doctor."

"If you can go see the doctor, you can make cookies."

Nothing strenuous. After what he'd done the last time he lost his temper, she didn't dare refuse. She'd never feared a child—but she'd also never taught a child who could kill her. She dragged herself out of bed and took her laptop into the kitchen, where she found black and orange construction paper and set Drew to cutting out pumpkins and hunchbacked cats while she put a batch of sugar cookies in the oven.

"This is nice," she said. She poured a glass of milk and sat next to Drew. The smell of warm vanilla filled the room. This wasn't so bad—maybe she could live with it. It was like having her own private classroom, a class of one.

He crumpled up the cat he was working on. "I messed up again!"

"It's for Halloween. There's no such thing as messing up; it's a monster cat."

"It's only got three legs and its ears are weird."

"We'll name it Frankenkitty. Look how ferocious it is." Lacey smoothed out the crumpled cat and made it dance along the table. "Look at me, I'm big and bad. Oh no!" Frankenkitty bumped against the glass of milk. "Poor Frankenkitty, he can't see where he's going, what shall we do?"

Drew looked sideways at the paper cat. "Make eyes for it?"

Lacey cut eyeholes in the paper cat's head: one, two, and then a third, right in the middle. She taped over the eyeholes and then colored the clear tape with red marker, adding a black slit to the center of each eye. "Monster three-eyed cat!"

"Cool," Drew said. "What's that smell?"

"Cookies!" Lacey lunged for the oven. She got to the cookies just before they burned, and by the time they were cool enough to eat, Drew had lost interest in making Halloween decorations.

"Bored bored bored bored," he chanted, kicking the table leg.

"Stop that."

"Don't have to listen to you. You're not my mother. Bored bored bored *bored*." He slowed down his chant and found a way to make the word even more ugly and irritating: he paused on the *r*, thrusting his chin forward, curling his tongue, and lifting his upper lip. "I'm borrrrrrrrrrrrred."

Boredom was only a step away from irritation on the noisy-boy emotional scale. Boredom, irritation, petulance, annoyance, anger. Greeley Honeywick fell down the stairs and felt her baby die. *Remember Beth Craddock,* a name Lacey hadn't felt safe searching for, with Drew breathing down her neck every time she opened the laptop. Discipline, distract, and redirect. "Let's play a game," she said urgently.

Drew stopped kicking. "What kind of a game?"

"Chutes and Ladders. It's in with my school stuff. Eric put it in the attic, in a cardboard box somewhere. Go get it, and we'll play."

Lacey listened to Drew's feet pounding up the stairs. How would he get into the attic? Would he float up or materialize there? If he just appeared out of nowhere, as he seemed to do so often, could he carry a real thing like the Chutes and Ladders game with him? What about the things he had, the bicycle and his clothes and everything else, did they only exist when he wanted them?

By the sound of it, Drew was dragging a chair from the master bedroom to the attic hatch. Then came the groan of the attic hatch opening, and the crash of the stairs sliding open. Seconds later, without closing the attic hatch or putting Eric's chair away, Drew ran into the kitchen with spiderwebs in his hair and the Chutes and Ladders game in his hands. "Can I be green?"

"Sure. You set it up while I check e-mail." Lacey logged on as Drew unfolded the Chutes and Ladders board, pausing to eat two more cookies. "You practice rolling the die," Lacey said. Now was her chance, while Drew was busy with the cookies and the game. She Googled Beth Craddock.

"Six," Drew said. He rolled a six. "Four." He rolled a four.

"No cheating," Lacey said. There were three Beth Craddocks. One came up on a genealogy website. She had seventeen children and died in 1783, probably of exhaustion, poor thing. One was an optometrist in Fairbanks, Alaska, offering a free eye exam with purchase of frames. Generous, but unlikely. The third was a South Carolina woman who had murdered her two-year-old son in 1981 by drowning him in the bath. Lacey's heart stood still and the baby's pulse beat in her veins like a hummingbird. She remembered the day she had washed Bibbits, how irrationally determined she had been that he must be clean, *now;* how she had held him underwater as his paddling feet slowed.

"Did you ever play with a kid called Tyler Craddock?" she asked. She moved her cursor to the minimize button, ready to vanish the page if Drew looked toward her.

"Three." Drew rolled a three. "You can't play with babies. They cry all the time, and they don't know the rules. Four." He rolled a four.

Beth Craddock said she put the baby down for a nap and then lay down herself, and when she woke up, she found him face-down in the tub, still fully dressed. She said someone must have broken into her house and drowned her baby while she slept, but the jury took only forty-five minutes to convict her. She was convicted in 1982 and killed herself in prison in 1986.

Had Drew done that, killed the baby and destroyed the mother? Greeley Honeywick thought so. Lacey followed the link to the newspaper archives. Beth Craddock looked like anybody's mother, in the picture from her son's second birthday party: she stood behind him, laughing, in a pink blouse and a denim skirt, while the dark-haired toddler blew out the candles. Six other toddlers sat at the table, with a smattering of mothers and older siblings in the background. There was a blond boy turning away from the camera, his face blurred. Could Drew appear in pictures?

"Did you go to Tyler's birthday party?" Lacey said casually. Drew glanced up at her, and she pulled a smile onto her face.

Not a good house for babies. The smile hurt, but she held it. She was good with boys. Maybe Beth Craddock had been impatient and careless. Maybe she'd told Drew to go away and leave her alone, she had her own children to take care of; maybe she'd snapped, *Leave me in peace for once.* Drew wouldn't take well to that, not at all. She wished she could take back the question about Tyler's birthday. She didn't want to raise any bad memories.

"Stupid baby birthday parties for stupid babies," Drew muttered. "Like I would even care. Six." He rolled a six. "Nobody ever makes *me* a birthday cake," he said.

"When's your birthday?"

"August seventh."

"Oh, honey. You should have told me. We missed it and I didn't know! I'll make you a cake next year."

"Big deal."

The boy in the picture must be some party guest's big brother. A camera couldn't capture what CarolAnna and Ella Dane couldn't see. Lacey closed her laptop. It was too dangerous. Drew needed all her attention now; he was on the edge, ready to tip over into rage. She knew the signs, the muttering and self-pity. He predicted four more rolls.

He was cheating. If she challenged him, would that push him over the edge, or surprise him into cooperation? She had to put her faith in his sweetness, his desire for connection. Through the ringing in her own ears, she said, "I'm not playing if you cheat."

"Whatever. Two." He rolled a five. "Okay? So can we play?"

Noisy boys were bad losers, and worse winners. Lacey played games with them all the time, as part of the process of civilizing them. Rainy days with indoor recess were her secret weapon. She urged the die on for every roll, her own or theirs, and she cheered for every ladder and groaned for every chute, no matter whose piece climbed or fell. If she brought enough enthusiasm to the game, the boys surrendered their desire to win, and enjoyed the game itself.

But it was difficult to play with Drew. For one thing, she saw him mouthing numbers as he rolled, and she was sure he was still controlling the die. Up the ladder, down the chute, her mind circled on Beth and Tyler Craddock. That lovely little boy, dead within weeks of the birthday party; the young woman in the pink blouse, smiling over the cake. Had Drew done that?

Perhaps he had loved Beth too. Perhaps he had slipped his hand into hers at odd moments, as with Lacey. He had sat at Beth's kitchen table—different table, same kitchen—watching her decorate Tyler's birthday cake with green icing and plastic dinosaurs. Nobody made a birthday cake for him, so he killed them. All children wanted to do these things. *Children are small psychopaths,* her educational psychology professor had told her. *If they could do what they wanted, we'd all be dead. This will not be on the test.*

Unlike other children, Drew could do what he wanted, and the Craddocks were dead.

He won two games in a row, avoiding every chute, landing on every ladder. "See," Lacey said, forcing her voice into a teacher tone of gentle guidance. "It's no fun if the game's not fair. Let's start over."

Drew rolled a four, which took him to the first ladder. He picked up the green piece, looked at Lacey, moved the piece back, and rolled again. He got another four. "I didn't do it this time," he said.

"I believe you. Climb the ladder."

The front door opened and closed, and Bibbits raced out of

Lacey's room and down the hall. "Who's a sweet puppy?" Ella Dane crooned. "Did you miss your mama?"

Ella Dane came into the kitchen. Lacey rolled a four, and the red piece joined the green one at the top of the ladder. "My sheets reek," Lacey said. "I think Bibbits had an accident."

"Poor little guy. He feels bad about it. Solitaire Chutes and Ladders, really? How bored are you?"

Lacey took a breath. Now or never. "It's not solitaire. I'm playing with Drew. You know, the kid who lives here."

"You stop that," Drew said.

"Oh, you're playing with Drew." Ella Dane sat at the table and hoisted Bibbits into her lap. She fed him half a cookie. Lacey thought of mentioning that the cookies contained eggs. "Who's winning?" Ella Dane said.

"We're tied. Drew's green. It's his turn."

Drew rolled a two and landed on a chute. Lacey provided sound effects as he moved his piece. "Oh no—here I go—I'm falling, I'm falling—aaaaaaah thump!"

Drew laughed as his piece landed all the way back on the second square. Lacey rolled a three and avoided the chute.

Ella Dane frowned over the board. "Why doesn't Drew move his own piece?"

"He is. Watch. Your turn, kiddo."

Drew rolled a six and clicked his piece along the board, square by square. Lacey looked at Ella Dane: What was Ella Dane seeing, if she couldn't see Drew? Was she seeing the green piece move alone, step by deliberately counted step? She was taking it very calmly; she looked more worried than surprised. Lacey took her turn and landed on another ladder.

Drew cupped the die in his two hands and shook it hard, the way children did, as if by hard shaking they could change its disposition. Maybe he'd forgotten that he could make it land the way he wanted, or maybe he was just playing along, acting out the game. And what did Ella Dane see: the die rattling in a three-inch globe of air?

The air was dense and hot, and the smell of sugar nauseated Lacey. Her mouth was sour with fear. She swallowed again and again, choking her sickness down, smiling for Drew. He threw a five, which brought him to a ladder. He and Lacey cheered as his piece climbed. Just as he reached the top step, Ella Dane's hand flashed out and grabbed his wrist. Lacey felt a sympathetic pain in her own wrist.

"Ow," Drew and Lacey cried together, "let go."

"Look," Ella Dane said. "Whose hand is this?"

"It's him. Drew." She saw Ella Dane's fingers squeeze the child's fragile wrist, and her own bones ached. "Can't you see?"

Ella Dane yanked Drew's hand in front of Lacey's face. "Can't *you* see? Look!"

Lacey looked. The hand was too big. Tiny pellets of cookie dough clung to the lifeline and the heart line. The fingernails were coral, and needed a touch-up, since the polish had begun to flake around the tips. . . . And the ring needed cleaning, the big diamond was looking dull.

Lacey touched the hand. She slid her fingers down to Ella Dane's hand, still clamped around the wrist. "That's my hand," she said blankly. "How did you do that?"

"I grabbed the hand that was moving the green piece. Your hand. You were shaking the die. It was all you."

"No."

She could not accept this. Hearing voices, acting on unseen commands—those were things crazy people did. She wasn't crazy; CarolAnna Grey, Greeley Honeywick, and Beth Craddock had all seen him. Ella Dane couldn't deny it, after what he'd done to her room.

"That was Drew. Drew was moving the piece."

"Is he still here?"

Drew's chair was empty. "He must have left. Let go, you're hurting me."

Ella Dane didn't let go. "You rolled the die. You moved the pieces."

"Drew was here. He ate the cookies." Lacey felt grease on her lips; she ran her tongue along her teeth, finding smears of chewed cookie. How many cookies had Drew eaten—eight, twelve? She felt bloated with sweetness, and she didn't even like cookies. "He went up into the attic and got the game."

Ella Dane threw Lacey's hand back to her. "You've been climbing ladders? What were you thinking?"

Lacey bowed her head over the game, rubbing her wrist. There was dirt on her arms and under her fingernails, and a smell of hot baked dust, an attic smell, on her clothes. She flashed to a memory of herself walking on the plywood floor of the attic, dipping her head to avoid the big silvery ducts, searching through four cardboard boxes of her old classroom things. This had not happened. She was on semi bed rest to save the life of her child. She had never been in the attic. Eric took the boxes up there—she didn't even know what it looked like. "Drew did it," she insisted.

"Nothing happened here but what you did," Ella Dane said.

No wonder the jury had convicted Beth Craddock so quickly. Probably her clothes were wet. Lacey felt cold all over, as if she had walked from a summer rainstorm into an air-conditioned room. Drew put his hands into Beth's as into a pair of winter gloves and used her to kill the baby. Because Drew was the child of the house, the only child. What had she known, what had she seen?

"Mom," Lacey said. "Does this mean he's inside me? He can make me do whatever he wants? What am I going to do?"

Before Ella Dane could answer, a car horn blared outside, long and continuous. Ella Dane ran outside, and Lacey followed more slowly, careful on the porch steps. Her question would have to wait.

Chapter Twenty-five

A BEIGE CHEVROLET bumped over the curb, crossed the sidewalk in front of Harry's house, crushed an azalea, and stopped with its nose pressed against a dogwood. The dogwood shook its leaves like a thousand agitated hands. The horn stopped, and in its silence came another sound, an alarm cry of, "Oh, oh, oh," a man's voice with the intonation of a distraught child. Lacey stepped forward by instinct, ready to hug someone and say *It's okay,* but Ella Dane held her back.

Harry came out of his house, violin tucked under his arm. He took one look at the Chevy, stepped back inside, and came out without the violin. "Lex?" he said, hurrying across the lawn. "Are you okay?"

A man got out of the car, still crying, "Oh, oh, oh," like a child. He was almost as tall as Harry but dangerously thin, with a face so drawn it was impossible to tell his age.

"I know him." Ella Dane let go of Lacey's arm. "He's the produce manager at MacArthur's."

Now it was Lacey's turn to hold her mother back. "Stay out of it! You don't know anything about him."

"Last week he saved me some really ripe mangoes. Beautiful,

like fresh jam. Hey, Mr. Hall—Lex! Are you okay?" Ella Dane ran toward the car, reaching it just as Harry did. "Oh, and thank you again for those gorgeous mangoes."

The surprise of this greeting finally stopped that awful wail. The thin man turned his blank, haggard face toward Ella Dane and said, "Mangoes?"

Lacey began to hear the sound of a crying baby. She turned to look behind her at her own house. Was this some trick of Drew's, or another voice of the house, little Tyler Craddock? No, it came from Lex Hall's car.

"She won't stop," Lex said. Harry pulled him away from the car, while Ella Dane opened the back door and lifted out a naked orange baby. "I can't make her stop."

Ella Dane sniffed the baby. "Yams?"

Bibbits joined them, dancing on his hind legs, trying to get a taste of the baby. Ella Dane set the baby down on the grass, and the baby promptly rolled over on her back, giggling while Bibbits dashed around her, licking any part of her he could reach.

"She won't stop crying," Lex Hall said again.

"She's fine," Ella Dane said. "Happy as a june bug."

"She's hungry."

"If she was hungry, the yam would be inside, not outside."

Bibbits licked yam off the baby's nose. She crowed with joy and grabbed his ears. He yelped but, to Lacey's surprise, did not bite. Lacey knelt and pulled the baby's hands off the dog's ears. "Don't hurt the doggy," she said. Bibbits barked, whined, and licked the cookie crumbs off Lacey's hands.

"Obby, oof oof," the baby told her.

"Doggy says woof woof. Good doggy."

"We'll clean her up," Ella Dane said. Emergency, as always, brought out the best in her. Lacey knew she had not forgotten

Drew, and as soon as she'd dealt with this baby, she'd turn her mind to the problem. "I need a towel. Does she have clothes?"

"They're at home," Lex said wretchedly, like a conscientious child who had forgotten his homework for the first time. "Her diapers and everything."

"Then you'd better go get them," Ella Dane said, and Lex hurried back to his car. Harry ran into his house and came back with a brown towel, and Ella Dane swaddled the baby. Seeing the dangerous hands restrained, Bibbits started licking the baby's face. Harry held out his arms for the baby, but Ella Dane held on to her and said, "Who is he, and why does he come to you?"

"Crazy nephew. Nobody else to go to when he needs help. And this is Theo."

"He's driving around with a naked baby in his car? Is there a mother?"

"They're getting divorced. I'll take the baby now."

"Let me do it. I'm going to be a grandma soon and I'm out of practice."

Lacey watched. Harry went inside for a bucket of warm water, soap, and a washcloth, and Ella Dane unrolled the baby from the towel and got to work with Bibbits's help, right there on the grass. She didn't seem that badly out of practice. In five minutes, Theo was laughing, trying to grab the washcloth. Ella Dane let her chew on it and laughed when Theo stuck out her tongue at the taste of soap.

"We live and learn," Ella Dane said. "What does she eat, cupcakes and bacon?"

"Fried chicken and white bread," Harry said.

Lacey sat quietly while Harry explained the situation. She hoped Eric was doing all he could to help Lex.

When Lex arrived with the clothes and diapers, she was happy to see Theo give a shout of laughter and crawl over to him, and even happier to see him smile as he swung her into the air. Theo landed in a laughing bundle on his chest, and she grabbed his nose and said, "Da da da," in a tone of clear delight. A baby that young had no tact. If she had reason to fear her father, she would have cringed from him.

Ella Dane took Lex and the baby into Harry's house, and Harry stayed to give Lacey a hand up from the grass. "Thanks," she said. "So what are you going to do?"

She followed him into his house, where they stood in the doorway and watched Ella Dane and Lex playing with Theo. The man was as innocent as his own child, but something had to be done.

"They can stay here tonight. I'm always here for Lex."

"Not if you move to Australia."

Lacey knew about crazy parents. She was still a certified teacher, and as far as she was concerned, a mandated reporter too. She could not go back to her house and pretend everything was fine. A child in the midst of a custody fight would have a volunteer guardian appointed by the court. She had briefly served as one herself, last year, for a girl whose noncustodial father had tried to take her from Lacey's classroom several times. She'd made contact and left a card with every member of the girl's extended family, so she said, "The guardian ad litem must have left you their number. This is when you have to call them. The guardian, or the police."

"Why get the law involved?"

"This is not okay." If Lacey had seen a parent like Lex with a baby like Theo in the car line at school, waiting to pick up a student—naked baby screaming, dad obviously decompensating—she would have called the police without thinking twice. She had no patience with anyone who put a parent's feelings above a child's safety, although she'd give Harry a chance to handle it before she stepped in. "I don't have the guardian's contact info," she said. "I'll be calling 911. I'm not leaving till it's done."

Harry pulled his cell phone from one pocket and his wallet from another, sorted through it for a business card, and made the call.

"You did the right thing," she said when he closed his phone. She still needed to ask him about Drew, but this was not the time. *Thank you for betraying your nephew, now tell me about the ghost*: like that would work.

"Lex has had such a hard life."

"When you're gone to Australia, and Lex panics, what's he going to do?"

"He's not dangerous."

Lacey wasn't so sure. She'd seen too many bullied children snap. Last year, she'd been first on the scene when a fourth grader, a quiet boy whose family was so poor that he wore his older sister's hand-me-down shirts and sneakers, decided his classmates had called him *gay* often enough. He took off his sister's blouse, knocked down his cruelest tormentor, and knotted the sleeves around the boy's neck. It was all so quick, neat and silent, none of the teachers supervising recess noticed. Lacey's class was in music, so she was in the teachers' lounge revising her rubric for the big Westward Expansion project, and her eye was drawn to unexpected motion under the slides. She didn't stop to call for help. She opened the window, kicked out the screen, and arrived at the slides as the bullied child inserted a stick into the knot of his improvised garrote and began to twist.

The look on that boy's face was one she would never forget. He didn't seem angry. He was intent, focused on his work, attentive to issues of torque and leverage—keeping his knees on the bully's upper arms, turning the stick in the knot—oblivious to thought or reason. She had to lift his fingers off the twisted shirtsleeves one by one, and then he turned that deliberate unconscious look on her and rammed his head into her midriff, knocking the breath out of her. He twisted the knotted shirt around the stick again. Breathless, struggling to fill her collapsed lungs, she had no strength to stop him or call for help. When the playground teachers finally noticed something was wrong, it took all four of them to pull him away.

Lex Hall's face had something of the same quality: thought beneath words, a human intelligence without the full faculty of language. He smiled, but she didn't believe him. He sat on the floor with Theo on his lap, watching as Ella Dane counted the baby's toes. "This little piggy went to market, this little piggy stayed home, this little piggy had roasted organic celery root, this little piggy had none, and this little piggy went wee wee wee all the way home." She tickled Theo's foot. Lex and the baby laughed.

Lacey felt warmth at her back. Harry stood behind her, uncomfortably near. "He'll stay if I cook," Harry said. "How about you?"

"No thanks," Lacey said. She'd take her chances with Ella Dane's roasted celery root rather than be here when Lex's wife's lawyer sent the cops for Theo. That intense listening look: she didn't want to get downwind of that. "What happened to him?" she asked, flicking her hand at Lex. She'd never seen anyone over the age of ten look so damaged. Adults learned to hide it.

"His parents died when he was little. You're sure you won't stay? I've got a frozen lasagna. Forty minutes in the oven. Keep us company."

"How'd they die?"

"One of those things," he said vaguely. "Lex, does Theo like lasagna?"

"See you later," Lacey said. "Mom, we'd better get home."

If this was going to turn into some sort of crisis, she didn't want Ella Dane in the middle of it. And there was Drew waiting for her at home. The Chutes and Ladders game spread on the kitchen table, the plate of sugar cookies half eaten; she had to get that cleaned up before Eric came home and asked what she'd been doing, had she climbed into the attic, risked the baby's life for a board game? But as Lacey reached down to shake Ella Dane's shoulder and hurry her up, Lex looked up at her, with the baby now cradled against his left shoulder, stuffing her fist in her mouth.

"He called someone," Lex said.

There was no point lying to him, not with that look full of dark less-than-language thought. She saw that look on some children racing on the playground, and others with crayons in their hand making bright private worlds, and they were as sensitive as dogs to any hint of falseness. "The guardian ad litem," she said. "He's worried about the baby."

"The guardian doesn't like me. Your husband is my lawyer. I'm a good daddy."

"I believe you." He knew to ask for help. She'd seen too many children whose parents believed they could go it alone to undervalue that. "You're going to have to learn some things before you can take care of the baby by yourself."

He stood up so carefully, the sleeping baby didn't even twitch. "I'm learning."

"I know. Come on, Mom, your dog's hungry."

They left Harry's house together, and Lacey watched while

Lex buckled the baby into her car seat, something else too many parents didn't learn. There still might be an armed standoff when the ex-wife's lawyer caught up with Lex, but with Theo the only available hostage, Lex would surrender rather than threaten her. "Can you lock the door?" she said to Ella Dane.

"You're not afraid of that poor man, are you?" Ella Dane said. "He's too scared of himself to be a danger to anyone. Fear is a sign of imbalance in the spirit."

"I know. He's unbalanced, so I want my door locked."

"Not his spirit. Imbalance in *your* spirit. Your third chakra is obscured. If you would just let me massage you with locust oil—"

Lacey surprised herself with a laugh. "Oh, come on. You just make this stuff up as you go along. Locust oil! Like I'd let you rub your nasty old squashed grasshoppers all over me." She had been pretending to misunderstand locust oil for years, along with royal jelly and anything made of hemp.

"Locust *bean*," Ella Dane said, as she always did. "I'm going down to the spa for a bottle of oil of cassia for spiritual cleansing. Also a vial of *Anacardium*."

"What's that?"

"A homeopathic remedy. It's good for body odor, poison ivy, and spirit possession. Also hemorrhoids and warts. You coming?"

Lacey wanted nothing more than to leave. But at Ella Dane's words, a wave of heat ran over the back of her head: that was anger—Drew angry at the thought of her leaving. Walking out the door wouldn't help. She'd seen him in the front yard, on the street, as far away as the hospital. He could reach into Lacey's hands, make her grab Ella Dane's steering wheel and crash the car into the maple, if he wanted.

"I'd rather not," she said lightly. "I'll stay here and see if Drew will talk."

"You're sure?"

"And I'm starving."

"Put this in your pocket," Ella Dane said, handing her an amethyst crystal. "Strong protection."

"See you later," Lacey said in a cheerful tone. She didn't want Drew to see her afraid. Ella Dane left, and Lacey went into the kitchen to fry up a couple of eggs and call Eric, to let him know that Lex Hall might be in trouble. The chunk of amethyst pulled her sweater down on the left. "You want an egg?" she said to the empty kitchen, and Drew did not answer.

Chapter Twenty-six

ERIC'S PHONE WENT STRAIGHT TO VOICE MAIL, so maybe he was already on his way to Lex's, or home. Lacey didn't leave a message. When she turned from the refrigerator with two eggs in her left hand, she came face-to-face with Drew. Usually he slid up behind her, or beside her, and she felt him before she saw him. This time, he flicked into existence without warning, dazzling like a camera flash. She flung her hands up, and the eggs splashed on the floor. "Don't *do* that," she snapped. "Look what you made me do."

"Let's finish the game."

"Let me . . ." No, not that voice—she sounded like a frantic child. She opened the back of her throat and let the teacher voice rise out, alto and firm. "Let me get these eggs cleaned up."

"I was winning. I want to finish."

On her first day of practice teaching, her mentor had warned that children, like feral dogs, could sense fear and would eat her alive if they had the chance. She stopped herself from agreeing with Drew, anything he wanted if he promised not to hurt her and the baby, and she held the teacher voice, the voice that ruled the room. "You see those eggs on the floor," she said.

"So?"

"So dried egg is way harder to clean than wet egg. It won't take a minute."

"So?"

"So I'm going to clean them up, and then we'll play." It was important to appear normal, to keep Drew in the mode of ordinary child, not angry ghost, until she worked out what to do next. She tried a smile and hoped it worked; the muscles above her lip didn't seem to be moving right.

"You're just scared of losing," Drew said. "Scaredy scaredy scaredy."

"Sweetie, it's Chutes and Ladders, not the Super Bowl. I'll get over it." Lacey scooped up the eggs in a paper towel, sprayed cleaner on the floor, and scrubbed with another paper towel. Bibbits patted in, busy little feet rapping on the floor. He stood on his hind legs and turned a circle for her, then stood up, with his front paws paddling in the air. Ella Dane had gone out without feeding him. And he was on another brown-rice-and-vinegar purge, poor thing.

"Let's see." Lacey opened the pantry. To appear normal—feeding the dog, that was a thing she'd normally do. "There's tuna, maybe." Bibbits dropped to the floor and stood with his head down, panting. That short dance had exhausted him; there'd been days when he skipped from room to room on his back feet, poor old boy. She wished she had something better than tuna to give him.

"Play with me," Drew chanted at the kitchen table, "play with me, play with me."

"I'm just going to feed the dog."

He stuck out his lower lip. "You said you'd just clean up the eggs."

"And now I'm just going to feed the dog. It won't take a minute."

"You said you'd play with me. You promised." Bibbits, seeing the can in Lacey's hand, was dancing again. "Stupid dog." Drew kicked out at Bibbits, and the dog's feet slid away from him. He fell heavily on his side, with a yelp.

"Drew!" Lacey picked Bibbits up and felt along his sides. He wriggled in her arms, trying to lick her hands. "Drew, sweetie, we don't hurt animals."

"You promised."

She popped the can of tuna and dumped it into a plate, stealing a chunk for herself and spreading the rest around with her finger for Bibbits. Her imitation of normalcy began to seem real. She was any woman on Forrester Lane, a woman with house, husband, child, and dog; she was feeding the dog, then she would play with the child. Bibbits had trouble with tuna, unless she broke apart the big pieces for him. He'd swallow it in chunks, only to regurgitate later, in her bed. "Almost done," she said cheerfully.

"And then there'll be something else that won't take a minute. Like your stupid husband might call, or your stupid baby might kick, or your stupid dog might need to go out, and then something else and something else, and you *promised*."

"Drew!" She put the plate down on the table, ignoring the now frantic dog, and wiped her hand on her thigh. "Look, it only took a—"

The telephone rang. Lacey made a motion toward it, but stopped herself. She couldn't turn her back on him. He might do anything. He might rush into her, as he had done before; take her baby by the throat and choke it inside her. "What do you want?"

"Go on, answer the phone," Drew said bitterly. "It's somebody who matters. You don't care about me, nobody does. And I didn't even cheat." He swept his arm across the table, and the game pieces scattered. Lacey flexed her hand. Had he done that through her, as he had played the game? She'd felt nothing. "Answer it!"

The phone rang again. Lacey let the answering machine take it, although she heard Eric's voice. "I'm listening to you," she said. "I'm listening right now."

"Nobody *ever* listens."

"I care about you."

"Nobody cares."

Lacey knelt in front of him, took his shoulders in both her hands, and looked into his face. What did he want, more than anything, what was all the noise about? He was the same as any other child. She knew about noisy boys because she had been a quiet girl; when she was little, she'd longed to do what they did, to demand along with them, *Look at me, listen to me, love me.* To be a person no one could ignore. She said, slowly and clearly, "I am paying attention to you, Drew."

He wrenched himself away. "Nobody listens, nobody cares, nobody loves me!" He grabbed the plate of tuna off the table and whirled out of the kitchen. Lacey and Bibbits followed him.

Drew ran up the stairs. He did not float or swoop or drift; his feet pounded hard and solid on every step. Bibbits raced after him, yipping with hunger and excitement, an old dog, not used to such games. "I accuse you," Drew shouted, from the darkness that gathered at the top of the stairs. Lacey held on to the curved edge of the banister and could not speak. "I accuse you," he said again, his voice now deeper and older. "You are guilty, all of you guilty, all, all, all." And Bibbits's desperate bark mingled with Drew's voice.

The front door opened and Ella Dane came in. "I meant to ask if you wanted . . ." she began. She stopped short, staring toward the noise. "Is that *Bibbits*? That noise?" She pulled the brown glass vial from her pocket. "Bibbits, honey, come get your meddies." She headed for the stairs, and Lacey clutched her arm and pulled her back.

Drew was a dark form among the shadows, starred with a single white gleam, maybe his bright hair, maybe his eyes, maybe something else—light on metal, Lacey couldn't tell—and he was taller, wider, larger. Or it was only the tumbling shadows that made him seem so big. "All of you," he shouted. Lacey had an impression of sound, terrible loud sounds that her mind could not name or remember.

Something pale flew toward her out of the noise and the dark. The plate smashed at her feet, and the lumps of tuna scattered. Oh, the mess, the smell; Eric would be so unhappy—she tried to gather up the pieces, maybe the plate could be fixed, here was a big piece, maybe as much as a third of the plate, the round edge fitting in her hand and the long dagger of ceramic, which she had to be careful of—something fluttered around her, beat into her, darkness and hands and voices, and she struck out at it with the piece of broken plate. It was Drew. He wanted to take the big pieces and break them into little pieces, so that plate could never be fixed and Eric would be miserable and furious, and it was all her fault.

"Get away, get away from me," she screamed.

Something caught her hands and wrists, something pulled the broken piece away from her.

Bibbits barked and barked. Strong arms held Lacey tight, crossing her arms across her body and holding both her wrists. "Hush, hush, baby, it's okay," somebody said.

"Drew?" she whispered into the black curtain that blew around her.

"Your fault!"

The black curtain blew over her. She threw off the binding hands. She was standing below the circle step at the foot of the stairs, and the banister should be at her right hand, but she couldn't find it. She stood in a black circle, struggling for balance—the baby would die if she fell, he would fall into the spinning shadow beneath her, he would fall forever—with Drew blazing gold and silver in front of her. Sunlight on his yellow hair, his white T-shirt and shorts, his yellow sneakers.

"Your fault," he said in his deep adult voice.

"Stop this," said the other voice. "Make him stop. *Now.*"

"Stop!" Lacey slapped Drew. "Stop it now!"

Drew's left hand flew to his cheek and he stared at Lacey. "You hit me."

She stumbled backward, as shocked as he was. She had never hit a child, not even the one who tried to strangle his bully. "I'm sorry, Drew, I'm sorry."

"You did it on purpose."

"No, no."

Tears kaleidoscoped her sight. The colors splintered, the child's yellow hair and white shirt, the golden floor and the red runner. There was blood on the floor, and the other voice was Ella Dane, saying again, "It's okay, baby, you made him stop."

Bibbits had barked himself into a panting stillness. Blood ran down Ella Dane's left arm, and Lacey's hands were sticky. "Mom," she whispered. "What happened? What did I do?"

"Can you bandage this for me?" Ella Dane was using her emergency voice, calm and competent and ready for anything. Something terrible must have happened.

"You need stitches." Lacey remembered the broken plate. She'd picked up the broken plate, that big piece. And then what? Something had attacked her, and she'd fought it off with the weapon in her hand. "Did *I* do that?"

Ella Dane squeezed her arm above the cut. "There's a first aid kit under the kitchen sink. We have to get out of here, Lacey; there's no time. Bandages. And can you grab my laptop, and Bibbits's blanket from the living room. Before he comes back."

"He's still here," Lacey said.

Ella Dane picked Bibbits up and the dog pressed against her, shivering, too exhausted even to cough. "Are you sure?"

She felt it, all the air in the house pressing in against her breast-bone, and the baby kicking in protest. Lacey closed her hands. He had used her to attack Ella Dane, stepped inside her as easily as entering an unlocked room. Never again. She was a teacher, and it was time he learned what that meant. It all began with con-trol. You had to rule the room, first thing on the first day. Lacey had never had trouble ruling the room. It was all in the look. The teacher's eye.

She'd let him get away with it. She'd let him think it was his house. "You go out and wait for me," she said, and Ella Dane obeyed as unthinkingly as any well-trained nine-year-old, out the door before the echo faded.

Lacey faced the stairs. "That will be enough," she said, in the mild but deadly pay-attention voice. Screaming never helped. The children who most needed discipline had been ignoring screams their whole lives. "Go to your room."

All the upstairs doors opened and slammed together. The feeling of presence lifted, as if a too-tight mask had fallen from Lacey's face. Something shook in her throat, a whimper flutter-ing to escape, and she held it down. Teachers did not whimper.

Rule the room. She let her gaze sweep left into the living room, up the stairs, to the right of the stairs toward the dining room and kitchen, deliberately moving her head and not just her eyes. Nothing moved.

"Stay here," she said, and she left the house.

Chapter Twenty-seven

ELLA DANE HAD PUT BIBBITS in her car. She took her laptop from Lacey and said, "You drive first, I'll follow you."

"I have to call Eric."

"First we leave. Call him when we get there."

"Where?"

"Columbia, my friend Jack—he'll know what to do."

Lacey shook her head. Drew had forced her from the house; there was no way Eric would leave Greeneburg, so she had to stay. "Somewhere closer," she said.

"It's not your fault," Ella Dane said.

Whose fault was it, then? Lacey had made cookies with Drew and taught him to draw. She had welcomed him without resistance into her loneliness; she had opened the door. She licked her lips, tasting salt. "Beth Craddock."

"Who's that?"

"She used to live here. She drowned her little boy. She said she couldn't have done it, someone came into the house while she was asleep."

No living baby since 1972. A green landscape kept rising in Lacey's inner vision, bright fields of sugar, populated by tiny dinosaurs. Tyler Craddock's birthday cake. *Focus.* "Those hotels out by the airport," she said. "They're all less than ten years old. Let's go there." Maybe Drew couldn't go to a new place, somewhere he'd never been in life, a building raised after his death. That made sense; she clung to it.

Ella Dane must have had the same thought. "How long has he been in the house, this spirit of yours?"

"Forty years."

"What happened forty years ago?" Ella Dane asked as Lacey got into her car.

"I don't know yet." She'd found 571 Forrester on her Internet searches: she'd found maps, the property taxes they paid, their school zone, a list of nearby homes for sale, even some beautiful pictures before and after renovation on Grey and Associates' website, but nothing about its history. No help there. How wide was Drew's reach? They had to get away from Forrester Hills before he caught them—she saw it again, his hands on the steering wheel, his foot on the gas pedal, accelerating her into a house, a tree, another car. In a crash, the airbag might kill the baby. She shifted the seat belt: lap belt low on the hips, under the belly; shoulder belt around the belly, under the breasts. She slid the front seat as far back as possible, getting every possible inch between airbag and baby. "Let's go to that new hotel by the airport. Skyview."

As Lacey reached the corner of Forrester and Forrester Hills, she saw a sheriff's cruiser coming the other way. So they'd come for Lex and Theo. She was glad Lex had already taken the baby home.

Could Drew walk in Harry's house? Harry had a picture that looked like him, so most likely he could; it was not as safe a sanctuary as Lex thought. Not a good house for his baby either.

As she turned, she glanced in the rearview mirror. The cruiser stopped at Harry's house. The late sunlight cast reflections of the surrounding houses and trees onto the windows of Lacey's house, and she could see nothing but a tossing chaos of other windows and other doors, masked and revealed by the rushing leaves.

Chapter Twenty-eight

AS THE NEW GUY, Eric volunteered for the Saturday shift on call. So far, it had been quiet, but it would pick up by late afternoon and spike around four A.M., after closing time, which estranged husbands considered the perfect time to repossess or vandalize their almost-exes' cars. He expected calls from the detention center, bail bondsmen, incoherent clients, and counsel for the party of the second part. What he did not expect was Sammie Vandermeijn, with her hair in a new, shorter bob and bright orange bangs, appearing in his office door on her day off to announce, "Oh my God, Eric, do you know what you did, you bought the Halliday house, and now you're living in it!"

"You know it's Saturday."

Obviously, she knew it was Saturday. She was wearing a turquoise tracksuit and no makeup at all. "I've been hearing about that place my whole life, and I've always wondered if any of the stories are true. And you're *living* in it. The Halliday house. That is so cool."

"Sammie," Eric said forcefully. He had to stop her babbling and get a clear answer out of her. "What are you saying? What's wrong with my house?"

"It's haunted. I didn't recognize the address at first, but it's the Halliday house for sure. I used to go there Halloween night with my cousins and throw eggs at it, after trick or treat." Sammie shook her head and laughed at her past self. "The things kids do. Awful things. We never thought about the people who were living there, how hard it must have been to clean up. 'Course, eggs are more expensive these days, so maybe you won't have it so bad."

"Sammie, please. Sit down and tell me. Sit." He gestured at the clients' chair.

She had written up her discovery in a tidy memo, and she handed it over the desk and waited as he read. "Are you sure this is the same house?" he asked once.

"Sure I'm sure. County tax records don't lie."

On the ninth of April in 1972, a high school history teacher named Andrew Halliday had come home, and for reasons never made clear he spent the afternoon murdering his family, beginning by drowning his baby daughter and finishing the job by shooting himself. Whenever he heard one of these stories, Eric wondered why the angry parent didn't save everybody a lot of trouble and pain by starting with himself. Somehow they never did. The children were Andrew Junior, James, Matthew, and Dorothy. The wife was Dora Rakoczy Halliday.

"Does this have something to do with Harry Rakoczy next door?" he said.

"She was his sister."

"And Lex Hall?"

Sammie snatched the paper from under his hand. "Didn't I put that in? I pulled up the title search to find out how Lex Hall got hold of the house. And he inherited it from his parents. Andrew and Dora Halliday. He changed his name from Halliday to Hall, but he's one of them, all right. He's the one who got out alive."

"There was another kid who wasn't home?"

Sammie seemed disappointed. He sympathized. Dropping a bombshell wasn't nearly as much fun if you had to stand around afterward and explain the bang. "There were four kids, three boys and a baby girl. Andrew Junior, James, Matthew, Dorothy. Nice normal family, but you know that's what the neighbors always say."

Eric didn't think Lex Hall's neighbors would say that. More likely they'd line up for the opportunity to say he was an obvious nut, and they'd always known it was only a matter of time before he cracked.

"Then one day," Sammie said, "Andrew Halliday snapped, drowned the baby, lined the wife and the boys up at the top of the stairs and shot them, one by one."

"And Lex is . . . ?"

"Andrew Junior. He survived. The Rakoczys adopted him. I tell you what, you are in big trouble, worse than I thought. You can't have that man as your client. Living in his old house, where all his people died. That's when they start mailing you dead possums and anonymous human thumbs. We'll find him a new lawyer, first thing Monday."

"You can't tell Lacey about all this."

Sammie snorted. "She doesn't know? Yeah, right, and Floyd's going to double my salary. Any day now he'll get around to it. I'll just hold my breath."

"I don't think she knows. She's never said." But it would be just like Lacey to find out some terrible thing and then keep it from him, believing she had to protect him. What was he going to do about this mess? A house where a whole family had died, and Lacey already nervous and unhappy. He'd have to do what Harry had done: live somewhere else, use the house as a rental, and eventually sell it, after the baby was born. Lacey was in no shape to pack up and move again. Depending on the housing market, which with any luck was hitting bottom right around now, they'd only have to keep it a couple of years to break even. And there'd be taxes, if it wasn't their primary residence. His mind spun along the numbers. They couldn't get another mortgage as long as they had this one, and how would they afford rent? They'd manage if the house had tenants, but not if it stood empty for long. Taxes, utilities, water . . .

It was all right for Sammie; she'd known the story all her life, and she wasn't living there. What did the tragedy of the Halliday family mean to her? She saw the same thing happen on CNN twice a week. Harry Rakoczy had told them people died there, but he'd never hinted at anything like this. His own sister, his niece, and his nephews all murdered; and he lived next door to it and owned it all those years, waiting for what?

Eric's phone rang, and Sammie answered it: "Moranis Miszlak." She frowned. "Have you been arrested? I'll let him know, and he'll get back to you on Monday." The phone gabbled at her, and she pulled a face. "Monday. He'll call you when he gets in. Good-bye." The phone kept on whining at her, but she hung up. "Speak of the devil. That was Lex Hall. Deputies just repoed his baby."

"He's got visitation."

"Cambrick MacAvoy filed an emergency order. Nasty. I told you. You don't want to be in court with that woman." The phone rang again, and she picked it up and said in a neutral, measured tone, "You have reached the offices of Moranis Miszlak. Our

office hours are Monday through Thursday eight A.M. through
five thirty P.M., Friday nine to noon, and Saturday," an infinitesi-
mal pause as she glanced at the clock, "two to five." The minute
hand clicked to twelve, the hour hand to five. "Please call back
during business hours. Thank you." She hung up on Lex's protests.

Eric was charmed. "How often do you do that?"

"As often as I want. What are going to tell your wife?"

"Nothing."

"Right, because it's so great for a marriage when people keep
secrets."

"I'm not keeping secrets."

"Sure you are. You're not going to tell her about the Hallidays,
are you? You know, what I'd wonder about is what she's not telling you."

"Lacey tells me everything." Almost everything. She hadn't told
him why she didn't want to buy baby furniture. She hadn't told him
Dr. Vlk said it was time to start birth classes. When she failed the
Praxis teaching certification test the first time she took it, she didn't
tell him until she took it a second time and passed, because she
knew how anxious he would be.

Lacey kept secrets, not to protect herself, but to protect him.

"Tells you everything," Sammie scoffed. "Sure she does.
When? You're always here. Just because you're on call, you don't
have to be actually *in* the office. That's why they call it a smart-
phone. Go home."

He couldn't go home. A thousand reasons jumped into his
mind. Files he might need to reference, research he might have to
do. The house pushed him out; the thought of the house repelled
him. Those three little boys, falling down the stairs, dying, dying,
dead—and if he could imagine it so clearly, how would Lacey

react? He'd never tell her; she could never know. He opened his laptop. "I've got work to do."

She slapped the laptop closed, and he pulled his hands away just in time. "I like Lacey," she said. "She's a sweetie. You should bring her round here more often. And now, go home."

Chapter Twenty-nine

"I'M JUST SAYING," Ella Dane said again, "get to the ATM. Cash, baby girl. Cash is a girl's best friend." The drama of their flight had taken ten, maybe twenty, years from her life, and she had flicked back to an earlier self, as if her personality were a deck of cards newly shuffled, and instead of the queen of diamonds (spiritual and refined), the topmost card was now the jack of clubs (vigorous and combative). She was the veteran of a dozen sudden flights from homes that had abruptly become unbearable. Never for exactly this reason, but she was no stranger to blood on the floor, the sudden seizure of all that was most precious and abandonment of everything else.

She even insisted on stopping at Little Pigs on Airport Road and eating a pulled-pork sandwich, the first meat she'd touched for years. Consequently, she now called to Lacey from the bathroom, where she and the barbecue disputed for possession of her body. More groans, another flush, and Ella Dane's voice again, now gray and dim: "They can use credit cards to follow you, baby."

"Who can?"

"Men." Another flush. "Cash tells no tales. There's an ATM in the lobby."

"We're not running away from Eric. We're running away from the house."

"It's the same thing. He'll never believe you. And if he *does* believe you, the worst that happens is you put the money back, no harm, no foul."

"There might be fees."

"Cash. Trust me. Go get it."

Lacey went down to the lobby and withdrew the daily maximum from the joint checking account: five hundred dollars. The machine charged a five-dollar fee. She pressed Cancel and thought about it. Five hundred dollars. She'd never had that much all at once, cash in hand. But this lively, powerful version of Ella Dane, this was the mother who got her enrolled in the best high school in the district when they were technically homeless, by parking the car in the school's parking lot and refusing to move until Lacey was admitted. This was the mother who paid the orthodontist even when the power was cut off, because they'd only have to take cold showers for a couple of weeks, but straight teeth were forever. This was not the mother who read auras and interpreted dreams. If Ella Dane said she needed cash, cash was what she needed. She withdrew the five hundred.

In the back of her wallet, behind the grocery-store membership cards, was the emergency Visa, the card she and Eric never used, except for dinner once a year on their anniversary to keep it active. She pulled it out and took a cash advance of fifteen hundred dollars, the maximum.

Two thousand dollars made an alarmingly thin chunk, not quite an inch in twenties. And the Skyview Convention Center charged a hundred fifty a night, once all the taxes were added in. This money wouldn't last them two weeks.

Ella Dane would know what to do. Lacey went back to the room, where her mother had logged on to answer her subscribers' questions about their dogs. "Here's one," Ella Dane said. "Her dog keeps looking at her in a meaningful way. She thinks he has a message from her last husband, who has passed on."

"Dead?"

Ella Dane read on. "Moved to Tucson. The dog keeps weeping."

"So what'll you tell her?"

"The usual. Check with the vet. Change his diet to the vegan food. Put her right hand on the dog's head while he's sleeping, and try to tune herself to his energies. . . ." So the aura-reading Ella Dane was still present. Lacey wished the woman would choose one persona and stick to it, instead of shifting this way.

Lacey felt, in her right hand, the warm hard knob of Bibbits's head, thrusting in for attention. He was panting hard, and his front paws quivered. She pulled him into her lap, and he sighed and laid his chin on her thigh. She rubbed his velvet ears and tried not to think about the house. The golden floors, the porthole window, the fifty-year-old maple; she was six years old again, anchorless, completely in her mother's hands.

Which mother? The otherworldly or the worldly-wise?

Ella Dane gestured to the table in the suite's alcove, where Lacey's laptop was waiting for her. "Pull up that stuff you were going to show me."

Lacey carried Bibbits over to the chair, sat with him on her lap, and logged on. As she pulled up her archived pages, Ella Dane read over her shoulder and eventually said, "Beth Craddock. Why was she convicted so fast?"

"Somebody broke into her house and killed her baby when she was sleeping? Who'd believe that?"

"Well, sure, but look." Ella Dane pointed out the third paragraph in the newspaper story. "They were out forty-five minutes. I was on a jury once."

"You were?" When had Ella Dane lived the kind of life that would land her on a jury? A tax-paying, fully documented life, registered to vote, with a stable address?

"Sins of my youth. It was a drunk driver. We all knew he was guilty, but it took more than an hour just to take the vote. People wanted to wait for lunch. And nobody wants to believe a parent can hurt a kid."

"It happens all the time."

"People don't want to believe it. Trust me on this. People who *should* know, they don't want to know. This Craddock jury didn't even take time to get friendly. Forty-five minutes? That's one unanimous vote. How could they be so sure?"

"Maybe the father knows." Lacey pursued the name Craddock down a couple of blind alleys. "His name's Everett," she said, and there he was, in Spinet Cove, just north of Charleston, owner of a bed-and-breakfast called La Hacienda. The website showed a Southwest-style cluster of pink adobe huts, palmettos in the parking lot, swimming pool, beach access, local golf, and a dark man with wings of gray hair at his temples, the older self of the smiling young husband in the Craddock family's Christmas portrait, taken four months before Tyler's death.

Lacey clicked Contact Us, and wrote, *I live at 571 Forrester Lane in Greeneburg, and there are things I need to know about the house. If you are the Everett Craddock who lived there, please call me.* She added her cell-phone number and hesitated, with her hands floating over the keyboard. "What if it's not him?"

Ella Dane reached over her shoulder to hit Send. "Then he won't answer. He might not, even if it *is* him."

Someone knocked on the hotel room door. Lacey laid Bibbits on the bed and opened it, and there was Eric, with his hand raised to knock. They fell back from each other, as if repelled by a magnetic force. "Wha-a-a-t . . . ?" she stammered. "Why?" She hadn't thought about him since taking the money; she hadn't thought he might wonder where she was or try to find her.

"Why?" He stepped into the room and pulled the door shut behind him. "Lacey, my God, what happened? You couldn't have called?"

"There wasn't time."

"Blood all over the floor; you can't imagine what I thought! I've been calling everyone. Dr. Vlk. The hospital. Everyone. I thought you were dead. You couldn't have even texted me?"

He didn't seem all that happy to find her alive. How dare he shout at her this way, like a parent who'd grabbed his kid away from a busy road—who did he think he was? "You didn't answer when I called," she said.

"Tell him," Ella Dane said. She was still online and had opened a new window to answer another e-mail from one of her dog owners, hiding the Craddock trial and La Hacienda.

"Tell me what?" Eric said.

He raised his hands, palms forward; he was making an effort to control his temper, and she tried to meet him halfway. "I should have called again. I'm sorry. But I can't go home. It's not safe. There's something in the house."

"Lacey. Lacey, please. Can we sit down and talk?"

She let him guide her to the bed; she even let him slip her sneakers off her swollen feet. She said again, "I can't go home."

He began to rub her feet. "When I went home, and there was blood on the floor, Lacey—" His voice cracked; he bowed his head and pressed her feet a little too hard. "You don't know what I thought. The things I thought— Whose blood was it?"

"Mine," Ella Dane said. "It was an accident." She paused in the doorway. "You'd better tell him." She left the room.

"When the hospital and the cops and Dr. Vlk didn't know anything, I started calling hotels," Eric said. He began to work on her feet again. "I started at the front of the alphabet, and Sammie started at the back. It took us an hour to find you."

"I took money out of the account. Five hundred bucks." Eric hated it when she used her debit card and didn't tell him. "But I can't go home. There's a thing in the house. A person. A ghost." There, she'd said it. Her hands tingled, and she felt her whole body prickling. Her heart closed in shame. It felt like confessing to infidelity. "A ghost," she said. "It's dangerous. It attacked Ella Dane."

Eric let go of her feet. She felt his weight lift from the bed, as she had felt Drew's weight so often. "Be serious," he said.

"It's a little boy. I can't go home, Eric, listen to me, I can't! He's hurt people. People died there—a baby, it drowned in the bath."

"That was a long time ago. It's our house now."

She wiped her eyes and glared at him. "You *knew* and you didn't tell me?"

"I just found out today. And it isn't even the same bathtub. Harry replaced it, remember? So you've paid for the room already, you might as well stay till morning, and then you'll feel better and you can come home." He sat down again, and she let him take her feet in his hands. "Look how puffy you are. Dr. Vlk says she wants to see you Monday; you'd better ask her about it. There's a spa. You and your mom can have a girls' day out tomorrow; you know you need a haircut."

"Well, I'm so sorry I'm not up to your standards," she said. But then he took her left foot in both hands and pushed his thumbs up along her sole. She sighed. "That feels so good. You can keep doing that. I'm sorry."

"What happened to Ella Dane?"

"It cut her. With a broken plate."

Eric's hands paused on her foot, and she wiggled her toes to encourage him. "You broke another plate?"

He *would* worry about the plate. "I can't go back. It's not safe for the baby." *No living baby since 1971,* Greeley Honeywick had said. How could she be so specific? "Please come with me," she said to Eric. "We can sell it."

"We can't afford to sell it. There wasn't five hundred bucks in checking. You went into the overdraft. The bank charges a seven-dollar fee and twenty percent interest, in case you want to know. You can't live in a hotel."

"I can't go home."

He was rubbing her ankles now, one in each hand. It felt wonderful. He said, "Where can you go? You can't get any more money from the bank."

"Why not?"

"There isn't any. The overdraft's maxed out. The fees pile up; you have no idea how much trouble we're in. And there's nothing wrong with the house."

She knew that tone. Eric was terrible at keeping secrets. "You've found out something," she said. "What's going on?"

"What's going on is, I'm going home, to our house that we bought together. You can take your weekend, get it out of your system, and come home. Somebody has to be the adult here." He patted her feet one last time and stood up from the bed. "Right now, Lacey, I'm walking out of here. I'll do everything I can to fix this, but you have to help me. Come home with me. Please."

Lacey shook her head, and her cell phone began to ring on the nightstand. She checked the number but didn't answer. It was a return call from Everett Craddock's motel in Spinet Cove. "Who is that?" Eric asked.

"Somebody who knows the truth. Eric, if you'd only listen."

"You are exactly like your mother. Exactly like."

Outraged, she bounced against the pillow. "You *said* that? You didn't say that."

"I did say it. But I don't want to walk out of here without you. Please."

She folded her arms over her belly. "If you loved me . . ." She hated to hear herself say it, but it was too late to stop. "If you loved me, you would believe me. Even if it was impossible to believe. If I go back, the baby will die."

"I can't do it. I can't believe that. Lacey, I'm sorry, I just can't." He stood in the door, waiting for her. She looked at her knees, not raising her face even when the door whispered along the carpet. He was going; he was gone. After everything. After she had made him face the world when Foothills Financial collapsed; after he'd refused to sell her ring. She twisted the ring, but her finger was so swollen, she couldn't get it off. He'd helped her with her job search, she'd called Uncle Floyd and asked him to hire Eric—after everything, he was walking out, because of a house, because of *money*? Lacey pulled the pillow from the head of her bed, hugged it tightly, and wept into it. But he couldn't hear her, and he wasn't coming back.

Ella Dane came back in and sat at the computer a few minutes after Eric left, and mercifully she said nothing either in comfort or blame. Lacey sat next to Bibbits, stroking him for the comfort of his small warm body. His fur felt dry, and when she rubbed his ears, there was something wrong. He was sleeping at last, poor thing; the shock of Drew's attack and the sudden removal from the house had upset him terribly. At least he wasn't coughing.

She touched his nose. It was cold and beginning to dry. She already knew what had happened, but she opened her palm in front of his mouth and waited for the touch of breath anyway.

"Mom," she said carefully.

Her mouth and throat filled with tears. Bibbits, how she'd hated him for so long, but he'd been a good dog, a comfort to her over the last couple of months; he'd kept her from being alone. Poor old boy. All those months dosed with *Taraxacum,* dandelion essence, instead of real medication, and then Drew had been too much for his thick, exhausted heart.

"Mom," she said again. "I think something happened."

Ella Dane was still surfing on Lacey's laptop. "Just a minute."

"Mom, there's something wrong."

"Don't worry, the arm's stopped bleeding. I probably won't need stitches after all."

"Mom." Lacey didn't want to say it. She wanted to crawl into the hotel bed, under the clean strange sheets and the scratchy blanket, and close her eyes and pretend she didn't know what was happening in the small body curled at the foot. She'd be careful not to kick him off the bed; she wouldn't have to say anything, eventually Ella Dane would notice. But Drew had done this. Drew had given the old dog's heart its final shock. And Lacey was responsible for whatever Drew did. She forced herself to speak. "Mom, there's something wrong with Bibbits."

Ella Dane came over with her brown glass vial. "Just a drop of *Taraxacum* and he'll be good as new."

"I don't think he's breathing, Mom. I'm sorry."

Chapter Thirty

IN THE SKYVIEW LOBBY, Eric turned on his heel and headed back
to the elevators. Away from Lacey and her outrageous complaint,
his mind worked clearly again. He had a plan, fully formed: sell
the house and take the loss—twenty thousand dollars, a hundred dollars a month, he'd borrow the money to get out of the
mortgage—rent some quiet apartment—ask Ella Dane to stay
when the baby came—Lacey could go back to work, subbing if
she couldn't get a full-time job in the district; or back to school,
to get her master's in special ed, as they'd planned she eventually
would. Money would be tight for a year or two, but by the time
the baby was in school, they'd be back on track.

Sell the house, take the loss. And the ceiling in Ella Dane's
room, he'd have to get that repaired and the whole room re-
painted before the house went on the market; they could even
use the same Realtor. Those were only details: sell the house and
take the loss, or Lacey would be the loss, and the baby with her,
leaving him with a house he'd never meant to keep more than
five years in the first place. He'd go back and tell her right now.

But as he turned toward the elevator, it opened. A blond child on old-fashioned roller skates swooped in front of him, pressed all the buttons with both fists, and swerved directly toward Eric. Eric stepped back, hands up to fend off or catch the child, who surprisingly bared his small teeth and gave a high whoop of exhilarated rage, a monkey shriek. The elevator door closed, and the other three elevators were all stopped on upper floors.

Another whoop echoed in the lobby. Eric couldn't see where the child had gone, and none of the other travelers in the lobby seemed at all distressed by his strange passage. Eric felt disproportionately troubled by the encounter, as if a stranger's voice had shouted in the dark to save him from an unseen danger, a cliff over deep water.

The pieces of his plan, broken by the child's shout, settled in a new pattern. What good would it do to sell the house? Lacey would take some crazy dislike to the next place, and the next and the next. Ella Dane had raised her that way, always moving, always leaving. Lacey complained about it, but she and Eric had lived together for three years, moving every year, once to a large apartment with two roommates, then to a smaller apartment with just the two of them, and last to married student housing, which was why they married when they did, and it was Lacey's idea to move, each time. She'd never settle. Year after year, for the rest of their lives, she'd uproot him.

Eric's cell phone rang. Someone was calling from his home phone, giving him a moment of weirdly dislocated horror—who, who, how?—until he remembered that Sammie had come to help him find Lacey, and she was still there. "Hello?" he said, and it was Sammie, wanting to know if he'd found his wife.

"She's here," he said. "She's staying."

Sammie gave him silence with room for words, information, confession, but he could do that trick in his sleep. He said nothing back at her, and she broke first. "I'll clean up this blood," she said. "Unless you need to keep it for the cops, for some reason."

"My mother-in-law cut her arm."

"You owe me dinner. Bring me something from Abernathy's. I'll call Floyd."

"Don't mind me, make a party of it."

Eric stopped at the lobby ATM to get two hundred dollars for the weekend, remembered the account was overdrawn, and decided to use Discover for his expenses until his next paycheck. Lacey didn't have a card for the Discover account; he'd opened it before they were married. On his way to the parking lot, he called his bank's emergency hotline and canceled both debit cards. He canceled all the credit cards except Discover, even the emergency Visa. It gave him a stinging, childish satisfaction: that would show her. But the baby was his as much as hers. He had to make sure she couldn't disappear with his son.

Driving home, he called ahead to Abernathy's and ordered a party platter of variety sliders to go. Sammie had an astonishing appetite for such a slender woman; she must exercise like a maniac. Any leftovers, he could reheat for breakfast, although if Floyd came over, there'd be no leftovers. A new plan formed as he drove. Saturday night's drivers—some of whom would be calling Moranis Miszlak from the detention center in an hour or two—swooped past him in the left lane, veering like the little boy in the Skyview lobby.

The new plan was, keep the house. It felt immediately, viscerally right. His house, not hers. He wasn't about to bankrupt himself to finance her craziness. Something was wrong with his rearview mirror. Small lights flicked and vanished. He adjusted the mirror. His breath gelled in his throat, and his car swung right; the passenger-side tires shuddered across the rumble strip and slid on the gravelly shoulder. Luckily, he was going the legal fifty-five, and not the community standard of seventy, so he was able to pull back into his lane. He adjusted the mirror again, but it was gone, whatever he had seen: the top of a fair head, low in the backseat, as if Lacey were there, huddled behind the driver's seat instead of sitting beside him with her seat belt on. He turned the mirror from side to side, and the backseat was empty. Of course it was empty. Lacey had left him, and when he went to find her, she refused to come home. He opened his mouth to take deep deliberate breaths, trying to control his slamming urgent heart.

The fear came from Lacey, her irrational thoughts infecting him. This was the power she had over him. She said *ghost* and he almost killed himself on the highway, because of a random something in the mirror. Ella Dane had brought it into their house, whatever it was, a chimera of her superstition—candle smoke and the echoes of chants—Lacey's childhood come to life. And it was his own fault. She'd warned him and he'd insisted on bringing Ella Dane into their home.

He couldn't live like that. Lacey had to choose. Him or her mother. He controlled his racing mind with conscious plans: debit cards, credit cards. Keep the house—that was the only reasonable plan.

Chapter Thirty-one

THE NEXT DAY, Sunday afternoon, Lacey and Ella Dane stood in the Civil War section of the Greeneburg Cemetery. Bibbits had led them here. Ella Dane opened the cooler, where the dog lay cradled in ice bags, paws curling toward his body, black lips locked in an eternal snarl.

Lacey recalled the dogs of her childhood: Henry who was hit by a car; Noodle who had a high fever and vomited for three days before closing his eyes forever; the smiling Pomeranian called Salsa who lived to the age of nineteen and simply stopped breathing one day. Each of these had a real grave, chosen with care. Bibbits deserved the same.

"Is this the place?" she said. A week ago, she would have sighed and rolled her eyes. But if Drew could throw a tantrum over a game of Chutes and Ladders, then Bibbits could pick his own grave. Maybe Ella Dane wasn't as crazy as she seemed.

On the other hand, maybe she was exactly that crazy. It was five in the afternoon, and this was the fourth place that Bibbits's finicky and indecisive spirit had led them. They'd been to the antebellum mansion-museum Gage House, then to the playground at Rosemont Park, which Bibbits approved until Lacey mentioned that the playground was soon to be remodeled and repaved, with a climbing wall, a bungee bridge, and a skateboard half-pipe. "Bibbits will get dug up," she said.

"He won't like that," Ella Dane agreed, and they visited Burgoyne Elementary, which made Lacey nervous—only three miles from home, could Drew sense her, so near?—because Bibbits loved children and wanted to be near them. This came as news to Lacey. Bibbits growled at children and had bitten several. Here, too, the problem was new construction. Sooner or later, the district would scrape up enough money to rebuild Burgoyne's termite-ridden gymnasium, and the project might involve any part of the school's grounds.

"Bibbits wants peace," Ella Dane said, so here they were at Greeneburg Cemetery, under a statue of a horse with an empty saddle. Lacey had researched this spot while writing up a sample lesson plan and field trip for her education portfolio, in her junior year.

One of Greeneburg's local heroes, General John Banister, was memorialized here. He had disappeared at Shiloh, leaving his horse wounded on the battlefield. The horse charged a Union cannon and trampled five of the enemy. The general's grieving family buried the horse, planting a garden of rosemary and lavender around the life-size bronze. When the lost general was discovered alive, operating a bakery under the name of Shemple in Princeton, New Jersey, in 1883, there was some talk of removing the statue. By then, it had become traditional for young men to propose marriage under the animal's eyes, and its muzzle was gold with constant stroking, and anyway, Fly-by-Night had been a true hero of the Confederacy, even if General Banister unfortunately wasn't.

"This is the perfect place for Bibbits," Ella Dane said. She knelt beside the cooler and touched the dog's head. "Isn't it, baby?"

Lacey's cell phone rang. She scrambled in her purse—was it Eric? She held the phone in her hands without looking at the screen and let it ring one more time before looking—make him wait for just a second longer—but it wasn't him. The number was unfamiliar, the area code 803. "Hello?" she said cautiously.

"Ms. Miszlak? Ev Craddock. You left this number."

Ev Craddock. How dare he call her, cluttering up her phone while she was waiting for Eric to call; he might call any second. Lacey bit the inside of her upper lip to keep from shouting at the man. "Thanks for getting back to me," she said.

"You'll want a room?" he said. "Off-season rates."

A room, room for what? Oh yes, his beachside motel. "No, I wanted to talk to you about the house where you used to live, on Forrester Lane in Greeneburg."

"You a reporter?"

"No. I live there."

"You calling from the house?"

"No, I wanted to ask you a question. About your wife. About her trial."

Everett Craddock gave a wet and rattling sigh. "You sure you want to know?"

Lacey instinctively wiped her own phone on her sleeve. "The newspaper said the jury came back in only forty-five minutes, and I was wondering why were they so quick?" Another death rattle from the phone. "Please," Lacey said. "I've been living in the house. I'm pregnant. I really need to know."

"I bet you do. Her clothes were wet. Tyler had bruises on his head, matched her hands. Couple of his hairs under her fingernails. She done it, no question. You want to know more, you come down here."

Lacey patted Fly-by-Night's golden nose. "Is there more to tell?"

"You left the house?" Ev Craddock asked.

"Yes, I'm done with it."

"It ain't done with you." He began to cough with a ripping noise, as if some wet and necessary vital organ had torn loose and was now working its way up to his mouth—a kidney, maybe. Lacey waited, flinching at the worst of the gurgles.

In the meantime, a group of children with cameras had gathered around Fly-by-Night. Lacey scanned the cemetery and noticed all the casual strollers, some snapping the more exciting monuments with their cell phones, others setting up careful geometrical shots with professional-looking outfits with big black lenses.

They'd never be able to bury Bibbits without being seen. And, worse, photographed. She'd never get a job in the district with something like that on her record. "Hello," she said into her phone. "Mr. Craddock, are you okay?"

"A room," he said.

"Bibbits doesn't like it," Ella Dane said. "Too many children. Too much noise."

Lacey blinked at this—they'd been at Burgoyne Elementary, not an hour ago. What happened to Bibbits loving children and wanting to be near them? "What about the beach?" she said.

"It's outside," Ev Craddock said. "That's where we keep it."

"Bibbits loved the beach," Ella Dane said.

"Two double beds," Lacey said into the phone. "Nonsmoking, and we can be there tomorrow afternoon." She'd have preferred to leave today, immediately, and get as far from Forrester Lane as she could, but she had an appointment with Dr. Vlk tomorrow morning, and Eric might still call. She'd left eight messages for him and she refused to try again. It was his turn. Surely, surely, he wasn't going to stop talking to her. Their marriage couldn't end like this. He had to call. Maybe he was calling right now and leaving a message.

Everett Craddock reserved their room, and Ella Dane worked her way through the crowd of children. "Another thing," Lacey said abruptly, as if she had been arguing with her mother, "we need clothes."

"You don't want to go back to the house, do you? Bibbits is scared of it."

This was the first rational message Bibbits had sent all day, and Lacey wasn't about to argue. "We'll pick up a couple things in the hotel," she said. Something new, something Drew had never seen or touched. There was a gift shop. They wouldn't have maternity clothes, but she could at least grab a new T-shirt and replace the rest of her clothes tomorrow at the mall on the way out of town.

They drove back to the Skyview. While Ella Dane replenished Bibbits's ice, Lacey sailed into the Skyview Shoppe, where her credit card was refused. She laughed. "Wrong card," she said, "sorry," and handed over two of her precious twenties. Thirty-two dollars for two T-shirts, and Eric had canceled the cards. How could he—how *dared* he, after she'd supported him and taken out loans for his education. He had income and she didn't, but six months ago it was the opposite, and she'd never thrown it in his face, not even once. Not even when he complained about how they were burning through their savings, when it was all money *she'd* earned. She kept the stiff, public smile stapled to her mouth all the way out of the shop and across the lobby.

Her phone rang in the elevator, and it was Eric. Too late. Canceling the cards, after all they'd been through. That was just mean. She turned the phone off without answering.

Chapter Thirty-two

THE LAWYERS SPOKE too fast and there were too many of them. And where was the green line on the floor? Lex had followed the green line to this room, which was Family Court, even though the judge was too young and wasn't wearing a black robe. How could you tell who the judge was when everybody was dressed the same? The judge wore a plain blue tie. Plainer than any of the lawyers' ties. Lex's lawyer, the young one, wore a brown tie with tiny gold squares in it, and sometimes the squares were floating and sometimes they were falling. Lex kept his eyes on the plain blue tie, but he was worried about the green line. Without it, he would never be able to find his way out.

"I have to go," he said.

The lawyer pulled at his gold-squared tie. He had a tiepin with a square yellow stone in it. It wasn't lined up with the gold squares in the tie. Lex had to look away. When he looked up, he couldn't find the judge. Where was the plain blue tie? Where was the green line that would take him back to the big glass door?

"I have to go," he said again.

Jeanne's lawyer, that scary woman, was staring at him. He

pushed his chair back and lunged for the courtroom door. It was a plain gray door, plain as the judge's tie.

Bangs and shouts. The young lawyer grabbed Lex's elbow and yanked him downward and sideways, back into his chair. "Mr. Hall, you have to stay here."

"Where's Theo?" They had to give Theo to him now. That was what the hearing was for. Lex's lawyer would explain everything, and then the judge would give Theo to Lex, and Lex would take her home. All these words, the story, the evidence, that was what had to happen, the only thing that mattered. Plain blue tie. There it was. He looked straight at the judge's tie—always look straight at the judge and keep your face up, the old man said, long ago, when Lex used to get in trouble.

"She's at home with her grandmother," the lawyer said.

That was wrong, because Theo's grandmother was dead. "There's no grandmother," Lex said loudly. He stood up again. "She died a long time ago! Where's Theo?" They had her in a room, maybe in a closet or some small place, the kind of place where a little kid would hide when there were too many words and the words were too loud. "She's dead," he said to the Family Court. Maybe Theo was nearby and she could hear him. "Theo!"

"Counselor," the judge said angrily to the young lawyer, and Lex recognized that voice; all judges had that voice. "Control your client."

"She's with your wife's mother," the lawyer said. "It's almost over; you've just got to sit down for a minute."

Theo was with Big Jeanne? "No," Lex said. "That's not right." Nobody would listen; they never did. "You can't do that," he said, and two of the courtroom cops dragged him outside and made him sit in a cold metal chair in the hallway, and they wouldn't even let him go to the bathroom.

But the green line went straight up to the Family Court door. He leaned forward in the chair so that he could look at the intersection of two gray hallways. The green line turned left, so that was the way out. One of the courtroom cops slammed Lex back against the wall and said, "Stay where you're put."

Lex was used to staying where he was put. That was what courts did. They put him places, and he stayed there. Eventually they would let him go, and he could go back to his house that he had bought, and his job that he was good at, and he would take his baby home and take care of her like a good daddy should. If he needed help, the old man would help him. He leaned back against the wall and began to hum.

"Stop that," the cop said, so he stopped.

Everybody came out of the courtroom. Jeanne walked past him with her lawyer, and she didn't even look at him. Here came his lawyer at last, looking tired and sick and alone. Something bad had happened to him. "When do I get Theo?" Lex asked.

The lawyer pulled off his brown tie with the gold squares. Lex was relieved. He wouldn't have to look at the squares changing direction anymore, or the sideways tiepin. "You didn't help yourself back there, but there wasn't much doubt how it would go."

"When do I get Theo?"

"Friday, from two to four, in MacAvoy's office. Supervised."

The lawyer didn't understand. Lex said patiently, "When can I take her home?"

"You've got supervised visitation in MacAvoy's office, two hours a week."

"I've got her room all nice for her."

"I'm sorry, Mr. Hall." The lawyer started walking along the green line, and Lex followed him. "Here's the thing. After what happened last week—"

"Nothing happened."

"You drove across town with the baby naked in your car, because you couldn't give her a bath. You'll have to let the custody issue lie for a while, that's all."

They waited for the elevator. Lex checked: yes, the green line ran toward the elevator doors. How did the judge know about Theo's bath that went so wrong? The lawyer's wife knew, but he was Lex's lawyer. The nice lady, the lawyer's wife's mother, she knew about it, because she had helped get Theo clean. Was she the one who told Jeanne's lawyer? He couldn't believe it. She didn't even ask him, *What happened, are you okay?,* the way the old man did, over and over; she just cleaned Theo and played with her.

The old man. The old man knew. He called someone. "The old man told Jeanne," Lex said as the elevator arrived.

"I really can't say," the lawyer said, and Lex knew what that meant. The lawyer pushed his foot against the elevator door to hold it open, but he didn't get in. "Mr. Hall, you're going to have at least a month before your next hearing. So you've got time. You're going to have to look into getting new representation."

"What does that mean?"

"You need another lawyer, Mr. Hall."

"Is it too hard for you? Do you need help?" Lex was disappointed. But the lawyer looked tired. Maybe he was scared of Jeanne's lawyer. Jeanne's lawyer was a very scary woman. If he needed help, then asking for help was the right thing to do. "Is it something you can't handle on your own?" Lex asked.

"Mr. Hall. This is something I can't handle at all. Here's a list of firms. As soon as you've got a new lawyer, I'll send your file. You need to do this right away."

"But you're my lawyer."

"I can't be your lawyer anymore." He pushed the piece of paper toward Lex. "You call one of these people, and they'll help you better than I can. Take the paper."

Lex took the paper.

"Call them today. They need to deal with spousal support, that's coming up next. Now you'll call them today, won't you? Say yes."

"Yes," Lex said. He folded the paper in half so he wouldn't have to look at it.

"Good." The lawyer pulled his foot out of the elevator and patted the doors as they closed. "I'm sorry I couldn't do more for you, Mr. Hall, and I'll have all your files ready for your new lawyer. You take care, now."

"Thank you," Lex said as the door closed. He closed his eyes. The elevator shook, and then it began to climb, slowly, in little jumps. He crumpled the piece of paper and dropped it. He didn't want a new lawyer. He already had a lawyer. He just had to make him understand. The elevator stopped, and he waited a few seconds with his eyes closed, hoping that when he looked, if he was patient and good, he would see the green line that would lead him to the big glass doors.

Chapter Thirty-three

LACEY KEPT COUNTING THE MONEY, and it came out the same every time. "Two thousand dollars," she said. "It's not much, considering."

"Something will come up." Ella Dane was in the bathroom, emptying the melted water from the ice bags. Lacey could smell the dog, not the usual dark smell of Bibbits, but a sharper odor, with a skunky, sulfuric overtone. The sooner they got the poor animal buried, the better.

Something will come up. For as long as Lacey could remember, that was Ella Dane's motto, and something usually did come up. They'd live in the car for a few days and then start traveling from one of Ella Dane's friends to another, sleeping on couches, in sleeping bags, in attic bonus rooms with no air-conditioning, in basements or converted garages. One of these friends would hook Ella Dane up with a friend of a friend who needed a house sitter or had a trailer sitting empty on family land. Once, they lived for three months in a model home in a new subdivision, the builder paying Ella Dane to keep it and the two other models clean and ready to show.

Mostly, Ella Dane earned a few dollars here and there, babysitting, housecleaning, gardening. And she could always work with dogs. She'd advertise *dog training in your home, house training a specialty.* They always had money, never much, just enough.

Lacey sat at her computer, trying to figure out what baby was born at 571 Forrester Lane in 1971—Greeley Honeywick had been so positive, surely there was a way to find this out—and thinking Eric-type thoughts about Ella Dane. Would she drift from one odd job to another for the rest of her life? Did she have any money saved? What kind of Social Security benefits could a person receive, who had practically no official income over her lifetime? Who was going to take care of Ella Dane when she was old?

Who else, but the daughter who had taken on thirty-eight thousand dollars of student loans (plus another ninety-seven thousand for Eric), in order to qualify for a stable career. Lacey was on the Census Bureau website, trying and failing to get into the records for 1980, when her computer crashed. She slammed the top down and snapped at her mother, "How are we going to pay for this hotel?"

"I'm going down for a facial and a mani-pedi," Ella Dane announced, "and I made an appointment for you, too."

"And how are we going to *pay* for it?"

"That's the advantage of traveling light. We'll walk out of here, and they'll send the bill to Eric. Let's go downstairs and get all girled up."

"Really?" Lacey said. "After all that's happened, that's all you can think of, really?" She knew she wasn't being fair. Her fear of Drew, her grief over Bibbits, her terror of the blank, solitary, Eric-less future were all part of the poisonous mix, but everything in her came to a point, aimed at Ella Dane. "Because here we are again," Lacey said, "stuck in some hotel that we can't pay for that we're going to sneak out of"—and where was Eric with his instinctive, bone-deep honesty, Eric who stood in line at the bank and argued with the teller if there was ten dollars too much in the account after he balanced the checkbook, where was he?— "and we're eating cashew nuts out of the minibar, and then we're going on the road with barely enough money for gas, and how are we going to eat, how are we going to survive?"

"One thing and then another," Ella Dane said placidly.

No, no, no. That was the way Lacey organized her school year. It couldn't be the way Ella Dane organized her life. Lacey was nothing like her mother, no matter what Eric said. Nothing like. "It's your fault," Lacey said. "If you hadn't brought that dog into my house. It was the dog that made Drew so mad. If it wasn't for you, I'd be home right now, and Eric would be frying me a pork chop and rubbing my feet."

"Bibbits was a good dog, he was an old soul; he was getting ready to move on but he wasn't ready yet. I came here for you, Lacey. I came because you needed me."

"I don't need you." Lacey felt breathless, but she hurried recklessly on, because Eric was wrong; she was nothing like Ella Dane. "I never needed you. I always used to wish I could go back and live with Grandpa Merritt like a real person in a real house, so I wouldn't have to grow up like I did, like a tramp. I never knew from one week to the next where we'd live and I hated it! All I wanted was a real home." She had a real home with Eric. What if it was over?

"I only ever thought of you."

"You only ever thought about what *you* wanted. Why couldn't you let me stay with Grandpa Merritt? It's the only real home I ever had."

"It was time to move on," Ella Dane said. She gave Lacey a serene, superior smile. This happened every time Lacey brought up the subject of Grandpa Merritt, and the white house with the green door: Ella Dane took a giant step backward and upward onto the moral high ground, leaving Lacey ready to cry with frustration. "It was necessary," Ella Dane said. "I forgive you. Bibbits forgives you too; he knows you couldn't help it. And now it's time to get our nails done. Everything in its own time."

"Oh, you are so selfish!" Ella Dane had her hand on the door-knob, ready to walk out of the room, taking her unsullied vegan temper with her, and leaving Lacey red-faced and screeching like a spoiled first grader, and Lacey couldn't let her go. She kept hearing Eric's voice. *Exactly like your mother.* "You were the worst mother ever," she said.

"I'm sorry you feel that way," Ella Dane said, which was what she always said when Lacey called her names. Never an apology, never an excuse; she just pushed Lacey's feelings back at her. It made Lacey frantic.

"I hated living with you. I hated never having a real home. It was *embarrassing*. I always wanted to stay late at school, so I wouldn't have to go back to you."

"I'm sorry you feel that way."

"All I wanted was a place to live. I used to wish you'd die, and I'd be adopted by real people and grow up normal. It was my birthday wish every year."

"I'm sorry you feel that way."

It was as pointless as arguing with an answering machine. "And another thing," Lacey said, "we should find a Dumpster. That dog of yours stinks worse than ever."

"Bibbits was a good dog, and he deserves a good burying."

That was better. At least it was a reaction. "Bibbits was a rotten dog. And you're a rotten dog trainer. What kind of dog trainer has a dog that poops on the floor?"

"Bibbits had special needs." Ella Dane was crying now, silently, with her chin up. She hardly blinked, but her cheeks glistened. "He was my dog, and I loved him."

"You always had a dog you loved better than me," Lacey said. She heard herself: she sounded just like Drew. Or any other spoiled, obnoxious child. She pressed her hands over her mouth and sat on the edge of the bed, then wrapped her arms around her belly and rocked the baby. "I don't know what's wrong with me," she said. "I can't think straight. I want to go home."

"Go home, then."

"You know I can't." Somehow, she wasn't sure how, but somehow, it was Ella Dane's fault. "Drew will kill my baby if I go home."

"Then stop whining about it." Ella Dane wiped her face with the back of her arm. She hoisted the cooler. Water sloshed from one side to the other, and the skunky smell wafted out, stronger than before. "Bibbits wants to be buried by the sea, so I'll meet you at that motel in Spinet Cove. And after that, you know what, since you're so grown up and responsible and everything, you can take care of yourself."

Ella Dane balanced the cooler on her left leg while she opened the door; she caught the door on her right forearm and spun out of the room, letting the door slam behind her. Lacey, dissatisfied and jittery, waited for her to come back and finish the argument, but she didn't.

After a while, Lacey went down to the parking lot. Ella Dane's car was gone. She returned to the room and e-mailed Greeley Honeywick. She stayed up until two, but Ella Dane didn't come back.

Ella Dane was still gone the next morning, so Lacey checked out on her own. She'd used the emergency Visa when checking in, and now that Eric had canceled it, she'd have to pay for the room with cash. She counted her money five times. After only two days, she was down to seventeen hundred thirty-six dollars. Two nights in the hotel would eat up three hundred of that. How was she going to live? She couldn't just drive to a new town and fall on her feet like Ella Dane—find someone she used to know, maybe one of the friends she'd completely ignored for the last four months, not even letting them organize a baby shower for her, and invite herself to sleep on their couch, pick up a few dollars here and there taking care of people's dogs. This money had to last till she'd worked things out with Eric.

Worked things out: whatever that meant. Another day with no conversation made it even less likely they'd get back together. Sooner or later, they'd have to talk about what came next. Was he going to pay spousal support to her? He'd have to. Maybe there was prenatal child support. This couldn't be the end. What was she going to do?

She could go home. She could persuade Drew. All he wanted was love, like any child. She'd keep him sweet, make sure he never again thought she loved someone else more than she loved him— No, she couldn't. As soon as the baby was born, he'd know the truth. He'd had a sister once, baby Dorothy who cried all the time. Lacey would never be able to convince him he was first in her heart, and the baby simply a tiresome responsibility.

She fanned through her handful of twenties again. Even if Eric paid spousal maintenance without fighting her—and if the court went by last year's tax returns, she'd end up paying him, she having worked while he was in school—it would be weeks before any money came. Seventeen hundred dollars wasn't much. Fourteen hundred was even less. Ella Dane was right, it was easy to walk out of a hotel with no luggage. So she did it.

It was easier than it had been when she was twelve or thirteen, and it was her job to haul the duffel bags down the stairs and out of the hotel while her mother came down the elevator and quizzed the desk clerk as to the best place to eat lunch. Now she came down the elevator herself, waddled through the lobby and out the front door, giving the desk clerk a tired smile. It was only nine thirty. She wasn't skipping the bill; she was stepping out for a breath of air. Out to the parking lot, and there was her car. Left and then right and she was on Airport Road with sixteen hundred dollars rolled up in the zippered inner pocket of her purse, and one hundred thirty-six in her wallet.

She pulled into a gas station for pork rinds, beef jerky, and barbecue potato chips. Back in her car, she tore open the bag of pork rinds, took a bite, and let it melt into grease on her tongue. The nausea she felt had nothing to do with the baby. This was the same way she'd felt when she took up shoplifting at thirteen.

She didn't steal for fun, the way her friends did—thirty, forty, sixty dollars in their wallets, and they'd snatch up here a lipstick, there a designer clutch or pair of sunglasses. No. Lacey stole only the things she so urgently needed, and Ella Dane couldn't or wouldn't buy for her. She stole bras, panties, and even shoes, putting on the new shoes in a style similar to her old, shoving her old pair into the box, and walking out in the new. She was careful and quick, and always knew when someone was watching. The shoes were the riskiest, but if she pulled out at least ten pairs and tried them on, first in pairs and then in mismatched pairs, walking up and down the aisles and eyeing her feet from every angle in the mirrors, the store employees lost interest. They were glad to see her go, grateful she had put all the shoes back in their boxes. The bras and panties she simply slid from their packaging, rolled tight in her hand, and shoved up her sleeves.

She needed them. Ella Dane shopped in thrift stores. Mostly, it wasn't so bad. The smell came off after a couple of washings. But the shoes never fit right, and as for thrift-store underwear, everybody had to draw the line somewhere. Lacey would rather steal.

When she was fourteen, she started babysitting, and then tutoring, and she didn't have to steal anymore. This was something she'd never told Eric. He claimed to have no secrets from her, and maybe he really didn't. He'd told her about the girls he'd been with before her (both of them), and how ashamed he was of the way he'd broken up with his first girlfriend (at her birthday party, just after the cake). He apologized to the girl and gave her a gold necklace for her birthday, and she forgave him and agreed that it was for the best—she was getting ready to dump him, anyway.

"I didn't feel right until I told her I was sorry," he'd told Lacey.

She couldn't tell him about the shoplifting, because he'd insist on her finding some way of making amends. Going back to the stores and giving them their money back, after all these years, like a little girl caught with a candy bar in her pocket. In marrying Eric she had married up, but she hated him to remind her of it.

He'd know about the hotel, because the bill would get back to him. Seventeen hundred dollars wasn't much, and fourteen hundred was even less, but she couldn't let Eric think she was a thief. She drove back to the Skyview and turned in her key card. "Thanks," the clerk said, and went back to tapping on his computer.

She waited. After a while, she said, "Excuse me?"

"Ma'am? Was there a problem with the room?"

"I need to check out." She put her purse on the counter and

dug into it for the roll of twenties. "Two nights. I need to pay cash, if that's okay."

He spent a few seconds on the computer. "It's paid already. Says here, paid in cash, for two nights."

Ella Dane. Ella Dane had been working, she must have built up a little bit of money, and she had paid Lacey's bill. Lacey tucked the roll back into her purse. "Thanks," she said. "I guess I forgot."

The clerk rolled his eyes, visibly thinking it must be nice to be some people, who couldn't remember spending three hundred dollars. Lacey returned to her car and discovered she had lost all appetite for beef jerky.

Chapter Thirty-four

DR. VLK GAVE LACEY PERMISSION to drive, walk, even swim, anything. The baby was strong and the placenta looked good. "So I can go for a vacation?" Lacey said.

Dr. Vlk gave her that straight blue stare, the look that needed no x-ray or ultrasound wand. "Absolutely," she said, and she didn't ask if Lacey's husband would join her on the trip. Instead, she looked in her iPhone and pulled out an obstetrician in Spinet Cove, "in case anything comes up," she said. "There's a good hospital, and the little one's viable. He's laying down fat. Getting big and strong."

"Merritt," Lacey said. Now that the baby was officially viable, she could say the name she had been keeping secret even from herself, ever since Dr. Vlk told her it was a boy. "That's his name. Merritt, after my grandpa."

"Family names are a good thing," Dr. Vlk agreed, and she didn't ask if Lacey would be traveling with her mother. So Lacey, with a clean bill of health and a bag of salty snacks, headed south, stopping only at the mall to pick up maternity jeans, a couple of smocks, underwear, and bras. On the way through the food court, she ate a Philly cheesesteak, which was suddenly the one thing in the world she absolutely had to have, it smelled so good as she walked by.

The weather had cooled, and for the first time since May, she didn't have to use the air conditioner. It felt wonderful to drive with the windows open, her skin softening in the cool, humid breeze. The landscape changed from the Upstate's pine and hickory woods and wide green fields, towns thickening together as the highway neared Columbia. She got through Columbia quickly, reaching the major confluence of highways at three in the afternoon, well before the afternoon rush. Twenty minutes south of the city, she saw the first palmetto tree.

As the land flattened, cornfields and vegetable fields gave way to cotton, gray with white puffs, and the golden tapestries of safflower fields. The soil had changed from red to brown, and soon, a full seventy miles from the ocean, gray sand spilled along the highway's shoulders. The trees were shorter, their branches airily spread instead of knotted and dense, and the palmetto palms looked like a child's drawing of trees, straight trunks and bushy bunches of fronds at the top. When she pulled into a rest stop south of Florence, the birds fighting over the trashcans were herring gulls, not crows.

And there it was, the magic castle of her childhood, the one place Ella Dane would never stop, no matter how much money Lacey had saved from babysitting. "Nothing but trash," Ella Dane proclaimed, "and no one but trash buys anything there," which was kind of snooty for a woman who was never more than one bad week away from homelessness.

SEASIDE EMPIRE, said the signs, LARGEST GIFT SHOP IN THE SOUTH! Lacey believed it. The front was all wheelchair ramps and wind chimes, and the Empire scrawled back from the road in a maze of poorly aligned rectangles, as if someone had bought three different houses standing close together, built covered walkways to connect them, and then surrounded the whole mess with deep porches and billboards. "See the Mermaid. Live Sharks. Souvenirs for All. Shelligami." What was shelligami? Lacey longed to know, but Ella Dane would never take her to Seaside Empire, and neither did Eric.

She'd never told him. They'd been to the beach five times in the years they'd been together, which meant they'd driven past Seaside Empire ten times, and Lacey hadn't said, "Let's stop there, it looks like fun." She wanted to but was ashamed. It was, as Ella Dane said, trashy, like sugar sandwiches. But Lacey could make long-term plans, as much as Eric could. For a moment, she set it all aside—Drew and Bibbits and Ella Dane and the terrible things she and Eric had said to each other—and she let herself believe everything would be fine. Someday, when Merritt was five or six, they would go to the beach—she could see them, herself having lost all the baby weight, Eric driving with sunglasses on, and maybe there was a second baby (a girl) in the back next to Merritt, in the silver Odyssey they would have—and she would say, "Eric, I forgot to pack Merritt's beach shoes. Let's stop here."

Seaside Empire, hers at last.

She pulled into the gravel lot. Instead of herself and Eric, Merritt and the little unknown in the silver Odyssey, it was just Lacey and Merritt kicking inside her. "Knock it off, kiddo," she said, and the baby did something sharp and awful. She gasped and clutched the car door. What was going on? Had he shoved a foot into her liver?

Eventually, he curled into a twitching ball. Lacey walked in, and Seaside Empire was all she had dreamed, and more. The clothes, shoes, towels, and Boogie Boards she ignored; but the shells! Tubs of loose shells, shell nightlights, shell jewelry, shell-encrusted pens, shell sculptures of everything from mice to the White House.

Even shelligami did not disappoint. It was origami folded out of thin aluminum and then encrusted with tiny cowries and snails. The mermaid was deliciously gruesome, a stuffed manatee shaved to the waist and wearing a black Halloween wig. The live sharks were baby dogfish; there were also dead sharks, eight inches long, formaldehyded in glass bottles. She fondled the mineral samples and the fossils. There were shark-tooth earrings; did she need shark-tooth earrings? Well, who didn't? Seaside Empire with seventeen hundred dollars in her pocket: childhood's wildest dream come true. Shark teeth. Giant fossil shark teeth! Lacey found the largest intact specimen.

"Megalodon," she said to herself. The fair-haired child beside her glanced up, startled at her voice, and she stumbled back. "No, no, no," she said, "it's not fair, no!"

"Ma'am? Are you okay?"

Lacey's heart settled. If she was going to have a panic attack every time she saw a blond child, she might as well go home now. This boy was older than Drew, taller, fatter, and he wore glasses with plastic tortoiseshell frames. He was looking at her with an open, adult-friendly expression, and he had chosen a baby hammerhead shark in formaldehyde from the shelf. Pure nerd. Teachers weren't supposed to say it, but for some children, no other name would do.

Lacey loved her nerds almost as much as she loved her noisy boys, and she yearned to bring them together, for the benefit of both. Last year, she'd experimented with selecting the leaders of both camps and giving them the joint responsibility of caring for the classroom's most interesting pet. Alpha nerd and noisy boy bonded over feeding crickets to Darth Venomous, the emperor scorpion. Alone of the fourth-grade classrooms, hers had no bullying.

"Ma'am?" the boy said.

"Sorry, it's nothing." She hefted the fossil tooth in her hand and smiled. "Megalodon. It's my favorite extinct animal."

"Mine's Andrewsarchus."

Lacey felt a chill at the name, but she controlled herself. Andrewsarchus was a real animal. She, like this sweet boy, had watched the *Ancient Killers* series last year on National Geographic. "That's the carnivorous sheep thing, am I right?" she said.

He smiled. "The biggest mammal land predator of all time!" he said. "Giant killer sheep! Do you think my mom will let me buy this shark?"

"Probably not." Lacey wasn't surprised that he asked her this. Children had always been drawn to her, confided in her. That was why she'd gone into teaching in the first place. "But maybe she'd get you this." She gave him the megalodon tooth. "It's the best one."

He turned the tooth, rubbing his thumb along the striations. She missed this so much, the conversations with children in all their variety. Eric had thought he was giving her a wonderful gift, letting her stay home while he worked, *till the baby starts school,* he said, which she interpreted to mean preschool at age two although she knew he meant kindergarten. Five years out of the classroom. If they had another child or two, it could be six, seven, ten years. If she'd had a job, two dozen children to handle every day, she would never have accepted Drew: he had used her solitude against her; he had peeled her like an orange.

She reached the sea at sunset. Spinet Cove was a one-road beach town, essentially a row of two-story motels with a scrabble of low square houses inland. La Hacienda was one of the beach-side motels and consequently had new bedspreads and an electronic marquee, advertising Continental Breakfast, Cable in Every Room, and Wi-Fi, all FREE. On the other side of the street, where the guests had to walk across two lanes of traffic to get to the beach, the motels weren't nearly so spiffy. A couple of them were closed, and the motel directly opposite La Hacienda had no roof. Its old-style movable-letter sign read PARDON OUR MESS WHILE WE REMODEL, which would have been more convincing had the building not been overgrown with kudzu.

La Hacienda was all Spanish arches, pink stucco, red tiled roof, geraniums in terra-cotta pots. Ella Dane's car was parked at the last unit. Lacey wanted to walk on the beach before dark, but Ella Dane came out, rubbing her hands, and gave a shrugging half wave. Lacey walked over to her. "Mom, I need to say something," she said. She had to apologize now, before it was too late.

"I don't think you do." Ella's Dane's voice was steady and firm. So this was how it was going to be. A perfectly reasonable relationship, Ella Dane using her telephone voice to Lacey, not letting their eyes meet.

Lacey went into the room. The necessary conversation with Ev Craddock oppressed her; she'd have to find out what he knew, tomorrow or the next day, after she'd rested and caught up with all these changes in her life, and after they'd dealt with Bibbits. She piled the pillows at the head of the bed and lay propped up, pressing the heels of her hands against her eyes until the tears sank deep. The baby rolled over, and she patted her belly. He pushed back, as if responding to her greeting. It made her laugh, even in her misery. It was worth everything, if she could save him—she'd give up Eric, the house, everything.

Chapter Thirty-five

THE SHINY GIRL'S FRONT HAIR was orange. Was she even the same girl? She took Lex to a room with a big table and a lot of mixed-up chairs. Some were office chairs on wheels, some were padded in different colors, some were wooden. Each had something wrong, scratches or torn cloth or broken legs or burns. "Wait here, Mr. Hall," she said.

She left him alone and he checked the mirror to make sure it wasn't one-way glass, with lawyers and cops watching him on the other side. The old man had taken him to dinner last night and had told him how to behave. "Act happy," he said.

"What if I'm not happy?"

The old man sighed over his pizza. "Just play with her."

Lex had bought a computer game a few weeks ago, a Chinese game called mah-jongg. It laid out a pattern of tiles, and you had to pull the tiles out in pairs, matching them up. He played it over and over again. When he lost, he went back and played the same game until he won it. Every game could be won. Everything lined up, everything matched, and there was nothing left over.

Theo wasn't old enough for mah-jongg. Maybe when she was five or six, they could play together. They could take turns. He could show her what to do. She would let him play his favorite tile, the eight of bamboos. He liked the way the eight bamboo sticks lined up, four on top saying W, four underneath saying M.

The shiny girl came back with a plastic crate. "We keep a box of toys," she said. "You didn't bring anything, did you?" Lex shook his head, and she sighed and said, not to him but to some invisible thing in the ceiling, "They never do. So here's a couple of dolls, some Duplo blocks, crayons and coloring books, and this noisy Elmo thing—they all like that. Oh, and this is a camera." She put a video camera in the middle of the table. "Stay where it can see you."

"Why?"

"And the bathroom's down the hall to your right."

She left. Lex laid out the toys on the tabletop. He sorted the Duplo blocks by color, and then by size within colors. They didn't come out even. There were seventeen crayons, and five of them were broken, but he liked the way they smelled. It reminded him of something.

The shiny girl came in carrying Theo, and the big dog lawyer came in behind her with a magazine under his arm. "Here you go, Mr. Hall," the shiny girl said cheerfully. She set Theo on the floor. Theo tipped forward until her hands reached the floor, and sat there, her legs spread, supporting half her weight on her thick little fists. "Anything else?" the shiny girl said.

"We're good," the big dog said.

"He's not my lawyer," Lex said. "Where's my lawyer?"

"You haven't got new counsel yet?" the big dog said. His voice was too loud, big dog barking so everyone could hear. "Eric's in court. You're a lucky man, Mr. Hall."

Lex backed up, trying to get as many chairs as possible between himself and the lawyer. "How's that?"

"Somehow that boy persuaded MacAvoy to change the visitation to this office. Pro bono, and there ain't a lawyer in a thousand who'd work so hard for a guy who's not his client. But you got to call those names we gave you, get someone new."

"I don't want a new lawyer. I want *my* lawyer."

"Any lawyer's yours that you pay for, and Eric says there's three hundred bucks left on your retainer. You don't want to do it, Sammie'll set something up for you."

"I don't want a new lawyer."

"Suit yourself." The lawyer sat at the other end of the conference table, leaned back and crossed his legs, and folded his magazine open. "We'll refund the retainer."

"But what am I supposed to do?" Lex asked.

"It's visitation. Visit. Stay where the camera can see you."

Lex looked down hopelessly. Theo was rocking on her fists. She tipped herself forward and landed chin-first on the floor. She burbled quietly for a few seconds, then got herself up on her hands and knees to crawl under a wooden armchair. She sat inside the cage of legs, slapping her hands on the floor and laughing at Lex.

"I see you," he said. He knelt beside the wooden chair and reached up onto the table for a Duplo block. Blue, rectangle. "Blue," he said, giving it to her. She chewed on it, made a face, and banged it on a chair leg. He reached for another block. "Red."

The lawyer moved the camera to the floor. "Good," he said. "Educational, interactive, all that happy crappy. Keep it up, Mr. Hall."

Theo tasted the red block. She dropped it and covered her ears. Then she pulled her hands away and looked at Lex with her huge, happy, wet smile and said, "Eep-boo!"

He covered her eyes and then uncovered them. "Peekaboo," he told her.

She tried covering her mouth. "Eep-boo!"

Playing with Theo turned out to be easier than he thought. She liked peekaboo, and after a while he realized she knew she was supposed to cover her eyes. She was playing a trick by covering her ears or her mouth. When he covered his own ears, she laughed so loudly that the big dog put his magazine down. "I don't recommend tickling," he said. "Got to watch out for the touching. That kind of thing don't look good on video."

"It's peekaboo."

"Good," the big dog said. Then Theo discovered some of the chairs moved. She spent the rest of the hour clutching the seat of a rolling chair and staggering around the room, while Lex followed, anxiously stooped over her to keep the chair from rolling too fast. He pulled Theo onto his lap and sat at the table, showing her the coloring books and the crayons. She tasted the crayons, ripped a page out of the coloring book, hooted loudly for a few minutes, and fell asleep with her head resting against his shoulder.

The shiny girl came to take her away, and he wouldn't see her again until next Friday.

"This is good stuff," the big dog said, playing through some of the video. "She's a sweet kid. A little chunky, but cute as a peanut pie. All that walking with the chair, that'll play well in the custody hearing. I'll have Sammie burn you a copy on disk. That wife of yours. She was raised by hippos, or what?"

"She lost some weight when we were married, but it's come back."

"Yes, and it brought friends. She's a lot younger than you, how'd you meet?"

"She was fourteen. I caught her shoplifting."

They were walking down the hallway toward the front office.

Lex tried to get a look at each office, because he wanted to talk to his own lawyer. He didn't realize the big dog lawyer had stopped walking until he crashed into the man's back. "Sorry!" Lex said, with his hands up and open. "Sorry, I didn't mean it, sorry, sorry."

"Fourteen-year-old runaway, you catch her shoplifting, and then?"

"I took her home."

The lawyer shook his head with his eyes closed. "Lord Jesus. Tell me you didn't."

"I told her mother where I found her."

"You took her to her *own* home. Excellent. And then?"

"She came to work at MacArthur's after school. First she stocked, and then when she was sixteen she got to be a cashier."

"How old was she when you got married?"

"Twenty."

"You had me worried for a minute. Old man, underage girl. Meeting her when she was fourteen; that's a little scary. But you weren't her supervisor?"

"I mostly never saw her at work." Was that his own lawyer's office, the one around the corner, with the closed door? The big dog was walking again, and Lex followed. "I worked night shift and she had afternoons."

"Great. Still, a girl that size." The big dog sighed and blew through his lips. "How do you do it? Roll her in flour and look for the wet spot, I guess. Here we are." He opened a door and led Lex out into the waiting room.

"Wait." The lawyer was trying to work Lex toward the door, but Lex set his heels and wouldn't move. "When do I get to talk to my lawyer?"

"He's off the case." His hand was on Lex's elbow, pulling him across the waiting room, closer to the door. "I'll be taking care of you till you get new counsel. We won't abandon you, Mr. Hall. Sammie'll line something up, and we'll let you know by Thursday."

Then Lex was outside, and the door was closing. He wanted to go back in and explain. The shiny girl and the big dog lawyer wouldn't listen. He needed his own lawyer, the young one. They said he was at court, and his office door was closed. That didn't matter. Lex knew where to find him. He knew where he lived.

Chapter Thirty-six

THE NEXT DAY, Lacey was finishing her third picture of Bibbits. There was no breath of Drew in the sea wind, and every day, Merritt was bigger and stronger. Maybe she could stay here in Spinet Cove until he was born. She'd looked for Ev Craddock earlier but the motel office had been empty, so she'd driven into the landward side of Spinet Cove to find a mall, where she bought textured watercolor paper, oil pastels, and fixative. Her first few pictures were stiff. As her hand began to move more easily over the paper, she produced a few versions that would have looked good on Valentine cards but did not express the quality of Bibbits, until she remembered dogs had eyebrows. She wrinkled the skin over Bibbits's eyes to give him the cautious, questing look with which he had greeted the smell of meat.

She layered pinks and reds and yellows, shaded in purples and greens, deepened his eyes. She smudged with her thumb and a paper torchon; she sprayed fixative and let it dry and then worked new layers over it. Now she was working on the final layer of color, adding white and lightest yellow to the highlights of his apricot-blond curls. It looked just like him, and she felt like herself for the first time in months, with flecks of color blending under her fingernails and staining the whorls of her fingertips.

The real Bibbits, meanwhile, looked less and less like himself, although Ella Dane kept him well iced. Lacey kept the door open for the sea air. Sand filtered in and blended with her pastel work, becoming part of the texture. Lacey wanted to know if they were going to bury the poor little thing. "When the time is right," Ella Dane said whenever Lacey asked, "when he tells me where." So far, apparently, Bibbits had not spoken.

It had rained earlier in the day, and the beach was solid gray, the sand pocked with rain above the tide line, clean and flat below it, with a scum of broken shells to mark the boundary. Lacey watched Ella Dane walking on the beach, and the eastern sky was green, a green unlike any other, like seeing without light. Ella Dane stood above the tide line, the wind pulling her hair and blue skirt north. She stepped forward, back, left and back again, spun in place, hesitated, like someone trying to learn a dance she had heard described but never seen. Then she drew a circle on the sand and came up to the room.

"It's time," she said. "Look what I found on the beach." She had two weathered sand shovels, one red and one orange.

"I made this for you," Lacey said. She laid the pad of watercolor paper on the bed. "It needs another layer of fixative, so don't touch."

"Oh." Ella Dane sat down slowly, beside the picture, running her fingers along the edge of the paper. "Look at that. His little nose. It's perfect."

"I'm sorry for saying those things," Lacey said. "I just lost it."

Ella Dane looked at the picture for a long time. Eventually, she said, "I went back to Columbia on Tuesday to pick up some

things from my friend Patty's garage." She had boxes of posses-
sions in garages and attics all over Columbia. "There's some pictures you need to see. Jack says it's time. He says the lies have
blocked your chi."

"What lies? I haven't lied to you."

"I've lied to you." Ella Dane pulled a manila envelope from
her duffel bag and handed six pictures to Lacey. They were Polaroids. Lacey recognized the thick paper, the broad white border
at the bottom. And old, the colors fading to yellow. Still, the
images were clear. A series of moments, a little girl changing out
of shorts and T-shirt into a blue swimsuit. One piece, halter back.
Lacey remembered the swimsuit, how the elastic had pressed
against her neck.

That was the summer before first grade, the wonderful year
with Grandpa Merritt. Six weeks into the school year, sometime
around the end of September, her mother had picked her up from
school and they had never gone home again.

Then what was this? Six-year-old Lacey, dressed, undressing,
half dressed, naked; the bare white buttocks and the brown legs,
the white ghost of the blue swimsuit on her skin, and then the
blue swimsuit drawn up. Lacey laid the picture of her naked self
above the others. "What does it mean?" she asked.

"One day," Ella Dane said. "One day I was sorting Dad's laundry, and I found a box of pictures. I tore up most of them, but I
kept these."

Lacey knew what these pictures would mean if she'd found
them in some child's book bag—they wouldn't be Polaroids now,
but printouts of digital pictures. Maybe not even printouts, but
accidentally forwarded e-mail attachments. She'd never found
such a thing, but she knew teachers who had. What did it mean,

when they were pictures of herself? What did it mean that Ella Dane had kept them? She fanned them, slipped the naked picture back into its place, and closed the fan, so only the first picture could be seen, the innocent image of the little girl in the blue swimsuit, a picture any proud grandpa might frame. The long tanned legs and the tangled yellow hair.

"Why?" she said.

"In case I ever needed them. In case he tried to get you away from me. If there was a custody fight between him and me—he knew I had these, so he never dared. In case something happened to me, to make sure he wouldn't get you."

"No, why, why are you telling me now?"

"I couldn't tell you before. And also . . ." Ella Dane reached out and touched the baby bump, and the baby kicked under her hand. "And I never knew till you told me the other day, how you felt about the way we lived. You were always so cheerful. All those adventures we had—I thought you were having fun. You looked like you were coping well. You know. Resilient."

"It wasn't all bad. But I didn't feel resilient," Lacey said. She still didn't, not a bit resilient. Shattered, maybe. Overwhelmed. And Ella Dane was dealing with all this—threats of a custody fight, from the man who had taken these pictures—during those first terrible weeks of homelessness and confusion. "That day you picked me up from school, was that the day you found these?"

"The very same day. I just flung our stuff in plastic bags and went for you. That was it, we were gone. Some of my cousins had told me nasty things, but I never believed them, till that day."

Lacey gave the pictures back. "I thought it was the worst day of my life."

"You'd have had a worse worst day than that, if we'd stayed."

"So why did you leave?"

Ella Dane looked startled. "What do you mean? It's what you do. Your kid's in danger, you get them away safe."

"Lots of women don't," Lacey said. She hadn't identified any victims of sexual abuse in her classes. She knew the numbers. About 8 percent of girls under ten were abused. Three years, twenty-five kids per class, thirty-eight girls altogether. The odds were she'd seen at least three victims. One every year had slipped past her, children she could have saved as Ella Dane had saved her. Some of those girls, those very quiet girls . . . She'd been so busy with the noisy boys, she would never know how many children in desperate need had sat in her classroom, quiet and mild, their suffering invisible to her teacher's eye. "Lots of women stay for lots of reasons."

"You didn't," Ella Dane said. "That's why we're here. I understand what you're going through, I really do. What he might have done to you. What that thing might do to your baby. Better to sleep in the car than one more night under his roof."

Were they talking about Drew or Grandpa Merritt? "I wish you'd told me," she said. All these years, she'd carried that vision of the white house with the green door, her perfect home. She'd painted her own door green. It made her sick.

"I'm telling you now. I didn't want you to grow up scared. I didn't want you to think you'd ever been touched. Because you weren't; you were never touched. I asked you some questions, not to give you any ideas but to find out what you knew. . . . He took the pictures, but he never did the next thing."

"What was that?"

"He would have dressed you up and taken more pictures.

That's what my cousin Maureen said. And then other things, but first it was pictures in costumes."

The swimsuit was almost a costume, in those Polaroids. Maybe he'd been further along than Ella Dane wanted to think. "He wanted to get me a special dress for Halloween, a princess dress. He said something." Lacey wasn't sure if she truly remembered this; she remembered that first night in the car, she remembered the palmetto bug in her book bag, and she remembered wanting to go home. She remembered the deep, bitter, adult rage she had felt against her mother for taking away that comfortable life. "I wish you'd told me."

"There was a silver dress in his closet," Ella Dane said. "Sequins and sparkles. I found the pictures, I saw the dress, I remembered what Maureen said, and that was it. We had to go. You'll do what you have to do, to keep that baby safe." She put the pictures in their envelope and handed Lacey the orange shovel. "Bibbits is ready."

Several days past ready. Lacey took the orange shovel and waited outside as Ella Dane hauled the cooler down to the beach. The courage it must have taken Ella Dane, with no money, no job, no skills, to take her child and run for safety. She had fled, but Beth Craddock hadn't. Maybe she hadn't sensed danger until too late. Greeley Honeywick moved to the other side of the country, but CarolAnna had stayed in Forrester Hills, and Harry lived next door. Lacey had to get Ev Craddock to talk to her.

"This is the place," Ella Dane said.

They dug into the sand. It was harder work than Lacey had expected, and she had to do most of it, because Ella Dane's arm hurt. Nine inches below the surface, she reached a layer of splintered shells. She put all her strength into digging so she wouldn't have to think about the little girl in the blue swimsuit, and the story of the life she hadn't lived behind Grandpa Merritt's green door. She had to recast all her memories. The things she'd been most bitter about—Ella Dane taking her away, Grandpa Merritt dying alone—were things she had to be grateful for, now. It was more than she could manage all at once, so she concentrated on the sand. It was like digging through broken glass. The green sky faded to gray-violet in the east, and then deepest blue, although the landward horizon was all in flames, great red and yellow clouds towering into a city of fire. The sea sighed in a quiet rhythm, shallow waves fainting along the shore, and the air crawled cold off the water.

Ella Dane opened the cooler. Lacey took a few steps back and upwind, hoping it looked like a gesture of respect. Had she ever thought Bibbits smelled bad in life? This was worse, a sticky smell, thick, gummy, an invisible glue. It clung, even in the sea air. She'd have a shower when they went inside.

"Bibbits," Ella Dane said solemnly, "was a good dog, even though a lot of people didn't think so. He had an old, wise soul and a loving heart. I have had other dogs before, and I will have other dogs again, but there will never be another Bibbits."

Ella Dane stood with her head down. Lacey did the same, wondering how long they would wait in quiet respect—and then, she realized that Ella Dane was waiting for her to speak. She took a deep breath, and the smell of Bibbits lodged in her throat, so her voice was thick and her eyes streamed as she said, "Bibbits wasn't an easy dog to get to know, but he was sweet." He'd kept her company. At the end, he'd tried to protect her from Drew. He had done everything a dog needed to do, but that was private, between the two of them. Ella Dane waited another half minute. Lacey said no more.

Ella Dane tipped the cooler over the hole, and Bibbits slithered reluctantly out, his hips catching on the cooler's rim. Ella Dane shook the cooler, and the dog came loose with a tearing sound. The smell blossomed. Lacey quickly shoveled sand into the hole while holding her breath, and Ella Dane stood weeping without sound or motion, like a statue in the rain.

Chapter Thirty-seven

ERIC'S ALARM CLOCK went off at four on Saturday morning. He lay for a moment moaning, feeling blunt pains in every bone; he felt about a thousand years old. Four in the morning, oh God, why? He had stayed up late Friday night to read Lex Hall's juvenile record, which Sammie Vandermeijn had unearthed. Interesting, even frightening in spots, but it could have waited.

Lacey. Ella Dane had called to tell him where they were. He was going to drive down to Spinet Cove and talk to her, just talk. And listen. More listening than talking would be good, no matter how crazy she sounded. Maybe there was something in what she said, something in the house. Maybe being pregnant, the hormones, the baby, something had opened the back of her mind, let the past blow in like leaves through the kitchen door. She'd been afraid of the stairs before she knew anything about the house's history. He'd swear to that in her defense.

They'd never had a fight. Not like this. Sometimes they argued, but they found their way to agreement, eventually, and he always remembered, no matter how annoying she was, that he loved her. He hoped she would do the same for him. Their marriage couldn't end this way, on their first bad fight. He drifted back to sleep and half dreamed that she was beside him in the warm bed. Lacey, not the Lacey he'd seen in the hotel, but the Lacey of last year, slim and cheerful and healthy, fearing nothing. She could be that girl again. She was still that girl.

The second alarm went off, 4:15; 4:15 on a Saturday morning, oh God. He shambled to the bathroom and looked at the mirror. That was a 4:15-in-the-morning face if there ever was one, a look at his future if the next fifty years went wrong. If *today* went wrong, if Lacey didn't come back. He swung the medicine cabinet open for aspirin, and halfway through its arc the mirrored door caught a reflection of something, a blond head turning swiftly away, the white edge of an arm and a hand.

"Lacey?" He turned to look back into the bedroom.

He'd have heard her car if she'd come home. He swung the mirrored door again, and there it was, the slash of fair hair and a pale arm. What did the mirror see? In the bedroom, dim and watery light spilled from the bathroom. Maybe the window's white blinds had caught the bathroom's cast-off light and reflected it blond and white. It could be nothing else. Over the last week, he'd been careful not to leave clothes lying around, after giving himself a shock by glimpsing a white shirt and seeing it as a body curled in a chair. This was a small house, but too big to live in alone.

He swung the mirror. It had to be the blinds. He couldn't keep his mind from slipping to the living room, the furniture with feet, creeping around in the dark. . . . He turned on the bedroom light and stood in the doorway to reach the hallway light switch. That was better. He needed a remote control that would turn on all the lights together. Four thirty. If he wanted to be at Spinet Cove by midmorning, he'd better quit daydreaming.

He hurried downstairs and put an English muffin in the toaster and three frozen sausage patties in the microwave. With breakfast in progress, he ran back up the stairs to toss a few things in a garment bag. Then down the stairs, slipping a little on the fourth step from the bottom; he caught the banister and bumped down the last three steps on his heels. Oh, that hurt, it jarred his teeth. He rubbed his jaw with both hands, just behind and under his ears, and what was that in his driveway, some immovable shadow?

The toaster popped. Eric made his sandwich: strawberry jam on the bottom muffin, sausage, a dribble of maple syrup, the second sausage, more strawberry jam, the third sausage, and wasabi mustard on the top muffin. Courtroom breakfast, his favorite, greasy and hot and spicy and sweet. What was in the driveway, blocking his exit?

He opened the front door. A beige car was pulled right across his driveway. He could see the tire tracks where it had driven across his grass. It was parked with its passenger door four inches from his back bumper. He'd never be able to get out.

Eric finished his sandwich, went back inside for his cell phone, and walked over to the beige car. He rapped on the driver's window. "Hey," he said. "You can't park here."

The beige car was greenish in the security light from Eric's porch, its windows dark as mirrors. For a moment, he was certain it was empty, that it had never been driven and someone had towed and abandoned it here, where it had taken root, never to move again. He rapped harder. Something moved in the dark inward space. "Hey!" Eric said loudly.

The driver's door swung open. Eric stepped back. For the space of five breaths, nothing moved. Then out came a worn sneaker, a denimed leg, a chambrayed arm and side, and the long dim face of Lexington Hall. "I need to talk to you," Lex said.

"What the hell?" Eric closed his hand around his cell phone, so Lex wouldn't see it. *He knows where you live,* Sammie had said. "You can't be here."

"You're my lawyer. I paid for you."

"Harry paid. I'm refunding your retainer," Eric said, and too bad if Floyd didn't like it. Eric would pay it out of his own pocket, anything to get Lex Hall off his driveway.

"You're my lawyer. I need my baby."

Eric took a breath to answer and stopped himself just in time. Never argue with crazy people. Arguing with crazy people makes you crazy. "You have to make an appointment. I can't talk to you here."

"That shiny girl won't make an appointment. She only lets me see the other one. You're my lawyer. I paid for you."

"I am telling you to leave," Eric said, clearly and loudly. A light came on in Harry Rakoczy's house. "Leave my driveway now, Mr. Hall."

Lex Hall's hands came up to his own chest, clutching and twisting the fabric of his shirt, as if he might tear the shirt off or pull it up over his head and hide inside it. "I didn't," he said. "I don't want. I didn't mean to. I didn't."

Eric was sorry. He ignored the feeling. Lex might be a poor sick damaged thing, but compassion was a luxury out of the Miszlaks' budget. Lex's sufferings, Lex's lost child couldn't be Eric's problem. "You have to leave," Eric said. "I'm not your lawyer. You can't come to my house. Go away or I'm calling the cops."

The light in Harry Rakoczy's house moved. The upper dormer light disappeared, and a new light appeared, green and yellow in the stained glass over his front door, then the door opened, and a broad yellow fan opened across Harry's grass. "Who's there?" he called, an old man's timid question in the dark.

Lex howled, wordless, in panic and pain. He jumped into his car and drove away across the Miszlaks' lawn and Harry's, tires grinding and spitting turf, and turned the corner with his lights still off. His car's single voice vanished into the murmur of the neighborhood: dawn air rattling the maples, the highway purring a mile away. Harry Rakoczy's door closed and more of his lights came on, a constellation appearing star by star, until his whole house was lit. Eric armed the security system, locked his house, and began his journey to the sea.

Sammie's illegal copy of Lex Hall's juvenile record lay on the passenger seat. The nine-year-old Andrew Halliday Junior had been taken in by Harry Rakoczy and his wife on his release from the hospital and had spent most of the next nine years in the system, mostly for arson. The last of these convictions came in 1975, when Junior was thirteen. Kid stuff. Backyard campfire that got away was his defense, and taken alone, it might have worked. Taken in context of a new fire every time the kid came home, not so much. In 1976, an assault on Harry Rakoczy's wife, Margaret, and later that year a much more serious attack on his young cousin. Junior Halliday, then fourteen, beat the five-year-old Teddy Rakoczy unconscious with a bag of toy cars. That was the end of his life with the Rakoczys. From then on, he bounced between detention, foster care, and group homes.

At least he'd outgrown arson. As Eric turned onto Austell Road, he surprised himself with the wish that Lex would relapse, that the Miszlaks would come home to a smoking ruin, 571 For-rester Lane burned flat to the ground, nothing left but a big fat check from State Farm. His grandmother's Ukrainian Easter eggs, all his books and clothes, he'd gladly let them go if it meant they could be free of the house and the debt.

He shook the thought away. That kind of thinking—avaricious, dishonest, unscrupulous—had led his parents step by step from undue optimism to creative accounting to outright fraud. He'd set the security system. If the house caught fire, the alarm would go off and the place would be saved, mortgage and all.

Chapter Thirty-eight

LACEY COULDN'T FIND THE BABY. She had laid him down on a towel so she could pick up a shell, just a few yards away along the beach. When she looked back, how flat was the sand, flat as still water barely shivering, with a dull gray surface and a yellow light floating on it. That was the towel. Where was the baby?

He was too little to crawl, too young to run away. The sand lay flat as the sea, and between sea and sand, the foam stitched and stitched again an endless seam perpetually torn, threadbare, ragged, beaded with tiny fish swirling up in the ripples and flicking themselves off the sand as the water pulled back. She'd left him in the dry sand, but the towel was wet.

"Where are you?" she said.

"Here."

It was Drew who answered her. He was digging with the orange plastic shovel. He wore black trunks patterned with white palmetto silhouettes, and he pushed his sunglasses to the top of his head, pushing the hair off his summer-brown face. "You left me, but I found you."

"I'm sorry, baby, I had to go."

"Everybody leaves me. Nobody cares. I'm all alone, all alone, all alone!" His voice rose higher; each word sounded again and again, hanging and beating in the air like wings, a flailing white storm, *alone, alone.*

Lacey pulled her lower lip into her teeth and held it. This could not, could not be. Though she felt the shell's weight in her hands, the sharp sand under her bare feet, even the salt pricking her skin, though the screaming voice whipped around her, though her baby was somewhere on the beach alone, it could not be.

"Alone, alone, alone," Drew wailed, tossing shovelfuls of sand to either side. Each syllable flung itself outward, a fierce white bird, and the white birds whirled up and down and crossed each other, a column, a tower, a cyclone of gulls stooping and rising, fighting over one particular spot on the beach.

The eastern sea turned gold on its far edge. The sun rose, and Spinet Cove's motels made a wall between sea and land, lit here and there as early risers went about their business. There was no wet towel, and the baby was safe inside her, kicking, alive. There was no shell in her hands, though she still felt it.

Her fingernails were clogged with sand. She had blisters on her palms and thin scratches, freshly bleeding, where the broken shells had cut her. She was standing on the beach with the orange shovel at her feet, and the only real thing from the dream was the noise, the towering battle of gulls, every bird in Spinet Cove drawn to one spot. As each gull landed, a dozen others stooped over it and beat it into the air. Lacey had to see what they were fighting over. Some small thing, torn this way and that, shredded in those yellow beaks. Bibbits, what else?

Could gulls dig so deep, or had someone dug down to it, using the orange shovel? Lacey's fingertips were abraded and sore.

There was a smell on her hands—she dug up handfuls of clean sand and splintered shells to scrub her palms clean and ran down to the water to rinse in the sea. Salt burned in every tiny scrape.

Drew was *here*. He'd followed her. Here, to the sea. How was this possible? She hurried up to the motel office, and there at last was Ev Craddock, lying in a recliner with his feet up, watching a shopping channel on the office television.

"Look at this," he said, as if he and Lacey had spent the last hour discussing kitchen gadgets as shown on TV. "The lids and containers are interchangeable." He shook his head, marveling. "The things people think of." His feet were bare, knobby and calloused, and his legs were woolly with old-man fur. He looked like he'd spent half his life climbing mountains barefoot. His wonderful hair fell to his shoulders in broad waves bright as steel. His face was so darkly tanned, he looked mummified.

The woman on television pressed a small device against a valve on the container's lid and explained how the system pulled air out of the container, creating a vacuum seal. Lacey felt a moment of pure longing—how perfect, exactly, *exactly* what she needed, until she remembered she didn't have a kitchen anymore. "Hi," she said, "I'm Lacey Miszlak. We talked on the phone."

"It's off-season. You missed the Clam Festival. There's not much here but the beach. We got miles of it, as much as you want."

Lacey sat in the other chair. On the television, the woman was now demonstrating an automatic folding spatula. "I didn't come for the beach. I need to know what happened on Forrester Lane."

"You can read it on the interweb. Anybody can read it." The woman on television had moved on from the folding spatula and was now demonstrating a small vacuum cleaner on the most unlikely messes: marbles, cocoa powder, modeling clay. It could also suck wasps right out of the air. "I got to get me one of those," Ev said.

"I need to know, because it keeps on happening."

"Been keeping on happening for years. My Tyler, he wasn't the first."

"Who was the first, then? How did it start?"

Ev worked his mouth as if he were chewing a small but tough tangerine. He knew the name; Lacey watched him decide. Every impulse pushed her to speak again, to demand the answer. She bit her lip to keep the words down. Ev grunted and lowered the recliner's footrest. "You think you got away, coming here," he said. "You think you got that baby safe. You ain't got away and that baby ain't safe."

Lacey shook her head. This she could not believe. The baby kicked, and she clutched the amethyst pendant and pressed it hard against her heart. "There has to be something I can do. There's always something."

"My Bethie, she lost a baby for every one that lived. Some blood thing went wrong and they failed. She felt them go, and it hurt her, but you got to take what you got coming. Not every baby can live. You got to let it go. Get away from that house before you start the next one."

"I can't accept that." The baby was viable, Dr. Vlk said. She'd brought him so close, come so far, left Eric to bring the child to a safe place, and now what—*let it go,* like a flawed recipe, toss out the first pancake of the batch and see if the second was better? "I can't do that," she said. She wanted to shout, but her voice had narrowed to a thread.

Ev shrugged. "That's all I got for you," he said.

So he wasn't going to tell her the name of the first child to die in the house. It mattered, she knew; a teacher's first step, when a child had trouble in the classroom, was to find out what had gone wrong at home. Something had gone wrong for Drew. She needed the name, his family's name, or she would never find him.

There was the edge of an idea. Home, school . . . "I need to go online," Lacey said.

Ev gestured at the desk. "You can use my computer. Knock yourself out. Wi-Fi's better here than in the rooms." He shuffled into the front office to start coffee and lay out yesterday's donuts, the free continental breakfast. He left the door open, and a sea wind blew through the room and through Lacey, clearing out the cobwebby hesitation of the last two months. She was a teacher. She knew how to find things out. It took her all of fifteen seconds: a website called myoldyearbook.com, whose users uploaded yearbooks—their own, their parents', books they found at yard sales and junk shops—searchable by school and year.

No living baby since 1972. Lacey searched for *Burgoyne Elementary 1972* and six yearbooks came up, one of them the Burgoyne in Greeneburg. She scanned the young faces, pausing at every blond head, looking for Matthew, James, or Drew.

Second grade: Matthew Halliday. The colors were old, changed with time, but she thought Matthew's eyes were hazel rather than blue. She moved on to the third-grade pages and hovered over another face. James Halliday. Closer, but Drew was thinner than this. Maybe James Halliday's smile made his cheeks so round. She'd never seen Drew smile like this. Fourth grade, the nine- and ten-year-olds.

Andrew Halliday Junior.

Drew. The name fit, and she had known from her first sight of him that he was small for his age. Among the other fourth graders, he had a young, soft look. He sat very straight against the photographer's blue background, giving a dutiful smile, anxious around the eyes, a careful, conscientious child, smoothly combed. This one turned his homework in on time and volunteered to put the art supplies away.

She cut and pasted the Halliday pictures, e-mailed them to herself, and logged off. The computer screen disappeared in a fiery haze, and she scrubbed at her eyes with a napkin. That sweet, careful child. What happened to him?

"Coffee?" Ev Craddock said. "I got a new pot on. It's the good stuff."

Lacey pulled up the picture of Andrew Halliday Junior. "Is this him?"

"Holy Christ." Ev collapsed on the sofa beside Lacey. "Can't be. That's any kid. Like a regular kid you'd see on the beach."

"Please, tell me what happened. I really need to know."

Ella Dane wandered into the office. "I feel a sense of peace," she announced, "like something good just happened. Like Bibbits is released from earth. Who's that?"

"Please," Lacey said again.

"I did the same as you," Ev said. "Got in the car and drove away. Me and the older kids, Joey and MacKenzie. The cops took Bethie and I ran for it."

"Where'd you go?"

"Camping at Yosemite. Every time I counted, there were three kids in the tent and one of them wasn't mine."

"He must have been there before," Lacey said. She clung to the idea of safety, Spinet Cove as a haven, Drew on the beach a nightmare brought on by the screaming gulls. Her torn hands? Injured by yesterday's burial. "I bet his family went camping. If they went to Yosemite when he was alive, then he could be there with you, right?"

"He talked to me. He was mad at Bethie, said she wouldn't play with him anymore. So I took Joey and MacKenzie to Vegas, got a job working for a landscaping company, put the kids in school. Bethie was on trial, and I went back one time to testify. I thought he, Drew, I thought he'd stay with her, but he followed me back to Vegas. He started riding in my truck. Got mad every time I picked the kids up from school. MacKenzie was six."

"Did you start doing things without knowing?"

"I'm allergic to peanuts. He wanted a banana split. I watched him eat it. Woke up in the hospital with a tube in my throat, turned out I'd eaten the thing myself, all those peanuts on top. It was just like Bethie said. I watched him eat it, but it was me."

"Me too," Lacey said, rubbing her wrist where Ella Dane had seized it during the game of Chutes and Ladders, feeling again that mingling of rejection and recognition when Drew's hand became her own.

"I sent the kids to Bethie's parents in Saskatchewan, and I stayed in Vegas with Drew till he left me, then I came here. Started a landscaping business, bought this place when I retired. He"— he tapped Andrew Halliday's face on the computer screen—"*this* kid was never here. Not with me. You seen him here?"

"Maybe."

She wanted to deny it. It was the tide—they'd buried Bibbits below the tide line, and the waves had exhumed him and left him for the gulls. The tide, not Drew.

"You think you got away, running away from the house? You ain't got away till he lets you go. Ten years he stayed with me in Vegas till he faded. Dimmed out, like when you lose a radio signal, driving. There were old people in the house those years, no kids, he wasn't interested in them, but when they died and a young family moved in, must have been early nineties, he got onto them and forgot about me." The telephone rang, and he went into his office.

Ella Dane sat next to Lacey and hugged her. "Baby, I'm so sorry," she said.

"There's got to be something I can do," Lacey said. But she had already done what she could do, in getting out of the house. It had cost her everything, and it wasn't enough. If Drew had reached the Craddocks in Nevada, she had nowhere to run. Ella Dane's crystals and candles had done nothing to protect her—or maybe they had; she was still pregnant, and she'd carried the baby all the way to viability, which was more than Greeley Honeywick had done. "Or is there something you can do?" she said.

"There might be rituals," Ella Dane said. "I've never done anything like that, but I can find out. I talked to Jack McMure when I went to Columbia for the pictures. . . . We'd have to go back to the house. You need to know who he was, and how he died, and why he can't rest. You need to know everything about him. And you have to be completely sure you've got the name right, that's what Jack says, otherwise it makes them mad. We'll have to go back to Greeneburg. Jack told me you have to face him where he's strongest. Can you do that?"

"I'll have to," Lacey said.

Going back to the house meant going back to Eric; a ritual in the house meant Eric would know everything. Oh, how he'd hate it; there was no coming back from that. It was the end of their marriage. The child moved under her skin. Someday he would be fourteen years old, sulky and angry, resenting her for everything she had done (things she hadn't even done yet), as cruel to her as she had been to Ella Dane. He would never be grateful. He would hate her for the divorce, as she had hated her mother for the loss of Grandpa Merritt. *I did this to save your life.* Sometime in those years, thirteen, fourteen, fifteen, he would leave her to live with Eric, happy to be free of his crazy mother. Her eyes were hazy with tears, and Drew's nearness prickled all over her skin; he was thinking of her, paying attention, reaching out. There was no time.

Chapter Thirty-nine

WHAT HE WOULD SAY TO LACEY: he planned it all the way down, four hours alone in the car, not even listening to the radio. He thought through his words and said them out loud, sometimes gesturing with his right hand. What he would say to Lacey—he would speak reasonably, which was the one thing none of his clients did, however often they were deposed; they *just wanted to tell her* or *needed to make her understand*; they never meant to hurt anybody, they *only wanted to talk*.

He only wanted to talk to her. He listed his points of argument:

First, that the life of a single mother was hard, hard on the mother and harder on the child, and she of all people knew that.

Second, that she needed him; although yes, she had supported him through law school, he had dragged her through her education degree, and she would never have passed her certification tests without his help.

Third, that there was nothing wrong with their house, except the ceiling in Ella Dane's room, and he would ask Dr. Vlk to recommend a psychiatrist.

Fourth, that everybody knew there was no such thing as a haunted house, especially if it had vinyl siding.

Fifth, did she think he had time for this?

Strike that.

Fifth, that a baby needed a father.

Sixth, that Lacey was barely competent to survive on her own, let alone take care of a baby, and her mother was even worse, and that if Eric went to court for custody, he'd have no trouble finding witnesses as to the character of the Kendall women.

Seventh, that he didn't want to spend another night alone, because he couldn't sleep. The house whispered.

Eighth, that he loved her.

Ninth, please come home.

A list of ten would be cleaner, but that was all he had. There were flaws in the progressive logic of his thoughts, but it would have to do. And here was Spinet Cove. What a dump. How could people live like this? La Hacienda: red tile roofs and black iron verandas, streaks of rust staining the fake-adobe walls. Whom did they think they were kidding? And why had Lacey come here?

Ella Dane had told him they were in 117, at the end of the row. Now he was here, he forgot his arguments, the structure, the clear reason walking from point to point. If he could remember, she would have to come home, because not even Lacey could disprove his logic, but it was all gone. There she was, in a red sundress, standing in the door of her room and looking out to the beach, where the gulls whirled. He ran across the parking lot before he had time to talk himself into turning around and driving back home.

"Lacey," he called.

She looked at him without surprise. "Okay," she said.

She turned and walked back into the room, leaving the door open, so he followed her in. "I need to talk to you," he said. "Can you please listen?"

"Okay," she said again, in a dull, uninterested tone, as if he had asked her if she wanted a boiled egg. "I'm almost ready."

There was a strange smell in the room, worse than the damp carpet and dirty seashell odors of beach hotels. Maybe some kind of sewer leak. He wouldn't be surprised, in this dump. Lacey's suitcase was on the bed, packed—if you could call it packing; she had just flung everything in and mashed it down—and ready to go. He'd caught up with her just in time. Where would she go? Probably she herself had no idea. "There's nothing wrong with our house," he said, remembering one of his arguments.

"If you say so," she said. "It doesn't matter now, anyway."

He remembered the eighth and ninth points of his argument. "I love you," he said. He took her hand. "Please come home."

"Okay," she said, in the boiled-egg voice. She looked at his hand, and he let go.

"What?" he said.

"I said okay. I'll come home. I'm getting ready, I'm packed. I just need a bath."

He had to agree: she really did need a bath. That strange smell in the room hung about her hair and her skin. He caught a wave of it whenever she moved. "I can ask Ella Dane to leave if you don't want her around," he offered, as if she had refused and he needed to bargain with her.

"No, I want her."

Feeling that something was required of him, he took her hand again. It lay in his as cold and wet as a pork chop, and he shivered, rubbing her palm to bring some life into her touch. "I'm glad you're coming home," he said. "I love you."

She snatched her fist out of his palm and clutched one hand over the other between her breasts. "Yes," she said, but she wasn't speaking to Eric; she was looking over his shoulder, at the corner of the room. "Yes, I love you, I'm sorry I tried to run away, I shouldn't have done it, I'm coming home." Her voice was dead, flat, like a hostage reading a prepared statement in a language she didn't understand.

"You don't have to sound so enthusiastic about it." He remembered another of his points. "A baby needs a father," he told her.

"Oh." She shrugged and looked away from him. "That baby. I don't want him."

"You're six months pregnant; you can't say you don't want him now!"

"You can have him. I don't want him. I don't love him." She was speaking to the corner of the room again. "Are you listening?" she said, and now he heard a thick urgency in her voice. "Can you hear me? I don't want him, I don't love him. Go home." She went into the bathroom. "I mean it," she called. Water gushed behind the door. "I don't want him. Go home."

That was the noisy tumble of bathwater, not a shower. "The doctor said you're not supposed to take hot baths," Eric said.

"It's not hot. I need a bath. Could you go? I'll follow you."

He remembered another thing he'd meant to tell her. "The new debit cards came yesterday," he said. "I got a cash advance from Discover to pay off the overdraft. I'm leaving your card by the sink."

"Fine."

Eric collected his handfuls of logic. Since she had agreed to come home, there was no further need to convince her, yet he felt she was unpersuaded, unwilling; she was coming home as a captive, resigned to imprisonment for a while, until the chance for escape came again. What had he ever done to her, that she should see him like this? "I love you," he said to the bathroom door. "Please come home."

No answer except the water. He thought she was crying and had turned the water up so he wouldn't hear. He tried the bathroom door: locked. He should break it in, pull her out of the bath or get in there with her, and take her face in her hands and make her look at him; he should ask her and ask her and ask her, until she told him the truth.

But he recognized this feeling. Lex Hall when he threw the camera through Jeanne's window must have felt exactly this. This was the feeling of the moment before *going too far*. His clients said, *I had to make her understand. I had to make her listen to me. I had to make her tell me the truth.* Nothing good ever began with *I had to make her.*

He had to make Lacey tell him the truth. Not to break through a locked door, no, that was going too far. "I'll see you at home," he said. He hated the weakness in his voice, but this was all he could do for her now, so he did it. He didn't wait for her answer. He closed the door loudly and revved his engine a few times outside room 117, so she would hear his car and know he was leaving.

All the way back to Greeneburg, he thought about what he should have said. If she didn't want the baby, why get pregnant in the first place? If she thought he would live with a wife who wouldn't sleep in his bed, and who gave him her hand like a piece of dead meat, she could think again. If she was just going to turn around and come back home, why had she left? If she wanted a week at the beach, she only had to say so.

Yet he was the one who had left the marriage bed. When she had to move downstairs, he bought her a twin mattress and stayed up in the bedroom, alone.

I love you, please come home. No, he'd said that. She was coming home, but nothing was settled, nothing was finished. He had no idea what to do next.

Chapter Forty

LACEY LOOPED AN ELASTIC around her hair. She squeezed a
pouch of motel shampoo into the bath, and the water battered it
into foam. She hadn't had a real bath since July, when Eric made
a list of things pregnant women shouldn't do. No soft cheese,
deli meats, sushi—not a big sacrifice there—no horseback riding,
skiing, skydiving, or trampolines—really—but she missed the
hot baths.

She turned the water toward cool. She liked a bath tingling
hot, but for the baby's sake, her someday child with sun in his
hair, her future teenage ingrate who would tell her he hated her,
she cooled the water until it was like a swimming pool in August,
not hot enough to melt the grease off her skin, the way she liked
it. She rubbed the hotel soap into lather and scrubbed her skin
red, and still the smell of Bibbits crawled on her.

Eric had smelled it, too. She'd seen the disgust in his face. He
said he loved her, please come home, and it must have cost him
something to speak so plainly, to open himself. She loved him
too, abstractly, as a fact she would think about later, when she
had time. He could live without her. The baby couldn't.

Ev Craddock saved his children by sending them away. She

could save the baby by giving him up, but she'd have to leave the baby with Eric and take Drew with her. If Drew would come with her. If he could. He could leave the house; how long would he stay away? If he went back and found another parent, another child, Eric taking care of the baby alone, how long before Drew demanded Eric's attention? He followed the Craddocks to Nevada, until a family moved in with children. That must have been CarolAnna's people, and after that, the Honeywicks.

If she divorced Eric and forced him to sell the house, if she gave up custody so he would take the baby and move, she could keep Drew attached to her long enough for Eric to get the baby away. Would Eric give up the house and go, stubborn as he was? Even though he called it their starter house, he might dig in his heels and insist on keeping it.

She could always try explaining it to Eric. Like *that* would work.

Just now, there was Drew, a shadow on the pebbled glass of the shower door. She'd known he was coming, and here he was. Tears rushed up. She splashed hot foaming water on her face and cleared her throat. Happy voice. "Hey. I know you're there," she said.

He slid the door back in its tracks. It moved and she saw his fingers come around its edge, she saw the silhouette behind the glass reveal itself as a naked child with a towel around his waist. She saw her own hands floating in the water, and yet, whose hand was on that door—her own hand, moving by his will in a gesture she could neither feel nor see? She swirled the water. The bubbles parted and closed, leaving a seam of finer bubbles where her hand passed. Even as she felt the water's resistance, the shower door slid open. Drew used her mouth to eat cookies, her hand to move the game piece and to attack Ella Dane with the broken plate, but he'd wrecked Ella Dane's room on his own, while she was downstairs, with Ella Dane her witness. Even if she could keep him out of her body and mind, she wouldn't be safe from broken furniture and flying glass.

"I heard what you said to him," Drew said.

"I know you did. I saw you. Don't you want to go home?"

"About the baby. You said you don't want him."

Lacey shrugged. She pulled the shampoo foam around herself, building islands of modesty. Her belly mounded up, a crayon color, Strawberry Cream. "I'm not going to be able to take care of him, am I? Not if I'm with you."

Drew smiled, bright and happy, the look of the little boy in the Burgoyne Elementary yearbook. "You won't leave me?"

"Never."

"You'll stay with me?"

Lacey took a breath as if it were her last, the sweet bubble-scented air. Drew was in the water already; he was inside her, cold on the underside of her skin. If she made this promise, she had to mean it. He would sense a lie.

"Always," she said. "As long as you want."

There was a flicker, a leap, and now the shower door was closed at her head and opened at her feet, next to the taps, although neither door visibly moved. Lacey shuddered in the cooling bathwater. Another soaping, and then she'd wash her hair, and maybe the smell would be gone.

"If you don't want the baby," Drew said, and she felt his warm hand on her belly, though he appeared to be standing in the bath, beside the taps, "he can go away."

The small invisible hand pressed, and the baby kicked. "Too

late," Lacey said lightly. "He's too big. I'd bleed and die, and then you'd be alone." The hand lifted. "It's only a couple of months. Eric can take the baby, and I'll stay with you."

"You were crying."

"There was soap in my eyes."

"You love him. You love them both, your husband and your baby, you do; they always do. Nobody ever loves me best."

"Yes, yes, I love them," Lacey said. No lie was possible now. "It doesn't matter, don't you see? I promise I won't leave you. I might have to leave the house, but you can come with me."

"It's my house. Why would you leave it?"

"Honey, I might have to. I might not be able to stay."

Drew's hand flashed, and the shower was on, full strength and steely cold, rods of water beating against her. She gasped and covered her face. "Andrew, listen! If I have to divorce Eric, I might not be able to keep the house. I might not get a job right away."

"What did you call me?"

"Andrew." She reached for the side of the tub. Everything was slick with a layer of soap, and her hand found only the glass door. "I found your picture on the Internet. You're Andrew Halliday."

"No, I'm not!" She could not see him through the water in her eyes, but she felt his hands on her ankles. His hands were hot, and larger than she had thought. She turned her face out of the streaming shower and caught a breath, and then he pulled her legs up, and her head slipped down, and the bathwater closed over her head.

Lacey opened her eyes. The shower pierced the water, every thread of the stream bringing a diamond-chain of bubbles. She saw Drew, a dark tall shape hundreds of miles away, and then the soap burned in and she closed her eyes. She kicked. Drew's grip yielded with the kick, but the upward pull never faltered, and his hands slid from her ankles to her knees; his hands circled her shin at the thin spot just below the knee. She kicked again, and her right ankle struck the tap, a numbing, stunning blow, a pain that shot all the way up to her hip. The soapy water stung in her nose.

She had time, many many seconds, before she began to drown, and Drew wanted her alive to take care of him. If he was holding her feet, he must be standing in the bath: he must be standing between her legs, holding her knees straight up. She reached her right arm down and sideways, straining along her body, grasping for his ankle. If she could pull him off balance—she felt only the bathtub's nubby floor.

Her chest caught and heaved, her lungs straining to force her mouth open. She stretched her neck and raised her forehead out of the water, not her nose—the bath was too deep. She squinted through the shower and saw nothing, nobody was there, no visible hands grasped her knees. Anyone walking into the room— Ella Dane, where was she?—would see a woman bizarrely drowning herself, legs raised and torso sunk.

Red lights crept inside her closed eyes. She released a bubble of air to soften the pressure on her lungs, and then another bubble. She had seconds, many seconds left, before she blacked out and opened her mouth underwater. Many seconds. Drew's hold was elastic and relentless. She could move her legs forward and back, even bend her knees within a small range; she simply couldn't bring her feet down.

She kicked again, and something drove in between the first two toes on her left foot, a shockingly hard, metallic blow. She gasped water in and clamped the back of her tongue upward against her throat to clear her mouth, and what was that thing, what had struck her, some part of the bathtub's machinery, not the tap—her fading mind cried out *the lever, the drain*. She hit it again, curled her toes around it, and pulled the lever down.

The water flowed along her body, and the sound of the pipes' starving gulp echoed through the walls of the tub. The shower came down as strong as ever, but Ev Craddock kept his drains clear, bless his heart, and Lacey's wet skin chilled in the air as the tub drained. She had many seconds left, four or five seconds, long enough for a lifetime, and then she was able to lift her head and take a breath of half water, half air.

Her feet fell into the tub. She sat up and turned off the shower. A breath and another breath, and she began to cough, deep shattering coughs that shook the baby. She tried to take careful, shallow breaths that wouldn't irritate her outraged lungs, but she was full of water, she had breathed it and swallowed it, water and soap and Drew's wild rage. She dragged herself to the toilet in time to vomit it all out, the soap and the foam, Eric and Drew and the house waiting in the hills, until nothing came but clear threads of slime. She flushed the toilet and leaned forward, pressing her forehead against the cool tank furred with clean water. And he loved her; this was what he did for love.

Chapter Forty-one

LACEY WRAPPED HERSELF in the big motel towel and set the hair dryer to low, hot, four inches from her left ear. She was safe for a while. Drew had a hit-and-run temper, like so many damaged children. She had a few hours, perhaps even a day, before he sought her again.

She hated the feeling of cold water worming down her back, and the water in her head was worse. Soap burned in her throat; her sinuses were full of sharp gravel, and the taste of bathwater rolled over itself, a hard slick thing. The hair dryer's warmth spread in her ears, softening and opening the constricted tubes.

When she was little and had earaches, Grandpa Merritt held her on his lap with her mother's hair dryer inches from her head. She tilted against his left shoulder while the warm air flowed into her right ear. He would tell her how when he himself was small, his own grandfather cured his earaches with hot smoke, lighting his pipe and softly blowing into the young Grandpa Merritt's ear.

It had made the child Lacey laugh to think of her grandpa as a little boy with an earache. He laughed too, and his stiff beard bristles scraped along her cheek. His arm tightened and she felt safe, loved and comforted and warm all through.

And then he took those pictures, those and how many others? Lacey turned the hair dryer off. She had been so angry at Ella Dane all these years; if Ella Dane had told her, she would have accepted it. Lacey was suddenly positive that Ev Craddock hadn't told his own children why he'd sent them away. There were no pictures in his office, no graduation caps or wedding gowns, no grandchildren. He saved them, but he lost them.

If they had known he loved them, Drew would have known it, too. Drew could travel, he could show up wherever he wanted. Ev kept his secret to set them free. He built a wall between Drew and his children. He himself was the wall. Ella Dane had kept her secret to preserve Lacey's innocence.

She would have to do the same, if Eric would let her. All the qualities in Eric that had drawn her to him—his honesty, his constancy, the firm architecture of his mind—all these qualities set him against her now, for he would never abandon the child or the house, or believe he couldn't have both. If she left the baby at the hospital, Eric would take him home, and in Drew's house there was room for only one child. She had to get herself into the house, and Eric and the baby out of it.

She had put him through law school, giving her a claim against his future income. If she gave that up, traded it for the house, and let Eric take the baby . . . How many months would he fight to get himself and the baby back into the house? The parent who took the children got the house, mostly. And family law was his specialty.

Or she and Eric could leave the house, rent it out cheap, and make sure the right people took it, a young family with children. Soon, Drew would shift his attention to them. The right family, a mother with a baby girl and a couple of elementary-aged boys, and the Miszlaks could get clean away.

That was life and freedom. That was everything.

"No," Lacey said. She put her hands over her ears, as if it were someone else's idea and she could keep from hearing it. No. Ella Dane had left her father's house, the security of life with Merritt Kendall, on the strength of a handful of Polaroids and a family rumor. She hadn't traded another child's future for Lacey's.

Hadn't she, though? She'd never reported Grandpa Merritt. In Lacey's case there was so little to report, pictures that barely flirted with the line of innocence, but she had cousins who'd been abused and she hadn't encouraged them to turn him in. He'd lived freely in a neighborhood with young families on every side, little girls in swimsuits wherever he looked. Ella Dane saved only her own child. That wasn't enough.

Lacey pictured herself in an apartment, turning on the local news a year from now, settling in the red leather armchair to read *Pat the Bunny* to the baby, her own healthy living child, and the announcer would speak solemnly of the unexpected death of a toddler or a young mother in a Greeneburg neighborhood. The screen would flash to a reporter standing under a tree, and Eric would say, *Isn't that our house? Aren't those our tenants?* She couldn't live with that.

The door opened, and Ella Dane came in, laptop under her arm. "Talking to yourself?" she asked. She scanned the room. "*Are* you talking to yourself, or is he here?"

"He left."

"You saw him here?"

"He was mad about Eric being here. He touched me."

"Oh, Lacey. I can't handle this alone. We need help."

Lacey nodded, not wanting to describe that lifetime underwater, twenty seconds at most. "He lost his temper for a minute. I'm fine." Ella Dane looked doubtful, and Lacey patted the bed. "Sit with me, Mom."

Ella Dane opened her laptop on the bed. "Look at this; I was online. Downloaded some old articles." She opened a folder on her desktop, selected a newspaper article, and turned her computer so Lacey could read.

It was the front page on April 10, 1972, the day after Andrew Halliday Senior drowned his baby daughter, shot his wife and three sons, and then turned the gun on himself. The picture was the family's formal Christmas portrait, 1971. The wife, Dora, looked about fifteen, slender in her tight-waisted checked dress, the baby a long fall of lace. Lacey recognized Dora, the tame trammeled adult self of the wild girl with the violin, Harry Rakoczy's sister. She was not looking at the camera, but down and away from the descending row of freshly combed little boys, down and inward to the unseen Dorothy. Her eyelids were long and pale, her cheeks and lips uncolored, her thick light hair pulled back off her face. No makeup, no hairstyle for this formal picture. How hard did a woman have to work to wear that narrow-waisted dress, with her fourth child not six months old? And then she didn't even put on lipstick.

Harry knew. Dora Halliday was Harry's sister. He knew everything and always had. Lacey filed that for later.

The row of boys sat with their hands in their laps and their knees together. None of them smiled, though the youngest, Matthew, had a smiler's dimples tucked into the creases of his mouth. Andrew Halliday, in a jacket and tie that matched his sons', leaned forward with hands on thighs, legs apart, elbows out, as if caught in the moment of springing from his seat. His hair clung in tense light-colored curls, clipped in polished waves. In 1971, a year of shaggy hair and long sideburns, that haircut made a statement. *Leave me alone. None of your business.* A military haircut, though the article said he'd taught American history at East Greeneburg High for the last six years and mentioned no military service. He stared straight at the camera, eyes open, brows fiercely lowered.

He was a teacher. Like Greeley Honeywick, like Lacey. How many teachers had lived at 571 Forrester? Teachers like Andrew Senior, young mothers like Dora. He'd drawn Dora's portrait, so he was an artist, too. Lacey knew, her knowledge both tentative and tactile, that every family had included either a teacher or a young mother, and someone who could paint or draw. It was like feeling her way down a stairway in the dark. Knowledge came piece by piece; she tested each piece and found it true. Drew gathered his family, time after time, and every time the family failed him.

Andrew's portrait of Dora reminded Lacey of that first day. Harry Rakoczy had seen her sketchbook; CarolAnna had mentioned the pregnancy; Lacey herself had told him she was a teacher. Harry *knew,* he'd always known.

"He looks like a murderer, that man," Ella Dane said. "Those angry eyes."

To Lacey, Andrew Senior looked shockingly young. Andrew Junior was nine, but people started families younger back then. He was thirty, thirty-two, maybe. He had a hot, eager look, full of energy, an odd match for the modest Dora, so saintly and pale. The scrawling energy of Andrew's portrait of Dora with her violin, in Harry's living room—that was Andrew's spirit, not Dora's. Or maybe she got quieter after she married him, maybe she put her violin away.

He drowned the baby in the bathtub, as Beth Craddock drowned Tyler, as Lacey had almost drowned herself (and Bibbits in his bath, that must have been Drew testing how far he could push her; it had seemed so urgently reasonable at the time). The article didn't say where Andrew Halliday had shot the family, but Lacey knew. Dying, they fell down the stairs. Greeley Honeywick fell, pushed by Drew using someone else's hand, probably her husband. Others had fallen, no doubt, many others. The question was not how many had died, sucked into the Hallidays' deaths, but how she could save little not-Merritt, and herself and Eric, too.

"The article says one of the children was found alive," Lacey said. If she could find that person, James or Matthew, and ask him to talk to his brother . . . Hard to find him by the name alone; there must be thousands of Hallidays named James or Matthew.

Ella Dane shrugged that away. "Shot in the head. One of them might have lingered a day or two. I e-mailed Jack McMure in Columbia. He's been doing spiritual realignment of houses. He'll come up to Greeneburg tomorrow and have a look. Three hundred bucks for the consult, and he'll tell you what the therapy costs. Couple thousand."

"Eric will never go for that. It's so much money." If only they hadn't bought that furniture. If they'd done a thousand other things, if they'd bought a different house, if Eric had taken a different job, if only. "Did you tell him what the problem is?"

"Sometimes tragic events leave imprints. Or there are demonic beings—they're, what does he call it, a concentrated impulse of nature; they destroy buildings."

Every impulse of nature was against houses, every gnawing animal, every tunneling root, ice and rust, wind and rain. "Like termites," Lacey suggested.

"But that's not Drew," Ella Dane said. "He's trapped. Jack

says he's a captive soul turned vicious, like a dog on a chain. He'll keep on hurting people till he finds a way out."

"Out where?"

"Out." Ella Dane waved her hands. "On. Move toward the light, all that. Jack says it's best not to get real specific, in case you get trapped in your own ideas. He says if you can find out what's been done before, that'll save him some time. Anything that other people have tried to get rid of the thing."

Greeley Honeywick had researched the house's history, so she'd know of any past exorcisms, cleanses, cures. Could this work? Calling an expert in to get rid of Drew, as if he were mold, asbestos, lead, any deadly thing that might lie hidden in a secret place—could it work? Clean him out, take the place apart, and rebuild it without him?

She went to Ev's office to e-mail Greeley, and to download directions to Jack McMure's home in Columbia, where she and Ella Dane would meet. It felt good to have something to do. While she waited for her e-mail, she pulled up the picture of the Halliday family. Not Drew, not the doomed children, not the father with his hands on his thighs ready to spring to his feet—it was the mother she wanted. Dora. That ivory face with the downcast eyes.

She could draw that. It could be beautiful. She felt the shape in her hands. Layers of oil pastels, white over yellow, green over white, building up to that translucent glow, like pure white soap. Those thick curved eyelids, a shadow of blue hinting at the eyes. She'd have to stop on the way home to pick up some more colors.

Chapter Forty-two

ERIC WAS HOME BY FOUR. Lacey should have been only a few minutes behind him. Half an hour to finish checking out of the motel. Four thirty, five, six. No Lacey. She didn't even call.

At 6:12, the phone rang. Eric grabbed it and said, "Where the hell are you?"

"Home in my little beddie," Sammie Vandermeijn said, "all by my lonesome." Scuffling and laughter, and she added, "Well, Floyd's here, but he don't count. Want to come over? Floyd'll put his pants on."

"Lacey's coming home."

"How happy you sound."

"She should've been here two hours ago." Eric cleared his throat. That thickness was congestion, maybe allergies, nothing more. All alone, a foreign thought kept running through his mind: she had left him all alone, gone on without him and never looked back; they all did the same thing in the end, they all left. "She hasn't called."

"Come on over," Sammie said. "I've got a pound cake and strawberries. We'll pour brandy on it and set it on fire. I *love* setting food on fire. Floyd bought me a fire extinguisher and he wants to try it out; he's so romantic, you can't imagine. Don't leave me alone with the old goat, or I'll have to spray him down."

The foreign thought rattled on. She would leave him, like all the rest. He would be alone without lights or food or voices, until people came again, alone, alone, alone. He pushed it away. Self-pity never helped anyone. Lacey's car turned into the driveway, followed by Ella Dane's, with an unknown head in the passenger window, so it wasn't Lacey's fault, Ella Dane had made her stop somewhere. "She's home. I've got to go."

"We'll save some pound cake for you. Maybe brandy, too, if you're lucky."

Lacey came in; she still had that bruised look around her eyes. Her week at the beach hadn't done her any good at all. He felt a pang of hunger for the flaming strawberry pound cake. No part of Lacey's attention was on him as she kissed him, and already she was moving away, pulling him toward the front door. "This is my mom's friend, Jack McMure. He's an architectural thera-pist."

He would have known the man for a friend of Ella Dane's, even without the introduction. He looked about three hundred years old, or a badly aged seventy, bald on top with a fringe of hair starting level with the tops of his ears. He'd grown out the fringe to its full length and tied it in a three-foot-long braid, thin as a pencil, with found objects tied into it: bottle caps, twist ties, candy wrappers. Birthmarks and age marks stained the top of his head in a pattern like a map of Indonesia.

"How nice to meet you," Eric said. "There are some motels on Austell Road."

"Oh, Eric," Lacey said, with disappointment in her voice, "he's here to help us."

Jack McMure whirled with his arms outspread. He was wearing some kind of poncho, handmade out of—could it be?—duct tape. "We don't need help," Eric said, hoping Sammie and Floyd would save a few strawberries. "We need to be alone."

"We're not alone," Lacey said. "We never have been. That's the whole problem."

"I know." Eric pulled her into the living room, leaving Ella Dane and her crazy friend to do whatever they were doing, walking up the stairs and banging on the walls. "I thought you needed your mom, and you told me she made you crazy and I didn't listen. We'll tell her she has to go." If Lacey would be reasonable. That was all he wanted.

"We've never been alone here. There's someone in the house. A ghost, okay?"

"No such thing," he said.

"People have died here. A whole lot of people. A whole family called—"

"Halliday," he said, and kissed her on the nose, ignoring her sudden stiffness. "Yes, it was terrible. We wouldn't have bought the house if we'd known. But it's just a house. Those people died a long time ago."

She was pushing at him all at once, all elbows and beating hands. "You knew? How long have you known?"

"Couple weeks, I guess. I asked Sammie to find out."

"You knew and you didn't tell me?"

"Why would I tell you?"

"You think you know so much! There's more than one family that had a kid die; how about Beth Craddock, do you know about her? There's this woman, she used to live here, she fell down the stairs—I just talked to her husband. He pushed her, but it wasn't him, it was the ghost. He gets inside people and he makes them do stuff. You're not *listening*."

Chanting came from the stairs now, as Ella Dane and her friend marched up and down. Eric wished he'd listened when Lacey told him she didn't want her mother in the house. "Get those people out of here," he told her.

"They're trying to help."

"That kind of help we don't need."

"It's probably no good. Greeley's kept a list of the things she hears about. This house has been exorcised twice by Catholics and once by Methodists, and once by a guy with a bag full of copperheads. There've been eleven deaths, nobody knows how many miscarriages. Four babies drowned, five kids and two women fell down the stairs—the same things keep happening, over and over."

"People die," Eric said. "People get hurt. About a quarter of pregnancies miscarry; I looked it up when you got pregnant. Who is this Greedy person?"

"Greeley Honeywick. She says the last baby born in this house was Dorothy Halliday." Lacey pulled a wad of paper from her purse. "She e-mailed me at the motel. These are facts. These are things that happened."

"I believe you." That shut her up for a minute. Eric spoke quickly. He had maybe ten seconds to get through before the craziness slammed down again. "People die, people get hurt all the time. Sometimes it happens a lot of times in the same place. That's statistics, it averages out. If you flip a coin a million times, you'll get twenty heads in a row. You don't start thinking you've got a magic coin."

"You think it's *coincidence*?"

"Maybe there's something real," he conceded. Not a chance, but if it kept her rational, he'd allow it. "People fall on the stairs. Maybe the light's bad. We can put in track lighting. Maybe there's something wrong"—he hunted for things that could be wrong with the stairs—"like the steps are uneven, so people keep tripping."

"And the bathtub, all the babies who drowned there? Dorothy Halliday and Tyler Craddock and the others?"

"Nobody's ever drowned in our bathtub. It's brand-new. Harry put it in when he sold the house. Maybe the old one was slippery. You can't look at a place that's had some bad things happen and say it's haunted. Bad things happen everywhere. Is the whole world haunted? That's just insane."

"Okay then."

"Okay then?" This was easier than Eric had expected, and he mistrusted her sudden compliance. "Okay then, what?"

"Okay, so you don't believe in it. But I want Jack to stay with us for a few days. Will you do that for me?"

Eric looked at Jack, who had stopped spinning and was now standing at the foot of the stairs, arms wide, head tilted so far back that the thin braid brushed the back of his knees. He hummed one tone in his throat and another in his nose, shatteringly out of tune. The geometry of the house came clear and Eric saw the walls and floors as a net of transparent wires. Jack McMure stood directly under the bathtub, staring up at it through the floor. The Hallidays had fallen, dead and dying, exactly where he stood. In spite of Eric's own certainty, it made him shudder; and did Lacey know where Jack was standing and where he was looking?

"They died here," Jack intoned. "I'm sensing water, the presence of water."

"Most of them died here." Lacey pointed at the ceiling. "Dorothy died upstairs."

Eric got ahold of himself. He gripped his elbows and pulled them tightly inward. Lacey knew how the Hallidays had died, and she must have told Jack; *the presence of water*—who did the old nut think he was fooling? The house was full of plumbing. Kitchen, bathrooms, sewer lines. It didn't take a psychic, or whatever he called himself, to know there was water nearby. That was an architectural fact. "This is great," Eric said. The psychic started to hum again, the double hum differently tuned, now, so that a third tone trembled into existence. "But I've got work to do. If you don't mind, I'll head down to the office." Maybe Sammie's offer of flaming strawberry pound cake was still open.

"It must be purified," Jack said.

"Will that get him out?" Lacey asked.

"No. It will pull his attention to us. We can open the way out and release him. I'll need to burn herbs."

"Herbs?" Eric asked suspiciously.

"Sage mostly," Ella Dane said.

"I need the spirit's name," Jack said. "His name in the smoke will . . ."

They waited for the end of the sentence, but that seemed to be all. "Drew," Lacey said into the silence. "Andrew Lexington Halliday Junior."

Eric laughed. Lacey and Ella Dane looked at him with their eyebrows drawn down and the lips tight; he had never realized how much they looked alike. "Something's funny here?" Lacey said. "I'm trying to save the baby's life and something's *funny*?"

"Is Andrew Halliday your ghost? Are you sure?"

"Yes."

"He's the one who's been drowning babies in the bathtub and pushing people down the stairs all these years? Andrew Junior."

"Yes, I'm sure; yes, it's him, yes!"

Lacey shook the wad of paper at him, and he took it, unfolded the pages, and folded them again with square corners and sharp edges. Immediately, he felt better. "Well, that really is funny. Because . . ." Eric looked at all three of them, Lacey's crazy mother, Lacey herself who would be just that crazy someday and was halfway there already, and the foul old nutcase the two of them had disinterred from under some moldy rock. "Because doesn't somebody have to be dead to make a ghost?"

"Yes, and so?"

"Andrew Junior's not dead."

"But . . ." Lacey gaped at him. "But it's him. It's Drew. One of the brothers survived, I tried to find him on the Internet but there are too many Hallidays out there; I haven't tracked him down yet. The one in the house is Andrew."

Eric pressed his advantage. "Andrew Junior's the one who survived. He grew up, changed his name, got married, had a baby. He's crazy as a weasel on meth, but he's not dead. He's my client. You met him at Harry's house. Andrew Lexington Halliday Junior is Lex Hall."

While they stared, Lacey and Ella Dane round eyed and soft mouthed, Jack with his lower lip folded over the upper as if he had no teeth, Eric turned on his heel, grabbed his briefcase, and left the house, not even slamming the door. Let them think about that, before they started burning their herbs. Sage mostly. Yeah, right.

Chapter Forty-three

JACK MCMURE SAID it was too late to turn back once the ritual was begun; they'd have to continue without knowing Drew's real name. Lacey trailed after them as they hunted Drew through the house. She thought they were wasting their time. She felt emptiness in each room. The rooms seemed taller, thinner too, as if the whole house had been drawn upward and narrowed. There were fewer shadows and less color. The burgundy leather in the living room dulled to a rusty brown, and the bright gold floors were a lusterless orange beige. Silence pressed in, so that she had to cough just to make sure she hadn't gone deaf.

Ella Dane and Jack were upstairs. "Mom?" Lacey said. She climbed the stairs boldly, right up the middle of the steps without even touching the banister, so confident were her feet. "Where are you?"

"Bathroom," Ella Dane answered. All the upstairs doors were open. In the center of each room, a smudge of herbs burned in a Mason jar. The herbs were mostly sage, with something brighter, maybe lavender, and a thicker, clotting scent that she decided to believe was not marijuana.

In the bathroom, Ella Dane looked up from her Mason jar,

cigarette lighter in hand. The center of this room was beside the bathtub, where a woman would kneel when washing a child. Or drowning one. Aching knees on the hard tile floor. Beth Craddock knelt there, holding Tyler underwater. And Andrew Halliday Senior with Dorothy?

Inconceivable. She couldn't make herself believe it. Men didn't drown babies. A father who decided the time had come wasn't afraid of blood. Andrew Senior shot the rest of them, but not the baby. That was a mother's murder.

She saw it as if she had sketched it from a photograph. The image moved from her hands to her mind. Dora Halliday dipped her elbow into the water, testing the temperature. She took off the baby's pink smock, unpinned the cloth diaper, rinsed it in the toilet, dumped it in the bucket, which was empty and smelled of bleach. She washed diapers twice a day, and had done so for the five years between the birth of her first child and the toilet-training of her third, and now she was doing it again. She laid Dorothy in the water, gently as if into bed. Those hands, hands that had played the violin with such ferocious passion, were now water wrinkled and soft and had spent more time cleaning human waste than practicing scales. She looked down, with her heavy white eyelids, her marble mouth so finely curved and yet so hard, and pressed her right hand against Dorothy's face as she lowered her backward and down, under the surface, and an island of bubbles floated across the child's body and rebounded off Dora's arms.

"Lacey!" Ella Dane said.

Lacey remembered her mother calling her, four or five times, from very far away. The bathtub was empty and dry. The baby kicked, and Dora Halliday's hand spread over the small chest and held her down—the baby kicked, and Lacey's own hand was spread over her belly, pressing too hard against the life inside her.

"Lacey!" Ella Dane pulled Lacey's hand away. "What is it?"

"I saw something." No. She had recalled it, not as her own memory, as if someone had told her *this is what happened.* "It was the beginning of the murders. I think maybe the mother killed the baby. Does that make a difference?"

Jack McMure said, "The name would make a difference." He leaned over the herbal smoke and wafted it toward his face. The smoke seemed stronger in here than in the other rooms, both the bright and the dark odors more intense, the clouds white and swirling, like cream poured into water, because this room was smaller.

Maybe some other reason.

"It's James or Matthew," Lacey said.

"We'll have to keep calling him Drew, since that's the name he chose," Ella Dane said.

"This is the fountainhead," Jack McMure said.

"Does he mean there are ghosts in here?" Lacey asked.

"Imprints," Jack said.

Lacey looked at her mother, who explained, "Influences, memories, stains."

Like a young woman, her saint's face rigid as her youngest child breathed water under her hand? A memory, a stain. Lacey stared into the smoke until her eyes smarted, trying to read messages in the white cloud.

The front door slammed. "Eric's back," Lacey said. As she left the bathroom, the fresher air in the hallway struck her like a shock of cold. She coughed and clutched the door. It wavered like cloth under her hand, and the whole house twisted, sucked upward into the smoke's plume, pressed down like a baby's head under a mother's hand. The door slammed again, and Lacey hurried toward the stairs. "Eric?" she said.

The entrance was empty, the welcome rug kicked to the side and crumpled. The door turned on nothing and crashed shut. Lacey walked down, not letting herself hurry.

She stood in the entrance, where the floor was a pool of gold. She looked up to the porthole window, a black circle, starless night quartered by the white frame. She had expected a moon. The front door opened to darkness. No light shone from Harry's windows across the grass, no windows gleamed from across the street, yellow from floor lamps or blue from televisions. The house's light stopped at the threshold. Lacey reached out, with a hand so cold that it felt like someone else's, and closed the door. Drew stepped out from behind it as it swung across the dark.

He glowered at her. He was so angry, and yet so small; at that moment she could not fear him in spite of everything. "You came back," he said.

"I told you I would."

"You said you loved me, but it was all a lie."

Lacey knew angry children. They would do the worst thing they could, but mostly she could cozen them out of their rage. And then there was Allan Montego. Two weeks into her first year, he refused, utterly and passionately refused, to take a note to his parents about his homework. She insisted and demanded, she asked him *why, why?*, and he swung his book bag against the Smartboard and cracked the screen. Although she argued on his behalf at the hearing, he was expelled, because it wasn't his first violent act, but it was her fault. She had pushed him farther than he could go.

And now she had pushed Drew. Allan Montego broke the

Smartboard. Drew could kill her. She said, "Are you Andrew Halliday?"

Drew opened his mouth. Starless night cracked open the creases of his lips, darted up the smile lines into his eyes, blackened and spread in the blue veins of his forehead. The blackness split and swallowed him, reached up and over Lacey like a raised fist, a tall wave on the point of breaking, the vertigo of nightmare balanced on the point of swallowing her forever. It shattered on her, sank into her body, pulled itself upward and out of her, and was gone. She spun in its wake, turned to follow the direction it had taken.

It was the thing that had fallen past her, the bloody screaming thing, now racing up the stairs, where Ella Dane was waiting with Jack McMure, ready to banish it from the house with— what? Burning herbs, mostly sage? What were they thinking?

She ran up the first five steps, and every muscle tightened, squeezing inward on the baby. She fell forward on her knees, grabbing for the banister to keep from falling downstairs on her belly. The pain tightened until she thought her spine would crack. Then, when she could bear no more, it sank down, water into sand. The baby kicked against this outrageous assault.

Thirty weeks. Too soon, too young, too small. "Please don't," Lacey said to not-Merritt inside her, not-Merritt not ready to be born. "We haven't bought a crib."

He wouldn't need a crib. He'd sleep in a bright womb of Plexiglas and white plastic. Too soon. Lacey waited for another contraction. The baby rolled. She slipped a hand under her dress to touch the wet spot on her underpants. Blood? No, it was colorless. Amniotic fluid? She sniffed her fingers and laughed. Imagine, that there could be time in her life when wetting herself was good news! She went upstairs on her knees, pausing on each step for balance before moving her right hand to the next banister post.

It took five minutes to get up the stairs. She knew, because she had marked the time of the first contraction on her watch, ready to time the second one when it came. She reached the top of the stairs at 7:21. Tightness rippled across her belly, but it wasn't really a contraction, so she didn't count it.

Just in case she had to tell a doctor, later, she noted the time. Six minutes.

Voices from the bathroom. A man's voice, loud and deep, and a lighter voice in a hurried response. Was Jack making peace with Drew? Could that actually work?

If the child Andrew had survived, then the spirit Drew might be Andrew Senior, a man who had worn a crew cut to teach American history in 1972. What was Jack McMure doing in 1972? Lacey would bet he wasn't wearing a crew cut, or if so, then not by choice. Maybe he and Andrew Senior could talk about it man to man, instead of the way she had tried to talk with Drew, teacher to child. She had to get to them. But the stairs were so steep, and if she stood, she would fall.

Lacey crawled to the first bedroom door and used the door-knob to pull herself up. It felt good to be on her feet, but there was something wobbly about her hips, the joint unlocked. She kept one hand on the wall as she went toward the bathroom.

It was a long walk from bedroom to bathroom, each step a deliberate act. Too quiet—she'd only lain down for a minute. Why hadn't the baby woken her up? The light on the stairs was the golden blond of late afternoon. She'd slept through lunch, slept through the afternoon feeding, slept until it was almost time to start cooking supper, how had she slept so long?

Lacey stopped, pressing her hand against the wall, feeling the texture of the paint against her palm. She looked at her watch, which said 7:23, so she'd only been in the hallway for two minutes, yet she could not shake off this heart-squeezing sense that it was too long, too much time had passed, she was too late. And the porthole window framed a starless night, clouded and moonless darkness, not the flood of late spring sunshine she had seen. Imagined. Not seen. Imagined. Remembered.

"Mom?" she said. So many children had stood outside this bathroom door calling for their mothers. "Ella Dane? What's going on in there?"

The door opened. Smoke twisted out, and Jack McMure roared out of the smoke, shouting in another man's voice, "You did this, you, you, you did this!"

Lacey's hand slid down the wall and she knelt with her hands over her face. "I'm sorry," she wept. "I didn't mean to, I just lay down for a minute, I was so tired!"

"After all I do, six hours a day with those freaks and hooligans, and I come home to this." He carried something in his left arm, pressed against his shoulder and his heart, something small as a cat. A clear stain spread from it, turning his white shirt to glass. She could not stop looking. Soon the stain would sink into him. His skin would fade away, his muscles turn pink, then white, then clear, his ribs would turn to glass and his lungs to water, until only the wild red heart was left, hammering unbearable pain. He grabbed her shoulder and dragged her to the top of the stairs. "Call them," he said.

She shook her head.

"Call them!"

"Junior," she said. "James. Matthew. Can you come here?"

Three boys came out of the smoke. The youngest had a smiler's dimples, even with his face pulled downward in concern and fear. The oldest came slowly, with his hands jammed into his pockets, looking at his feet. The middle child came most fearfully, tucking himself into his older brother's shadow. His black-framed glasses slid down his nose, and he pushed them up and coughed, and then ducked his head, as if the cough were a guilty secret he wished he could deny.

"Your sister is dead." The wet, clarifying stain was a baby's body wrapped in a white towel. Blue lips pulled back from purple gums, blue irises gleaming under the half-shut eyelids. "How did this happen?"

The boys shuffled their feet, all but the oldest, who flashed a glance to the kneeling mother and shook his head.

"She did it." There was a gun in the man's hand and a sense that time had passed. The light in the porthole window had deepened to red. "She put the baby in the bath and then she—lay—down—for—a—nap. She's guilty. Say it."

"Guilty," all three boys muttered, one after the other by age, youngest to oldest.

"But is she guilty alone? Because there's such a thing in the law as a conspiracy. She killed the baby by her laziness, but she didn't do it alone, boys." The baby's hair was dry, now, and one small hand was fisted against her left cheek. "No, you were here, too. And didn't I tell you to help your mother, didn't I tell you all?"

"Yes," they said, oldest and youngest, but the middle boy's answer was an exploding sob.

"Look what you did. All of you did it. All of you."

He held the baby up in front of them. The towel fell off her bare body. In death, she had drawn herself inward, legs and arms folded into the chest, as if she still slept in her mother's body. The wedge-shaped feet were crossed at the ankles. He held her up to show her to them, then he dropped her, threw her down the stairs. "No," the mother said. She heard the three shots, one after the other, but she felt the fourth shot as a surge of white in her mind and body. She fell after the falling children. It was like flying.

Something caught her by her left elbow and shoulder. She cried out, struggled and kicked against it, but it pulled her back, and a panting voice in her ear called a name she did not know, "Lacey, Lacey, Lacey, listen to me!"

The pain pressed harder, a crushing and grinding intensity, and Lacey looked at her watch. Seven forty-eight, and if the first one started at 7:16, that meant, what? For the moment, she couldn't remember how to subtract, she couldn't remember anything. The pressure eased, and she said, "Thirty-two minutes."

"Lacey, is it you?"

Lacey was leaning against her mother's body on the top step. "Is what me?"

"Are *you* you? Because you and Jack said awful things— Jack! We've got to call an ambulance. If I let you go, are you going to throw yourself down the stairs?"

"Why would I do that?"

"Stay here and don't move." Ella Dane pulled Lacey backward down the hallway to the bedroom door. "I'm getting my cell phone."

"Where's Jack? What happened?" Lacey hadn't felt this disoriented since coming out of anesthesia when her wisdom teeth were pulled. As then, she felt a sense of weird loss, something hollowed out that had been solid, some pain already present though not yet perceptible. She touched her belly, and the baby pushed her hand.

Ella Dane ran into her bedroom and came out with cell phone

in hand. "Let me call 911 first. We need an ambulance! 571 Forrester Lane. My friend fell down the stairs." She covered the phone with her hand and said to Lacey, "He started yelling at you. Saying things that didn't make sense. You were both falling. I grabbed you."

"Did I push him?" Lacey asked. "Did he push me?"

"Nobody pushed anybody," Ella Dane said. She repeated it into the phone, as the dispatcher asked another question. "Nobody pushed anybody! It was an accident."

"I'm having contractions," Lacey said. "I might be in labor." She lay against the wall and looked at the ceiling, the corner of the hallway above the bathroom. The shadows crawled over each other; the air whispered *guilty, guilty, guilty*.

"I don't believe it," she said. No mother would walk away from a baby in a bathtub to lie down for a nap. And the other vision, Dora kneeling by the bathtub to drown Dorothy. They couldn't both be true. Maybe they weren't either of them true.

"I haven't touched him," Ella Dane shouted. "I'm up here with my daughter; she's pregnant. Can't you send the ambulance and quit asking me these questions?"

"He's dead," Lacey said. "He killed them all and he killed himself. Because he was guilty too." Something occurred to her. "You'd better get rid of the herbs before the cops come." She pushed her mother away and stood up. "I'm going next door. The hospital's not safe. Drew's found me there before." She saw the picture, the small fair boy next to the great piano, tucked in with a dozen other pictures on Harry's windowsill. "I need to find out what Harry knows." And this time she wasn't going to be polite and let him change the subject or slide her out of his house. This time she was going to keep asking until he answered.

Chapter Forty-four

UNLESS HE WAS GOING TO VISIT the old man, Lex avoided Austell Road. It sucked him toward home, where he could not go, no, never. It was worst in April, when the dogwoods bloomed white and pink, each one a tall fair woman in a wide-skirted dress, and memory rubbed like a stone in his shoe.

Tonight, he found himself on Austell Road driving west. He knew the names of every side street (Green Acre, Valley Church, Eston's Farm), because his dad taught him to read maps, and made him draw maps of the neighborhood, with all the streets and names. There was no church on Valley Church Road and no farm on Eston's Farm Way. "Names remember," his dad told him, "even when people forget."

Lex forgot names. That didn't make him crazy. He could remember if he tried. On Austell Road, the streets said their names in his father's voice, remembering, as he followed Jeanne's gray Corolla, license plate PTY 796. PTY for pretty, he said when he bought the car for her, so she would remember. Where was she going, seven at night, fifty-eight miles an hour when the sign said forty-five?

She slowed at Burgoyne's Crossing; Lex jammed his brakes,

and the car behind him honked. If she turned left at Burgoyne's Crossing, she'd drive past his school, and then she'd turn left on Forrester Hills Avenue and right on Forrester Lane and go home, and take the baby inside where everything was waiting for her and for him. Everything, a shadow full of names, remembering.

Still honking, the car behind him changed lanes and pulled alongside. Jeanne carried on past Burgoyne's Crossing, and he accelerated after her, cutting off the other car just as it swerved to rejoin his lane. Honking and shouts followed him. Jeanne passed the big mall and the little mall. She turned left without signaling into a confetti burst of yellow, green, and red, neon and trumpets, a building with a roof like a huge Mexican hat and some kind of party in the parking lot.

Jeanne found a spot near the entrance. Lex nosed his car past hers and parked far back in the lot. He turned his lights off and stayed in the car. It looked dangerous. Jeanne slammed her door and turned her face toward the party.

No baby. Was the baby at home? Big Jeanne's car was gone. That was why he followed Jeanne, to find out where she was taking the baby. And he'd seen her put the car seat in the back.

He should go home. There was no time. Time, time, time; his dad kept them all on a schedule, homework from four to seven and if you run out of homework, boy, I'll pick a name from the encyclopedia and you can write me an essay on him, remember all the names, remember; Lex hadn't heard his father's voice so clearly for years. He used to set fires, and the roaring voice of fire would swallow up his father's roaring voice. Time, time, time is running out. You forgot something. What did you forget?

It wasn't just a party, here in the new building with the Mexican hat for a roof. It was a fiesta. With a mariachi band, men in bright colors with gold braid on their shoulders, and trumpets tongued with gold. Not just the building, but all the people wore broad-brimmed Mexican hats with bright striped ribbons around the crown.

Remember the names of things. *Sombrero.* "Bienvenidos, amigo!" a girl said. She had long, straight hair, pure red from root to tip, and she jammed a sombrero onto Lex's head. "Arriba!" she trilled. "Welcome to the grand opening of Taco Mania." She swung her hips, and her wide striped Mexican skirt spiraled around her, released itself from her knees, and spiraled the other way. Her beauty amazed him. "These are Taco Pesos." She gave him a book of coupons. Buy Two Tacos Get One Free, Free Coffee with Purchase of Donut Burrito.

"I'm looking for my wife."

"She's wearing a hat," the red-haired girl said. She laughed. "There's free tacos inside, beef, chicken, bean, and our fudgy dessert taco! Kids' meals come with a free bean." She pressed a large plastic bean into Lex's hand.

His thumb found a button on the side. The bean opened to reveal a smaller bean dressed like a mariachi musician with a tiny plastic trumpet. Time is running out—what did you forget? "Free tacos," he said. That's where Jeanne would be.

The red-haired girl pushed him toward the huge sombrero and turned from him to meet the next new customer. "Bienvenidos, amigo; would you like a hat?"

The building was too bright, too crowded, and everyone wore a sombrero. Where was Jeanne? Young people carried trays of tacos through the room, and mariachi music crashed through the speakers, louder than the band outside. In the old man's house, there was always music. The steam of so many hungry bodies pushed Lex against the wall, where a smiling young face offered him a tray of tacos, and he took one. He put it in his pocket.

Somebody gave him another taco, this one spilling chocolate goo onto his fingers, and he put that in his other pocket.

He saw Jeanne near the counter, with three tacos neatly rayed between the fingers of her left hand while she ate another, in two bites, crunch through the middle of the taco, four chews and it was down, and she poked the rest of the taco into her mouth, sucking her finger clean as she pulled it out. She snatched two more tacos off another tray. Lex leaned against the door and forced himself out of the building, against the crush of customers crowding in. Where was Jeanne's car? "Adios, amigo," the red-haired girl shouted as he passed her, and for a moment he was tangled in the mariachi band, guitars everywhere and a trumpet right in front of him.

Then he was through the crowd, out among the cars, next to Jeanne's car. Theo was in the back with a bag of minidonuts. All alone in the cold and the dark, with donuts she could choke on, choke and suffocate and die. Drowning in sugar.

Lex banged his fists on the car window. Theo smiled through sugar. He wanted a rock, but the parking lot was smooth and black. Mariachi trumpets thronged in his mind. He pressed the button on the toy in his hand, and his own tiny musician played silently. The real band in the parking lot started "La Cucaracha." The simple melody helped him think, and he laughed at himself. He didn't need a rock. He had keys to Jeanne's car, because it was half his car. He opened it and took Theo out of his half.

Chapter Forty-five

LACEY SAT AT HARRY'S KITCHEN TABLE. "A friend of my mother's," she said, as the ambulance pulled away from her house. "He had an accident." Harry stood with his back to her, pouring boiling water into two mugs. Now that she was here, she found it hard to begin this necessary conversation. *Why did you sell me your haunted house?* wasn't easy to say, just like that. She had to work into it. She said, "He fell down the stairs."

Harry's shoulders pulled up and in, a slow flinch, and he said, "Tea or cocoa?"

"Cocoa." She was surprised to see him dump an envelope of powder into a mug; she'd thought of Harry as a man who made cocoa with milk, from scratch, whisking sugar and real cocoa powder into the hot milk, whisking continuously so it wouldn't scald. He poured boiling water over the Nestlé mix just like everyone else. "Thank you," she said.

He must have caught the tone of disappointment, because he turned toward her with his eyebrows high in his long face. He set the mugs on the table, said, "Hang on a second," and pulled a jug of cream from the refrigerator. Real cream, in a white ceramic jug. "I'm glad you came to me," he said.

The cocoa slopped over the edge of Lacey's mug and scalded her knuckles as the contraction began. It began with a grinding shift in the bones of her pelvis, bones she had not thought could move. Agony yawned and swallowed her whole. She pushed the mug away. It wobbled on its farther edge, took half a turn, balanced, and tipped, spilling cocoa all over Harry's table. This pain, so much worse than the others, ran out more quickly, a foaming wave, already gone. She rubbed her face.

Harry was all around her, fluttering with a damp washcloth, a dry tissue, paper towels for the table, and a second mug of cocoa for her, while his own cup cooled and the cream separated into a scum of oily bubbles on its surface.

"Honey, what's wrong?" he said.

So he was going to play innocent to the end. She was tired of him. Her right hand worked the tissue, rolling it hard and tight. "Because it used to be your house and you lived in it and you left it and you lived next door to it and you saw what happened to them, the Craddocks and the Honeywicks and all of them. Where's that picture?"

She roamed the kitchen, scanning through the family snapshots of children on the beach, children in plaid uniforms, a little girl with a giant white rabbit, a boy next to a bicycle with a big red bow on it. So many pictures. The refrigerator was paved with them, and pictures of every dimension, from wallet-sized school photos to ten-by-fourteen portraits, paneled the kitchen walls. These hundreds, every race and age, many of them posing with violins, must be students and children of students, a teacher's gallery.

The picture of the boy who looked like Drew had stood on the windowsill, above the sink, tucked behind three or four others.

There was the frame on top of the microwave, clean silver with a beveled edge, but it held an Asian girl aged about twelve, in a plaid Christmas dress with violin at port arms.

"Where is he?" She shook the frame at Harry. "Where is he, *who* is he?"

Harry took the frame. He turned her to face the opposite wall of the kitchen and guided her to the middle, and there he was, the serious blond boy beside the gleaming piano. Drew. Not Drew. So much alike. "I told you last time. That's my son, Ted, when he was seven."

"It looks just like Drew." Not quite. Drew's eyebrows were straight, as if drawn with a ruler, but this boy's eyebrows lifted in a curve of slight surprise, giving him a look of mild and pleasant eagerness, as if someone had unexpectedly given him candy.

"Everybody says so," Harry said. "Everybody who's seen him. I never saw him. I used to go over there, in between tenants, and call him and call him, and he never came."

"Then why don't you live in the house yourself?"

"When we lived there, my wife saw him. Teddy was six. She got scared. She went back to her family in Australia. Whenever I'm in the house, Drew goes after Ted."

"In Australia?" And she'd thought she could escape by driving to the beach.

"He's got kids. My grandchildren. I can't live in that house."

"Burn it. Tear it down."

"You think that'll stop him?"

"Maybe." But if Drew didn't have a home of his own to return to, maybe he'd go to Australia, a cuckoo in Ted Rakoczy's nest. "I don't know."

Harry put an arm around Lacey's shoulders and urged her

back to the table. As she drank her cocoa, her right hand worked the tissue, her thumb rubbing and rubbing along the oily dent in the felted paper. "So he's still calling himself Drew?" he said. "You know he's lying, because Junior survived?"

"Eric found out. I wondered if he was the father. Andrew Senior."

"He was an artist. Andy Halliday. He was my best friend in high school. He drew that picture, Dora with her violin. She was fifteen . . . oh God, fifteen. I have students older than that. Sixteen when they got married. They had to. You had to, back then, if you got a girl in trouble. Not in some places, but in Greeneburg you still had to."

"What did they do?"

"He enlisted right out of school and broke both his ankles on an obstacle course in basic. Dora was seventeen and Junior was a baby then."

Injured in basic training and discharged, still wearing his crew cut nine years later. Lacey felt a remote pity, like an archaeologist finding a mummified murder victim. A tragedy, so long ago. "What did they do?"

"He went to college, got a teaching degree. She waitressed all those years, put him through school. Twelve hours a day on her feet and a baby every year."

Greeley Honeywick broke both her ankles and lost her feet. Lacey put Eric through school. The house knitted them together, all their lives in the same pattern. The same life, repeating itself in fragments. Mosaic, pastiche, collage.

"He never forgave her," Harry said.

"*He* never forgave *her*? She did everything for him!"

"And he couldn't get over it. Those years when she was earning and he was in school. I sent them money, but they wouldn't take it. So young and so proud. Andy was a hard man and he got harder. His students hated him."

Lacey wasn't surprised. Her students were too young to hate their teachers, but she knew of people who'd left the classroom forever, driven out by the mob revulsion of middle-school and high school students. The stories, repeated by older faculty to student teachers as cautionary tales, always ended with the failed teacher entering some more lucrative field. *And he got another degree and became an accountant, but he never taught again.* She checked her watch. If the contractions kept coming every half hour, she was due for another in four minutes or so. "What did he do?"

"Beat up a kid. So he was fired, just after Dorothy was born. Dora went back to work. I sent them two thousand dollars, all the money I had on hand. They never cashed the check. Next thing I knew, they were all dead except Junior. Margaret and I moved down here with Teddy. And then, well . . ." Harry opened his long fingers. "You know the rest."

Lacey sat back, thinking. "My mom's friend Jack," she said, "the guy they took away in the ambulance. He was trying to help. Greeley says it's been tried before."

"I tried once. Got a fellow in, a psychology professor from a college in Indiana. He wasn't in there but five minutes."

"What did he say?"

"He said Drew is lost. He's trying to get out, he's, what was the word? He's *recruiting* mothers and children, to be his guides, but he's too hurt and too slow to follow them. The fellow said Drew would keep doing it unless someone could take him the rest of the way. Then he refunded his fee and never came back."

Lacey laid the crushed tissue on the table, beside her empty mug. She checked her watch. Eight forty-five, forty minutes since the last contraction. Was she safe, was the baby safe? What a question. Safe. "Do you think . . ." she said, and the house was suddenly full of noise, hammering and shrieking.

"Let me in, let me in," a wild voice shouted from the porch.

Lacey grabbed Harry's arm. "Who's there?" she whispered.

"It's just Lex. And he's got the baby with him." Harry pushed her hand off his sleeve. "Don't worry, he's harmless." He went to open the door.

Chapter Forty-six

ERIC SLEPT MORE DEEPLY than he had in months, a sleep so black that he became conscious during it, aware of himself floating, a leaf on a quiet sea. Blue-black weightlessness heaved and he drifted on the skin of it, breathing the pulse of its slow caress. As the night rolled toward morning, a sparkle of memory-dreams crowded behind his eyes, warmly vanilla scented. The Christmas morning when he and his brothers all got bicycles, three in a row, blue Schwinns with a red bow on each; the cornmeal pancakes his mother made for special mornings, first day of school, birthdays, and sometimes just Wednesdays. The first day of third grade, when he turned away from her good-bye-and-good-luck kiss, too old to be kissed in front of everyone. All that long day he felt heat on his face, the kiss he had rejected burning him, and when he walked his brothers home, he walked into the smell of sugar and vanilla. She had made cupcakes.

Sleep sank away, and Eric struggled for reason in the swarming dreams. He had no little brothers. His brothers were fourteen and seventeen years old when he was born; they'd gone to college, one in California, the other in Texas, and had never come back. He hardly knew them; he'd grown up practically as an only child. His mother never made pancakes or walked him to school. He got a new bike every spring, not Christmas. Even as he puzzled over them, the dreams shredded, leaving a sense of affectionate nostalgia that he reflexively distrusted. When he was in third grade, he toasted his own Pop-Tart and walked out to catch the bus. His parents were already at the office, so he locked the house and set the security alarm. His mother had never made a cupcake in her life. Millions of dollars, yes, imaginary and criminal millions. No cupcakes.

The dream scent remained, and he was in an unfamiliar room, small, lined with bookshelves full of secondhand paperbacks. He had slept on an airbed with a puffy pink quilt and a flat pillow that smelled of cat. Somebody was cooking something.

Someone tapped on the door. "Are you decent?"

Sammie. "Yes," Eric said, hoping it was true. *Was* he decent? What was he doing in Sammie's apartment? He identified the quality of his hangover: red wine and self-pity. He fell back against the pillow, shaken by shame. Sammie came in with a small tiger at her heels, and the scent of his dream came in with her. "Waffles?" he said. The cat jumped on the bed and sat with its paws curled under its chest, staring at him with golden eyes full of inexpressible thought.

"Donnie Osmond says you're in his bed," Sammie said.

He pulled himself up against the pillows, working around the cat. It purred so loudly its shoulders quivered. "I dreamed about my mother," he said.

"That's pathetic. Get over it and eat your breakfast."

Uncle Floyd came in, wearing a knee-length blue bathrobe that suggested all too strongly that he wasn't wearing anything else. Eric fixed his eyes on the tiger-cat in order to avoid any more wrinkled pink glimpses. The cat stood up, hunched its back, and patted Eric's hand with one heavy velvet paw. "Coffee," Floyd said to Sammie.

"In a minute. Donnie Osmond likes waffles." Sammie left, and Floyd sat on the bed with his knees a little too far apart. Eric tore off a bit of waffle for the cat, who took it delicately, with his whiskers fanned forward.

"You still working for Lex Hall?" Floyd said.

This brought back a third element of Eric's hangover: red wine, self-pity, and a bracing lecture on marriage from Uncle Floyd. "I guess," Eric said. "He's supposed to get a new lawyer and call me for the files."

Floyd shook his head. "He'll never do it. You got to find a new lawyer for him. And you got to hire Cambrick MacAvoy yourself, before that little girl gets her."

"You said having Cambrick on a case is like having flesh-eating strep."

"Get her on your side, it's the other guy watching his ass melt. You want Cambrick, and you can't have her if she's against you on the Hall case. Get rid of the nut and latch on to that woman. Best advice I can give. Or you'll be paying off your ex for the next twenty years. She's got her hooks into your future income and don't you forget it."

"She's not my ex."

"It's all over but the shouting."

"Coffee!" Sammie called from the kitchen.

Floyd leaned forward to pat Eric's shoulder. Eric shut his eyes, half a second too late. "You'll be good," Floyd said. "It's only the first divorce that hurts."

Floyd and Sammie passed in the doorway. Sammie slithered up against him and shimmied in a way that made Eric close his eyes again, his body impaled on a pulse of emotion either lust or envy, he couldn't tell which, but definitely sin. Gluttony, the tiger-cat, patted his arm, and he fed it another piece of waffle dripping with butter. Sammie took Floyd's place on the bed.

"It's not necessarily over," she said. "Half the people who come through Moranis Miszlak, if I could give them a cup of coffee"— she handed him his coffee—"and a piece of lemon chess pie, or a pile of cookies, I could talk sense into them. Go home."

"Try talking sense into Lacey. She's trying to exorcise my house. Her mother dug up some shaggy old bum with trash in his hair. You have no idea."

"You are *not* ready to walk away from her. You're all up in each other's mess."

Donnie Osmond took advantage of Eric's distraction to slide his head under the coffee cup and seize the waffle. The cat whirled, kicked off with both his hind legs against Eric's arm, and shot from the room, leaving a trail of melted butter. The coffee fountained from his cup, scalding the fresh cuts. "Oh, grow up," Sammie snapped, and Eric bit back his moan of pain. "Grow up and go home."

"I can't." The phone rang in the other room. She kept her eyes on Eric, and he kept talking. "I can't go back to that. It's crazy. It's messy. It's wrong." *It's low-class;* but he wouldn't say that about Lacey to anyone.

Sammie heard it. "So she didn't come up like you. Why did you marry her?"

"Because she ate three doughnuts without even worrying about it."

Sammie handed him tissues to clean the blood and coffee off his arm, and he thought about Lacey and the doughnuts. It was their third date and he had reservations at Amaranth, Columbia's most expensive low-country restaurant, a test for Lacey:

Did she have the clothes, the shoes, the manners? She wore a dress obviously bought for the occasion, white eyelet lace, light blue low-heeled shoes, and a necklace of blue glass beads, summery and modest. She smiled too much but didn't say, *This looks real fancy,* as he had feared. The evening was perfect, until the maître d' said, "Miszlak? I think not."

"I called yesterday. We have reservations." The man was immovable. All the tables were booked and there were no cancellations; Eric, feeling the evening slip away, said, "Can we wait?"

"There will be no cancellations," the maître d' said.

Lacey waited in her bright new dress and perfectly appropriate shoes. He'd meant to test her, and now she would test him, find out if he was the man he meant to be, or only a kid with his daddy's credit card. She touched his arm and said, "Let's go somewhere else." A moment of pure grace and he loved her. She didn't test him; she didn't even know there were tests. They went to Krispy Kreme and bought half a dozen doughnuts, fresh hot now, and she ate three and never said a word about the fat and the sugar, nor a syllable of regret for the elegant dinner they were not having.

The third date, and he was hers. That moment at Amaranth when she touched his arm, and the second moment, when she took the third doughnut.

She was still that same Lacey. When the money disappeared, she planned for how they would live now. Crazy and messy she might well be. But she was true. He needed her, or he'd look in the mirror in thirty years and see Uncle Floyd.

"I'd better get home," he said.

"Did I tell you what happened the last time I went to the Halliday house?"

"You threw eggs."

"Another time, later, I was twelve. There was a kid standing in the front yard."

"What happened?"

Sammie shivered and pulled her arms across her chest. "Nothing. He just stood there. It was horrible. I slept with the light on for a week."

"Did anybody else see him—did anything happen?"

"We all saw him. It was the single creepiest thing that ever happened to me in my life." She huffed impatiently. "I can't say it the way it was. But it was awful. Awful, that's all. It's something you don't forget. Anyway. That's my story."

"It's not much. As stories go."

She gave him a nasty look. "I just can't tell you how it was."

Floyd came into the room. "That was Cambrick MacAvoy," he said.

Sammie blanched. "She knows my number?"

"She's got the devil's own Rolodex; she knows everybody's number."

"What's a Rolodex, old man?"

Floyd said to Eric, "Theo Hall disappeared last night."

Eric's mind tilted sideways for a moment. Theo, Theo, he didn't know anyone called Theo. "Lex Hall's baby? Disappeared how?"

"Out of Jeanne Hall's car, in the parking lot of Taco Mania on Austell Road. So Jeanne waits till morning, and she calls Cambrick, and Cambrick says you'll have the baby back to her in an hour, or she's calling an Amber Alert. You get shut of that man."

"I'll call Lex."

"Already done. He's not home. Where else would he go?"

Where else, in the whole of Greeneburg, would Lex Hall take Theo? "Harry Rakoczy's house. I'll go see if he's there."

Chapter Forty-seven

LACEY SLEPT IN HARRY'S HOUSE, in the reclining chair with her feet up. She called Dr. Vlk's answering service at midnight, and Dr. Vlk called within five minutes to explain that these were Braxton Hicks contractions and she was not in labor; it was perfectly normal. "Should I take two aspirin and call you in the morning?" Lacey asked.

"No aspirin," Dr. Vlk said briskly. "Do I hear a baby crying?"

Harry was settling Lex into his guest bedroom, and Lacey had volunteered to hold Theo, who hadn't stopped crying for the last three hours.

"It's Theo Hall."

"Hall. Not one of mine. How old?"

"Eleven months. I've changed her diaper, I've given her food and water and formula and burped her and everything, and she won't stop!"

"Hold the phone closer." Dr. Vlk listened for fifteen seconds and said, "She's teething. Give her a peeled carrot, and keep an eye on her so she doesn't choke."

It worked. Theo gnawed the carrot, and the hard, cold sweetness soothed her inflamed gums; she mumbled herself to sleep.

Lacey laid her in the makeshift bed Harry had prepared—a nest of blankets on the floor, as if she were a stray puppy—and settled herself in the recliner with her feet up, letting the contractions roll through. Dr. Vlk was right about the carrot, and the contractions, too. They didn't hurt so much when Lacey relaxed. After a while, they were almost pleasant, and the baby's flutterings afterward seemed like laughter.

He wouldn't be like poor Theo. He would have a bright nature and a happy heart, the kind of child who hugged his teacher for no reason, everybody's favorite and friend to all, his temper a summer storm quickly past, a sturdy boy with a quick mind, her dear son. She drowsed, dreaming his life.

Bars of light flashed across Harry's lawn as the lights in her own house turned themselves on and off, Drew's summons to her. For months he had walked quietly in her life, with cookies and crayons and tantrums, a natural child; now that she knew him, he was showing her, *This is what I could have done. Would you have known me then?* And would she? Answering her thought, all the lights turned on at once and stayed bright. She had to go back. Where else could she go? She'd take her baby with her, carrying life into death. Her thoughts floated in Harry's dark living room, sweet with orange oil and violin rosin. Good-bye, golden child. This beautiful life never lived. Ev Craddock would tell her there'd be another baby. She didn't want another baby. She wanted *this* baby.

"Good-bye," she whispered. Her nose was running; she wiped it on her wrist. At the sound of her voice, he moved upward, pushing hard into her ribs.

By morning she achieved a light, whirling state of mind near sleep. The tears kept sliding, and her cheeks were raw with salt.

At some unreasonable hour, Lex came howling down the stairs in the clothes he had slept in, shouting, "Where's my baby?"

"She's asleep," Lacey said. At the sound of her father's voice, Theo raised an animal howl, and this time she rejected the carrot with contempt.

"She's hungry," Lex said. "I'm going to give her oatmeal and applesauce."

"Good luck with that," Lacey said. She yawned until her jaw hinge popped. Had she ever been so tired? Five thirty. She used to get up at this hour every day, to be at work in time to super-vise the early arrivals in bus-holding. She was out of the habit now, and early morning was a foreign world. She leaned against the kitchen wall, watching as Lex pushed oatmeal at Theo, who squalled and struck the spoon away. Clots of oatmeal flew across the room in every direction, and the applesauce was no better received.

"Please," Lex begged Theo. "It's good for you."

He shoveled in a spoonful of applesauce. Her mouth hung open, and the applesauce dribbled out until she expelled the last slimy smear with her tongue. "It's hopeless," he said. "She won't eat good food, and she's going to get sick and die and I can't help her." He set her on the floor, and she tipped forward to hold her weight on her fists. "She'll die," he said. "It's all my fault, and there's nothing I can do!" And hungry Theo lifted her shrill cries into his wail of despair.

Harry came into the kitchen. "Let me feed her," he suggested. "Go on into the other room and think quiet thoughts. Discipline your mind, Junior, or at least your voice."

Lex fled, and Lacey followed him, wanting to help. As she left the kitchen, she heard Harry ask, "If I put sugar in the oatmeal, would you eat it?" Soothed by his slow voice, Theo squawked. "You're a roly-poly baby doll, aren't you," Harry said. "How about just a taste of brown sugar, pudgy puss." He sang to a melody from *Mary Poppins,* "Just a spoonful of sugar helps the soluble fiber go down, the soluble fiber go down, the soluble fiber go down . . ."

Lacey found Lex in the living room, Harry's teaching room, pulling stacks of music out of the bookshelves. "What are you looking for?" she asked.

"Paper. Somebody showed me. It made my eyes feel good." He ripped out the end sheet from the piano accompaniment to a book of Mozart sonatas. He snatched a pencil from Harry's music stand and sprawled on the floor, scribbling like a child. Lacey watched the shapes forming.

They were her own shapes, her circles that the soft edge of the pencil shaded into spheres, her cones and cubes. They were the shapes she taught to her wild children, her noisy boys, to keep their twitching hands busy, a soothing habit for their mind. She had taught dozens of children these shapes. Most recently, Drew.

Lex ripped the end page out of another volume of sonatas. His pencil moved slowly, and the shapes had a darker edge, sure and firm. She loved this moment, whenever it came: exactly now, when order bloomed in a disordered mind. The shapes moved from hand to eye to heart, and she could touch the shoulder of the noisy boy driven wild by his own mute passions, and say, "Tell me about it," so she did it now, though the suffering child was forty-eight years old.

"She'll be fat like her mother," Lex said. He drew an oval, pulled two lines downward to create a curve-topped triangle, and shaded it into a cone. "Jeanne's got the diabetes already, and so does her mother. Theo could die. People die of it."

"They do," Lacey agreed. "You know she's eating oatmeal now?"

Lex hunched his shoulders in a child's sulking shrug.

"Harry's your uncle, isn't he?" Lacey said.

Another child's shrug. Lacey felt irritated. He had no right, a grown man with a wife (almost ex) and a baby, to pout on the floor and tear up other people's books, like a little kid. "You're Andrew Halliday," she said. "Junior."

"Not anymore."

"You used to live in my house."

"Not anymore, no no."

"Somebody's still there. One of your family. He says he's called Drew. He's stuck there and he can't leave. He needs you." *He needs you to go home and die for him.* "He needs you to tell him it's not his house; he has to go on to where your mother is. He needs—"

The pencil ripped through the paper. Lex squeezed both pages into a ball and threw it across the room. He surged to his feet and Lacey pulled herself away, instinctively folding both arms across her belly. She had to get Lex into that house. Lex would recognize Drew and say his real name; this had to work.

"No," Lex said. "I'm not allowed to go back there. Other people live there now."

"*I* live there. I want you to come home. Please."

Lex mirrored Lacey, his arms folded across his body, his shoulders pulled in around his chest. "No. Not allowed. No."

"He needs you."

Lacey touched his arm, and he exploded. He flailed and battered, punched her as if he were beating at a cloud of wasps, wild directionless blows around her shoulders and head. With every blow, he cried out, as if some other, heavier hand were striking him. "Leave me alone," he shouted. He shoved her into the corner, catching her between the fireplace and the bookshelves. He hit her with slanting, diagonal blows, more of rejection than attack. She sank down, clasping her legs against her body to shield the baby.

Chapter Forty-eight

ALTHOUGH THEY COULDN'T serve alcohol on Sundays in Greene-burg until after two, Abernathy's opened at ten thirty with a brunch buffet of everything greasy, crunchy, and fried. The kitchen was experimenting with twice-fried cheeseburgers—a beer-battered cheeseburger, deep-fried—and anyone who was willing to critique it could have one for free. By late afternoon, Abernathy's usual crowd would drag itself in, returning like dogs to roll in their own stink. But at 10:45, when Eric arrived, the place was full of families, satiny girls, boys in Sunday suits with clip-on ties, their halos almost visible. They'd just come from church. Not just church, but early service. They'd earned their twice-fried cheeseburgers, their caramel-apple pie.

Eric's Bluetooth kept slipping off his ear, and Cambrick Mac-Avoy's voice faded, but he wasn't missing much. Cambrick liked to repeat herself when she had the upper hand. "Custodial in-terference," she kept saying, as if it were some playground game she was winning and not a family in pain, a confused baby, and poor crazy Lex who had already suffered so many losses. Even Jeanne. He wasn't representing her interests, it wasn't his job, but was anybody looking out for her? Nobody would ever care for her as Lex had. Sammie was right. If there was just a way to get them together and talk sense to them . . . "I'll call the cops on him," Cambrick said.

Once, in another life, she had been his aunt Marian. On one of his birthdays, when he was very small, she had given him a Thomas the Tank Engine train set.

"I want," Eric said, and then realized he was standing at the cashier's desk, with three respectable families lining up behind him and a four-year-old girl in an Alice-in-Wonderland dress kicking his ankles. "I need two boxes to go, please. Three boxes."

"Six dollars a pound, no crab legs," the cashier said, handing him a stack of Styrofoam boxes.

"I'm hungry *now,*" the Alice-child said, and so was Lacey hungry at home. She needed him to feed her, to take care of her and tell her he was sorry; he'd bought the house for her, and if she didn't want it anymore, they'd sell it. He had to get moving.

"I want to know," he said to Cambrick MacAvoy, "how long was the baby missing before Jeanne called you?"

Silence from the Bluetooth. Eric wove through the crowd at the buffet, sliding between indecisive children, cutting in front of the slow-moving fat people, who took all-you-can-eat as a command and not an offer. Lacey wanted an onion blossom, roast beef, fried shrimp, crab cakes, a twice-fried cheeseburger. She'd never feared food, unlike the slim expensive girls he had dated before her.

"What do you mean?" Cambrick said.

"Two hours, three hours, not till morning? How long?" Eric felt the taste of truth in his mouth, thrilling and hot, someone else's blood. "She thought she left the baby in the car overnight, didn't she? She doesn't even know for sure if Lex took her. She doesn't know *where* that baby is. I'll see your custodial interference and raise you criminal neglect."

"I'll get back to you on that," and Cambrick hung up on him.

Eric dropped a tongful of ribs into the second to-go box. The boy standing at his elbow said, "I like coleslaw. And beans, the spicy ones."

Eric caught himself with the spoonful of beans lifted over the steam table, red-brown sauce dripping from the underside of the spoon in a translucent amber ribbon. He hated baked beans. "Where's your family?" he said. The boy looked familiar.

"I'm waiting for them."

"They're meeting you here?" Ridiculous, a stupid thought. Ten-year-olds did not meet their families for brunch. Eric shook his head, as if he could shake his ideas into place. The taste of truth was gone.

"I'm waiting for my mother."

Some kind of post-divorce child exchange. Parents who couldn't stand to be in each other's presence, the shared air turning to poison in their throats—one would leave a child and the other would pick him up. What if the pickup parent happened to be late? If the mother's car crashed on the way to Abernathy's, it could be hours before anybody knew the child was missing. An open, friendly child like this, who would talk to strangers so readily. Terrifying, the risks people took with the thing they should most treasure. Whatever you could say about Lex, he'd never leave Theo alone in a car, not for a second. "How long have you been waiting?"

Tears came into the blue eyes, but not easily. The boy had to squint and wrinkle his nose, hauling them up from some deep well. "Can you help me find her?" he said.

None of this made sense to Eric. Something unsound came off this boy in waves as palpable as smell. He wanted no part of it. He wanted to be gone. Far away, home already. "I guess you'd better keep waiting," he said.

"I want to go home." More false tears, dragged up and pushed out onto the bright clean face. "Can you take me home?"

Eric dropped the spoon into the beans. Cries of protest and disgust came from the people around him as the sauce spattered on their Sunday best. "No," he said. "Go away." He left his containers at the steam table and pushed through the crowd to the door.

In his car, he locked all the doors and leaned forward to press his forehead against the steering wheel. His heart jumped and skipped, as if he'd escaped a wreck—hit the brakes just in time and barely hard enough, swerved around the spilled bicycle, felt the tires grip the road after two rotations on black ice. He remembered them all at once, his there-by-the-grace-of-God near misses, and felt in a confused way that if things had truly gone wrong, his airbag would have deployed. No airbag, so he was safe. Lie down, lie down, he said to his skipping heart, nothing happened, lie down.

He'd seen that child before—in Dr. Vlk's office, in the Skyview, in the backseat of his own car, in the bathroom mirror. Was this what Sammie had tried to describe? Had Lacey seen and felt these things, all these months in the house? Nothing happened, yet nothing ever felt more dangerous. He speed-dialed number one but Lacey wasn't home, and she didn't answer her cell, so he tried Ella Dane. She answered on the fifth ring.

"I left Lacey with Harry when I went to the hospital," she said coldly.

"Why are you at the hospital? Are you okay?"

"Jack McMure fell down the stairs."

People fell down stairs all the time. Second-most-common household accident, after drowning. There was no such thing as bad luck; it was just the way truth looked, working itself out in a messy world. How else were people supposed to die? There was nothing wrong with his house. "Is he hurt?" Eric asked.

"Concussion. He'll be okay."

"Does he have health insurance?"

"Do you have homeowner's insurance?" Ella Dane asked, with a sarcastic tone he considered unnecessary, even redundant. It was going to cost him. Everything cost him; people thought because he was a lawyer, he'd built a tree house in the money tree. Everybody wanted something, and they all wanted it from him.

Harry Rakoczy wasn't answering his phone. Lacey was in Harry's house, with Lex and Theo, and if Cambrick MacAvoy called the cops, what might Lex do?

Anything. He might do anything. Eric peeled out of the parking lot, ignoring the no-right-on-red sign and the honks and shouts of other drivers. Home. Now.

Chapter Forty-nine

"SHE DIDN'T MEAN IT," Harry said.

Lacey pressed a bag of frozen peas against her right shoulder, where one of Lex's wild blows had connected. Lex squirmed and cried in his seat like a bee-stung child, furious and unwilling to be helped, as Harry tried to press a cool washcloth on his red face. Lacey resented it. What right did Lex have to fuss? *She* was the one who'd been hit, so where was her cool washcloth? But no, Harry just shoved the bag of peas into her hand. Theo, under the table with three copper-bottomed saucepans and a wooden spoon, made an intolerable noise.

"Junior!" Harry caught Lex's flailing hands. "Look at me." Lex didn't raise his head, but Harry lowered himself awkwardly on his old knees to meet his gaze. "She didn't mean it." He pressed the washcloth against Lex's forehead. Lex flinched it away. "Close your eyes." Lex closed his eyes, and Harry spread the damp cloth over his face.

"Excuse me," Lacey said in the coolest tone she could muster. "Hello?"

Harry pushed a small white bottle across the table to Lacey. "Have an aspirin."

"Pregnant women can't have aspirin."

"There's Tylenol in the cabinet over the sink."

Lacey waited. Did he mean that she should get up, in her condition, and walk across the kitchen, and get her own medication? Yes, apparently he did. "Thank you so much," she said. She meant him to notice the sarcasm, and she meant it to hurt.

"Look what you've done," Harry said reproachfully. "He hasn't been this bad for years. He's been doing so well—even with Jeanne—I could have got him through that. Look at this."

Lex wailed from under the washcloth, "She tried to make me do a bad thing!"

"I only want him to come and talk to Drew."

Lex wailed again. He tore the washcloth off his face and ran upstairs. A bedroom door slammed, and the noise of his sobs came muffled through the walls. Theo banged her saucepans with her spoon. Lacey wished they would all shut up and let her think. She almost understood . . .

"We couldn't handle him when he got into his teens," Harry said. "Whenever he wasn't in detention, the county put him in a group home. He used to run away and go back next door."

"Did he ever talk to Drew?"

"He never went in. He set fires in the yard, but he never got close enough to the house to do any damage. Mostly he'd just stand across the street and shout. I finally made him understand he could never go there."

"Sounds like the lesson took," Lacey said, listening to the cries from upstairs. "What'd you do, beat it into him with live wires?"

"Repetition and discipline," Harry said. "You can teach Lex anything eventually."

"Well, isn't that nice."

"It's too dangerous for him. I owe it to Dora to keep him safe."

"Too dangerous for *him*? What about Tyler Craddock? What about Greeley Honeywick's baby?"

"He's my sister's child; he's all that's left."

"Drew's left. He says they left him all alone. Do you owe it to Dora to help him?"

"Why do you think I held on to the house all these years?"

"Why'd you sell it to us?" Lacey asked the question quickly, without letting any tone of anger or accusation color her voice. Harry would talk about Lex when he wouldn't talk about Drew? She was fine with that. Not *why did you sell me the house when you knew it would kill me* but *why did you sell the house, after you kept it so long?*

"You were perfect, you even look like Dora. Your hair's the same color. And you were a teacher and an artist. I thought you could help Drew, if anyone could."

"Help him? How?"

Harry ducked under the table to give Theo a metal spoon. He showed her how to hit the pans with the metal spoon, and how the two spoons made different noises. Theo gave a baby screech of pure joy and banged louder than ever.

"You thought I would die there," Lacey said.

"No, no," Harry said from under the table.

"Yes, yes. I'd die and I'd go on and Drew would go with me. He would recruit me to be his guide, like you said."

"No, no." Harry came up from under the table. His face was red. "I never wanted anyone to get hurt. I thought you could talk to Drew."

"Talk to him? You sold us the house so I would die there, me and my baby both. Don't you lie to me." This sweet old man, whom everyone liked and respected: she was going to make him face what he had done.

"So many people have died." Harry leaned across the table to grasp Lacey's hands. She pushed her chair back. "When I put people in the house, people die, babies die. When I live in the house myself, Ted's kids start seeing him in Australia. Same thing when I leave it empty. They're my grandchildren. If only one more person had to die, I thought, someone who could take Drew away, it would be the last one."

"Two people," Lacey said. "You had no right."

"There wasn't any other way."

"Why not take Lex inside and let him talk to Drew?"

"No. I owe it to Dora. He's all that's left."

Lacey rolled her shoulder. It was only bruised, and the frozen peas had soothed away the pain. "He's all that's left? Then you won't mind if I do this." She stood up and dragged Theo from under the table. Lacey got her hands under the baby's armpits and hauled her up to balance her on her right hip. Theo's left leg pressed against the undercurve of Lacey's pregnant belly, and the baby kicked in greeting. Lacey turned toward the door, and Theo gave her a wet, soft kiss.

Harry started toward her, but the telephone rang, and Lex raised a new shriek of despair, and his uncertainty trapped him in the conflict of demands. "What are you doing? Where are you going?" he called after her.

At the front door, Lacey looked back. "Home," she said. She walked out of Harry's house with her double burden, her right leg almost buckling with each step. She crossed their two lawns and hurried up the front steps, getting herself and Theo inside and the door locked just as Harry reached the front door.

"I'll call the police!" he shouted.

"You do that." She slid the dead bolt home. "I'll call them myself. Lex kidnapped this baby and he beat me up. Call them."

Silence. Lacey set Theo down in the hall and ran through the house, reaching the kitchen door just as Harry did on the other side. She locked it as the knob began to turn. "What do you want?" he said through the door.

"Send Lex over here, and I'll give him his baby," Lacey said.

"Or what?"

"Or nothing. I'm not making any threats. Here's me in the house, a teacher, an artist, a perfect fit, and here's Theo. She's Drew's cousin or his niece or whatever; you think she's got an hour, ten minutes, how long before he notices her?"

"You wouldn't."

"CarolAnna Grey never told me what happened to her. I bet her mom looked at her funny one day and said, *This little girl needs a bath*. CarolAnna was smart and fast, and she got away. Maybe Theo needs a bath."

"No!"

Lacey waited twenty seconds, long enough to have carried that heavy child up the stairs, and then she turned on the kitchen tap. The kitchen door shivered under a variety of blows, flesh, metal, ceramic; Harry must be using the patio furniture and the planters to hit the door. She opened it. He was covered in dirt, bloody handed in the wreckage of the planter, chrysanthemums at his feet. "What," she said fiercely.

"I want it to stop. I want it to not happen anymore."

"I can't stop it. You can't stop it."

Theo crawled across the kitchen floor to grab a chrysanthemum from Harry's foot. She crammed it in her mouth, then took it out, and poked her tongue in and out, clearing the dirt from her lips. "You think Lex can stop it?" Harry asked.

"It's his brother. One of his brothers, using his name. Or his father."

Very quietly, in one of the empty rooms upstairs, a door opened.

Harry picked Theo up and gently pulled the chrysanthemum from her hand. "I'll send Lex over," he said. "Give me a minute."

It was more like ten minutes, long enough for Lacey to shovel her mutilated chrysanthemum back into its broken pot, shaping the dirt into a rough pyramid and laying the terra-cotta fragments over it. She stood in the kitchen doorway and the sense grew in her that someone was behind her, staring at the back of her head. She did not turn.

Bringing Theo into the house!—what was she thinking? She told herself it made no difference. If Drew had a hit list, Theo was on it already. If he could reach all the way to Harry's grandchildren in Australia, then Dora's granddaughter on the other side of town had lived in deadly danger from the moment she was conceived.

Lacey accepted no excuses in her classroom. *Never mind telling me why you did it,* she said to her guilty children, and if she didn't hold herself to that standard, what kind of teacher was she?

She had tried to save herself and her baby by putting someone else's baby in danger. Theo Hall, human shield. That was no different from what Harry had done, renting the house out to young families for all those years.

"No, no," she said out loud, and the maple tree shook its yellow leaves at her in the afternoon sunlight. *Yes, yes.* She was guilty. But what else could she do?

What else could Harry Rakoczy have done?

He could have gone into the house and faced it himself.

She could do that, too. Her whole body shouted *no* and the contraction took hold of her pelvic bones again. Slowly she sat in the doorway and waited for the pain to sink. It didn't change the truth. She could do what she demanded of Harry: she could go back into the house and face it herself.

Yes, and take her baby into danger with her? She wasn't living for herself alone.

Neither was Harry living for himself alone. Drew could touch his grandchildren on the other side of the world. There was no way out. She could go into the house, face Drew, and die; she could hold on to him and not let go, take him with her and leave the house clean. Eric wouldn't understand, but Ella Dane would. The baby—but the baby had no chance anyway. *Sometimes you have to let them go,* Ev Craddock said. Her golden child.

Lex wandered across the back lawn, kicking his feet every third or fourth step, reluctant, sulky and slow. She resisted the urge to call him to hurry up, because he had the look of a child who would slow down even further. *You're not the boss of me.* Every inch of his body said it, a six-foot-tall gray-headed pouty preteen. She was not ready for this, not one bit.

"I'm here," he said as he climbed onto the patio.

Lacey gave him her sweetest and most welcoming first-day-of-school smile. "I'm so glad you came."

"The old man sent me."

She pulled him into the kitchen. "Can I get you something to drink? Coffee?"

At once, she knew it was absurd to offer coffee to this man, and he said, "Pop?"

"I don't think so." Lacey checked the refrigerator. Eric drank Pepsi, but Ella Dane had a habit of draining Pepsi bottles and refilling them with her own concoction of dandelion root and powdered carob. "There's orange juice, guava juice, some kind of sugarcane thing that my mom likes, and milk."

"Milk."

She gave him a glass of milk. She'd been so eager to get him into the house, and now here he was, and what could she do with him? She'd expected some sign—doors slamming, water running, noises, voices—but the house sat quiet in the October sun. Every gust of wind was followed by a light pattering as a wave of leaves jittered across the roof. Occasionally a car drove by, and the more distant sound of Austell Road was a constant faraway surf. Where was Drew?

Lacey cleared her throat. She took the empty glass from Lex's hand and rinsed it in the sink. "So," she said. Now she had him here, she wasn't sure why she'd wanted him. It had felt important. Now she felt nothing. "It's a long time since you were here."

"I was never here."

"I guess not." Lacey looked around the kitchen. What was the same as 1972? Nothing but the walls, the size and location of the windows—only the bones of the room, and those were identical to Harry's kitchen next door. "How about if I show you around?" she said, as if he were any ordinary guest.

"I don't care."

She led him across to the future dining room, where she'd been sleeping for the past three months. "I'm going to move upstairs when the baby comes," she said. "We'll get a real table in here." The air in the room was thick, not precisely foul, but heavy with animal presence. She needed to change the sheets. Bibbits had slept beside her for weeks. "This was your dining room, right?"

Lex shrugged.

She hurried him past that spot at the foot of the stairs—did he remember lying there, brothers dying beside him, sister already dead? She hoped not. Maybe the bullet had torn the memory from him. "This is the living room." Stupid. He knew that.

He didn't answer, and she talked into the increasingly dangerous silence. "So this is where Harry teaches lessons in his house;
that's the most beautiful room, with that gorgeous picture. . . ."
Dora Rakoczy, by Andy Halliday. Harry said she looked like
Dora. Maybe Lex thought so, too. What about Drew? Did he
think she looked like Dora and would it matter to him?

"Would you like to see upstairs?" she asked.

"Can I leave now?"

"Don't you want to see your old bedroom?"

"I'm not supposed to be here. Can I leave now? Please?"

"Do you remember the Honeywicks? A family called Honeywick?"

"I don't remember anything. Something bad happened to
them."

"What about the Craddocks?"

"Can I leave?"

"What about—" What was CarolAnna Grey's maiden name?
She'd forgotten, if she'd ever known it. "A little girl called Carol-
Anna, do you remember her?"

"A bad thing almost happened. Can I go?"

"What about the Hallidays?"

"I don't remember anything at all."

These answers. How could he know these things? She stopped
looking for Drew and instead stared straight at Lex. His face was
tired and anxious, old, so old. His eyes were those of the girl
on Harry's wall—Dora's eyes, no, *Drew's* eyes. Stupid, stupid,
stupid. Here she was watching and waiting for Drew, and he was
right in front of her all the time. Recognition poured over her
skin, combing every hair upright.

"I know you," she whispered.

"I don't remember." He sank before her, slowly to his knees, and crossed his arms over his face, shaking his head, a child's gesture, a child's misery. "Please," he said. "Please can I go. Oh please."

"But I know you. It's *you*." She touched his shoulders, then pulled him in, pulled his head against her belly, cradled the back of his head in her hands. His breath was hot between her breasts, and he clutched the sides of her dress, pulling it tight over her shoulders. "Don't be scared," she said into his thin, light hair. Poor thing, poor thing. He hadn't meant to hurt anyone. "It's okay, you can tell me."

And it was almost there, the truth, the answer, gathering around them. Lacey sensed its geometry, the turning of a kaleidoscope, lines and angles clicking into place. "I know you," she said. "I know who you are."

"I remember," he said, "Mama lay down for a nap, she was so tired."

"And then?"

But the door opened and Eric came in with the October wind around him, yellow leaves scurrying at his feet. Lex wailed and pushed himself away from Lacey, and the moment passed, the memory unspoken.

Chapter Fifty

"WHY ARE YOU HERE?" Lacey asked. She'd known the truth, but it was gone, blown out in the sudden wind.

"What's going on here?" Eric said. "What is this guy doing in my house?"

"Visiting," Lex said. He scrambled away from Lacey on his knees. "She made me come here. I didn't want to."

"You. I'll talk to you later. Lacey, where have you been?"

"Next door, at Harry's."

"And don't you ever answer your phone? That's what it's for, so I can get in touch with you. I've been calling and calling." He pulled his cell phone out of his pocket and speed-dialed two to show her. Lacey's cell phone tinkled the "Ode to Joy" on the kitchen counter. "You went out of the house and didn't take it with you?"

"I was in a hurry." She couldn't remember why. Eric was so loud and so sudden. Couldn't he just shut up and listen? She almost had the answer. "I didn't have time."

"How much time does it take to pick up the damn phone?" Eric turned to Lex. "And you. Do you have any idea how much trouble you're in? Why did you take that baby out of that car?"

"Jeanne left her all alone, all by herself alone in the dark! What could I do?"

"You could have called 911. You could have called *me,* for God's sake. You had Jeanne right where you want her. Child endangerment, neglect, the whole nine yards, that was your whole custody case in that parking lot, and you took the baby, why?"

"I don't know," Lex said. "I don't know what I did."

Something changed in the air. Lacey looked up, already knowing what she would see, and Drew was there, standing at the top of the stairs. Though he looked as solid as ever, the light from the porthole window flowed through him unimpeded, casting a block of white on the red carpet on every step. "Can you stop, please stop?" Lacey said.

"What were you thinking?" Drew said.

"What were you thinking?" Eric said to Lacey.

"Listen to yourself," Lacey said. "These aren't your thoughts. He's trying to control you, can't you feel it? Get out of here *now.*" Hopeless; she'd never felt Drew's approach, there was no way Eric could resist.

"All you have to do is take care of the baby," Drew said.

"All you have to do is take care of the baby," Eric said.

Lex pressed his hands over his face and ran up the stairs. Drew flicked out of sight. He reappeared halfway down and said, "I gave up everything for you."

"I gave up everything for you," Eric said.

Lacey couldn't let that pass. "No, you didn't. This is our life together. Our money, our house, our baby—we did it all together. It's what we both wanted. Nobody gave up anything. Eric, don't listen to him!"

"I take care of everything for you," Drew said.

"Don't say it."

"I take care of everything for you," Eric said.

She turned to run for the door, but he was too quick for her, both of them were too quick. Eric caught her arm just on the elbow and squeezed it hard. Drew said and Eric echoed him—and now the echo came closer, so that she was hearing them both at once, converging—"I want you to understand what you've done." They said the last word together, and Drew disappeared. Lacey and Eric were alone, at the foot of the stairs. "Come and see," he said, pulling her toward the stairs.

She swung her fist against the side of his head—a soft and clumsy blow, because he was still Eric, and she couldn't hurt him—but it was enough to surprise him. He let her go, and she ran for the kitchen. She had a second or two, she'd never reach the front door. Long enough to reach the drawer beside the sink. She pulled out a knife at random—a vegetable peeler, no—and the second knife she seized was the spare chef knife, still new, in its cardboard sleeve. She whirled and held it out in front of her just as Eric reached her. He stopped. She waved the knife, absurdly sheathed in white cardboard. She'd entered the house ready to die if she had to—maybe, hoping it wouldn't be necessary—but she couldn't let Drew use Eric as he had used Beth Craddock. What it must have been like for Beth, when Drew stepped out of her body and she realized what her hands had done, no, she'd do anything to spare Eric that. If she could separate them, surprise Drew out of Eric—if she could ask Eric a question Drew couldn't answer, if she could do for Eric what Ella Dane had done for her, she could save him.

"What's the third-most-common household accident?" she said.

"What?" he said, two voices together, man and child in unison.

"There's drowning in the bathtub, and falling down the stairs, happens all the time." She waved the knife again. "How about kitchen accidents?"

"Third," they said together; and Eric's voice alone clarified, "Mostly burns."

"Listen to me!" she said. "Eric, listen. You don't have to do what he wants. You can move sideways."

"Sideways," Eric said alone, and Drew shouted, "Shut up, don't talk to him!"

She was alive because she had opened the drain with her toes. If only she could get through to Eric, make him listen. "Do something he hasn't thought of," she said. Footsteps upstairs, but Drew was inside Eric, so how—? Lex. She'd forgotten him. "Lex!" she screamed. "Go next door and get Harry, go now!"

A door slammed, but he didn't come down. Instead of fleeing the house, he must have shut himself into a bedroom. Eric caught her left wrist. With the last moment of freedom in her left hand, she snatched the cardboard sheath off the knife. Eric turned her wrist, and the knife sliced across the web between her thumb and her finger. He took the knife from her right hand and held it against her head, alongside her right ear, with her left arm pulled painfully back and twisted against his body. "All right then, if you like," and the voice was entirely Drew, there was nothing of Eric here, Eric would never hurt her, "let's move sideways. Up the stairs."

"I'd rather not," she said, as if politely refusing a reasonable invitation. "I'd rather stay here."

He spoke in the double voice again, Eric and Drew together. "I need you to know what you've done. I need you to be reasonable."

Those were Eric's words. Drew had turned his thoughts against him, as Lacey's thoughts had been turned. Ella Dane had shown Lacey the truth by holding Drew's hand until Lacey knew it for her own. Whatever Eric thought he was doing or seeing, she had to find a way to touch him. "Listen," she said.

They came to the foot of the stairs. Her left hand was slippery with blood. She pushed herself backward against him with all her weight, into the knife instead of away from it. The cut was a fiery line against her cheek and forehead, but she hardly felt it. Eric stumbled and let go of her, and she broke for the door. That same slippery hand slid off the dead bolt, and he came up behind her and held the knife under her belly, blade up, where one stroke would bring the baby's birth and death at once.

"Upstairs," he said.

"You don't want to hurt me," Lacey said. She walked slowly up the stairs, stopping on each step until he pushed her. The knife traveled around her belly, nudging her forward, and her dress fell from it in ribbons. Why did people have to make knives so sharp these days, why? "Eric, listen. I need to see Dr. Vlk now. Can you drive me to her office?" Some way to distract him, surprise him out of Drew's control.

"We can't afford the copays for you to run off to the doctor every five minutes," Eric said. "This house, we can't afford this, not with the student loans."

"I taught summer school every year you were in law school."

"That paid for my books, no more. I'm not making the kind of money you think I am. We're barely keeping up with the interest. The house. All that furniture."

Maybe he thought they were sitting at the kitchen table going over the checkbook. Maybe he thought they were sanely negotiating their future. In his mind, the hand with the knife held a ballpoint pen, tapping a row of subtracted numbers.

"Look at yourself," she said. "Look at your hand. *Look.*"

He urged her up another step. They were too high. If she fell back on him, made them both fall, down and backward and into the knife, all three of them would die. "It was for you," he said. "It was all for you. The hospital bills. All I get from Moranis Miszlak is my salary. They've got me working the pissant lawsuits and the trailer-trash divorces; there's no money there. I've got to bring in big cases, and how can I, if I have to run home whenever the baby kicks wrong or you see a shadow you don't like?"

"That is not fair."

"And I brought your mother here and she's worse than you are. And that loony-tune who fell down the stairs, do you know what that could have cost us? Thank God we've got liability, but it's only a million bucks, and if he'd broken his neck we'd burn through that in a year. We are *broke*."

They should have had this conversation three months ago. She knew from his voice that these were not new thoughts. He'd been ruminating for months, and meanwhile buying furniture they couldn't afford to keep her happy, just as she had kept Drew secret as long as she could. "I'll go back to work next August," she said. "We're keeping up. Eric, please. I might even be able to get a job in January. Don't listen to him. Don't do what he wants. Don't push back. Move sideways. I know you can."

He couldn't, that was the truth. He was not a flexible thinker. He was going to kill her and the baby, be tried and convicted for it—death for her, worse than death for him, all their lives wasted, for nothing. She'd lost contact with Drew, he was entirely Eric's now. When her family died, Drew would, once again, be left behind.

They were at the top of the stairs. Was he going to push her down? She grabbed the banister with both hands. He kept cutting, a silver whisper, light through the cotton dress, heavier at the gathered pleats on her shoulders. A hard snap, and he was through the elastic back of her bra. Frowning in his concentration, his tongue sticking out between his lips like a little child trying to draw equilateral triangles, he cut the bra straps and pulled it off her. Two last snicks, one at each hip, and she was naked.

"You need a bath," Drew said. "Let's go."

He pointed the knife at her belly button, and she let go of the banister and walked into the bathroom.

"We're broke," Eric said. "We can't go on like this."

"Eric, you can't listen to him. Look around you, look at what you're doing."

He waved the knife, and she got into the bathtub. He leaned over the tub, keeping the knife, sideways in his left hand, between Lacey and the shower curtain, while he reached over with his right hand to turn on the tap. In that moment, when he was so badly balanced, she could have tried to kick him and escape, but by the time she thought of it, it was too late. The water was running in, cold around her toes. He turned the tap to hot, and it began to steam at the other end of the bath.

"Sit," he said.

"No." She should have done this ten minutes ago. Drew didn't want to cut her, he'd never used a knife. She should have made her stand in the kitchen, where he'd never hurt anybody yet. "No, I won't."

"Sit." He pressed the point of the knife at the notch of her collarbone and pulled it downward, and the skin opened in a long straight line between her breasts. She felt a line of cold but not pain; she decided to let it hurt later. "Sit down in the nice hot water."

"No." She'd take the blade in her hands if she had to, but she wasn't getting in a bath with Andrew Halliday again. "Eric, listen!"

"Listen," Lex said. He stood in the bathroom doorway, his hands kneading the air in front of him. "She didn't do it."

"Shut up," Drew said.

"My mama didn't kill Dorothy."

"Shut up, shut up, shut up!" Drew shouted.

"Now you can tell the truth," Lacey said. "You can tell the truth right now, you've waited so long. Now you can do it." Repetition and discipline. "You have to do it." She threw her voice at him, the teacher's voice that ruled the room. *"Now."*

"Mama was asleep. I wanted to help. I put the baby in the bath. And I went to my room to get a boat for her. And I came back. And she was under the water and she wasn't moving. So I turned the water off and I went back to my room. I didn't know what to do."

"Shut up." Drew turned away from the bathtub and held the knife up as if it could protect him from Lex's words, cut them from the air. "I didn't do it," Drew said.

"I did it," Lex said. "I let her die, and Daddy killed everybody and I never told, I never told that it was me; it was my fault and I never told."

"It wasn't me," Drew said. He ran at Lex, head down and fists waving, a child so angry he had forgotten how to fight, forgotten the knife in his hand. Lex fell back before him, both hands out, backward into the hall.

Lacey turned the water off and pulled Eric's brown bathrobe from the hook beside the towels. She ran out of the bathroom but stopped in the doorway as a contraction turned her knees to water. Braxton Hicks, not real labor—if only she were in Dr. Vlk's office right now, anywhere but here. She sank to her knees in the hallway between the bathroom and the stairs. Sideways, Eric, sideways. Lex Hall is Andrew Halliday Junior, and Drew is all that he could not bear to remember, Drew is all that he left behind; let them fight it out between them. Move sideways.

"Make him stop," she said. "Don't let him hurt himself."

"Stay back," and she couldn't tell anymore if it was Eric's voice or Drew's. "Stay back," he said again, whoever he was. "Lacey, stay back."

They were at her feet. She put out her bleeding hand as if she could stop them. Lex clung to Drew, arms and legs wrapped tight, and Lacey pulled up the teacher's voice one last time: "Sideways. Now."

They rolled over each other at the top of the stairs, and Eric's foot shot out and felt for the banister post, braced and pushed. They fell, Eric and Lex and Drew and the knife together, into blood and silence. Lacey waited for the contraction to pass, so she could go and call for help.

Chapter Fifty-one

THE NURSE ADJUSTED THE STRAP around Lacey's belly, and the baby's pulse flashed on the monitor's screen, *183*. "Is that fast?" Lacey said. She preferred the other machine, the one that said *hush-hush*. This one showed the baby's pulse in a jagged blue line with a red number. She tugged the strap; the line flattened, the red number dropped to zero, and the nurse made an impatient noise and pulled it back into position. The number jumped to 208, and adrenaline prickled in Lacey's veins. She pretended not to see the watcher by her bed, the cop with his clipboard, waiting to question her. "It's getting faster," she said. "What's wrong?"

"Nothing. It's normal," the nurse said. She turned the machine so Lacey could see the screen without craning her neck. "He's fine; you're both fine. Dr. Vlk will be here soon. I'll go find out how Dad's doing, okay?"

Lacey had come to the hospital in the ambulance, holding Eric's hand; he was unconscious but breathing, the EMTs said, monitoring his breath, flashing lights into his eyes. He was stretchered into the emergency room, and a nurse came with a wheelchair to take her up to Labor and Delivery, depositing her in a curtained cubicle with a frighteningly narrow bed. She clutched the sides to keep from rolling off. Lex had come in a different ambulance, followed by police.

"Can you talk now, Ms. Miszlak?" There were two cops. One was waiting in the ER for news of Eric, and this one had followed her upstairs. She liked him; he had a warm, basset-hound face, creased by years of sympathy. He was not her ally, she reminded herself. He was no friend of hers. "Tell me what happened," he invited.

Lacey settled into the pillows. After everything they'd gone through, they weren't out of danger yet. She was exhausted; she wanted to cry, she wanted to sleep, but first she wanted an ultrasound to tell her the baby was safe. What did the police want from her—what kind of trouble was this? She needed time to think.

"I need to know if my husband's okay," she said. She had squeezed his hand in the ambulance, until the EMT pushed her aside, and his hand had been utterly unresponsive, all expression and personality wiped out of his face; she had never seen him like that, even in his deepest sleep.

"The man in your house. He's someone you know?"

"Lex Hall. My husband's a lawyer, he's a client. And he's my neighbor's nephew. What about Lex, is he okay?"

Oh, that sympathetic look; she didn't trust him at all. "We don't know yet."

That meant he was dead. Lacey laid her hands over the monitor belt and made her fingers relax. The baby's pulse stayed steady at 179. Lex dead. Surely this meant Drew was gone, Andrew Halliday was made whole, the lost child and the broken man. Her eyes overflowed, and she reached for the tissues on the table and blew her nose.

The curtain opened and Eric's uncle Floyd sailed in, jovial in his pink seersucker suit and a maroon bow tie. "You answering questions without me, girl?" he boomed.

Lacey gaped at him. "Why not?"

"You been cautioned?"

"She needs to be cautioned?" the cop said.

"*Does* she?" Floyd said.

That was all the caution she needed. Drew had killed Lex, destroying the memory he could not endure. For the world and the law, there was no Drew. If Lex was dead, Eric had killed him. His freedom, their future, depended on Lacey's words. She gathered her shattered thoughts. Water in the tub, blood on the stairs—Lacey in a bathrobe, Eric with a knife. What narrative could make sense of this? The stranger in the house, always the same stranger, from the beginning.

"Uncle Floyd," she said. "How is Eric? Have you seen him?"

He dragged a metal chair through the curtain and sat at the head of her bed, where he could watch the fetal monitor. "Baby's still good," he said. "I'll tell him."

"He's conscious?"

"Not yet. Docs say there's a bad concussion and a lot of broken bones. They're putting him back together. The knife stayed in Hall. I knew he was trouble. We told him to get a different lawyer," he said to the cop, "and he took it bad."

"What bones?" Lacey said. "He's not—it's not his spine? He's not paralyzed?"

"Legs, hip, arm, skull fracture. Don't worry, girl, he'll pull through."

"Tell me what happened," the cop said.

Someone was interviewing Harry Rakoczy, right now. Someone was interviewing Lex Hall's wife. Ella Dane, somewhere in this same hospital with Jack—someone would find her soon and question her. Lacey braced herself and said, "Okay, so. This is how it is. I only met Lex a couple times at Harry's house when he brought the baby over. Something happened last night with him and his ex, I guess, maybe. I don't know."

"Don't tell me what you don't know, ma'am. Tell me what you know. Where were you last night?"

"I stayed at Harry's." How odd that must sound to them; why hadn't she been in her own house, right next door? "Eric and I had a fight. Mom's boyfriend fell down the stairs so she was here with him, and I didn't want to be alone. You know, in case I went into labor."

"Lots of people fall down those stairs, seems like," the cop said.

He had no idea. "We need to get a contractor to look at them," Lacey said.

"What did you and your husband fight about?"

"Money. It was stupid. He spent the night I don't know where . . ."

"With me," Floyd said, to Lacey's surprise. "At my girlfriend's condo."

"And this morning?" the cop said.

The baby's pulse surged to 210. They all watched it, the living lie detector. What would Harry and Ella Dane say—what *could* they say? Ella Dane might say anything. "My mom thinks the house is haunted," Lacey said. Floyd buzzed his lips, and the cop gave him a reproachful look. "I can't help it, that's what she thinks. She and her boyfriend were doing a ritual to make it safe; that's when he fell." The baby's pulse fell to 180. "It sounds crazy, I'm sorry, but that's what they did. I stayed with Harry. Lex came over with his baby."

"When?"

"How would I know? I had a lot on my mind. In the morning I went home." Theo. Theo had gone back and forth between the Miszlak and Rakoczy houses. There would be evidence of that. "I took Lex's baby for a few minutes so Lex and Harry could talk. Then Harry came and took her back. And then Lex came over, and he was shouting, crazy." And he was dead, the one witness who could never refute her testimony. "Yelling, screaming, I don't know what. He broke a plant on my porch." Would Harry admit to breaking the plant? If he did, she'd say she'd only heard the smash and had assumed it was Lex. "I don't know what he wanted."

"I do," Floyd said. "He wanted Eric."

Corroboration. She must be doing all right. "So Eric came home and they talked, him and Lex. I was . . ." And where was she? If they questioned Eric before she had a chance to talk to him—his concussion would cover any discrepancies. "I was running a bath. Lex came upstairs, and he had the knife." Eric had been holding the knife; her fingerprints were on it, too. Her knife from her kitchen, why not. "Eric got the knife away from Lex, they were fighting and they fell down the stairs."

"Did you let Hall in?" the cop said.

"I might have left the door unlocked, I don't remember."

The cop shook his head at her, *Stupid woman, leaving the door unlocked, you think your neighborhood's so nice but if you knew what I knew,* and she knew he was convinced. Floyd patted Lacey's hand and said to the cop, "You got enough? This girl needs to rest, now."

"We might have some more questions later."

"You got more questions, you come to me," Floyd said. He waited until the cop left and added, "That goes double for you. They got questions, you call me. Got it?"

"I've got nothing to hide," Lacey said.

"You keep telling them that." He leaned over and kissed her forehead. "You done good. I'll keep an eye on the boy for you."

Left alone, Lacey watched the baby's heartbeat on the monitor, steady at 180. Safe and whole. She grabbed the sheet with both hands and pulled it up, bunching it in a mass on her knees. The thought of the house she now possessed, the family she had defended, left her desolate. Dropping her face into the bundled sheet, she sobbed for that wasted, lost, and ruined life, the child she had failed to save, for Lex, for Drew.

Chapter Fifty-two

ON HER RELEASE from the hospital, Lacey spent a few days at the Skyview, until it was time for Eric to come home. She stood for three minutes on the front porch, waiting for the courage to open it. Then she got tired of waiting and opened it anyway, the adrenaline running so hot she could almost see the nerves blazing under her skin, and the house was empty.

Harry had been busy while she was gone. He'd brought in some young people—college-aged students and former students—to build a ramp from the driveway to the front door, and stained the wood and painted the railing to match the porch. He also brought over some orange chrysanthemums, and two purple curly-leaf cabbages in stone urns, one for either side of the front door.

"In May, you can replace them with geraniums," he said.

"Stop giving me things," she told him. They stood in the doorway between the cabbage urns, watching the road, waiting for Ella Dane and Eric. She'd seen those urns at Home Depot, seventy dollars each. "No more things. I don't want anything from you."

"How's the baby?" Harry asked.

"You don't have the right to ask me that."

She had pictures of the baby in her wallet, yesterday's ultra-sounds. The lower part of his body was a blur of angles and loops, but Dr. Vlk assured her he wasn't half octopus, he had tangled himself up in the umbilical cord in an entirely normal way.

"I had to protect my grandchildren," Harry said.

"You can't come to my house anymore. I can't have you here."

"I'll be leaving soon."

She'd seen CarolAnna's car in Harry's driveway. Was he selling and moving to Australia, as he'd said he wanted? She wouldn't ask.

"I can't file for custody," Harry said, and Lacey's mind whirled. Custody? Of whom? "But there's a grandparent relation-ship, so I can get visitation. Floyd Miszlak's working it out with Ms. MacAvoy."

Theo Hall. "You're not her grandfather."

"Legally, I am. I adopted Lex when he was twelve." Harry took a shivering breath, and Lacey turned away. "It's my fault," Harry said. "If I'd gotten the truth out of him, all those years ago . . ."

"I don't think he knew it himself, until just then."

"Ah, poor Lex. He never meant to hurt anyone. The things that happened in the house; he couldn't have known what he was doing. It wasn't really him."

"Yes, it was," Lacey said. "Drew was real, and he was really part of Lex. I don't think Lex knew about it. Not consciously, anyway." She hated that she had yielded to Harry's pain, let her-self be drawn into his future. "Where are you going?" she asked.

"I'm moving downtown. You won't see me anymore."

"Good." Ella Dane's car turned onto Forrester Lane. "They're here," Lacey said. She waited until Ella Dane parked, and then she walked, large and stately, belly first, down the ramp. Ella Dane popped the trunk and unfolded the wheelchair from it, like a magic trick, and she got Eric from the backseat into the chair as Lacey reached them.

They hadn't mentioned Drew in the hospital. Eric had been unconscious, then heavily medicated, then more lightly medicated but worn out from the first stages of physical therapy. And there were always people watching and listening. Cops at first, then nurses. Two weeks, and they hadn't said a word about it, and every day made the words harder to speak, the memories more distant and estranged. They had to talk about it—only once, but it had to be spoken. She wasn't sure how to begin. He might not even remember.

"So," she said, hands on hips, shaking her head in mock accusation, "this is an extreme way to get out of diaper duty, don't you think?"

"Extreme?" Eric said. He laughed, winced, groaned.

"Some people might even call it *lame*," Lacey said.

"Oh, Lacey!" Ella Dane said with reproach, but Eric and Lacey were both laughing now, Eric in light, painful syllables and Lacey effortfully, but it was better than nothing. "After what he did for you," Ella Dane said.

"Look at this ramp; some of Harry's students built it. He's moving."

"You know I'll only need it for a couple of months," Eric said. "Two more operations on the left ankle, and I'll be on my feet again."

"It'll be good for the stroller after that. I'll push you up to the door."

"No, you won't," Eric said. He rolled from the driveway to the ramp, and Ella Dane took over from there. "Did you know I could hear you the whole time?" he said.

So he remembered. "Why didn't you do something?"

"I did. He was so strong. But you kept saying *sideways,* and I thought, when my parents took me to the Isle of Palms when I was little, my dad said if you get caught in a rip current, you don't try to swim inshore, you swim sideways till the current lets go. He wanted to push you down the stairs, but I made him think the bathtub was better."

"Thank you so much, I was really looking forward to drowning."

"It was a little more time. I didn't mean those things I said; it was all for more time. I kept looking for *sideways,* like you said. There had to be a way. I listened to you all the time, Lacey, I did. All the time. Then when he was fighting Lex, there it was, a way to get us both down the stairs, away from you. I pushed, and we fell."

"You could have died," Lacey said. They reached the top of the ramp, where Harry was waiting, smiling between the cabbages.

"I didn't care. Somebody had to die. As long as it wasn't you."

Harry opened the door for them with a flourish. Eric put his hands on the wheels and stopped Ella Dane from pushing him inside. He looked at Lacey. "Is it safe now?" he said. "Are we going to be able to live here?"

"Look," Lacey said. The afternoon light spilled through the porthole window and pooled brightly at the foot of the stairs, as it always did, and the house stood empty, remembering nothing.

About the author

About the book

Insights,
Interviews
& More . . .

Meet Sonja Condit

Photograph by Brent Coppenbarger

SONJA CONDIT received her MFA from Converse College, where she studied with Robert Olmstead, Leslie Pietrzyk, R. T. Smith, and Marlin Barton. Her short fiction has appeared in *Shenandoah* magazine, among other publications. Condit plays principal bassoon in the Hendersonville Symphony Orchestra and for the Greater Anderson Musical Arts Consortium. She teaches at the South Carolina Governor's School for the Arts and Humanities. ∽

Author's Note

THIS BOOK HAD ITS ORIGINS about ten years before I wrote it, in a dream I had when pregnant with my first child. I was sleeping with a teddy bear, because we had a very devoted cat (Siamese, affectionate but possessive), and we were afraid the baby would upset him. Our plan was to sleep with the bear in the bed with us for a couple of weeks, then put it in the bassinet in the hospital. Before bringing me home with the baby, my husband would give the bear to the cat. We thought that in this way, the cat would recognize the baby, by scent, as being part of his family.

One night I woke up in the middle of a dream. In the part of my mind that was still dreaming, I thought the bear was the baby. In the part that was awake, I knew it wasn't breathing. So I believed I had rolled over on the baby and suffocated him. This dream seemed to go on forever and is still one of the worst experiences of my life. When I started to write a ghost story, I tried to capture those feelings of horror, grief, and guilt. ❧

Author Q & A

What inspired you to write this particular book?

Pregnancy was hard for me, especially the first one. I had four months of bleeding and seven months of nausea, and for most of that time I was certain the baby would die. There is nothing in the pregnancy books about how to get through a situation like this. It was lonely; my husband was right there with me, but I felt completely alone. The baby was fine in the end. When I wanted to write about a haunted house, I instinctively made the protagonist a pregnant woman, because I knew that a pregnant woman is a haunted house. My son was ten when I started putting together the idea for this book, and he was fairly noisy, so Drew and the baby really are the same person.

Have you ever lived in a haunted house?

Supposedly, yes. Our house in London had a ghost. People would hear a crying baby. I never heard it, and I don't really believe in ghosts. But I was terrified of the stairs. The stairs in *Starter House* don't look anything like those stairs, but they have the same feeling.

Are you a southern writer?

I didn't grow up in the South. I grew up mostly in the UK and Canada, but I had a southern grandmother who told stories, and maybe that's all you need. My stepgrandfather used to threaten me; he'd tell me that if I wasn't careful, I'd end up in South Carolina. And he must have been right, because here I am in Greenville.

So where is Greeneburg?

Greeneburg is my sandbox. I have set several short stories there, and places and even characters reappear from one story to another. I erased the northwestern corner of South Carolina, brought the Blue Ridge Mountains a little farther south to make the summers five degrees cooler and keep the spring flowers blooming a little longer, and put the combined population of real-life Greenville and Spartanburg into my Greeneburg. And the extra *e* is for our Revolutionary War hero Nathanael Greene. In downtown Greenville, on the corner of Broad and Main, there is a lovely statue of Greene holding a telescope; he was famous for saying he would recover the country or die in the attempt. Using Greeneburg instead of Greenville frees me to have only what I need in the stories, without having to worry about real-life geography. And returning to the same places grounds the stories, I hope, in a sense of larger reality. The characters aren't trapped in their own story. They can show up in the background of someone else's life. ▶

Author Q & A *(continued)*

Does the ghost represent something?

Sometimes he does. There's the hauntedness of pregnancy, the fact that you have another human being alive inside you, yet you really don't know anything about this person. Haunting in general makes me think about the ways that violence, drug addiction, and other kinds of abuse are passed down through a family, as if behavior were inherited just as much as hair color. But mostly I just wanted to scare people. ᘓ

Reading Group Discussion Questions

1. What do you think about Lacey and Eric's marriage? How does their relationship change through the story?

2. How do their different backgrounds affect their ability to communicate with each other?

3. Why is Lacey so reluctant to leave the house, long after she knows how dangerous it is?

4. Do you think Ella Dane Kendall is truly psychic, or is she pretending? If she *is* psychic, why can't she see Drew?

5. Drew has killed many children and young mothers over the years. What does he want from them, and why is it so difficult for him to get it?

6. Lacey knows she can save her family by moving out of the house and renting it to someone else. Why won't she do this?

7. Lacey sees herself only as she relates to other people, as a teacher, daughter, wife, and mother. She even perceives her professional persona, the teacher voice, as a separate mind, not really herself. Is there a true, integrated self inside her? If so, where in the story does this self appear? And if not, what is she? ▶

Reading Group Discussion Questions
(continued)

8. What do you think these characters will be doing five years from now? Will Eric and Lacey still be married? Will they be living in 571 Forrester Lane? 〜